PRAISE FOR

JOHN S. McFARLAND'S

THE BLACK GARDEN

"...a brilliant writer...,"

—Jodie Rhodes

"Classic horror, worthy of H. P. Lovecraft. You'll love it—or my name isn't Cthulu."

—Michael Gerber, author of the million-selling Barry Trotter series

"...evocative, literate, character-driven,"

—Catherine Rankovic, poet, essayist, author of *Fierce Consent*

"*The Black Garden is* literate and suspenseful, a complex and lyrical story drawn from the dark traditions of Southern Gothic horror. John McFarland has written a grand opera of a tale."

—Elizabeth Donald, author of *Nocturne*, *Setting Suns,* and *The Cold Ones*

THE BLACK GARDEN

John S. McFarland

The Patrice Press
Tooele, Utah

Cover illustration by the author.
Cover design by David Lancaster.

The Patrice Press
319 Nottingham Drive
Tooele, Utah 84074
1-435-833-9168
email: books@patricepress.com

Printed in the United States of America

For my kids,
Megan and Evan

The Black Garden

A NOVEL BY

JOHN S. MCFARLAND
novelguy12@gmail.com

ACKNOWLEDGMENTS

Sure, the internet is a great resource for research. But as one who prefers dusty, antique libraries manned by underpaid bibliophiles and filled with centuries-old books, maps, and newspapers, I wish to thank the staffs of the Ste. Genevieve Public Library, the St. Louis Public Library downtown, the Mercantile Library, the Golden Eagle River Museum library, and Jason Stratman at the library of the Missouri Historical Society. Early editors and bearers of encouragement and invaluable bits of information include Connie McIntyre, Elizabeth Donald, Michael Gerber, Mark Golding, Tom Makeever, Patrice Stribling Nelson, Lisa Buese, my agent P. T., and, for "taking possession" of the project, Elisabeth Luaders. For her careful and enthusiastic reading and great encouragement, with much love I thank Carlye Hoese, the one and only.

For great nuts-and-bolts editing and always managing to see things I don't see; for her great patience, since she witnessed the very beginning of this effort, I thank Anne Makeever.

Emphatic and enthusiastic thanks to my old friend, David Lancaster. His careful and impassioned readings and long-considered suggestions made this a much better book than it started out to be. I wondered at times how he might have counseled Shakespeare: "*Hamlet* is a good story, Bill,but I wonder if you might liven it up a bit with more conflict?" In addition to his literary advice, David was also vital to the spirit and even the look of the novel you are about to begin. Lifelong thanks to a lifelong friend.

—John S. McFarland
March 2010

THE BLACK GARDEN

1

LaRochelle, 13 April 1656

Medullinus, whom I was,
Palimpsest of these centuries
On whose page the
Heretical years rewrote
In an ever refining hand,
Deft and complacent savageries . . .
Fragment rediscovered, Montsegur, 1882

Night was like a heavy mantle threatening to suffo cate her. It surrounded her, walled her off from the rest of the world, and left her vulnerable, without any chance of help or salvation. Claire tried to comfort herself in the darkness, in these dead hours, by thinking of a time twenty or thirty years in the future when she, as a middle-aged woman, would have no night fear greater than insomnia brought on by too many household responsibilities.

"You are exhausted, Madame," Estelle, her maidservant, had said. "If you could just *rest*, you could see your fears are groundless."

Claire became convinced that if she could envision herself still alive in twenty years, it would happen. Surely, in a few months, or a year, all of this would be over. Her husband had promised to take her to Paris late in the summer to meet Bartholdi, who was creating the great statue to be erected in New York harbor, and there were promised trips to America and the Middle East, and a honeymoon, delayed by business, to Italy. She was giddy with excitement when her husband, her Guibord, had described all of the places he wanted to show his new wife. And it would begin soon, as soon as his business allowed. But each night until then—until these night terrors faded away and her usual life resumed—had to be faced.

Claire told herself, as she did each night, that if she could make it until dawn, she could survive. Although it was well after two o'clock, she was wide awake, though exhausted. She lay on her left side watching Estelle sleeping restlessly on the chaise in the moonlight. Tonight was the fifth night Estelle had slept there, and Claire took great comfort in it, although she still had no idea of going to sleep herself.

Each night in the beginning, before she'd settled upon a self-imposed insomnia as the nightmare returned and became more terrifying, palpable and suffocating, she could not convince herself it was a dream, as she'd been able to do in the past with lesser night terrors. It couldn't be a dream. The smells, the sounds, the sights were unquestionably real. Yet they were of a place and time she couldn't dredge from any part of her own mind and experience, as she could her other dreams. And she had come closer to the terrible end each of the last four nights. She'd come to know somehow she had to make it to sunrise, that the gray dawn would evaporate the terrors, and later in the unequivocal sunlight of Languedoc, she could safely recover and get the rest she needed. But she soon discovered sleep in the daytime was also difficult, if not impossible, without sleeping draughts from Dr. Valle, which she dared not take. She could not risk taking a drug that would make it impossible to awaken and extract herself from the mortal dangers of the nightmare. And what part did Bastide play in all of this? Why did Orien

Bastide, the strange American who seemed more French than even her own husband or her father, appear in each of the nightmares? It seemed it was her connection to him that was causing this. Guilt for betraying her husband, perhaps. Betraying him in the sense that she had given to Bastide a part of her self—her thoughts and ideas—which she had never given to Guibord, only because he had never sought them.

The suffering and horror of the images she saw every night, and which she knew would soon engulf her, suited Bastide more than herself. Knowledge of such things could be found in his face. He seemed to carry the burden of it sadly on his slightly misshapen shoulders. In some way he'd made these things hers.

She never intended to betray Guibord, not in her thoughts, nor with her body. He had rescued her and her family from a life of decorous poverty in Carcassonne. Her father, like so many of his friends, had lost his fortune in Mexico in the days of the Second Empire. Guibord had reestablished it, after they had married, by allowing her father to manage his business interests in the ancient town, limited though they were.

Guibord brought her back with him to his village of Montsegur, to a new house he'd had built for her out of the white limestone quarried from the mountains surrounding them, and had given her a better life than she'd come to expect. It was a practical match, beneficial to her family. She loved him enough to be satisfied with her situation. She never intended to betray him.

She hadn't really succumbed to Bastide. She was overwhelmed by him. By the time she'd come to the village, he was already there, and had been in France for nearly fifteen years. He'd taken the medieval chateau built by Raymond VI, Count of Toulouse. The great house stood at the edge of the meadow called Prat dels Crematz, the Field of the Burned, at the base of the mountain citadel where a band of heretic

Cathars made a last stand in 1244. The citadel, a ruined castle atop a five hundred-foot pinnacle of rock, held the last orange rays of the sun at dusk long after the village below was lost in darkness. That was how Claire remembered it from her first visit to Bastide.

Guibord was a man without suspicion or reproach, and he had encouraged the friendship. He wanted a friend and companion for Claire when he was away on his frequent business trips to Toulouse and Marseilles. Bastide had been a guest in their house many times since her arrival in the town. She'd been a little startled by his appearance at first. His face was lifeless, without expression or personality, and framed by a shock of gray hair. Her first impression was that it was a face which had no more evidence of a soul behind it than the glazed, milky eye of a long dead goldfish she'd buried as a child. This effect was conveyed, she soon realized, by a wax prosthesis that formed pieces of a face, which he wore on the rare occasions when he ventured outside his chateau. He'd noticed her surprise at first seeing him, and had explained he'd been diagnosed by a physician in Berne who specialized in degenerative and deforming diseases of the muscles and bones, as having an incurable condition that would one day leave him, in Bastide's words, at best "as twisted as one of St. Anthony's fiends" and, at worst, kill him.

Claire was a little surprised by Guibord's obvious and immediate liking of Bastide. Bastide was a person of refinement and high intellect, and unlike anyone else of her husband's acquaintance. Guibord had invited his new friend to dinner twice. On the second evening, Bastide had felt at ease enough to remove the lower part of his prosthesis in order to eat his meal more easily. Bastide told many stories from ancient and medieval history in detail so amazing it seemed to Claire he must be enlarging upon the facts with his own imagination. He made a diligent and obvious effort to include her in the conversation; Guibord was barely a participant.

When the men moved into the front parlor for brandy, Claire was surprised at Bastide's insistence that she join them. Guibord seemed a bit mortified and apologetic that he hadn't thought of this himself. Although he generally observed convention without question, he was by no means closed to the possibilities of looking at familiar things in new ways. The men had their brandy. Claire preferred a white Burgundy and took her preferred seat closest to the fire. Bastide was intent on continuing a conversation he had started about the causes of the revolution. Claire watched the fire, as was her habit, glancing occasionally at Bastide and then at Guibord, whose eyelids, she saw, were becoming heavy.

Bastide was always aware of her and her reactions to his observations, and he seemed increasingly determined to draw her more fully into the discussion. She was an educated woman, but this made her ill at ease at first, as though something were expected of her that she could not quite provide. Eventually, though, as Guibord nodded off, she began to give her guest her ideas, ones she was formulating on the spot, about how the concepts of liberty and fraternity might have affected women and family life in those heady days of change and terror.

After a second brandy, Bastide left, graciously thanking Claire for an elegant and engaging evening. And as she helped her husband out of his chair and up the front stairs, she had a confused sensation of well-being tinged by unease. After she put Guibord to bed, she went back to the parlor and had another glass of Burgundy.

It was an evening near midsummer when Bastide first invited her to his chateau for a light Provencal supper. Guibord was in Marseilles, personally checking vegetable dye lots from Guiana on samples of his woolen goods before accepting them for shipment to his weavers in Carcassonne.

The chateau was a huge Romanesque structure that had been left intact by the French crown after the Albigensian Crusade and the disgrace of the Count of Toulouse in aiding the Cathar heretics. The large oaken door was opened by Bastide's tall Haitian manservant, Tertius, and as she crossed the ancient threshold, Claire felt an instantaneous and unaccountable sensation of loss, of the brevity of everything material and spiritual that she owned, and a perverse desire to destroy it all.

Tertius delivered her into the library to wait for her host. "Monsieur Bastide is in the conservatory."

Tertius's voice, a deep, refined growl of perfect enunciation, filled the room. "There is a repotting situation."

He smiled vaguely and started toward the door. He stopped for a moment just inside the room and turned back to face her. He smiled slightly once more.

"Madame," he said quietly, almost informally, "Monsieur Bastide relishes company and conversation. So much so that his sense of generosity is often incited by an evening's companionship. He may wish to offer you some token of friendship before you leave tonight, some gift. An old Roman coin, for example, a silver *denar*, or even a gold *aureus* are usual. Forgive me, but by no means accept this gift."

He paused for a moment. His voice became more formal again.

"These gifts to married ladies are improper, and have caused talk in the past. Please accept no token from him of any kind. Pardon my intrusion…"

His voice trailed off, and he turned away before Claire could answer. He closed the door silently as he left.

The room was of an enormous size. Ceiling-high bookshelves on every wall were filled with thousands of volumes, and the last indirect rays of the orange sunset crossed the room through narrow, stone-edged windows, illuminating the cracked leather bindings of *Malleus Malefacarum, The Origin of Species,* and Sinistrari's *Demonality,* as well as many other titles she could make out on sacred and scientific subjects. On shelves of dark wood beneath these, as well as on several large tables placed in the center of the room, were scattered the bones of oxen, birds, wolves, cats, and other creatures, including what Claire took to be the enormous skull of a hippopotamus.

There were also many lidded jars scattered about filled with murky liquid, in which floated grotesque and pallid specimens of fish, rays, and various fetal mammals. Elsewhere around the room, as well as in the great entry hall through which she had just been led, were many objects of antiquity, including fragments of classical, Egyptian, and Assyrian statuary, medieval limestone saints, and painted icons of Christ and the Holy Family.

On a cluttered table near her lay a thick, leather-bound journal kept open by a stone that held the fossil impression of some large type of snail. The day's entry seemed to be half finished in an expansive, nervous hand: "Large specimen dead leaf mantis, *Gongulus Gongyledes,* described by J. Loten, arrived from Ceylon, as well as Scorpionfish, *Scoroena Patiriarcha*, in good condition..."

This entry was written about three quarters of the way through the enormous book. Claire began to casually leaf backwards through it, noting many hand-drawn sketches of exotic creatures and rough maps of strange landscapes, some with notes and observations scribbled across them and in the margins of the pages. Near the beginning of the book, written in brown, faded ink, a scrap of what appeared to be a poem or song caught her attention:

LaRochelle, 13 April, 1656

Medullinus whom I was,
Palimpsest of these centuries
On whose page
The heretical years rewrote
In an ever refining hand
Many deft, complacent savageries . . .

She heard a footstep in the hallway and quickly closed the book. Bastide threw open the heavy library door as if it were a sheer curtain.

"I've never seen such a collection outside a museum," she said, somewhat insipidly. She had determined on first seeing him not to say anything vacuous, as she had on their few brief meetings previously, but she had failed herself. She felt superficial and silly in his presence, even though she sensed an effort on his part to allay those feelings.

"There is nothing more valuable than time," Bastide said didactically. "We've been given so little of it in which to learn about, to know the world. Anything worthy of human investigation is of interest to me; high-toned as that sounds, it's true."

He was drying his hands on a linen towel, hands that reminded Claire of the tangled, visible roots of ancient trees pushing out of the ground or overhanging a riverbank. He was not wearing his prostheses, an indulgence he had asked of her in his invitation to supper. One other time she had seen him completely without them, and she'd tried to prepare herself for this encounter. He looked puzzled for a moment, although she had found it difficult to read his expressions because of the downward twist of his mouth, the slight, bony prominence of his brow and forehead, and the mystery of his large, round, watery eyes.

The first time Claire had seen his face complete, she had been aghast to realize that the startling, round look of his eyes was caused by the lids being held open by small wires, owing to the degenerative effect of his disease. Every so often he had to place drops of fluid in his eyes from a small vial he always carried with him, to restore their moisture.

"Did it sound high-toned?" He dropped the towel on a chair.

"No."

Although his accent was flawless for Languedoc, he was in the habit of using phrases like that, Americanisms, she imagined, which confused her.

"I certainly don't claim everything is understandable. It's the pursuit, the effort that matters, isn't it?"

He shook her hand graciously. Through his slight smile she could see the glint of his narrow teeth. They looked unnaturally long, or abnormally exposed, perhaps, from the receding of the gums. His grasp was gentle, but warm, almost feverish.

"But I suppose none of this would do for your house?"

Claire could see no tactful way to answer the question. And he was looking at her in a way that made her ill at ease, made her struggle for words. To make small talk seemed like a ridiculous waste of time. Often, in his presence, she found herself dismissing her life as bourgeois and ridiculous, and concluding that her education must have been a farce.

His eyes appeared to take in all of her at once, darting up and down and from side to side at a rapid pace until they settled on her eyes. It was a gaze she could not return for long. In that light she noticed, as she had once before in another advancing dusk, that his eyes appeared almost amber. He quickly averted them in a way that was almost apologetic.

"Excuse me," he laughed, "for asking such an impossible question!"

"My house is the house of a merchant and his wife, you see? This is the house of a...naturalist. A historian..." Claire felt she had made a satisfactory response.

"An industrialist and a dabbler, a dilettante on all counts. Particularly the industrialist. But my good fortune in inheriting American lead mines without the bother of having to run them myself, has permitted the great indulgence you see around you."

"Who does run them for you?"

"Mr. Morisot. A very clever and resourceful Creole fellow from Martinique by way of New Orleans. He takes care of it all."

"He must be very trustworthy."

"I trust him with everything. He and Tertius. They have a discretion that I've found to be essential over the years. I'll be seeing Morisot next month. I'm going back to Ste. Odile. And it will be good to see my old house again. I actually think it may be the oldest house west of the Mississippi. Construction was begun in...1694, or was it 1699, by another Orien Bastide, the first of my line to be named for a prince of Hell! Such a long time ago. The local people call it the Jardin Noir."

Tertius refilled Bastide's glass with the aromatic Burgundy he had been drinking, and Bastide quickly drained it. He seemed to take no pleasure in the act. It reminded Claire of the manner in which her father used to drink after his fortune had been lost.

"I am familiar with that name, Ste. Odile. It is an amazing coincidence, don't you think? Out of all the towns in America, we would both have a connection to that one?"

"How do you know of it?"

"My brother, Prosper, lives in Boston. He has since he was a boy. My father wanted him educated in the new land with its new ideas, you see?" She smiled. "We saw each other only for a few weeks in the summers as we were growing up. He was my mentor and my example. I miss him so! His fiancée has taken a post in Ste. Odile, teaching at a female seminary. I assume he'll follow her there, though he was unclear on that point. Her name is Perdita, as in Shakespeare. I'd love to see the Mississippi someday myself. I've read about it in Chateaubriand. Is it still a great wilderness?"

Bastide laughed. "It is nothing like that. There are steamboats up and down the river every day. The riverbanks are denuded to feed the boilers. Americans are in love with new machines and how they enhance commerce. They will sacrifice the beauty of a landscape or the peace of a countryside, if they can find a way to mow their grain faster or get their pigs to market sooner. In a land whose history looks back only a couple of hundred years, novelty and newness are ends in themselves."

He emptied another glass. "Except for our village. Our Ste. Odile. The progress of this frantic century has hardly touched it. There was a great earthquake in 1811. It was like the world was ending. The course of the river was changed, shifted east. The main body of the river, and the traffic and commerce and progress it carries, is now to the east of de Castres Island, leaving only a shallow channel to flow past Ste. Odile. Our town can hardly be seen beyond the island by the passengers on those elegant boats. At any rate, Ste. Odile was always more French than American. A relic of our presence in the Mississippi Valley. A two hundred year old …oddity."

"Are there Indians?"

"Most are gone. There are still a few Sac and Fox, and even the occasional Osage to be seen. There is still an old mission there for them, built when the village was a few years old, and the female seminary you mentioned, attached to it to educate their daughters, and now those of freed slaves."

"Jesuits?"

"At first. Then Franciscan Recollects. Since 1780, the Sisters of Perpetua."

An hour or so later, after an aperitif and discourse about whether or not Claudius should be considered to be homologous with the later "good" emperors, Tertius announced dinner.

"Surely no emperor could be called 'good,' who allowed gladiatorial games and the persecution of Christians," Claire said, as they moved into the large but rather shabby dining room. Bastide held her chair for her and then seated himself at the head of the enormous oak dining table.

"The gladiatorial games were mere entertainment," Bastide noted, "presenting little or no moral dilemma to most Romans. And the Christians had scarcely been noticed at that time. When they were noticed, they were seen as barbarous, heretical, and blasphemous. But really more a threat to order than religion."

"Blasphemous! What did pagan Romans who murdered people by the thousands for the sake of "entertainment" know about religious—" she searched for the right word—"propriety?"

Bastide looked at her for a moment, and leaned toward her. "They had only to consider the nature of evil. And its emissaries. Celsus asked: 'In a universe that operates according to the will of God, is it not blasphemous to suggest there would exist adversaries with the power to constrain His capacity to do good?'"

Claire considered a response, a repetition of her catechism about free will and the need for temptation to prove our worthiness to God, but the subject had seemed to agitate her host, so she said nothing.

Conversation continued through four courses, arousing Claire's imagination in a way that again surprised her, as it had done on that previous evening in her home. Subjects ranging from history to the arts to the natural sciences eddied and pooled around game hens, salads, and assorted fruits, and extended into a large salon before a limestone fireplace, with brandies and more liqueurs, late into the night.

Throughout the evening, Claire found herself noting Tertius, in his comings and goings with trays and decanters, glancing at her, sometimes indifferently, sometimes catching her glance instantly with a trace of some inference in his eye she could not quite read. One moment she would see something empathetic in it, another something that seemed intended to communicate some secret knowledge or admonition.

Just after midnight she walked home alone, cordially refusing Bastide's surprisingly insistent and concerned offer to accompany her. He extended his hand to her as she stood at his door. She noticed Tertius stop with his tray behind him. He looked at her with an expression she could not fathom, as she took Bastide's hand. In his hand Bastide had hidden an old gold coin that he passed to her.

"I would like you to accept this small gift. A remembrance of this pleasant evening we have passed together. Will you accept it?"

Claire looked at the coin. A Roman *aureus*. It was heavy, thick, and worn, but still brilliant after two thousand years. Claire could see no harm in accepting the gift. To refuse might be seen as an insult. She knew Tertius was paused behind her host to see if she would honor his request to her and refuse the gift. His comments seemed presumptuous now, and out of place. She hesitated a moment, then smiled at Bastide and nodded. Tertius returned his attention to his duties, disappearing into the library.

Bastide's hand was warm, as it was the first time she'd taken it. Again she felt the sensation of loss she'd noted before, and the same perverse desire to bring it all about quickly. This time, the sensation seemed specifically connected to Bastide somehow, as if taking his gift had sealed some unspoken bargain between them.

She'd never had an evening like this one, one devoted solely to her, to challenging her mind and ideas. She'd never known a man like Bastide. He was superficially repulsive, but his mind was keen, active, and hungry in a way unknown in her small circle of family and merchants. She scarcely noted the houses and familiar streets in town as she passed them.

As she walked she slowly became aware of subtle movement in the hedges along the street. A low, chittering growl, punctuated by short barking sounds, could just barely be heard. In an instant, in a liquid blur of violent movement, a small, hunched shape darted, or more accurately flowed, from the hedge across the dark path in front of her, followed by a second, apparently identical creature. In the darkness she could make out no details or features. She could only assume they were small wild dogs or perhaps martens or sables of some kind, although her impression was that they were unlikely to be any of these. She stared into the dark undergrowth for a long time, but saw no further sign of the creatures. She decided to hurry her pace down the hillside.

Suddenly she found herself at her own iron gate. Glancing back along the route she'd just walked, she could see the pinnacle and its castle black against the stars, and could picture Bastide's chateau in the darkness far below it. How was he regarding her now? Was the connection she felt to him now real? Was it mutual? She felt it must be. Some barrier had been crossed.

As she prepared herself for bed, the excitement of the evening faded a little, and this new connection began to frighten her. There was something about the way Tertius had looked at her as she was leaving that made her wish she'd taken his advice, although why he would disapprove of this simple act of friendship, she could not tell. And those strange impulses to throw off everything that had contented her up to this day terrified her. She felt as she had as a child when she'd scarcely escaped falling from a high scaffold when she and her family were touring the restorations which were being done to the cathedral at Carcassonne. It took several hours for her to empty her mind and fall asleep that night.

It was the first night she felt the presence. She slept in short, fitful stretches for a few hours. She dreamt of a room with whitewashed stone walls, a dungeon or castle, filled with people archaically dressed, some in black ceremonial robes, others in medieval jerkins and homespun skirts. All were sitting or standing quietly, calmly, as if they were all resigned to some great doom. There was a table, or altar, covered in white linen, upon which lay several white napkins and a book of the Gospels. A minister, flanked by two assistants, was preaching to the crowd, instructing them about the sacredness of the sacrament, the *consolamentum*, which, under these special circumstances, they were all about to receive. Claire suddenly understood that the castle was the citadel of Montsegur. And these people, of whom she appeared to be one, were the heretic Cathars. The minister, the *perfectus*, assured the people that by accepting the sacrament, and therefore death at the stake, they had chosen the right course, and that soon the dual nature of God would be apparent to them.

Claire found herself suddenly awake. She realized she had awakened herself because she was aware of an odd sensation that someone must be near, watching her sleep. But the room was empty. A breeze lifted the curtains slightly, making a sound in the darkness like the rustling of clothes on a heavily draped figure. That must account for the sense of a presence near her, she thought. It was nothing.

She thought about the images of the dream she'd been having and was surprised she remembered them so well. She usually remembered little, if anything, of her dreams.

But these images were as clear in her mind as if they had just happened. Her mouth was dry. She sat up and poured herself a drink of water from a carafe at her bedside. Exhausted, she settled back into bed and quickly fell asleep. Her dream seemed to continue in the same place she had left it. She was back in the citadel chamber with its whitewashed stone walls, surrounded by the doomed Cathar faithful.

In a far corner of the room, apart from the ceremony, another *perfectus* was giving hurried instructions to four men, the four who had been chosen to escape, to preserve the fortune and writings of the Cathars. She knew their names. They were Amiel Aicart and his companions, Hugo and Poitevin. And Orien Bastide.

Claire began to rouse herself again from the dream. She knew nothing of the history of the region. Where did these images come from? She must have been stimulated by the evening's conversation and the proximity of the citadel. She seemed to drift in and out of sleep, and again felt a vague sensation of being watched. She slowly became aware of the fact that she could not move. Her breath became short and pressure from a great, inexorable weight on her chest and hips was increasingly painful as it was suffocating. A stinking waft of breath passed over her, but she could not open her eyes. She became conscious of a slow pressure on her inner thighs, a pressure she could not identify as warm or cold or gentle or rough, but a pressure she was horrified to realize was slowly pushing her thighs apart. She had too little breath left to cry out, but she managed a small, growled "no," and freed her body slightly from the pressure by twisting toward her right side. Suddenly the pressure was gone, and as she opened her eyes, she thought she saw a dark form disappearing through her doorway, its features half seen. It appeared to her to move fluidly from one point in space to another, rather than to physically walk or run. If it had been real at all.

Claire sat up in bed and lighted her lamp. She could find no mark or bruise on herself, nor could her serving girl, who examined her thoroughly the next morning.

By nightfall the next day she had decided the sensation of a presence, the shortness of breath, the images of the Cathars and Montsegur, had been parts of the same dream. She slept heavily that night with no dreams of any kind she could remember, and awoke the next morning in the same position in which she had first fallen asleep.

The next day she received an invitation to lunch from Bastide, including the promise of observing the rare blooming of an obscure type of orchid he'd received from Venezuela a year ago. She walked to the chateau late in the morning, and enjoyed the lunch and conversation immensely, although the hoped-for blooming did not occur.

But early in the afternoon she began to feel uneasy and distracted. She watched Bastide's lips move as he talked, but heard little that he said. The dream she'd had two nights before and the terrifying presence afterward began to fill her thoughts. Why would she have such a dream? And why did Bastide, looking very different than he did now, but undoubtedly him, appear in it? What stimulus in her agitated mind had included him in such a vision? He seemed different to her today. There was something insincere about him, and almost guilty. And she imagined she could read on his face a possession of some knowledge that was vital to her well being, but which he refused to share.

She refused the custard Tertius offered her. She soon felt faint and short of breath, and she gladly accepted Bastide's offer to have Tertius drive her home in the carriage.

She recovered somewhat in the evening and was able to eat a small supper. She went to bed just before eleven and slept well until the vision of Montsegur returned. This time, the *consolamentum* was finished, and the congregation received a blessing and began to file out and down the mountain path toward the soldiers waiting for them. Bastide and his three companions were gone; through the fissure and tunnel to freedom. Claire could see the enormous pyre being prepared in the meadow hundreds of feet below them, upon which each of them would be burned, delivered at last from the evil of the world.

This time she believed if she could not extract herself from the dream, the nightmare would become real and she would die in the flames, die without the faith and resolve from which the Cathars took comfort. As the terror of this understanding took hold of her, she felt the return of the presence. Again she felt paralyzed and suffocated, and could not open her eyes. The warmth radiating against her now sweating back and side must be coming from a body near hers. She thought briefly about Guibord and how in some way this was a retribution for having sinned against him, however minutely. But it was Bastide that her mind fixed upon. This confusion, these night terrors, and even the strange creatures in the hedges, all drew her back to him, all seemed to proceed from him. And she had an urge to be with him now that defied her dread. Tomorrow she would see him again. She had to see if another meeting would resolve or allay her fears.

She gasped for breath as she felt her thighs being pushed apart. The pressure against her was more constant and irresistible than it had been before. And as she resisted she felt a stab of pain as if from barbs or claws that would only be relieved by yielding to the pressure. A scream choked in her throat as she tried to gulp air at the same time. An urgent and insistent pounding on her door broke the oppressive silence, and her lungs filled with air.

"Madame…fire! Fire!"

Claire opened her eyes. She caught a glimpse of something slipping past the curtains and over the balcony outside.

"Madame! Fire! Can you hear me?" It was Estelle.

Claire slid off her bed and onto the floor. She pulled herself along the carpet toward the door. She was too weak to stand and struggled for breath.

"Yes, Estelle. I'm here." She knew her voice was too weak to be heard.

Estelle was pulling futilely on the door handle. "Madame, can you hear me? The door is bolted."

"I'm here, Estelle." Strength was returning to her voice.

"Pull the bolt. I must get you out!"

Claire found the bolt in the darkness and pulled on it with all the strength she could manage. Guibord always insisted the bolts be kept well oiled. It easily slid free. Claire fell against the door as Estelle pulled it open.

"I didn't lock the door," Claire whispered, as Estelle helped her to her feet, noticing spots of blood at the knees of her mistress's nightgown. "I didn't lock it."

The fire was easily contained in the kitchen chimney where it had started, and the household was back to normal by midday the next day.

Claire felt increasingly nervous and sick through lunch and was unable to eat. Estelle tried to convince her that the wounds on her thighs must have been somehow self inflicted during the dream. Claire struggled to accept this explanation, but could not convince herself.

"If only Prosper were here," she mumbled. "I need my brother here to help me through this. I'll write to him. Yes, I'll write to him and ask him to come as soon as he can. I know this would all pass if he were here to make me feel safe!"

"But, Madame," Estelle said diplomatically, "you are a married woman now. Monsieur Guibord will be home soon, and together we will see to your needs until this bad time passes. Your brother is across an ocean. It would take him weeks to get here..."

"I will write to Prosper. I must write to him tonight."

As Claire stared at her lunch on its Limoges plate, at a small fish looking back at her like the one she had buried as a child, everything became suddenly clear to her. Neither her brother nor her husband could help or protect her. There was no more room for suspicion or fear. There was only certainty.

"It *is* him! I've got to face him," she mumbled. "Let him look me in the face and tell me none of this is his doing!"

Early in the afternoon, Claire, accompanied by Estelle, walked out of the village to Bastide's chateau. The two of them pounded on the door for many minutes, but there was no answer.

"Perhaps they've gone, Madame," Estelle said, scanning the windows for any signs of life. "You said they were going to America."

"No. Not so soon. Bastide said they weren't going for a month. I know he's here!"

Claire stepped back onto the drive, and, looking up at a small second story window, saw Tertius looking back at her. He watched her gravely for a moment and then disappeared. Claire threw herself against the door and began to pound on it frantically.

"BASTIDE! You will see me!" Claire's hands were soon bruised and scratched.

"He refuses to admit you." Estelle, startled by her mistress's vehemence, tried to pull her back from the door.

"He must say what is happening to me! He can stop it. You see?"

"No, he cannot stop it."

"Yes, he can. I have never been so certain of a thing. I can see it when he looks at me!"

"How can Monsieur Bastide have anything to do

with…any of it? It isn't sensible."

"I know it is his doing. I don't know how it is, but it is. He means to kill me. My dreams are telling me—"

"But what sense do dreams make? He has no power over—"

"I haven't betrayed my husband, and I won't!"

Estelle enclosed Claire's hands in her own strong hands and led her away from the door. "They will not admit us," Estelle said soothingly, seeing her mistress could not be reasoned with, only calmed. "We should go home. I'll sit with you tonight."

Estelle made her bed in the chaise near Claire's window that night, but Claire could not close her eyes until dawn. Estelle returned the next night, and again Claire managed to remain awake, having rested fitfully in the afternoon.

On the fifth night of this arrangement, it seemed to Claire that she was forgetting her husband and her family, and what it had meant to have a normal life with them. It seemed ages since she'd seen Guibord. He was expected back in two days, a length of time that now seemed intolerable. She decided to travel to Rennes to meet him.

Estelle huddled uncomfortably on her chaise. The ivory mantle thrown over her shoulders glowed in the moonlight washing through the casement. Claire smiled a little as she watched her sleep. Poor Estelle! As soon as Guibord was safely home, she could return to her room. Claire would give her a month's paid holiday in Paris to reward her loyalty.

Staying awake had become much more difficult the last two nights. Resting during the day was a skill Claire had not yet mastered. Her mind raced day and night, but after midnight, exhaustion was taking the edge off her clarity and focus.

She lay on her left side, watching Estelle sleep for

more than an hour. She began to feel more at peace, and her mind began to wander. She wondered if Guibord's trip had been a profitable one, and if her father had yet mastered the responsibilities her husband had given him. She marveled at the patience and kindness Guibord had shown him and her whole family. She thought of Estelle's basic goodness and how this quality had managed to appear again and again in human history in spite of the persistence and inevitability of evil. The Cathars sought a goodness in the world and were persecuted for it. They were consigned to the flames of the heretic, put living into the fires that blistered flesh and boiled their living fluids before they died. Flames she could feel even now…

The great hall clock struck two and Claire opened her eyes. She gasped for breath, but could scarcely draw it in. Estelle had not moved on her chaise. But as Claire's eyes began to focus, she could see the ivory mantle had fallen away, revealing the high, dark neck of Estelle's chemise. Claire became conscious of the movement of the hairs on the back of her neck and head, stirring in waves, as if there were a great breath upon them. She could feel warmth against her back from a form, a body which seemed to extend beyond both her head and feet. She heard the guttural snarl of a voice, perhaps behind her, perhaps reverberating from some other plane altogether; heard it growl something that sounded like "you." Pressure on her shoulder was pulling her onto her back.

"Estelle," she whispered. But she could hardly hear her own cry. As she tried to resist the pressure, she saw that the dark area at Estelle's throat was not her chemise. It was raw flesh.

Claire's eyes closed as she was forced to her back. A pressing weight that she knew Guibord would never have the chance to protect her from nearly crushed out the last of the breath she had left. The flesh of her thighs tore as they were forced savagely apart. As if far removed from herself, she heard a faint, final gurgle of air in her own throat.

"Bastide—"

2

Letter from Perdita Badon-Reed to Moira Keane Parnell

Miss Perdita Badon-Reed
Hotel Essex
St. Louis, Aug. 2, 1882

To: Miss Moira Keane Parnell
14 Newgrange Circle
Boston, Massachusetts
8 P.M.

Dear Moira,

Settled at last in what I must call a "sensibly situated" hotel. Arrived by train from Chicago this afternoon. I am a day in advance of the *Abyssinia*, which I am to board at eleven A.M. tomorrow, provided my stone block is already safely on board (the second block, the one I intend for the Havilland Library commission, is coming up from Tennessee, and will meet me soon, I hope, at my destination). I will proceed on the packet downstream to Ste. Odile, a trip of eight to ten hours I am told, depending upon the river conditions and how frequently we must stop along the way.

I am taking this time to write you an intelligible letter to allay the neglect I am sure you must feel from having received from me recently so many unintelligible ones.

My only excuse is the distraction and exhaustion of traveling, not to mention the circumstances that provoked my departure in the first place. But more of Prosper later.

I call the Hotel Essex "sensibly situated" because it is an easy walk from the train station and the levee, but comfortably removed midway between the sounds and smells of both. The city is larger than we thought, and at least at the first glance I've had of it, less backward. Now it must be clear to you why I spoke so much of St. Louis and my Uncle Tancred and his work in Ste. Odile in the weeks before I disappeared. Knowing each other's thoughts as we do, I could see you were becoming suspicious. I am so sorry for having misled you. It seemed necessary at the time.

I took the opportunity, soon after finding my room, to walk a few blocks north to a private library on Locust Street called the Mercantile, which the desk man at the Essex, Mr. Schiller, told me possessed a respectable collection of art, including, as we had heard, a *Beatrice Cenci* by the great Harriet Hosmer. As I told you several weeks ago, I knew the statue was here, but I had no indication of exactly where, or even if, it would be available for public inspection. I can only hope my own version of the tragic heroine, when fully realized, is in some part as exquisite as Miss Hosmer's.

The piece is white marble, somewhat larger than life-size, of a chained and recumbent figure lost in despair. It is perfectly finished, more in the style of Bernini than Michaelangelo, and fairly breathes with life. And with these qualities it captures effects which I had sought after in my *Cordelia*, and again in *Cleopatra*, but, as you know, did not achieve to my satisfaction.

There were other statues and many paintings to see at the Mercantile, though most of the latter were scenes of frontier and river life, and are, I suspect, romanticised views of the lives of Plains and Woodland Indians. Moira, with whom shall I share these small adventures, these little discoveries, now that I am so far from you? With whom shall I discuss, far past the witching hour, the ideas they excite? With my uncle, who awaits my arrival with such apparent gloom? Will there be anyone in this unknown hamlet who has even heard of Hosmer? Or Bernini, for that matter?

After the Mercantile, I struck out toward the levee, but soon thought the better of it. The streets here, though considered by the locals to be paved, are mostly covered with a fine white gravel called chat, which in some spots is not so much like a gravel as it is sand. Rain in the last few days has made these streets muddy and difficult of passage, and I felt that in the space of a block or two my shoes as well as my hemline would be soiled beyond my ability to satisfactorily clean in my hotel room. There is extensive work going on, however, to pave these areas with red granite cobblestones in some quarters, and brick in others. I decided to return to my room.

On the way, I passed an open air market, where I bought a roasted chicken leg to take back with me to the hotel. Mr. Schiller offered me a glass of sherry to go with it, and I've just finished a light but satisfying supper.

The overall feeling the city has given me is that it isn't of the West at all. It is older and even more European than many cities I've seen in the East. Many of the streets and boulevards have French names, and many of the people German ones. But this is all preamble, and surely not what you hoped to read on receiving this letter.

I can tell you my state of mind is much more tranquil and at peace since I saw you last in Boston. I hardly know how to explain or excuse my emotions then, either to you, my lifelong friend, or to Prosper, whose expectations I have destroyed. Of course, I hardly need mention the disappointment my parents must feel. First, in my failure to find a vocation in the holy orders, and second, in my desire to make my own way in the world by a means all but unknown to my sex, except amongst the communities of anarchists and nonconformists. Yet, I feel if all this had happened fifteen years ago, it could more easily be forgiven (those are fifteen years I've lost), but for a woman, a few years removed from forty and a spinster, to set aside a respectable proposal of marriage, to abandon friends and family, and in the opinion of some, God Himself, in something like the pursuit of a career, is neither to be understood nor forgiven. And Heaven knows, if I may be truly honest with myself, often I do not understand it either!

And such a career, too! A sculptor. A carver of stone. Was there ever a more unlikely profession for a woman? Except for Miss Hosmer, Edmonia Lewis, and a few others, stone carving, with its need of a strong arm, planning, and perseverance, is entirely the province of men. And do I need mention my lack of formal training?

As I sat in your parlor that rainy Sunday in June, surrounded by your loving family, with Prosper on my right, it suddenly occurred to me, as a result of some casual phrase spoken then about aging and the passing of time, or perhaps the news of the terrible death of Prosper's sister, Claire, that we had recently received, or something else which I can't even exactly remember now, that my life had reached, or even passed, its midpoint without my ever having attempted to live the life you know I've hoped for. It was all too much, recognizing that failure to act, which has always been as you know, my greatest flaw. Prosper has been exceedingly patient and kind. Even excessively so. I surely don't deserve such considerations. And I mean that most literally.

Is my middle-aged Frenchman also feeling his mortality? Am I merely his last hope for domestic complacency? The murder of his sister at Montsegur has affected him so terribly. It has disoriented his thinking and made him even more dependent upon me. But what would a life with him have been? A retelling of the one my mother and father knew?

He is a good man, and I know you bear him much affection, but he has truly and surely not an idea of his own. His interest in the arts, such as it is, is a mere condescension to me. So too his interest in books. I know you do not want to hear these things. That is why I write them now. I lacked the courage to discuss them with you face to face. And I know, with your influence on me, you would have dissuaded me from my purpose.

You asked me, in the telegram you sent me in Chicago, why I must leave Boston to make this expression of myself. What culture will I find in a forgotten backwater like Ste. Odile? What fulfillment in teaching the daughters of freed slaves and Indians on the banks of the Mississippi, living with an uncle who approves of my choices no more than my father? The only answer I can make is that there I will have the opportunity to make my own "culture" and my own living, freed from old connections, most of which, with the exception of you, my friend, I am more than ready to break. I will have very much leisure time and few distractions. There will be nothing but my own character and habits to prompt my failure.

I will close for tonight. It has been an exhausting day. I will write more tomorrow, as I expect to have many hours of idleness on the boat.

Aug. 3, 1882
2:15 P.M., aboard the *Abyssinia*

Dear Moira,

I had little sleep last night. As you can imagine, knowing my temperament, I was far too anxious to rest. By the time the chambermaid knocked upon my door at 8 A.M., as Mr. Schiller promised, I was dressed and packed, and ready for my breakfast. A small restaurant next door to the Essex filled the bill with cold ham, biscuits, and an egg, which I ate while Mr. Schiller sent a boy to the levee with my trunk.

After breakfast I made my way toward the levee. The streets had dried somewhat since yesterday, as an oppressive heat has settled over the region. Walking toward the river, I encountered rows of warehouses, many dilapidated, in which are stored great flasks, bales of cotton, farm implements, and other things, items which either have recently come off of, or will soon go onto, a riverboat. The tracks of the St. Louis and Iron Mountain railroads form a boundary at the outer edge of the grade of the levee, which slopes toward the river, paved as far as the eye can see with pink granite cobblestones. And the levee! I don't think I have ever seen such a spectacle of activity and confusion. Stacked everywhere on the cobblestones are the products of commerce: more cotton bales and grain, produce, flour, sugar, architectural iron work, leather goods, casks of beer and ale, all attended, added to or subtracted from, by hundreds of day laborers and roustabouts. It truly seems that everything made on this continent must pass through this city! And everywhere was a cacophony of languages and dialects, people speaking in many cases broken, accented English, or none at all. There were Germans, Irish, Negroes, Bohemians, Italians, and many which I took to be Greek or Lebanese.

It was with some difficulty I made my way through this crush of people and products toward the great bridge lately built by Eads. The *Abyssinia* was berthed, as I was told, in the first spot on the north side of the bridge. And resting there, it was the central boat of scores similarly berthed, bows upstream, run up nearly upon the cobblestones, with gangplanks lowered, each accepting or disgorging passengers and cargo. Many other boats were berthed parallel to the riverbank, in some cases two or three deep, waiting for the attendance of the roustabouts to relieve them of their burdens, or to add to them. All of these formed a white line of what could almost be taken for enormous, floating, lacy wedding cakes, extending at least one-half mile north and south from the spot on which I stood. The air was full of steam, and the smell of coal smoke, tar, and pine.

It was too soon to board when I arrived at the berth, as the roustabouts and day laborers were still loading cargo. I joined a small group of passengers waiting out of the way of the urgent loading and securing of crates and parcels large and small on the deck. My marble block had safely arrived as promised and was clearly visible on deck already, partially wrapped in burlap and secured with hemp ropes.

I lay my bag and leather purse momentarily on a large crate next to me to remove my jacket against the heat. Being one of only three women amongst the twenty or so waiting passengers, this simple and practical act attracted more attention than it warranted, I must say. Momentarily, four roustabouts arrived to remove the crate, and as I retrieved my bag from it, I noticed the markings, from an address with which we are both familiar: FROM HERTER BROS., 479-85 FIRST AVENUE, NEW YORK, NEW YORK, TO: MR. ORIEN BASTIDE, NUMBER 1 THERMOPYLAE ST., STE. ODILE. I was more than a little surprised to see a crate of furniture from the renowned Herter Brothers heading downriver to a tiny backwater village almost at the edge of the western frontier. I wondered who this man might be, to reside in such a place and yet be prosperous (and tasteful) enough to furnish a home from such an exclusive source.

Soon the holds and decks of the *Abyssinia* were loaded, and the passengers began to file up the gangplanks. My trunk was carried on board, nearly dropped once by what I took to be an Irish gentleman carrying it. He was more concerned than I, as the only breakable contents were a looking glass, my old glass-covered engraving of St. Cecilia's martyrdom, and my carriage clock.

As soon as the passengers had boarded, we were asked by the mate, a nervous, stocky little man, to give our tickets to the clerk who awaited us at the foot of the forward stairs, and then to ascend to the boiler deck where the staterooms are, until we were under way.

There were reputed to be more than thirty staterooms on the *Abyssinia*. As you may guess, I resolved to spare myself the expense of one of these. My infamous discomfort in small rooms may be manageable on dry land, but I could not predict what effect it would have on me on the water. As the trip downriver was said to take an average of ten hours, and there were many chairs to be had on deck, I didn't see the need of a room. I found a group of four of the chairs on the starboard side. That is where you find me now. I will close in hopes of posting this at our next stop.

Always your friend,
Perdita

Perdita waved her letter dry in the breeze, folded it, and returned it to her lap desk. She placed the small desk beside her chair, next to her tiny leather bag, and stretched her legs from under her chair across a varnished deck. A prosperous-looking couple approached her from the aft. They stopped at her side and nodded courteously, introducing themselves as Mr. Cooke and his wife from Davenport, Iowa.

"Do you mind if we sit?" Mr. Cooke asked in a flat, Midwestern accent.

"Not at all; please do." Perdita smiled and straightened herself in her chair. She thought she and Mrs. Cooke could almost be sisters. Mrs. Cooke was also of average height, with green eyes and red hair that still showed no sign of gray, despite that she was, like Perdita, approaching middle age. The Cookes sank slowly into the two chairs to

Perdita's right.

"I'm in real estate," Mr. Cooke said. He went on to explain, in some detail, that he and his wife were traveling to Natchez to settle some disputes that had arisen among Mrs. Cooke's family regarding the terms of her great aunt's will. As the boat waited for its turn to depart, the heat seemed even more oppressive on the water than it had been on the levee, and Mrs. Cooke soon followed Perdita's example and removed her jacket.

Mr. Cooke told Perdita he was a frequent packet traveler on several rivers, owing to his business. He said they were fortunate to be on the *Abyssinia*, as the boat, its captain, and most especially, its pilot Mr. Eccles, were highly regarded. Perdita was struck with a momentary wish that Moira could meet the Cookes. They had a charming Middlewestern way of talking and bickering back and forth, which she knew her friend, as a student of language and idiom, would have enjoyed.

"Boat this size will carry about two hundred tons of cargo and maybe a hundred and thirty passengers," Mr. Cooke said, as he tried to make himself comfortable on the hard chair. "This boat used to run from New Orleans to Vicksburg in about forty-five hours. I was on it once when it did. Then it was sold to McQuarrie in St. Louis for this run."

"Joda, I'll swear I don't know when you're telling the truth anymore!" Mrs. Cooke said, smiling at Perdita.

"No, forty-five hours it was, or maybe forty-nine, but it was absolutely less than fifty!"

"It don't hardly seem possible, upriver like that."

"It's possible. But you got to watch your boiler pressure. This one might do a hundred and fifty pounds or so..."

"Well, Miss Badon-Reed, I'm just as sorry as I can be, but Joda could talk the paint off a barn when it comes to these boats."

Perdita tried to make mental notations of the Cooke's

sayings so she could write them down for Moira later.

"If you got a good engineer, you'll probably be all right." Mr. Cooke was unfazed. "We got a good one. Can't think of his name, but he was on the *Prester John* until the ice broke her up. Anyway, you got to have a fellow who can control the pressure. You don't want to be on one of these when the boiler blows. I was on the *Teutonic* in the Ohio River when it blew up four years ago. It was fifteen crew and thirty-one passengers killed. Scalded to death, burned up, blown to bits, or drowned. I was thrown off the boiler deck into the river and caught a snag in my leg right here." He touched a spot on his left thigh.

"Joda!" Mrs. Cooke interrupted sharply. "Nobody wants to hear all that!"

"I have never been on a steamboat before this trip," Perdita said. "It is all new to me, and very interesting."

Mr. Cooke appeared grateful for what seemed like a diplomatic intervention on his behalf.

"How far down the river are you goin'?"

"Ste. Odile."

Mr. Cooke thought for a moment. "I never stopped there. Property never comes up for sale. Old French town. They speak as much French as English, and they have their own way of doing things. There's a few French towns down that way: Cahokia, Kaskaskia, Prairie du Rocher, Fort de Chartres. They do things different there, not much like Americans. I rode to Memphis with a priest from Kaskaskia once. He said the whole area was French until the English run them out in the 1760s or so. Ste. Odile was so out of the way nobody bothered with it. But like I said, property don't come up for sale. Nobody comes or goes."

"Is there much trade?" Perdita asked.

"Oh, they ain't poor, most of them. They mine lead. The war was the best thing that ever happened to them. They produce salt and quicklime, too."

A bell rang out above them, startling Mrs. Cooke and Perdita.

"That's their twelve hundred-pounder. We're ready to go," Mr. Cooke said.

A voice boomed down from above: "Break up!"

The squeaking of the pulleys was heard and the gangplanks started to rise to their storage positions. Deck lines were cast off, and one of the roustabouts called up, "All ready, Mr. Eccles." The message was conveyed to the hurricane deck, then up to the pilot house by another mate with a strong voice. The great steam whistle sounded.

The boat backed slowly out into the channel, and the three companions were momentarily engulfed in a cloud of black smoke and the smell of steam and tar as the breeze shifted. In a few moments, the boat's backward movement stopped. The whistle sounded a second time and the boat was on its way, under the legs of the great bridge and out into the sunlight again.

As Perdita watched the often shabby riverbank sliding past, she thought that the riverfront of any great city is not the most attractive foot it can put forward. She recalled the distinct sights and smells she and Moira had discovered in their wanderings along the Charles in Boston. In that regard, this stretch of the Mississippi looked much the same as the Charles. The whole of the riverfront as they passed it seemed given over to warehouses and industry, and the great hubris of activity. As the breezes shifted, the smells of the boat were often intermingled with foul and dank odors from the factories, slaughterhouses, and open drainage ditches and pipes that emptied into the river.

Once the *Abyssinia* was clear of the main body of the city, the breezes were most refreshing and provided a much needed relief from the heat. Recent high water had left tangles of debris in the channel and many snag boats were active, removing the masses of logs and other detritus that present such a hazard to all steamboats.

Within a half hour of its departure, the *Abyssinia* made its first stop, a matter of no more than five minutes, at Carondelet to take on two more passengers, and to offload a spinet and a sack of mail. Soon after the boat had maneuvered back into the channel again, Mrs. Cooke began to complain of uneasiness in her stomach brought on, she thought, from the smells and motion of the boat. Mr. Cooke took his wife's unsteady arm and the two of them made their way tentatively back to their stateroom to rest.

At a village called Kimmswick, the boat offloaded a crate of hurricane lamps and several plows, an elderly couple, a sack of mail, and took on another sack of mail and a young woman with a small child. The young mother and the child, a girl of about four, made their way slowly past Perdita and disappeared aft behind crates and cotton bales stowed on the deck.

Several times since leaving the city, Perdita had noticed a man in a linen suit walk past her on deck, stand for a moment looking out across the river, move away and then come back again. Soon after the Cookes returned to their stateroom, the man made his way slowly back toward her and stood at the rail looking down at the water churning under the side wheel. He was eating an apple. When he finished it, he tossed the core back toward the wheel and watched it disappear under it, into the roiling water. He turned and looked at Perdita in the eye for the first time and touched the brim of his hat. He looked at her in an almost brazen way, even though he did not hold her gaze for long. She began to feel uneasy. She thought about the changes in herself and her temperament that she was resolving to implement, that she needed to make, to make her new life possible. To avoid the man's gaze, she looked to her belongings sitting under her chair and thought she might add an addendum to her letter to Moira. To her horror, she saw her small leather bag was gone. She stood in a panic.

"Oh, my God!" she gasped.

The man in the linen suit approached her with a grave expression on his face.

"What is it, Miss?" he asked.

"My purse is missing. My bag! It had all of my money in it!" Perdita was suddenly lightheaded. She gasped for breath. "It was here, under my chair but ten minutes ago." She started to hurry forward, then aft, then stopped, not knowing how to begin to look for her bag. "The mate," she said. "I'll report this to the mate or the captain. I'll go up and speak to the captain!"

"That's a good idea," the man said. "Before you do that, though, wait here a minute. Just a minute, then I'll help you notify anyone who can help you—if need be."

Perdita stood, puzzled, as the man made his way aft quickly, past the crates and cotton bales. In less than two minutes, Perdita saw him approaching her again. He smiled.

"Here you are, Miss," he said, as he reached into his jacket pocket and withdrew Perdita's bag. She smiled in relief and took the bag from him.

"Oh, thank you, sir!"

"I thought the first place to check was that little girl who came through here a while ago. I found her and her momma on the other side. The bag was too pretty for her to leave alone. Is everything there?"

Perdita drew the bag open and looked inside. "Yes, it's all here. Thank you again." She felt suddenly drained and returned to her chair.

"Do you mind if I sit?" the man asked in an unctuous fashion. Perdita did mind, but said she did not. He sat and crossed his legs.

"I am Virgil Alsop."

"How do you do?" Perdita said flatly, but not impolitely, discouraging any implied rapport by conspicuously withholding her name.

"I am with the Cerberus Assurance Company in Memphis. On my way home."

"You are a salesman, then?"

"Well, yes. An agent."

"There seem to be a lot of salesmen up and down this river."

"But not too many women traveling alone." He shrugged. "I thought you were with that couple, who were here. But now I see you're not."

"No. Mr. Cooke is a salesman too. An agent."

"So. You are traveling alone then."

"Mr. Alsop, why should you be at all interested in the circumstances of my trip? You have done me a great service just now. Without being rude, I must say I was hoping for some time on my own." Perdita was surprised to hear the words leaving her lips. Her cheeks flushed and her voice began to quiver.

"Oh, just making conversation. Just trying to be friendly. I approve of women doing independent things."

"Acting on necessity is hardly an act of independence."

"But still, I approve of —"

"I neither seek nor highly regard your approval, sir!" Perdita stood. She wanted very much to control her emotions, but found herself suddenly on the verge of angry tears. She could not understand her own vehemence.

"There's no need to—"

"Your service to me has not given you latitude to presume familiarity, to impose attentions on me. And now you have taken from me a most comfortable point of vantage. I will take the matter up with the mate should you choose to annoy me again!" Her voice broke and her whole body quivered as she turned from him and walked forward toward the stairs. She climbed to the Texas deck and stood forward facing the breeze until she could regain her composure.

Another steamboat, a sternwheeler, as Mr. Cooke called them, approached the *Abyssinia* on the port side, and Perdita was startled by a blast of the huge whistle in greeting. The pilot house was behind her and she heard the door open. A small man in a black swallowtail coat and derby hat, whom she took to be Mr. Eccles, the pilot, descended the stairs with a teacup in his hand.

"Good afternoon, Miss," he said, touching his hat. "I didn't mean to startle you just now!" Perdita smiled, rather embarrassed. "It is loud, isn't it?" he asked.

"Yes, when you're not expecting it."

"I was going to have this," he said, offering her the teacup. "Why don't you have it? It relaxes me." He directed her to a small bench just in front of the pilot house. She sat.

"Thank you," she said. "I think this is just what I need."

"I have to get back upstairs. I hope you enjoy the rest of your trip." He touched his hat again and disappeared.

She found the tea to be most soothing and was grateful for this small act of kindness. She slowly finished the cup.

Perdita sat transfixed for several hours, facing the breeze and watching the landscape slide slowly past. She watched the sworls of viscous, opaque water, and the occasional white egret, as well as hawks, muskrats, and herons in stretches where the riverbank subsided into great dreary marshes with spectral, dead oak trees and varieties of grotesque evergreens. At five o'clock, the dinner bell sounded. Hours later, after the meal and a brief reunion with the Cookes, Perdita returned to her solitary deck chair with her lap desk under her arm. She had decided to add the addendum she had considered to her earlier letter to Moira:

Later, on deck

It is getting late, and the Texas deck is nearly deserted. I thought I would sit a moment under one of the bright deck lamps to let my dinner settle and enjoy the breezes a bit longer in solitude before my river trip ends.

I remained forward on this deck, the Texas deck, as I said, for several hours this afternoon, enjoying the sights along the river and those landscapes which remained unscarred by the heavy hand of man. I sat here until the dinner bell was rung and I made my way down to the grand salon. The salon is a long, elegant room with a lush red carpet, and white and gold tracery around the windows and doors. The Cookes, a very affable couple I had met earlier on deck, were seated at a table near the main door and they invited me to join them.

Mrs. Cooke was recovered from an earlier illness and was full of conversation. Mr. Cooke insisted on buying my supper of a pork chop and steamed vegetables. As Mrs. Cooke prattled on about fashion, the appointments of the salon, and the greediness of her family regarding settlement of a will, and Mr. Cooke interrupted her with comparisons of the load capacities of sidewheelers versus sternwheelers, my attention wandered around the room. I noticed a creature whom had first aided me, and then annoyed me on deck earlier, a Mr. Alsop, seated at a table across the room with a young woman who had boarded at a village called Kimmswick with her small child.

After supper, the Cookes and I resumed our former seats on deck. We talked for several hours about many things, touching on no subject of much importance, certainly nothing worth recording here.

2 A.M., at Ste. Odile, my room

Moira, it is obvious I will have little sleep tonight. I have been trying to settle in for two hours in the cozy bed and comfortable room which my uncle has provided for me, with no success. I may as well give up the effort!

The *Abyssinia* arrived in Ste. Odile a few minutes past eleven. The Cookes had retired at ten, and after adding a few lines to this letter, I watched on deck alone for the lights of the town, which I was told by the mate should soon appear on the western bank.

Soon, in the darkness I saw the black hump of an island ahead and the boat began to turn to the right of it, by all appearances heading into an empty shore. The calls of whippoorwills drifted here and there above the dark barrier of forest on both banks of the river, mixed with the chirruping of tree frogs and other night sounds. There was a sliver of moon in the sky, and as we cleared the point of the island, it illuminated a channel I hadn't seen before. As the channel widened and the boat headed deeper into it, I began to see the few dim lamps of Ste. Odile.

There were lanterns and oil lamps at the landing, and the boat sounded its whistle and made its way toward these slowly and carefully. There was a high prominence just north of the town that rose black against the sky. There appeared to be tall trees and a large house on its summit, and a few dim lights glowed orange in its irregular silhouette.

I was the only passenger whose destination was Ste. Odile. I made my way forward and down to the main deck. Two deckhands had already secured my marble block in a harness suspended from the forward hoist. We sidled into the levee, a smaller version of the one in St. Louis, smoothly and effortlessly, as if sliding along the surface of an ice-bound lake.

A platform spring-wagon with a two-mule hitch awaited us on the levee, and with surprising ease the block and my trunk were loaded onto it. The driver, Aristide, was an old black man with a French accent who had been hired by Uncle Tancred to meet me. I climbed up onto the seat next to him, without his assistance, I might add. As the wagon was turned around, I noticed a second wagon arriving down an adjoining street with the odd name of Mal Ardents. This wagon was driven by a tall, well-dressed black man, there, it became apparent, to pick up the large crate from Herter Brothers which I had seen in St. Louis.

Aristide had little to say as we made our way along the dimly-lit cobblestone streets. Do you remember, Moira, when I was eight and my father took me by ship to New Orleans to see if I might be enrolled in the Ursuline School? Ste. Odile reminded me immediately of that trip. The air was heavy and damp, and very hot. The streets were narrow and dark, and had a foreign feel about them, for want of a better way to say it. They were lined with shops and shuttered houses made of stone or brick, or poteaux-en-terre, in the Creole style. I felt as if I had stepped out of the United States and into some misplaced European town.

As the wagon slowly turned onto a street called Bucephalus, a courthouse with a small brick jail came into view. There was a small group of seven or eight men in front talking to another who was holding a lantern and wearing a badge on his lapel.

"Dem men still dere," Aristide mumbled, as if he was speaking to himself, not to me.

"Who are they?" I asked.

"Oh, dem men is after Miss Chardin."

"*After* her?"

"She kill her daughter. A nine-year ol' chile."

"My God—"

"Hit her in the head with the edge of a shovel. Then she lay her in bed in a new linen dress and walk to the jail."

I gasped at the horrible image conjured by what Aristide had just said.

"Dem men wants to lynch her. Dey jus' layabouts

with nothin' better to do. Dey ain't goin' to cheat the packet company out of dere money."

He reached down to the floorboard of the wagon and found a handbill which he gave to me. It read:

> AN EXCITING EXCURSION IN THE CAUSE OF JUSTICE! VIZIR PACKET LINE OF STE. ODILE OFFERING PASSAGE FOR ONLY $1.50 PER PERSON TO de CASTRES ISLAND ON AUGUST 22 AT 9 A.M. TO ALL PERSONS WISHING TO WITNESS THE EXECUTION BY HANGING OF MARIE DELAPORTE CHARDIN FOR THE HIDEOUS MURDER OF HER ONLY CHILD. INTERESTED PERSONS SHOULD SEE MR. REMY AT OUR OFFICES AT NUMBER ONE HUNDRED AND ONE BOSPHOROUS STREET, STE. ODILE.

I folded the paper and put it in my bag. It seemed a unique keepsake of human cruelty, and I thought I must enclose it with this letter so you can see for yourself my introduction to this village. Moira, I scarcely knew which event was more ghastly, a woman murdering her child, or a town turning out in a festive mood to watch her execution.

"I can't imagine a mother hating her child so much as to—," I began.

"She didn't hate that chile—"

I wondered to what kind of place I'd come. Had I decided upon Ste. Odile too hastily? Aristide guided the mules around the corner of Constantinople Street, and the Church of the Holy Mandillion came into view. Behind it was the small, Gothic brick rectory of my Uncle Tancred. The house was dark, and so I assumed him to be asleep. I hoped my arrival would not disturb him.

I will close for now. I am exhausted, and I think perhaps I can sleep. I will try to post this tomorrow, and be assured there will be many more letters to come.

With greatest affection,
Perdita

3

Moira felt she had done all for Prosper that she could do. She'd been more than sympathetic. She, too, was shocked by Perdita's sudden disappearance, as much by the fact she hadn't foreseen it, as that it had happened at all. She felt somewhat betrayed by it. They were the closest of friends since their earliest years as schoolgirls at the Academy of St. Thecla. There were never any secrets between them. For Perdita to disappear like that, deceiving her family and fiancée, and without the consultation of her closest friend, was almost completely contrary to her character, at least as Moira had always known it.

Moira loved Perdita like a sister, but knew her to be occasionally indecisive and irresolute, and often in a quandary about what course of action would serve her own best interests. It had been Moira, after all, who recognized Prosper's true feelings for Perdita, and encouraged her to respond to them. Left on her own, Moira knew Perdita would have failed to identify the signs, or questioned their truth and failed to act, allowing an opportunity, perhaps never to be repeated, to fade away.

Moira embraced the life of a spinster, and found an ironic sense of independence in continuing to live with her parents. But this was not the life for Perdita. Her family situation was difficult. And she lacked, in Moira's opinion, a strong sense of her worth and her talents, although Moira saw an undeveloped inner strength in her friend that she sometimes realized she envied. But Perdita lacked confidence and boldness, which made her disappearance even more surprising. She would have a hard time making her way in the world without a husband's emotional attentions and reinforcement. Moira felt Prosper was of a temperament to suit this purpose very well.

As for herself, Moira had rarely come across a man whose nonsense she could tolerate for long. She didn't imagine all men were of the same species as the few with whom she'd had any degree of intimacy, but somehow those more worthy souls never crossed her path. She had no interest in becoming a house servant, a cook, a breeder of children, of living at the beck and call of some man whose intellect bored her, or in having to minister to him in his old age. She didn't feel any of this was beyond the latitudes which Perdita could reach. But Moira knew it was not for her.

Moira was amazed at the level of deception Perdita had employed to effect her disappearance. She had reestablished contact with her uncle, Father Tancred Condell, the parish priest at Ste. Odile, had asked him for a position at the seminary, arranged her trip and the shipment of her marble blocks, packed and slipped away, all on her own, without the knowledge of her friends or loved ones. Given all she thought she knew of Perdita, Moira would have scarcely thought her friend capable of conceiving and executing such a plan independently. Perdita often seemed rather helpless to Moira, and lacking in the practical skills necessary to cope with life's many details. And she had never known Perdita to be deceptive, except perhaps once or twice when Moira had pressed her hard on some lapse of judgement or common sense, as when she'd been cheated by a tradesman or shopkeeper, and been too embarrassed to readily admit it. In spite of her friend's mortification in those circumstances, Moira found she could not, in good conscience, allow the incidents to pass without making her feelings known.

Moira could hardly make Prosper understand something she didn't understand herself.

"I didn't hear a word from her until she'd been gone for four days," she said, offering Prosper more cake. He refused it, and finished the last of his tea. He was sitting miserably in her father's overstuffed chair. "And that was scarcely more than a note," she continued, "just a few lines to say she was well, and generally where she was, and to promise more of an explanation later. She asked me to show the note to her parents, but she's sent nothing to them. Not a word."

"Nor to me." Prosper smiled painfully as he said it.

"Not yet. But I'm sure she will."

Moira set the tea tray on a side table. "Give her time. She means to, I'm sure of it. She's still very confused and unsettled in her mind. Another few weeks will do the trick."

"I've done something to turn her away from me." Prosper cleared his throat repeatedly, as he always did when his emotions were getting the better of him. "It is such a terrible time for this to happen. I had the letter and wire from my poor sister back home asking me to come to her, but I sensed something was wrong with Perdita, and I refused Claire's request. Who knows if Claire would not be alive now if I had gone to her as she asked."

"You must put it all in the past. None of it was your doing." Moira had told him this many times in the last few days. "Perdita is confused. I think the signs have been there for a year or two. Now I understand them. I think she'll never be content unless she knows whether or not she could truly live as an artist."

Moira refilled her teacup. "It's a fancy she and I have shared," she continued. "In that sense, you could say I am more responsible than you. To me it was nothing more than a fancy. Girlishness. Foolishness. But I'll be sunk if she didn't believe it!" Moira quickly ate the last bite of her cake.

Their long conversation had extended tea into suppertime. "We talked about founding a colony of artists and writers, of being self-supporting." Moira frowned in confusion. "I can't believe she took any of it seriously. And she was always banging around on some piece of stone—"

"I didn't approve of it." Prosper cleared his throat again. "But I said nothing. I thought I must needs keep quiet about it. I thought it distracted her too much, and upset her."

"And, Lord, the pieces didn't amount to much. They never looked quite right to me." Moira took a long sip from her cup. "I mean, the *Cordelia*. A person can't turn her head like that. And the proportions on the *Cleopatra*, with the leg going from here to there!"

"I didn't want to be the one to discourage her," Prosper said as he rose from his chair. He put his cup on the red serpentine mantle. "What chance will she have of success? Who will seek out a woman to commission a stone statue?"

"The Havilland Library did, but I'm not certain if it is a serious commission. There is no contract. Mr. Tedoni told her to make clay models first," Moira said, "but she never had the patience to do it. She attacks the stone and hopes for the best."

Prosper moved to the tall front window and looked out on the shady, well-kept arc of lawns, ornate front doors, and gigantic elms that made up Newgrange Circle.

"I should be back home now." His voice was weak, and Moira noticed that the remnants of his Provencal accent were a bit more in evidence than usual. "I should have gone home as soon as I got word of Claire's death. My mother is distraught. My father scarcely leaves the house. He's drinking too much again. I get a letter every two days from my brother asking me why I'm not there. When Perdita seemed so distant and uncertain, I told him business was preventing my departure. Since she's gone, I've told him I'm ill."He filled his pipe from a pouch Claire had once sent him as a birthday gift. "It's terrible to deceive them at such a time. I just don't know what to do."

Moira could see his hand trembling slightly as he held his pipe. She recognized in him some evidence of the melancholia she'd seen as a volunteer nursing war veterans. She remembered Sergeant Larkin, a man she had nursed at the Cole Street Hospital. He had lost his left foot and hand at Antietam, costing him his trade as a tanner. His family was reasonably well off, and his business, run by his father, had even prospered during the war years. But idleness and a sense of uselessness slowly enveloped him in despair, driving his wife away from him, and ending in his suicide a month after Moira had first taken up his care. She knew Prosper's mind needed an occupation, a mission toward which he could re-direct his thoughts and energies.

"There's never been any question about it in my mind. About what you should do, I mean." Moira stood and retrieved Prosper's teacup from the mantle and stacked it on top of hers on the small side table. "There will be no use in talking to Perdita for awhile. I feel her mind is set. We have often been able to sense each other's moods, and I feel, for now, she is intractable. She must have time and opportunity to consider what she has done. To go chasing after her now would be the worst thing we could do, and would profit nothing. You must go home to see your family, and pay your respects to your poor sister."

The bell was rung for dinner. Prosper tapped out his pipe on the fireplace wall. The smell of roasted beef filled the house. Moira could hear the creak of the servant's staircase, the one her parents preferred to use, as they descended. Moira took Prosper's arm and led him gently toward the dining room.

"I can't believe she took any of it seriously!" she said.

4

Perdita's first impression when she opened her eyes was of void. Nothing but a pale gray emptiness was visible through her double-casement window, as if she had awakened in a room perched at the edge of the world. For the first few moments, she could not remember where she was nor how she had come to be there. Then she remembered: Uncle Tancred, Ste. Odile, the beginning of her true career as an artist. Her trip had ended, and now it was up to her to create a new life.

She sat up. Perdita found herself in a simple iron bed in a room just large enough for comfort: not too enclosed, not too dark. The large double window with leaded panes helped allay any feeling of confinement, and seemed to open up the room. A small desk was situated before the window, in front of which sat a plain walnut chair on casters. A chiffonier, a moderately sized wardrobe, a bedside table, and a small bookcase completed the room's furnishings. She arose from bed and moved to the window to get a better look at the grounds. A dense fog had settled in; nothing was visible through the mist but a suggestion of a large tree, some branches of which reached vaguely toward the window.

Aristide had placed her trunk at the foot of her bed the night before. She opened it and dug through to the bottom. There she found her etching of the martyrdom of St. Cecilia, wrapped in a petticoat for safety. She had found the etching in a curiosity shop in Boston ten years before and always carried it with her on the few occasions when she traveled. She carefully unwrapped the picture and studied it for a moment. It was at least a century or so old. The ink had turned brown, but was still very dark and distinct. The saint lay crumpled on the street, on her right side, presumably in front of her large house. Although the body faced the viewer, the head was twisted backward, in a position which looked impossible until the gash on her neck was noticed. Two Roman soldiers stood watching her, waiting for her to die, as they had done for three days. One of them, perhaps, was the one who had botched the beheading, and now, afraid to finish the job, both stood by helplessly as she preached with a failing voice to onlookers, winning many converts to her new Christian faith in her last hours.

Perdita found an old nail in the wall between the windows. She carefully hung the etching on it, then removed her carriage clock from the trunk, wound it, and placed it on the night table. She then began to unpack her clothes and few books from the trunk.

In fifteen minutes she had organized her things, put away her clothes, and dressed. She could hear a clattering of dishes toward the front of the house and could smell fish frying. She smiled. Uncle Tancred's taste in food apparently had not changed in the nearly twenty years since she'd seen him: fish for breakfast; his old English breakfast. Even though he was from the Midlands, a Warwickshire man, he had developed a taste for breakfast kippers during his years as an assistant pastor at Brixham. Perdita's parents, who had emigrated after her uncle, had given up many of their Old World habits almost as soon as they set sail from Bournemouth, before she was born. She heard footsteps approaching her door. She pinned her hair quickly. There was a knock.

"Miss Perdita?" It was a young woman's voice, sweet

and a bit uncertain.

"Yes. I am here."

"Breakfast is ready, Miss. Father Condell wants to know if you'll be a-comin' out for it?"

Perdita opened her door quickly. A young girl of sixteen or seventeen in a pressed, white apron stood before her in the hallway.

"Good morning." Perdita smiled, feeling for stray, fallen hairs as she stepped out of her room. "I was just coming. I wanted to organize my things, you know—"

"Yes, Miss. He sent me to fetch you. It's breakfast at seven-thirty every morning. Don't think he'd wait on it long. He hates tardiness."

"I remember that about him." The girl's face was well-scrubbed and pleasant. "And what is your name?"

"I'm Bess, Miss. Mrs. Moon's daughter. She is the housekeeper. I help out here when I can be spared at home." Bess began to lead the way toward the front of the house along the whitewashed hallway, the walls of which were unadorned save for a grouping of small lithographs depicting New Testament scenes.

"He has mass at six and some days again at eight for the girls at the seminary," Bess said. "That is, when Father Vannier ain't here. Those are the days he don't eat at seven-thirty, because of communion. Then he has his Divine Office and all the things priests have to do. He ain't much used to guests. Not ones that live here, anyway. I hope you'll do all right with him. I mean to say, I'm sure you will."

"Does he have many friends in town?"

"I don't know. I remember, Sheriff Aubuchon's been here a time or two, and Mr. Morisot from the mines. Mr. Robert is here every so often. Hypolitte Robert. They talk about books and religion."

"Are they friends?"

"Oh, I don't know, Miss. Mr. Robert is an Episcopalian!"

The hallway ended at the dining room, which was of a moderate size with white plaster walls and dark oaken chair rails. Uncle Tancred sat at the near end of the table. With some difficulty he turned toward Perdita as she entered the room, then started to rise from his chair. She was surprised at how small and old he looked.

"No, please, Uncle, don't stand." Perdita embraced him tentatively from behind, lightly touching his shoulders, to prevent him from rising. She kissed him lightly on the cheek, which seemed to startle him a little. "Good morning," she said cheerfully. "I hope you haven't waited breakfast on my account."

"No."

He may have smiled slightly, but Perdita wasn't certain.

"There isn't much time for waitin' meals 'ere, my girl!" His Warwickshire accent was as thick as it had been thirty years before. "I've too much to do for that. No lack of courtesy intended."

"No, of course not. I promise to have no effect whatever on your routine. It is so good to see you!"

"Aye." He nodded emotionlessly.

"And it is so generous of you to take me in like this."

"We'll zee what comes of it, my girl. Not much good, if I may zpeak plainly!"

Perdita avoided the inclination to be ruffled by this statement. "Your kindness has not been misplaced or wasted, Uncle Tancred. I'll prove it to you, as quickly as I can."

Tancred took a long sip of a murky brown liquid in a small glass in front of him. Perdita smiled.

"You are still sipping your nectar, I see," she said, nodding at the glass.

"Aye. Ztill favor a glass of zoider with my kippers

of a mornin'. Do you good, too."

Perdita took a place at her uncle's right hand. Mrs. Moon quickly brought in a plate with two fried eggs and bacon, and placed it in front of her.

"Do you take coffee, Miss?" Mrs. Moon asked. She was slim and well groomed, a thin-lipped woman of about fifty.

"Yes, thank you, with little cream. And I'll have a cider, also."

Tancred finished his cider in a single gulp, making sucking and swallowing noises which Perdita imagined offered no affront to manners in the opinions of elderly gentlemen used to living alone. And her uncle did seem elderly now. He had aged greatly in twenty years. His back was bent, causing him to hunch over his breakfast plate. His complexion was more sallow, his hair much grayer than she remembered. After he had gone west, when Perdita was still a young girl, she had overheard scraps of stories her parents had apparently resolved to keep from her, about some great calamity Tancred had faced and barely survived. She wondered if the effects of that experience had contributed to the decline she saw in him now. Tancred's coffee cup shook a little as he raised it, and a bit of the brown liquid dribbled on his chin from his drooping lips as he sipped.

"'Ow was your trip, then?" Tancred asked, not looking up from his breakfast.

"Oh, tolerable. Pleasant enough. The last part, the river travel, at least. Once you are accustomed to the smells, and the noise—"

"I 'ate those boats. The zmoke and the racket. Rattle your zkellinton apart. I'll take a zail and rudder any day and twice of a Zunday!"

Perdita laughed. She noticed his accent seemed to grow more or less severe as he became animated and then calm again.

"Well that's 'ow I feel on the zubject of zteamboats," Tancred said defensively and humorlessly.

"No, I agree. It is so exhausting. I am glad the trip is over and that I am finally here…with you!"

"Aye." Tancred finished his coffee.

Perdita was suddenly hungry, and ate her eggs quickly. Tancred looked through some mail Mrs. Moon had placed beside his plate. He dropped the letters abruptly on the table and looked seriously at Perdita.

"Are you in good graces with the church, then?"

Perdita was surprised by the question. "Yes…I haven't made confession in two weeks, but I will as soon as you'll hear it. Nothing much to say, really. Then I will receive Holy Communion, of course. Tomorrow, I suppose. I can't now…this morning…because we've eaten, obviously."

"No eight o'clock mass today, anyway. Father Vannier 'as been doing it more these days. 'E comes through three times a week from Kaskaskia and Prairie du Rocher. Rather that 'e be your confessor."

"Well, of course, if you prefer. As I said, there isn't much to say—"

"Would be more proper."

Mrs. Moon appeared from the kitchen, rustling noisily in her starched apron and skirts. She began to gather up Tancred's dishes.

"Saw there was a letter from the diocese there, Father," she said.

"Aye," Tancred grunted.

"Has the Archbishop improved any?"

"No," Tancred said wearily. "Ztill paralyzed on the right zide and bedridden."

"Dear me, that don't sound good." Mrs. Moon shook her head. "His Eminence had a stroke a month ago," she said to Perdita. "I'm afraid he's had it, God bless him. He'll have to resign or be replaced by the Holy Father. The sooner the better, too."

"We'll leave that to God and to the Holy Father, eh, Mrs. Moon?" Tancred sounded peevish. "Zince I've zeen no telegrams lyin' 'ereabouts from Rome zeeking your advice, I assume the disposition of His Eminence is ztill at zixes and zevens, as far as the Pope is concerned, though the matter may be in no doubt to Effie Moon!"

"I was only stating the obvious." Mrs. Moon was unfazed.

"Our Lord's ways would be zoooo much less mysterious, if only He'd listen to you, would they not?"

Mrs. Moon winked at Perdita as she carried the dishes into the kitchen.

"No difficult questions in the world at all," Tancred grumbled, opening another letter. "Zimple as pie, they are; just ask Mrs. Moon!"

Perdita smiled to herself and finished her cider. Tancred again dropped his mail on the table suddenly.

"And what about young men?" he demanded. Perdita was puzzled. "We 'ave to broach that zubject, don't we?"

"No, Uncle. You have nothing to worry about on that account."

"A propriety must be maintained in this rectory."

"I understand, of course."

"You left a young man behind, as you zaid, to come 'ere."

"Yes. I can promise you I have no interest in emotional entanglements. I wanted to be away from that…from those."

"You zay it now; if we dig up what the dog buried zix month from now, will it zmell the zame, I wonder? As long as we understand each other." Tancred returned to his mail.

Perdita collected what were left of her dishes, and

would have risen to take them into the kitchen had not Bess appeared and whisked them away from her with a smile.

"Aristide was waitin' for you with the wagon when you landed?" Tancred mumbled.

"Yes. He helped me in with my things."

"'E's a good man, and 'as many zons like 'imself. The English don't appreciate men like 'im as they should. The native peoples. The ones in a place before our ilk arrives. Aristide's folk 'ave been 'ere two hundred year!"

"He told me about the woman, Chardin, who murdered her child."

"Aye. Marie Delaporte Chardin. A lost zoul, if ever a creature fit the description."

"Why in Heaven's name would she do such a horrible thing?"

"It may be difficult for you to understand, my girl." Tancred looked at Perdita for the first time with an expression that conveyed affection. "It's terrible, truly. Don't judge the poor wretch too harshly. She made 'er confession, and I can zay nothing. There was madness in 'er family, 'er grandmother and aunt. She feared that curse, too, I know. She doubts 'er own zanity at times, I think, though she 'as told me she was aware and in 'er right mind when she did the deed. It is a great tragedy, to be sure, for both child and mother."

"And the execution will be public?"

"Aye," said Tancred sadly. "The packet-line is making an excursion out of it. A dollar-fifty a ticket to watch this shattered woman, once a friend and neighbor, get 'er desserts, be they just or unjust."

"Yes. I heard about that. It's appalling. I always try to think the best of people, of their goodness, then you hear of something like this—"

"And they've near zold every ticket!" Tancred shook his head as if in disbelief. "These aren't bad people 'ereabouts.

I don't understand why they would be a party to zuch a thing."

"The poor woman. Although I can't imagine what would have driven a mother to have done—"

"I must minister to 'er today, 'ear 'er confession. And Mrs. Moon 'as baked 'er zome tarts, though I imagine Aubuchon will end up with most of those."

"May I go with you, Uncle? Do you think it would be appropriate? Do you think she would mind seeing a stranger?"

Tancred looked surprised. "No 'arm in it, I guess. If you're of a mind to. She would be grateful for the company. Particularly a woman's company."

"I will go then, if you will allow me."

"But touch on no zubject relatin' to 'er crime or zentence. If she mentions them, that's different."

"Of course. And I must check with the packet-line office about my block of marble from Tennessee. I'm doing a Heloise and Abelard for a library—"

"You told me in your last letter. The block hazn't arrived az yet. I checked yesterday."

"Ah. Thank you for checking, Uncle. I hope it isn't too delayed. I have to finish that statue by spring."

After the breakfast dishes had been washed and put away, Mrs. Moon prepared a basket with her tarts, a jar of peach preserves, and a tin of ground cinnamon for Perdita to take to the jail. Tancred disappeared into his room for a moment and soon reappeared with his biretta on his head and a valise in his hand.

The air was still and humid as Perdita and Tancred stepped out of the rectory and onto the flagstone walk alongside the church, which emptied onto Constantinople Street. The church, as Perdita could now see, was a beautiful old Gothic structure of brick and stone with intricate carvings and tracery surrounding stained glass windows, buttresses, and niches housing marble saints. It stood at the corner of

Constantinople and Mal Ardents streets.

"It is a beautiful church," Perdita said, as her eyes scanned detail after detail, from cornices to mullions, to corbels along the façade.

"Aye," Tancred agreed, following her gaze. "This izn't the original building. That was ztone and hewn logs built, they zay, within the zecond month after Mouzzaut, I mean to zay Moussaut, the first priest, landed 'ere. That one burned to the ground."

"What does the name signify? The Holy Mandillion?"

"Zaid to be a cloth upon which Our Lord left an image of 'is face and zent to the king of Edessa to cure 'is leprosy. We 'ave a fragment known to come from the cloth that 'as been in the village from the earliest days."

Constantinople Street formed a western boundary of the town's mercantile district. There were a few shops to be seen, including a cabinet maker and a blacksmith, with houses of various sizes situated between them. Further north along the street and to the west, behind the church, there appeared to be more homes than businesses, with the commercial district, such as it was, lying closer to the river.

A farmer driving a team of oxen, and a woman leading a large sow along the street nodded to Tancred, though they appeared to be looking at Perdita. He returned their greetings, grunting something unintelligible, as he guided Perdita around the corner onto Bucephalus Street. A clacking of hooves resounded on the cobblestones behind them, approaching at a slow, steady pace. Perdita turned in time to see a pair of chestnut geldings pass them pulling a large, maroon Rockaway carriage. The tall black man she had seen at the landing retrieving the Herter Brothers crate the night before was driving. She caught only a glimpse of the figure inside the carriage, but she had the odd impression that the figure was not a living person, but a mannequin of some kind. Tancred looked sternly at the carriage as it passed.

"I saw that driver at the landing last night," Perdita said, "picking up a crate for a…what was the name?"

"Bastide." Tancred said the name slowly.

"Yes, that was it. The crate held some piece of very expensive furniture. I was surprised anyone in a small town like this—"

"That gentleman can afford anythin' 'e desires. 'Is family 'as owned the mines zince the beginnin'. Now 'e's the only one left. I don't know what to make of 'im. Left Ste. Odile before I arrived and 'as only just returned. Almost never zeen in the town."

"He sounds like an interesting, or at least mysterious, character."

"Aye. It iz my opinion that you would do well to zteer clear of 'im."

"I can't imagine our paths ever crossing."

"I'm told 'e 'as a way of crossing paths with young women if 'e 'as a mind to."

Perdita smiled. "I do not think that I would be the kind—"

"My girl," Tancred stopped and faced her, "it is not my intention to flatter you or to tweak your vanity. Nothing as zilly as that. It is a fair warning and for your own good."

"Oh, of course." Perdita felt the color rise in her neck and face. She was embarrassed at her presumption and a little angry at her uncle's unsparing manner.

"I zee our friends are ztill 'ere." Tancred nodded toward two men sitting on the curb in front of the jail. Perdita recognized them as half the party she had seen confronting the sheriff the night before.

"They've been layin' about 'ere for a week."

"Yes, Aristide told me."

"Orville! Tector!" Tancred called harshly to the men. "You look like a pair of 'ounds waiting for a scrap to fall from the table."

The men looked at Perdita. Their gaze unsettled her.

"Scrap might fall," the older man said. He was thin and sunburned. and wearing a torn straw hat. "And if it don't, may hafta take it anyway."

Both men continued to look at Perdita. They seemed to be enjoying her uneasiness. "Somebody needs to do somethin' about this…murder. Ain't right to wait for the packet-line to make money on it."

"What do you two care about this woman and her child?" Tancred was growing angrier. " 'Ave you no work at Laubardemont's to occupy you?"

"Nope," the younger man said. "We done earnt our fifteen dollars this month."

Tancred took Perdita's arm and hurried her toward the jailhouse. The heavy jailhouse door was open now. Sheriff Aubuchon stood in the doorway.

"Never mind those two, Father," Aubuchon called. "Come in. Come in, Miss."

The jailhouse was dark and humid inside. Aubuchon's office was a cluttered, square room. Tiny barred windows provided most of the light and all of the ventilation. Aubuchon bolted the door after them. He was a tall, unshaven, middle-aged man.

"I know what you are going to say, Father," Aubuchon said, smiling. "I'll tell you like my mother told me: '*Si vous ne voulez pas dormir avec les rats, mis inviter dans!*'"

Perdita looked puzzled. "My French isn't—"

"If you don't want to sleep with the rats," Aubuchon interrupted her, "don't invite them in!"

"They ought to be in jail!" Tancred was adamant. "They are malingering, disturbing the peace! What about their zervice on the county roads? 'Ave they done that yet this year?"

"You can't enforce it, Father," Aubuchon said. "And that would only clear them out for four days at any rate. I've run them off a few times, but they come back. They're afraid Floyd McCready's boys are going to beat them out. Get to her first. This territory was better off when it was just the French here!"

"No, it wasn't. Not what I've 'eard," Tancred said, as if the idea were absurd.

"I don't want them in here with me," Aubuchon continued. "Don't want to feed them." He smiled at Perdita. "You must be the Father's niece."

"I am pleased to meet you." Perdita extended her hand. Aubuchon took it, seeming a little surprised by the gesture.

"I hope those two didn't upset you?" he asked.

"No. Perhaps a little. I am fine, thank you."

"They are harmless alone. '*Sans tete, un corps se repose tranquillement*.'"

Again Perdita was puzzled.

"Without a head, a body zits quietly," Tancred translated. "Aubuchon thinks I'm losing my wits in my old age. 'E likes to azzail me with these ridiculous French phrases, and expects me to translate on the zpot."

"Father does the same to me with Shakespeare." Aubuchon smiled.

"A test 'e fails abysmally!" Tancred huffed. "I do not understand why 'e enjoys playing a game for which 'e is zo catastrophically ill prepared." He looked out a small front window at Orville and Tector. "It isn't the yawning churchyards breathing out contagion upon the earth today," he said, "it's Laubardemont's farm!"

"Hmmm," Aubuchon puzzled. "*Macbeth*?"

"*Hamlet*," Perdita said. Aubuchon nodded in approval. "With Mother and Uncle being Warwickshire people, I was expected to know my Shakespeare."

" 'Ow is Marie today?" Tancred asked.

"Hardly hear a word out of her," Aubuchon said. "I think she'll be glad for a lady's company. Come on. We'll go back now."

Aubuchon opened a heavy, iron-barred door at the rear of the room. He led them along a short corridor, which had two empty jail cells on either side. The corridor appeared to end at the wall opposite the barred door, but, in fact, turned sharply to the left past the last cell.

"This is a private cell for special cases," Aubuchon said. "Marie! Visitors!" he called. Perdita noticed the private cell was smaller than the four general cells they had passed, and appeared to be in an L shape, affording the occupant some measure of privacy. Aubuchon stopped.

"You know I have to check your valise, Father," he said.

"Yes, yes," Tancred said irritably. He opened the valise. Aubuchon glanced through it quickly, appearing to Perdita to not really be looking for anything.

"And you, miss," Aubuchon said to her, indicating the basket. She lifted the linen covering it.

"Hmmm. Mrs. Moon's tarts."

"Yes," Tancred sniffed. "There's a-many there with your name on it, I 'ave no doubt!"

Aubuchon laughed and unlocked the cell door. He swung the door open, allowing Tancred and Perdita to enter ahead of him. Perdita glanced nervously around the room. It was uncomfortably confined and very dark. An alcove to the left, a few feet past the cell door, formed the L shape of the small room. Along the far wall was a plain but comfortable-looking cot, neatly made. The alcove was illuminated by another barred window on the wall opposite the bed. On the bed sat a tiny woman in a plain muslin shift. Her hair had been roughly shorn off. She stood, looking at Perdita with an expression of surprise and disbelief that quickly seemed to transform into gratitude. She couldn't have been more than an inch or two over five feet tall.

"This is Miss Perdita...," Aubuchon hesitated.

"Badon-Reed," Perdita said.

"Father's niece," Aubuchon continued."She's brought more of Mrs. Moon's tarts with her."

Perdita held out the basket. After a moment Marie took it, nodding her thankfulness, and placed it on the bed. Marie seemed to be suddenly aware of her appearance. She smoothed her shift and passed a hand over her mottled, scabbed head.

"She did that to herself," Aubuchon said. "I'll leave you alone." He left the cell and closed the door behind him.

"How do you do?" Perdita said.

Marie nodded self-consciously. "I am very pleased...and grateful to meet you. Father told me his niece was coming to stay with him. I didn't expect...it's very kind of you to come." There was the slightest hint of a French accent in her speech.

"Not at all." Perdita smiled awkwardly. She had never spoken to a murderer before. She could scarcely believe this frail, tiny woman had committed such an abominable crime. But the fact of her crime did not seem to be in question, and Perdita was now confined in this small, dark space with her.

"I haven't spoken to a woman since my sister was here," Marie said.

"She zmuggled in the shears," Tancred said, "at Marie's request. Aubuchon has zince forbidden her to visit anymore."

"It is the women who abandon you first in Ste. Odile," Marie continued. "The ones who should understand the most. They see you as fallen, a threat to the order of things, and they abandon you first. I've had nothing but the company of men for weeks. Their understanding can only reach so far."

"Are you eatin' well, and zleepin'?" Tancred asked.

"Not sleeping, Father. I wouldn't dare sleep even if I could. I have not eaten yet today."

"Good," Tancred said. "I'll 'ear your confession, then you can receive the Holy Eucharist." He looked at Perdita. "You'll 'ave to ztep outside for a moment, my girl."

Perdita nodded. She pulled open the cell door and stepped into the corridor. She thought she might feel less confined there, but quickly found she did not. Immediately she could hear the soft murmur of Marie's voice as she made her confession and the low hum of Tancred's as he bestowed absolution. After a few moments, Perdita could make out a phrase or two of Marie's, and the Hail Marys which Tancred always gave as penance. After a while, Perdita could hear Tancred mumbling in Latin as Marie received the Holy Eucharist. Then there was silence, followed by the low murmur of conversation. The air seemed to grow more stale and thin to Perdita as she waited. She started to feel she could not breathe deeply enough to fill her lungs.

"You may come back in now, Miss Badon-Reed," Marie called.

Perdita reentered the cell. Tancred was putting his stole, chalice, and prayer book back into his valise.

"She'd like a few minutes alone with you," Tancred said to Perdita. "I wanted to talk to Aubuchon anyway. I will zee you in a day or two, Marie." He closed his valise and left the cell.

An old pine milking stool sat in one corner of the cell near the window. Marie sat on it. Perdita's compulsion was to leave the cell with Tancred. She felt she'd had enough of this small room, and was suddenly uneasy about being alone with a murderess. Marie looked at her expectantly and smiled.

"Please sit on the bed. It is more comfortable," Marie said.

"Thank you." Perdita sat. She was glad to be facing the window, the light.

"I can scarcely thank you enough for your visit. It is such an act of true Christian charity!"

"It is a small thing. Nothing."

"Do you have a child?"

"No. I have never been married."

"I am sorry to hear it. Bearing a child gives a feeling of fulfillment that cannot be compared to anything else. There is still time for you, though."

"I don't foresee motherhood in my future." Perdita was a little insulted. "My fulfillment will come in other ways."

"Forgive me, but it won't compare with motherhood. It is God's will that we be mothers. He has structured our bodies and our feelings perfectly for that purpose."

"It is not intended for everyone. I am certain I do not have the temperament for it. The urge, the impulse to care for children has eluded me."

"Yet you have come here to teach children."

Perdita had often thought of the contradiction of this, but had not yet fully formulated an answer. "It is true," she said. "I feel my detachment, if I may call it that, will make me a better teacher. Perhaps I will be less likely to compromise my expectations of children out of pity or affection."

"It would be a shame to deny yourself. To never develop this gift of motherhood, this blessing that is within you."

"Still, it isn't likely to happen."

"My husband was in the war. He was one of the men who stayed behind to blow up the powder magazine at Pilot Knob when the Confederates came through."

"The town was with the North? I thought—"

"Our sympathies were divided. There was a garrison of Federals here when the Confederates threatened. We profited from both sides. Otherwise both sides would have overlooked us. My husband was shot as he escaped. A bullet pressed his spine for many years. He was in much pain. Eight years ago he died."

"I am sorry to hear it."

"I am glad he didn't live to see all of this. But I think he would have acted as I did under the circumstances. Or worse, perhaps."

"Oh?" Perdita said awkwardly. "Of course I don't know what those circumstances were."

"When the war came, and after the war, many people lost everything. Towns and villages were nearly destroyed. Livelihoods were lost or decimated. Some have yet to recover, even after seventeen years. None of that happened here. We had the lead mines, the salt and lime that the army—both armies—needed. No one went hungry here. No one who wanted work could fail to find it. This security, this prosperity, all of it was the gift of the Bastides."

"Yes, I have heard that name."

"Things have changed here in the last few months. If I were your guardian angel, I would carry you away from Ste. Odile."

"But my uncle hasn't said anything—"

"He doesn't know. He is an outsider. Even in confession he hears little. I have my sister and her family to consider. They could suffer."

Perdita was puzzled. She was unsure of whether she should press for an explanation, or wait to see if one was offered.

"My daughter's name was Michee," Marie said. Her face brightened, and her spirits seemed to lift. "She loved to work in the garden, to sew, and care for the animals. We had goats she raised and milked, and pullets. All in her care. She made this shift I'm wearing."

Perdita forced a smile. She could not fathom how

this woman could speak so affectionately of a child she had murdered.

"There is a purity in children," Marie continued, "that is almost...what is the best way to say it?... heartbreaking. Through war, through mistreatment, through the loss of home and family, they keep that spark of purity, of hopefulness, of the expectation of goodness. There is no more terrible moment than when that purity is lost. It is lost soon enough in the natural course of things. A mother cannot let it be wrenched away."

Marie stood and approached the foot of the bed. She reached under the mattress and withdrew a small, paper-bound journal. She handed it to Perdita. Perdita held the book awkwardly for a moment, unsure of what Marie intended.

"This is where I have written everything, explained what has happened. For my sister's sake, I have not spoken of it, but it needs to be expressed, put down so that it is understood."

Perdita opened the book to a page near the front:

> "...the mountain fortress. I have seen *Le Vorace*, have heard them. My mother explained these as signs that one has been chosen.
>
> April 17.
>
> Last night was the third night of..."

Marie quickly but gently took the journal and returned it to its place under the mattress. "There must be a record," she said. "I wanted you to know of it."

A crash against the bars of the window startled the women. Fragments of glass sprayed across the cell. Perdita jumped from her seat and gasped for air. Shouting could be heard outside, followed by another crash and more broken glass.

"Perdita! Marie!" Tancred called. He burst into the cell out of breath. "Get into the corridor, away from the windows. The other two are back, drunk!"

"Who?" Perdita asked. She embraced Marie and led her into the corridor.

"Levon and Tobe have joined with their friends outside. They mean to get Marie!"

"Where are the deputies?" Marie asked. A small cut bled above her left eye.

"Across the river, in Prairie du Rocher, extraditing a prisoner," Tancred said. "I'm going to talk zense to them! They're rabble, cowards!"

"Uncle!" Perdita grasped his arms. "Leave this to the sheriff. Do not go outside!"

"They won't hurt a priest, an old man."

"It isn't your place," Perdita insisted.

"Aubuchon won't let him go out," Marie said. Tancred pulled away from Perdita and returned to the office. Perdita gasped for breath. She knew she could not remain in the dark corridor.

"Stay here, away from the windows," Perdita said to Marie. "I have to see my uncle." She walked around the corner and up the corridor to Aubuchon's office. The door was ajar. She pushed it open slowly. She saw that the jail's front door was open. Aubuchon stood in the doorway holding a Sharpe's rifle, identical to one Moira's father displayed over the mantel in his study. Tancred stood behind Aubuchon.

"Levon," Aubuchon said calmly, "you're drunk. I'll give you one chance to take your boys here and get out of my sight. You know you'd have to kill me or burn the jail down to get at this woman."

Perdita moved to one of the small windows.

"Get away from the window, girl," Tancred said. Perdita didn't move. She could see a large, rough-looking man outside facing Aubuchon, and another a few feet behind him. Perdita noticed a well-dressed young man watching the confrontation from under the awning of a general mercantile store across the street. The young man stood beside a selection of staves and pick handles displayed for sale in a wooden barrel. He selected one of the pick handles and stepped into the street, making his way slowly toward the jail.

"Mr. Aubuchon," Perdita began, "There is another one coming."

"Aubuchon," Levon shouted. He was unsteady and bleary eyed, and held onto the low-hanging branch of an elm tree. "If you think we're jus' gonna give up on this and leave her here, you don't know me like—"

Perdita saw that Aubuchon was holding the rifle with one hand now. He swung it casually, as if it were a pistol, toward Levon and fired. The blast was deafening. Perdita flinched at the noise, and, at the same instant, saw a spray of red explode from Levon's thigh. He collapsed on the ground instantly. Tobe, Orville, and Tector were motionless for a moment, in disbelief. Levon lay stunned on the ground, silent, staring at the sky and blinking, as though he had just awakened from a deep sleep. Tobe rushed to Levon's side, pulled off his slouch hat, and crushed it onto the bullet wound.

Orville and Tector stared at Aubuchon. Simultaneously they moved toward him. The young man with the pick handle was directly behind Orville now. He swung the handle quickly in a downward arc. It hit the backs of Orville's thighs with a meaty thud. Orville collapsed, screaming in pain. Tector turned to face the young man, looking at him blankly for a moment. Orville was writhing on the ground. "Git him, Tector," Orville screamed. "My leg is broke!"

Tector lunged at the young man who jumped to his right and crashed the pick handle against Tector's shin as the drunken man stumbled past. There was a loud crack and

Tector crumpled onto the flagstone walk. Tector gasped, sat up and looked at his shin. A thin splinter of shattered bone protruded from his trouser leg in a widening halo of blood. He fell back onto the flagstones unconscious.

Aubuchon leaned his rifle against the door frame and stepped outside. "*Est assez, assez*," he said.

Perdita looked at her uncle, speechless.

"Yez, enough iz enough," Tancred agreed, and he stepped outside to look after Levon's bullet wound.

The well-dressed young man dropped his pick handle on the ground. "The infirmary at the mine is closest," he said to Aubuchon. "May as well take them there. Doctor's busy with Duval's baby right now."

Perdita rushed through the jail door. She barely knew how to react to what she had just seen. "Mr. Aubuchon," she said at last, "you shot this man!"

"Yes, Miss, I did."

"Was there no other way to contain him?"

"This must be your niece, Father," the young man said cheerfully.

"Aye. Miz Perdita Badon-Reed."

"I am Hypolitte Robert, Miss. I am very pleased to meet you."

"You've broken these men's legs!"

"Yes, and I'm sorry for it, too. At least no one was killed. And these four will be out of the way until after the execution. So, it all worked out fairly well, to my way of thinking, since, as I said, no one was killed. I am sorry you saw it all, though. What you must think of us, I can't imagine!"

Again Perdita could think of nothing to say. She pulled her handkerchief from her sleeve and pressed it to her cheeks and forehead. She noticed her hand was shaking. Tancred stood and took her arm, guiding her back into the jail.

"Welcome to Ste. Odile, my girl," he said.

5

Letter from Moira Keane Parnell to Perdita Badon-Reed

Moira Keane Parnell
14 Newgrange Circle
Boston, Massachusetts
August 16, 1882

My dear Perdita,

I received yours of the 2nd, etc., this morning with great excitement. What an adventure you are having! Traveling halfway across the continent, and alone too! To say that I am amazed at what you have done would understate the matter to an absurd degree. I always said you had a hidden courage and resolve in you, and I think your escape proves my point. You make no mention of a letter I posted a day or two after you left. I sent it to the address which you left in your note, the rectory at Ste. Odile. Perhaps the letter went astray? In it I only mentioned my surprise, and Prosper's dismay, at your disappearance. This has, of course, had a great effect upon him, and upon your parents. But of course this was not unexpected by you. How could it be otherwise?

It pains me to say it, but your mother is most distraught and often inconsolable in her distress over your departure. She is concerned for your welfare and angry that her brother Tancred would keep such a confidence with you at her expense. You often told me about the bad blood between your parents and uncle. Perhaps that animosity made this familial transgression, if one may call it that, easier for your uncle to justify. Would you agree? You will question the sincerity of your mother's remonstrations, knowing her as you (we) do, but there it is. Your father has been most inscrutable. I'll be sunk if I can fathom his mood. He says little and conveys nothing by way of facial expression or bodily attitude. Perhaps a week after you'd gone, your parents invited me for dinner and to talk over the situation. (It was beef, but boiled, of all things; a dismal, somber meal. Your mother's dogs were filthy pests, of course!) I watched your father all evening, and if I had to divine a single impression from all that I observed of him, I would have to say that he didn't seem surprised.

I, on the other hand, and Prosper were quite surprised. It is hard for me to believe you would not take your dearest friend into your confidence. You say if you had told me of your plans, you believe I would have dissuaded you from your purpose. You know I am not one to meddle in the affairs of others. Surely I have made that element of my character clear to you over the years? If not, I cannot help but feel that I have failed in our friendship in some way. What it amounts to, after all, is that you do not completely trust me.

But, I do not want to fill my letter with scoldings or rebukes. You had your reasons for leaving. They made sense to you at the time, and at this moment we cannot undo what you have done, can we? We will sort all of this out when next we meet. Perhaps then I will make some sense of it.

I can truly say I miss you terribly. I attended a lecture last week on *The Feminine Myth in Northern Italian Art 1450-1600* and another on *The Destabilization of the Familiar: Liszt and His Circle*, both at the Hibernia Club. Two nights ago, I heard an evening of Chopin polonaises at Clarendon House. Lord! If you've heard one of those, you've heard them all, don't you agree? At any rate, these evenings seemed empty and unsatisfying without you along to share them. I know I will not take as much joy in these sorts of things again until we once more experience them together. And I expect we will experience them again, once the "charms" of life in the hinterlands have faded in your estimation. At least this is my sincere, and undeniably selfish, wish.

I was both horrified and amazed by your reference to the woman who has murdered her child, and aghast at the handbill you sent encouraging the town to turn out for her execution. Have you learned any more of her story?

In spite of my own dismay at the loss of you, and your mother's sympathy-engendering distress, I truly think it is Prosper who feels your loss most severely. He took it as an undeniable reflection upon himself, as a sign of a failure, or a flaw in his character. He feels he has done something to drive you away. I have assured him that essentially this is not true, and I assume I am correct in this, but he is unconvinced. The murder of his dear sister so recently, and then the withdrawal of his fiancée with no explanation, has left him disconsolate. I felt he was in need of a purpose, an occupation. I therefore encouraged him to go home. It is what he should have done a month ago or more. He has gone to console his family and hear for himself what happened. He will press for an interview with the commissary, or at least the inspector in charge of the case. I saw him off yesterday morning. He's on the *Egeria* bound for Marseilles by way of Lisbon, Gibraltar, and Palma de Majorca. The ship is a steamer fitted with sails: the type of craft that has made ocean crossings such a matter of brevity and convenience these days.

The accounts written in his brother's letters describes Prosper's family as having been nearly destroyed by this tragedy. His parents have lost all desire for human society, and his father has forsaken the position created for him by Monsieur Guibord, the dead sister's husband. The family has been truly ruined, or soon will be.

Prosper has shared few details of the murder with me. Murders, actually. As you recall, a maidservant was killed also. Prosper either did not have the details to share, or he wished to spare my "feminine sensibilities," as he sometimes says, from the gruesome facts. I suspect the latter. I know the family's physician examined the body and provided a report to both to the family and the court clerk. I also know the murders were excessively violent, that the attack on Claire was of a sexual nature, and that similar attacks, though intermittent, are not unknown in the region. Prosper has promised to wire me when he arrives in Marseilles, and to write frequently.

My, what a sad tone my letter has taken on. I do not wish it to end so. Have you begun preparations for your classwork yet? As you may recall, when I taught the orphans at St. Brendan's, I didn't find an excess of preparation to be necessary, or even advisable. Even well-disciplined children (and Lord knows there are few enough of these!) have an innate skill for distracting a teacher from her mission. As orderly and fixed a person as I am, I have found that to allow a bit of latitude in the classroom seems to encourage learning more than an utter lack of it. This, at least, has been my experience. You will learn to marry method and situation as you go along. Of course, with children you never know. Like gray-eyed Athene, "I do not know the ways of birds clearly."

I must close now. The dinner bell has been rung. It is beef tonight. Remember: a week without a letter from you will be a week of little consequence to me.

With all affection,
Moira

Also: if you abandon this adventure by Christmas, you can be back in time to enjoy Von Bulow's return to Boston with a program of Mozart and Beethoven (the Allegretto from the Seventh Symphony) at Clarendon House, AND Gilbert and Sullivan's *Iolanthe*, all in the same fortnight. Incentive indeed!

6

"This will do admirably, Uncle. With no walls, I won't feel so stifled and confined as I work."

"It were a blacksmith's lean-to at one time. Make use of it az you zee fit."

The sun in his face was obviously bothering Tancred. He stepped under the cedar-shake roof of the lean-to and mopped his brow with his handkerchief. The block of Perdita's Carrara marble was resting atop of a pair of sturdy oak benches. "I 'ad Aristide and 'is boys put it there."

"Thank you, Uncle. That's perfect."

"T'other bench is 'ere." Tancred indicated a smaller bench for Perdita to sit upon as she worked near a split-rail pen which once held horses waiting to be shod. "Your tools I 'ad put in this chest to keep the rust off." Tancred kicked a wooden chest that sat on the ground next to the rusted anvil. He nodded toward a grindstone at the far end of the lean-to. "And the wheel was gatherin' dust in the shed, zo I 'ad it put 'ere to sharpen your chizelz with."

"Uncle, you've been so kind!" Perdita's inclination was to embrace Tancred in gratitude, but she thought the better of it and just touched his arm. "I only wish my block for the Havilland commission would arrive. I would start it today! Thank you for helping me with this."

"Couldn't very well lug all o' this back 'ere on your own, could you?" Tancred turned and began walking back toward the rectory. He stopped and pushed open a skeletal door which connected the lean-to to the shed against which it was built. "Use the shed as a ztudio, if you like." Tancred stepped back into the humid sunshine and crossed the back garden and gravel drive toward the kitchen door at the rear of the rectory.

"Thank you," Perdita called after him, but he made no acknowledgment that he had heard her.

Perdita opened the tool chest. With both hands she lifted out an oilcloth in which her stone-carving tools were wrapped. She placed the parcel on the anvil, opened it, and spread everything neatly out on the cloth: points, toothed chisels, flat chisels, rifflers, separating tool, and hammer. She picked up each piece and turned it over in her hands. There were no signs of rust. She had sharpened the cutting tools the week before she left Boston. Everything was ready to use.

From a pocket in her apron, Perdita removed a small, leather-bound sketching diary and a stick of charcoal. She opened the diary to an ink drawing she had done near the back. It was the reclining figure of a woman. The figure lay on her back, draped in chains, with her right arm thrown over her face.

"My *Beatrice Cenci*," Perdita whispered solemnly. She studied the drawing for several minutes. "There is nothing more important than this!"

Perdita laid the diary open on the ground below her marble block. She ran her hands along the sides and top of the block, relishing its smoothness where the stone saws had cut, and its roughness where the block had broken free of its mountainside. The characteristic lush opalescence of the Carrara seemed to glow, even in the shade inside the lean-to, as if all of the light that had ever penetrated its creamy translucence, like the gray-blue suggestions of veining throughout, was still trapped and nearly visible within the density of the block.

Perdita studied her ink drawing for a few moments. She then began to sketch the figure onto the side of the block with the charcoal. She worked quickly and nervously, breaking pieces of the charcoal off in her enthusiasm as she drew. She could quickly see she had drawn the figure too short for the block. She wanted the figure to fill the block, so she rubbed the sketch off with her hands and started again. This time she drew the figure too large and had to rub the drawing out a second time. On her third attempt, she started by roughing in landmarks: the top of the head, the chin, breast, waist, knee, and toes. Then she was able to fill in the figure proportionate to the block. She repeated this process in reverse on the opposite side of the stone and roughed in a top view where the irregularity of the surface permitted.

Seven years earlier in Boston, when she had decided, contrary to Moira's opinion, that sculpting stone would be her means of creative expression, she had made the acquaintance of Mr. Tedoni, a Florentine expatriate who carved figures and architectural details in limestone for churches and government buildings. Tedoni's family had been stone carvers and quarrymen for three hundred years. He was one of the only persons of her acquaintance, and the only man, who had not actively discouraged her from her chosen career. He had helped her select her points and chisels and had shown her how to use and care for them. He put her in touch with suppliers in Vermont, Tennessee, and Italy, from whom she had ordered stone. He showed her the use of the separating tool, of rasps and rifflers. Most importantly, he had taught her to make *maquettes*, scale models in clay, of the proposed sculpture, on which proportional problems could be resolved before the first chisel blow is struck. But Perdita found she did not have the patience to make clay models, nor the skills in mathematics to accurately project the dimensions of a model onto the stone. She much preferred to attack the stone directly and take her chances.

Perdita grasped the separating tool in her left hand and her two-pound hammer in her right. She placed the sharp edge of the separating tool into a groove left by a saw blade in the front edge of the block and struck it firmly with the hammer. A triangle of marble about three inches across broke free and fell to the ground. Perdita smiled. "I'll find you in there, Beatrice," she said. She repositioned the tool and struck it again and again until the corner of the block began to show a rounded profile.

After twenty minutes of work, Perdita had rounded off most of the front edge of the block. "I really should be working on my lesson plan," she mumbled to herself. "The term is starting soon…really should go into my room…" She moved the separating tool to the edge of the block opposite her and began to round it.

"You're not one to waste time, I see."

The voice startled Perdita. She turned and saw Hypolitte Robert approaching the lean-to.

"Getting right at your work," he continued. "The world has been denied many a magnum opus, I'll wager, for lack of discipline. Not a factor for you, apparently, Miss Badon-Reed."

"My failure, if it comes, will have nothing to do with a want of effort." She noticed her hands were sweaty and covered with a film of stone dust. She imagined her face and neck were in a similar condition. "You aren't seeing me at my best, Mr. Robert."

"I think I am. If you see someone engaged in something they are passionate about, surely you are seeing them at their best."

"That isn't what I meant."

"I think I know what you meant."He studied the sketch on the side of the block for a moment. "A figure, I see. Anybody I know?"

Perdita pointed toward her sketch diary on the ground. "*Beatrice Cenci*."

"Hmm, the tragic heroine." He nodded. "Art is full of tragic heroines and allegorical figures these days, isn't it? Two hundred years ago it was shepherds, a hundred years ago it was Natural Man in his native situation, now it is Dido, Queen of Carthage, and allegories of industry and progress!"

Perdita felt the color rise in her neck and face. "I'm sorry if you find my subject trivial, Mr. Robert."

"Oh, no, not at all."

"But it is my opinion that if we are only today preoccupied with the tragic heroine, it is high time, after centuries of neglect of her in favor of the male model!"

"I haven't expressed myself very well—"

"I believe I know what you meant."

Hypolitte smiled at her. "I am not sure you do. What I meant was public art: things you find in public squares and the rotundas of public buildings. Personal expression, whatever form it takes, is another matter."

"I'm not certain I see the difference."

"It's a question of…fashion. Public officials will commission a subject they imagine is fashionable, not because of a love for, or understanding of it."

"How do you know I'm not doing the same thing, Mr. Robert?"

"Because I saw you working just now. I don't think you labor under the pall of fashion."

Perdita laughed. "I suppose I will concede that you've talked your way out of a quandary, Mr. Robert."

"Thank heaven for that!" Hypolitte laughed.

"At any rate," Perdita said, blowing a strand of hair away that was dangling in her face, "this isn't the piece I should be working on. I have my commission to do, a double figure, *Heloise and Abelard*. The stone was supposed to be here when I arrived, but the packet-line seems to have lost it. I checked with Mr. Dufresne this morning, and still nothing."

"I am sure Mr. Dufresne will look into it thoroughly for you. I used to know him well. He is a good man."

"Uncle Tancred is in the rectory, if you are looking for him." Perdita wiped the stone dust from her face with her sleeves.

"It is you I came to see, actually."

"Oh?" Perdita was a little surprised. And she knew her voice sounded more apprehensive than she would have liked.

"Yes. I have a friend who would very much like to meet you."

"A friend?"

"Yes. You will get to know her very well this term, as I understand you will share some teaching duties. Her name is Sister Solana."

"Oh yes, Solana."

"She joined the Sisters of Perpetua in Baltimore. She's young, intelligent, and lively. I am sure you will like her."

"Well, I am not in any condition to go now. Surely it doesn't have to be now?"

"I took the liberty of telling her I'd be right back with you."

"Why would you have done that?"

"She's made arrangements to meet Marie Delaporte Chardin. She'd heard Marie has become attached to you."

"I met Mrs. Chardin once! I am not attached to her."

"Marie apparently feels you are. Sister was hoping she could both meet you and ask you to make her introduction to Marie. And though she asked me not to mention it, she has a kind of welcome gift for you, as a new friend and teaching partner. A good dusting off and a damp cloth on your face and you'll be as prim as a Dutch woman!"

Perdita looked at Hypolitte angrily for a moment, but her expression soon softened. She began to dust off her arms and walk briskly toward the rectory. "Well, I am certainly going to change clothes first!"

In fifteen minutes' time, Perdita had changed and washed her face, brushed and repinned her hair. She emerged from her room pinning her small straw hat to her head. She found Hypolitte in the parlor with Uncle Tancred. Hypolitte rose as she entered. Tancred began to rise, but gave up the effort halfway through and settled back into his leather chair.

"Zo, you're goin' to meet Zister Zolana, then?" Tancred asked.

"Apparently." Perdita nodded. "I seem to have very little say in the matter. I am to introduce her to Mrs. Chardin, based upon my long and intimate association with that lady. The sister is shy, I suppose."

"Not shy," Hypolitte interrupted. "Well, yes, she is rather shy. But also a great believer in etiquette. Proper form, which is a bit odd when you think of her temperament, don't you think, Father?"

" 'Ardly know the girl. The zister, I should zay."

"Well, I mean," Hypolitte continued, "she is so full of energy and humor. You'd think conformity would not mean that much to her."

"Picked a poor life for 'erself, if that is the case," Tancred scowled.

"A poor life?" Hypolitte was puzzled.

"Becoming a nun," Perdita said.

"Ah." Hypolitte nodded. "Possibly. But I do think, in fact I'm certain, she has a true vocation."

"We are always grateful to get the fallen-away Anglican view of Catholic vocation. After all, anyone who would willingly follow a religion invented by a zyphillic, murdering, debauched glutton must be of a first rank intelligence, and of course 'is opinions must be valuable!" Tancred sniffed.

Hypolitte laughed heartily. "Episcopal. Not Anglican."

"God bless the young woman if she has a true vocation," Tancred said. His eyelids appeared to be getting heavy.

"Shall we go then, Mr. Robert, and meet this conflicted young woman?" Perdita asked, a bit irritably. Hypolitte put on his black hat.

"Yes," he said, moving toward the door, "providing we can come to an agreement. I have no wish to call you Miss Badon-Reed. It is euphonious, but a mouthful. May we use first names?" He opened the door for Perdita.

"Of course," she said.

The day had become warmer, but a breeze had stirred up. Perdita made no attempt at first to hide her irritation from Hypolitte. She had started on the *Beatrice*, made real progress, and could have accomplished much more, if not for this intrusion, this presumption. Still, Moira had always said one must strive for acceptance in circumscribed communities such as small towns. Better to be true to oneself within a system, if possible, rather than reject all customs and dogmas, and make a real struggle out of daily life and self-expression by being an outcast. And Mr. Robert's intentions did seem to be in the right place. She knew it was important she respond to any offered cordiality, particularly from persons such as Sister Solana, with whom she would be working so closely, and Mr. Robert, who was a close friend of Uncle Tancred. And Mr. Robert was personable, though a non-Catholic, if a bit insistent. He obviously had some degree of taste in his clothes and his reading. He was certainly a reasonably intelligent, educated person.

"So," Perdita said as they crossed Bucephalus Street and continued south on Constantinople, "Sister Solana is a young woman with a true vocation?"

"Without doubt, in my pagan opinion." They both laughed. "But it hasn't…drained the life out of her, if you know what I mean."

"I know very well."

"Ah, yes." Hypolitte remembered. "You have spent some time behind the sacred wall."

"Very briefly. I wondered if Uncle might have mentioned it. I was with the Ursulines in New Orleans for a time."

"For a time?"

"I painfully discovered that, unlike Sister Solana, I did not have a true vocation."

"Well, I am glad of that. It isn't a life I'd wish on anyone."

"Don't you believe in piety? In the sacrifice of the self to God?"

"No. Not in that manner. Not in the cloister." Hypolitte frowned.

"It is a sacrifice one chooses to make. What of the saints whose entire lives were sacrifice?"

"And self-denial to the point of death, or self-flagellation, or some other form of self-torture? What must we think of a God who requires that? Or even approves of it? I do not mean to offend you, but I will tell you as I told Tancred: I am sure most of the great saints and hermits of the past would find themselves, rightly, in lunatic asylums, were they alive today."

Perdita burst into laughter. "You didn't say that to Uncle Tancred!"

"I did, and got a half-hour dressing down for it, too!"

"And you not even a Catholic."

"Oh, I was, upon a time. That just makes it worse for him." They paused a moment in the street to allow a wagon filled with green hides to pass. "I'm glad you are out here in the world with us," Hypolitte continued, "not buried alive in some convent. Your vocation is here, with that stone. Your task is to liberate *Beatrice Cenci*!"

In the block south of Bucephalus Street, the sidewalk became wider and paved with wide limestone slabs worn smooth by decades of foot traffic and edged in the reddish-pink granite that had become so familiar to Perdita since she had first seen it in St. Louis. Bordering the walk on the western side was a high brick and ironwork fence.

"That is the convent and the school." Hypolitte nodded toward the building.

Beyond the fence, Perdita saw an expanse of partially maintained grounds populated by ancient, gnarled elms, great drooping pines, and gigantic oaks with splayed and twisted limbs, many of which sagged to the ground as if burdened with great weight and age. Beyond the trees could be seen a sprawling and dreary series of buildings: the school, chapel, gymnasium, and convent, all built of brick and limestone, and in the same Gothic style as the church and rectory. Midway along the city block, a large brick and ironwork gate in the wall opened onto an avenue of ancient cypresses lining a gravel drive, which led back to the rather gloomy-looking school building. Perdita stopped for a moment halfway through the gate. She studied the buildings, the trees, the grounds.

"I've often wondered what a little girl of six or seven must think when she sees all of this for the first time," Hypolitte said. Perdita looked down the avenue of cypresses toward the substantial and forbidding façades of the buildings.

"Fear," she said as she slowly began to walk again. "And dread. And a sense of being alone. Abandoned like you've never felt before. You understand that you are actually and truly not connected to any other human being: not mother, father—no one. You know you are alone."

"Remind you of the Ursulines?"

"Yes. It is very familiar."

Beyond the cypresses, to the left of the avenue, Perdita could see the irregular but well-kept headstones of a moderately-sized cemetery. Most were limestone crosses or tablets situated above old, sunken graves. But at the far edge of the cemetery, against an ironwork wall which formed the southern boundary of the property, stood a small but stately mausoleum, with red serpentine columns and a Romanesque arch on the front.

"That is the tomb of Sister Maria Phillipa, a mother superior of a hundred years or so ago," Hypolitte said. "She brought much recognition to the order and is responsible for the acquisition of the saint's relics the convent owns."

"Relics?"

"Yes. Perhaps Sister Clotilde will give you a tour. She is the current Mother Superior."

A brick walkway intersected the avenue of cypresses just past its midpoint. Hypolitte guided Perdita onto it, and they walked toward the convent, across the lawn toward the north end of the property. The walkway encircled, at its midpoint, a large stone statue of St. Perpetua Flavia. The docile and adoring lions that, at the saint's command, would devour her for the amusement of the Roman crowd and the greater glory of God, were moss covered and in a poor state of repair, unlike the saint herself, who seemed to Perdita to show few signs of age and weathering.

The main door of the convent was oak, unadorned except for heavy iron hinges and a bronze knocker in the shape of a woman's hand holding an apple.

"Should we knock?" Perdita asked.

Hypolitte nodded and reached for the knocker just as the door flew open. A young nun with a pretty, round face stood in the doorway smiling at them.

"Miss Badon-Reed?" the young nun asked.

"Yes." Perdita smiled.

The young sister rushed through the door and threw her arms around Perdita.

"I'm so glad to meet you, at last!" she said, beaming. "I've been watching for you for the last hour, waiting in the vestibule. I am so excited that we will be teaching together! I've told the girls what an honor they should regard this opportunity to be taught by a real artist!"

Hypolitte laughed. "Perdita, this is our demure and solemn Sister Solana!"

"I am very pleased to meet you, too, Sister," Perdita said.

"Oh, I know we'll be such good friends! Father has told me a bit about you. He isn't one to go on and on, as you know, but he has told me about your work, a little. A stone sculptor! What a time we are living in that a woman can claim such a profession! Mrs. Wollstonecraft would be proud, don't you think? That is such a smart walking-about outfit you're wearing. And that hat is perfect for the shape of your face!"

Perdita began to laugh as she touched her hat and adjusted it a little on her head. "Thank you. I am glad you like my hat and outfit."

"Please come in, come in."

Solana took Perdita and Hypolitte each by the arm and led them through the vestibule into a large, wainscoted sitting room. Perdita and Hypolitte sat on a padded oak bench and Solana on a bentwood chair, facing them.

"I would invite you to my room," she said, "but it is just a garret, and I only have one chair. Really, this is more comfortable."

"This is fine. Very pleasant," Perdita said.

"I found Perdita hard at work already this morning," Hypolitte said, "murdering a block of marble."

"Oh, and I've interrupted!" Solana gasped. "I knew

I should have sent a note first."

"No," Perdita said. "It wasn't an interruption. I had done all I should today. And I am so glad to be meeting you."

"Well, it is kind of you to say so. Please tell me if I ever intrude upon your privacy. I forget myself sometimes. Now, I have a little welcome gift for you, if I can remember what I've done with it. Ah, I left it on the stair." She stood. Hypolitte stood at the same time.

"I'll fetch it," he said, and left the room. Solana moved to the bench and sat next to Perdita. She put her hand on Perdita's hand.

"I am so glad that you and Hypolitte—Mr. Robert—are friends," she said. "One of the few people in town, I'm afraid, that you can really talk to."

"Yes," said Perdita, "I've enjoyed the few conversations we have had."

"No trouble for the eyes, either, wouldn't you say?" Solana smiled at her and winked.

Perdita was a little surprised to hear a nun say such a thing.

"Oh." Solana seemed to notice Perdita's reaction. "Was that inappropriate? Was it the wrong thing to say? Like I said, I forget myself sometimes and say naughty things."

"No, not at all."

"No, I should not say things like that. A bride of Christ gives up the things of the world. Pretty outfits. Handsome young men."

"You are a nun, but also a young woman. What could be the harm?"

"These things distract one from purpose and vocation. I was always silly that way as a girl. Naughty. That is why I took Holy Orders."

Hypolitte reentered the room carrying a small parcel wrapped in paper. He handed it to Perdita and sat in the bentwood chair.

"Sister," Perdita said, "this really was unnecessary." Solana squeezed Perdita's hand.

"Nonsense," she said. "It will give us something more to talk about."

Perdita untied the string binding the parcel and unwrapped it. Inside was a thick book attractively bound in blue leather, the title embossed in gold.

"*Moby Dick*," Perdita read.

"Do you know it?" Solana asked excitedly.

"I have heard of it, yes." Perdita answered.

"Wasn't sure what to make of it, myself," Hypolitte said.

"Oh, it's wonderful," Solana said. "Wise and complex and rich. It isn't known much, but it should be. 'To the last I grapple with thee; from Hell's heart I stab at thee. For hate's sake I spit my last breath at thee…!' It speaks with such authority about man and the suffering to which our natures condemn us. Like Milton, or…or—"

"Shakespeare?" Perdita said.

"Yes."

"Or the Bible?" Hypolitte said.

"Yes," said Solana, a little embarrassed. "The Bible."

"Well, I cannot thank you enough." Perdita smiled at Solana and squeezed her hand. "I am very eager to start reading it. In fact, I will start tonight after I write my letters and work on a lesson plan. Actually, I thought we should discuss that soon, if you'd like."

"Oh, yes." Solana smiled.

"I am a little surprised at the curriculum the archbishop has requested. The arts often suffer in these schools," Perdita said.

"The archbishop, God restore him," Solana touched her lips with her fingers as if she were kissing her rosary, "visited us last year before he took ill. He thought we did well with the basics, but said young ladies need refinement. More arts, he said. They had another young lady, a lay person, to take up the task, I have heard, but she died, poor thing."

"Yes, she died," Hypolitte said somewhat wistfully. "Enter Perdita Badon-Reed and Sister Solana, more than equal to the job, I'll wager."

"That is still to be seen," Perdita said, "at least for my part."

"Together I am sure we'll do well." Solana smiled. Footsteps could be heard on the stair just outside the parlor. "This could be Mother Superior," Solana said. "She was coming down to meet you, too."

"Oh."

"You will just love her," Solana whispered. "She truly is a mother to us!"

There was a tap on the door as it was slowly pushed open. Sister Clotilde was a tall, elegant-looking woman of about sixty.

"Sister," Hypolitte said, rising.

"Good morning, Mr. Robert."

"Mother Superior." Solana grinned.

"Miss Badon-Reed, I am Sister Clotilde, Mother Superior here, as you've surmised. I am so glad to meet you."

"Thank you, Sister," Perdita said. "Everyone is making me feel so welcome. I am overwhelmed."

"We don't get many newcomers to Ste. Odile," Hypolitte noted.

"Well, there is more to it than just that," Solana laughed.

"Of course," Hypolitte said.

"To have a real artist here to teach our girls, that is a real privilege for us," Clotilde said.

"Thank you." Perdita smiled. "I'm anxious to meet the sisters and the girls."

"Perhaps we could show you around now?" Solana asked, looking at Sister Clotilde.

"But you have an appointment, do you not?" Clotilde remembered. "You're going to see Mrs. Chardin at the jail?"

"Not an appointment, exactly," Hypolitte said.

"I've just asked Perdita to introduce me," Solana said.

Clotilde smiled at Perdita. "Mrs. Chardin is very attached to you, I have heard."

"Yes, Sister, I have heard that, too. I have only met her once. Poor woman. I think she is just desperate for… understanding."

"And a sympathetic ear," Hypolitte said. "And you've given her that."

"Yes." Clotilde nodded. "We haven't done our Christian duty by this lost soul. You have shown us our failing. Sister Solana has wanted to visit her for some time, but I have not allowed it. I thought it would be inappropriate. I was wrong. So I thank you for accompanying her today. Would you have a free hour or two tomorrow, at about midday?"

"Yes, certainly," Perdita said.

"Good. Come then, and I'll show you your classroom and introduce you to some of the girls. They are starting to return for the new term now."

"Yes. I will be here. Thank you, Sister."

"I'll leave you now." Clotilde extended her hand to Perdita, who took it. "Tomorrow at about noon, then." She smiled and turned gracefully to leave the room, reminding Perdita of a ballet dancer she and Moira had admired in a production of *Figaro* they had seen in New York a few years before.

Solana touched Perdita's arm. "So, I have not imposed upon you by asking you to come with me today?"

"Not at all. If it will make you more at ease in meeting Marie, then I am glad to do it."

"Oh, thank you!" Solana beamed. "Should we go now?"

"Why not?" Hypolitte said, and led the way into the vestibule and out onto the walk.

He guided them south on Constantinople Street and east on Endymion so as not to retrace their steps, and to allow Perdita to see more of the town. Solana was full of benevolent gossip about her new sisters in Christ, and the few townspeople she had met since her arrival at the convent six weeks before.

"...Well, I had no idea Sister Ruth had such difficulty with loganberries, I mean I have never heard of such a thing. Strawberries, yes, and a few other things, but never loganberries. I mean, you don't see them much in this part of the country—"

"Yes, they're more of a western fruit," Hypolitte said offhandedly.

"Yes, that is right, so how was one to know? Anyway, I put the loganberries into the fruit salad sliced, so she did not recognize them, I suppose, and my word: in an hour she was as red as a sow's belly after nursing time and twice as swollen!"

Hypolitte burst into laughter. After a few seconds, so did Perdita. Solana looked perplexed for a moment, then smiled in embarrassment.

"Shouldn't I have said that?" she asked timidly. "Was that naughty?"

"You are a pip, Sister." Hypolitte laughed. "I do not know how we got from day to day here before you arrived! We never knew we were at such a loss to be ignorant of these important little facts."

Perdita took Solana's arm affectionately, reassuringly, as they turned north on Bosphorus Street.

"So, what do you hear of Mr. Robert's employer?"

Perdita asked.

"Do you mean the Creole gentleman?" Solana asked. "What is his name?"

"Morisot," Hypolitte said.

"No," Perdita said. "I mean Bastide."

"I know a little." Solana shrugged. "Very wealthy, of course. A naturalist. Aesthete, they say. Collector of art and antiquities. But a mystery, as his father and grandfather were, I hear."

"Yes," said Hypolitte. "I've been in his employ for nearly ten years, and I have never set eyes upon him. Owns an estate in France and spends much of his time there and traveling, as, apparently, his forebears did."

"But, I will soon know him better," Solana said.

"Oh, how is that?" Perdita asked.

"I will be meeting him. I am something in the way of being a minor authority on late medieval sculpture." Solana smiled with a mock coyness. "Especially of the Low Countries. I have had a letter from Mr. Bastide. He has heard of this avocation of mine and has asked me to visit him."

"Has he?" Hypolitte sounded surprised.

"Yes. He purchased some finely carved wooden figures in Dijon and wonders if they might be the work of Claus Sluter."

At Bosphorus Street they turned north.

"I don't know if I will be able to tell or not," Solana continued. "I am not sure Sluter worked in wood, but—"

"Did Bastide write to you personally?" Hypolitte interrupted.

"Yes. And the note was delivered by that tall black man. Tertius, I think he is called."

"That is extraordinary," Hypolitte said. "He has never made any personal contact with me or anyone in his employ below the level of Mr. Morisot, so far as I know."

"Have you ever been to his house?" Perdita asked

Hypolitte.

"No."

"I cannot wait to see it!" Solana said. "I have heard he has collections of pictures and statues and artifacts of ancient and natural history that would be the envy of museums anywhere. Jardin Noir, it is called. I am going on Tuesday evening after dinner. Mother Superior has given permission. Mr. Bastide has been a great benefactor of the convent and school."

"He is a philanthropist?" Perdita asked.

"Selectively," Hypolitte said. "An occasionally generous, rich man."

As they turned the corner of Bucephalus Street, a commotion could be heard coming from the vicinity of the jail. There was a crash of glass or crockery and a splintering of wood, a woman's scream, and Sheriff Aubuchon's voice raised in anger or excitement, though his words were unintelligible. Hypolitte ran ahead of the women into the jail. Perdita and Solana followed as quickly as they could.

Inside, the office was empty. The door leading to the hallway and cells was open, and through it Perdita could hear Marie screaming and crying.

"No, let me do it! I must do it!"

"Hold her," Perdita heard Aubuchon say. "Hold her arms!"

"Watch her feet!" It was Hypolitte's voice. Perdita and Solana ran down the hallway to Marie's cell. The cell door was open, and Marie was thrashing wildly. Her hands and arms and her neatly pressed smock were covered in blood. Hypolitte was trying to hold her arms still from behind. Aubuchon was attempting to hold her feet and tie them together with a leather cord. Marie's small, three-legged stool had been smashed and there were shards of a broken ewer scattered about the floor.

"Marie!" Perdita shouted. "What have you done?"

"I won't die in front of all of those people!" Marie screamed. She tried to break free again, driving her head into Aubuchon's stomach. "I won't have them all looking at me!"

"She cut her wrists," Aubuchon said, trying to catch his breath.

"Have to restrain her..." Hypolitte said. "The doctor needs to be sent for."

"I'll go," Solana said, and she rushed down the hallway and disappeared.

"I did what I had to do!" Marie screamed. "It was my duty to my child. Sacred! No one else has anything to do with it! I won't be an amusement, a spectacle. I won't let you defame what I did, cheapen it that way!"

Perdita rushed forward and tried to hold Marie's face in her hands.

"Marie!" she said. "You must calm yourself! Calm yourself. I am here. I am your friend. You have hurt yourself severely. You must let us care for you. Let me care for you!"

Marie instantly went limp. She looked deeply into Perdita's eyes for a moment and burst into tears.

"You are here!" Marie sobbed, as Perdita pressed Marie's face against her breast. "You are here!" Marie continued hysterically. "You are my friend...you understand... I know it. You understand I can't die in front of those people."

"Yes," Perdita said, looking evenly at Aubuchon. "I understand that. It would be grotesque."

"It's out of my hands." Aubuchon shrugged. "It's the law."

"NO!" Marie screamed, writhing to her right, nearly breaking free of Hypolitte's grasp. Perdita stumbled backward at the movement and fell onto the floor. She shrieked a little as she fell on her right hand, and as she arose from the floor, she saw she had gashed her palm on one of the broken shards. When Marie saw the blood on Perdita's hand she again went limp.

"Oh no," Marie sobbed weakly. "You're hurt!"

"It is all right, I think." Perdita pulled her handkerchief from her sleeve and dabbed at her cut. "It is nothing. It is you we are concerned with."

Marie sank to the floor, sobbing. Hypolitte relaxed his grip on her. "I didn't mean to hurt you," she cried.

"Do you have a knife? A penknife or something?" Perdita asked Hypolitte.

"Yes."

Hypolitte reached into his pocket and withdrew an ivory-handled penknife. He opened it and handed it to her. Perdita picked up a towel lying on Marie's cot and sliced through the hem. She ripped the fabric in half, handing one half to Aubuchon.

"Help me," she said, as she began to bind the gash on Marie's right arm. Aubuchon did the same to the left.

"Missed the arteries," Hypolitte noted. "That's lucky."

"Lucky we saved her life, isn't it?" Perdita said coldly.

"You'd better see to your cut," Aubuchon said to Perdita.

"The doctor will be here in a moment," Hypolitte said. "Let him take a look at it."

"No." Perdita stood, helping Marie onto her cot. "I'll go home and tend to it there."

Marie was still sobbing quietly to herself. She rolled onto her left side, facing the wall.

"Sorry about all of this," Hypolitte said. "Since you've arrived…everything…I think she'll be all right now. Go home and wash that cut."

Perdita nodded and brushed a strand of hair out of her face. She smiled weakly, picked up her *Moby Dick*, which had fallen on the floor, and left the cell. As she walked down the hallway, she realized she was crying. She stopped in the jail's doorway to dab at her eyes with her bloody handkerchief before she stepped outside. In the sunlight, she noticed her dress was spattered with blood. Ruined. One of only three sets of clothes she owned.

She was unaware of meeting anyone as she walked along Bucephalus Street to Constantinople. She did not notice the rectory or the church as she passed them. She continued along the walk, back to her shed and lean-to. Under the lean-to she removed her hat and was unaware she had let it fall to the ground. She ran her left hand along the rounded profile of the marble she had carved that morning and glanced at her sketch beside it.

"There is nothing more important than this," she said.

7

"I have had a report that Mrs. Chardin's injuries to herself were minor and she is resting now." Sister Clotilde sipped her coffee and returned the cup to its saucer, which was sitting on the walnut table between them.

"Yes," Perdita said. "She is sedated. I think she is beyond hysteria. I visited her on the way here this morning. She is resigned, at peace."

"I can better understand the thoughts of suicide—remorse for her crime—than I can the murder she committed. How could she have murdered her child?" Clotilde said gravely.

"I don't know." Perdita sighed. Her right hand was bound in a clean bandage applied by Mrs. Moon that morning. "She wants to tell me, but is fearful for some reason."

"Fearful?"

"For the safety of her sister and her family. She did not explain why. She has made a journal of it all, though. She wants me to have that," Perdita said, sipping her coffee.

"But really, to have any crime bring one to commit suicide, when it means certain damnation—" Clotilde shook her head.

Perdita smiled thinly and placed her cup on the table.

"But, Mother Superior," she said, "if one were so distressed, so confused and beyond reason as to kill oneself, if someone were clearly not in her right mind—how could

God, who knows and loves and forgives all, condemn her for it?"

"I do not know," Clotilde looked evenly, but warmly at Perdita, "but He does. Unless the doctrines of the church are mistaken, which, guided by His hand, through the infallibility of the Holy Father, they cannot be. It is a mystery to be solved, somewhere in the scriptures." She stood. "And I am ashamed to confess I cannot put my finger on the passage at this moment. But it is there. Now, let me show you around the grounds. I would like for you to meet some of the sisters, and some few of the girls are here, too."

"I would enjoy that." Perdita rose and followed Sister Clotilde through the vestibule and out the large front door. Sister Clotilde's gait was elegant and poised, and soon Perdita found herself imitating it.

They followed a brick walkway that bordered the lawn just in front of the convent and continued on to the gymnasium, chapel, and school. The day was warm but breezy, and Clotilde's habit and veil fluttered in the wind.

"I won't bore you with the gymnasium today. There isn't much to it—an expanse of wooden floor. The girls take their exercise there, and often we have pageants and plays, if they prove to be too large for our small theatre." A few steps more and they had reached the limestone stairs of the chapel.

"This is of interest." Clotilde climbed the stairs with Perdita behind her. She opened the double Gothic-arch doors and stepped aside, allowing Perdita to enter first.

The chapel was of a moderate size, with a capacity to accommodate perhaps a few hundred, Perdita thought. The pews, wainscoting, and ribbing in the ceiling were all of a golden, finely carved oak. There was ornate, gilt plasterwork throughout. The Stations of the Cross hanging on the walls were carved marble, punctuated by huge, brilliant stained glass windows depicting scenes from the lives of the saints, including St. Paul's conversion and the crucifixion of St. Peter. There were statues throughout, all above life-size, all marble. Perdita was speechless for a moment.

"It is beautiful. Gorgeous," she said at length.

"Most of what you see is a restoration of twenty years ago or so, paid for by Mr. Bastide," Clotilde said.

"Bastide?"

"Yes. The windows are Bohemian, the statues Italian, and the woodwork mostly German. Very lavish for our simple needs."

"I cannot imagine the expense of this. Bastide paid for it all?"

"Yes. A bit much for our needs, I've always thought. How many souls could have been fed and clothed with that money? Still, benefactors usually have very clear ideas of how they want their money spent. Two of our young sisters died around that time, I am told. Mr. Bastide felt our loss and thought his gift would—"

"Compensate?"

"No, never compensate. Ameliorate, perhaps. Ameliorate the sense of loss in the convent at the time. The restoration was dedicated to them."

A polished granite holy-water font stood to the right of the main door. Perdita dipped her fingers in and made the sign of the cross, dripping a little of the water on her bandage. She took a few steps down the main aisle and turned around to look up at the choir loft. Silhouetted against the large rosette window that dominated the front wall, Perdita could see the head and shoulders of a young girl. The child seemed to start at being seen, and sunk to the floor, disappearing beneath the loft railing.

"Hello . . . ?" Perdita called. Clotilde joined Perdita and followed her gaze to the loft.

"Who is up there?" Clotilde shouted. "Anatolia Montes, is that you?" After a moment of silence, a rustling of papers could be heard in the loft.

"Yes, Sister." The voice was small and timid.

"Come down immediately! Didn't I tell you not three days ago that the chapel is for reflection and prayer, not for drawing and idleness?"

"Yes, Sister." Small footsteps could be heard descending an unseen stairway.

"One may as well lecture one of these stone images as to talk to some of these girls," Clotilde said. In a moment a shadowy door opened in the corner to the right of the main door. The child's dim form could be seen emerging from it, carrying a tattered sketchbook.

"And does not using God's house for idleness and pleasure diminish it and mock its purpose?"Clotilde went on.

"Yes, Sister," Anatolia said. She stepped into the light, and Perdita could see her for the first time. Anatolia was a slight girl of about twelve. She was small for her age, Perdita thought. Her complexion was a flawless café au lait, and her eyes were large, dark, and fathomless. Perdita could see, in spite of the child's modest uniform, that her body was just beginning to change, to mature: there was a small curve at her hips, and a slight suggestion of breasts.

"I'm sorry, Sister," Anatolia said meekly. "I like the...privacy. There is always someone bothering you in the common rooms, and Lillian won't leave me alone in the dormitory. And I like to draw the angels in the window up there." She pointed toward the rosette window above the loft.

"I have heard all of this before, have I not?" Clotilde asked. Anatolia nodded shamefully. "I want you to say an extra rosary today. I am extremely unhappy when you girls force me to use prayer as punishment—it is such a contradiction. But I dislike spankings and harsher punishments, so what am I to do?"

"I don't know, Sister," Anatolia mumbled, looking

at the floor.

"Neither do I," Clotilde said. "But next time it will have to be something more harsh."

Anatolia nodded her agreement. "I will understand if it is more harsh next time, Sister," Anatolia said earnestly, glancing up at Clotilde with a furrowed brow.

Clotilde smiled a little. "Thank you for your commiseration with my plight. Now, Anatolia Montes, I want to introduce you to Miss Perdita Badon-Reed, who will be teaching you this term."

For the first time, Anatolia looked directly at Perdita. She smiled timidly.

"I am very pleased to meet you, Miss," Anatolia said. "The sisters have told us you are a real artist."

Perdita smiled warmly. "I attempt to be. I am pleased to meet you, Anatolia. What a pretty name that is."

"Thank you, Miss. I am named for a country of olden times."

"And which country is that?" Clotilde asked.

"The land of the Turks," the child said dutifully.

"May I see what you were drawing?" Perdita asked, extending her hand to the child.

Anatolia pulled a loose leaf of paper from her sketchbook and held it up to Perdita. Perdita took it carefully and studied it. The sketch was a finely rendered, if in spots uncertain, head of an angel that was just visible in the rosette window above the loft railing. At the top of the page were notes written in a small, self-consciously neat but childish hand: "hair the color of angel hair—yellow. Eyes the color of angel eyes—blue. These are God's helpers, much like the ones who speak to me."

Anatolia was looking up expectantly at Perdita. Her eyes were so dark Perdita could not distinguish the pupils from the irises.

"Your drawing is excellent," Perdita said, handing

it back to her.

Anatolia smiled slightly.

"I am most impressed, Anatolia. I am sure it will be a pleasure to have you as my student."

Anatolia smiled a little more broadly and looked at Perdita almost affectionately for a long moment, then seemed suddenly embarrassed and looked away.

"Why do you like to draw angels, Anatolia?" Perdita asked.

"They are always so pretty in the pictures we see, like they are in the windows of our church," Anatolia said thoughtfully. "They must be the prettiest of all of the heavenly hosts. And I think what a wonderful place heaven must be if angels, who are so beautiful, live there. And I feel sometimes they are speaking to me—perhaps they speak to all of us."

"Well, that is very true. I am sure the sisters have taught you there are many more reasons to hope to enter heaven than besides how pretty everything is. Although I suppose that is a good reason, too." Perdita smiled warmly at the child. "And I am sure our guardian angels speak to us often."

"Thank you, Miss," Anatolia said. "Should I go now, Sister?"

"Yes," Clotilde said. "And remember the extra rosary."

"I will." Anatolia hurried out the front door and into the sunshine.

"Her drawing was outstanding," Perdita said.

"Yes, she has some talent," Clotilde said. "She writes verses, too. Rather an unpromising student otherwise. Cannot follow a thought from A to B. She was hurt as a child. I do not know the whole story, but I feel it has affected her interactions and concentration. At least that is my opinion. And she claims to see things, hear things, if we are to believe her. Half of the time we find her in the choir loft. She claims the angels called her to be there."

"Is she an orphan?"

"No. Abandoned. Her father was a free black man from Baton Rouge, I think. And her mother is a Tamaroa Indian. Both are still alive. I don't know which world she will live in, her father's or her mother's, or if either will have her."

Clotilde stepped outside and down the front stairs. Perdita followed. They continued along the brick walkway to the school building. Clotilde directed Perdita into an inconspicuous door nearly hidden among untrimmed bushes. Inside, they stood in the center of a plain, plastered corridor.

"The north corridors are the classrooms," Clotilde said, "first and second floors. The third and fourth floors are dormitories. Some of the girls must go home to help during the summer. Others have no homes, and stay here year round."

"Like Anatolia?"

"Yes. Come this way." Clotilde took Perdita's arm and led her to a shorter corridor to the left. "This way are the common rooms, library, dining hall, and kitchen."

Clotilde opened a large, square double door and they entered the dining hall, a room sixty- or seventy-feet long, about forty-feet wide, and at least fifteen-feet high, lined with wooden tables and benches. A large painting of St. Perpetua Flavia, serene in spite of the torture of being devoured by lions, looked down upon the room from high on the western wall.

"The kitchen is this way." Clotilde walked toward the far end of the room where a pine counter and swinging door could be seen. "In a community of women, you will not find housekeepers or cooks," she continued. "I have never seen either in a convent. We take care of everything ourselves. Of course men—priests—are not brought up to care for themselves in a household. They are incapable of it. Helpless in many ways—" Clotilde stopped short and looked at Perdita. Perdita wondered if Clotilde regretted her last statement, if she thought it might be considered slighting to Uncle Tancred.

"I shudder to think how Uncle Tancred would manage, left to his own devices," Perdita said. "What a catastrophe it would be! Now Mrs. Moon can keep him shipshape during the day, and I take over in the evenings!"

Clotilde seemed to recognize this indulgence, this offer of rapport, and smiled in appreciation. She pushed open the swinging door to the kitchen. Inside were two nuns in aprons. The younger was washing dishes, the older scrubbing a cutting block. They dropped their sponges and rags, and dried their hands on their aprons.

"Good afternoon, Mother Superior," they both said in unison. Clotilde nodded and smiled.

"This is Sister Patrice," Clotilde said to Perdita, as she put her arm around the older nun, a pretty woman of about forty with striking green eyes. "And this young woman is Sister Rose Agnes." She indicated the younger nun, who was plain, with a bad complexion, thick nose and uneven teeth. "Sisters, this is Miss Perdita Badon-Reed, of whom I have told you."

Both nuns extended their hands at once to Perdita. Perdita shook Sister Patrice's hand first, then Sister Rose Agnes's.

"How do you do?" Perdita said.

"Sister Patrice is our cook, chiefly, and Sister Rose Agnes is her assistant," Clotilde said.

"We are so glad you arrived safely," Patrice said, "from...was it Philadelphia?"

"Boston." Perdita smiled.

"You don't have an accent, do you?" Sister Rose Agnes asked suspiciously. "They have such an odd accent up there."

"None that I know of." Perdita smiled more broadly.

"It is so lucky your steamboat didn't explode," Rose Agnes went on. "Not lucky, I guess, but God's will. I would be afraid to get within a thousand yards of one of those boats!"

"No incidents. I suppose I was lucky. Or blessed."

"Yes, you avoided the accent and the explosion." Clotilde smiled.

"Thank God you are here, safe and sound," Patrice said. "If you need anything at all, don't hesitate to ask either of us."

"Thank you, Sisters." Perdita nodded.

"You are at the rectory, then?" Sister Patrice asked.

"Yes, for the time being. I will find my own rooms soon before I wear out my welcome with Uncle—Father Condell."

"Will you be having your meals at home, then, breakfast and supper?" Patrice continued.

"I assume so, yes," Perdita said. "I often have no breakfast."

"Oh, you mustn't skip breakfast," Rose Agnes said almost sternly. "Sister Patrice has told me many times, have no luncheon or supper, if you've no stomach for it, but have breakfast, by all means."

"That is true, Sister," said Patrice. "Thank you. But Miss Badon-Reed, if you ever feel . . ."

"Peckish is what the English say," Rose Agnes interrupted.

"Yes, thank you, Sister," Patrice said patiently. "Count on luncheon, Miss Badon-Reed, but, really, come to see us any time you need a bite of something."

"Thank you, Sisters," Perdita said.

"Let's go through this back door," Clotilde said. "I want to show you our hidden treasure."

The kitchen door opened upon a small herb garden. The garden beds were arranged in patterns radiating around a central bronze sundial, on the face of which could be seen a skull in low relief with the words "Tempus Fugit" under it. Perdita recognized the scents of thyme, sage, and basil as she followed Clotilde along the path that bisected the garden, and through a small iron gate that opened onto the lawn beyond.

Clotilde led Perdita toward a stand of oak and hickory trees, which deepened into a forest running up a hillside a few hundred feet back. There was a suggestion of a walkway, paved and edged with bricks, covered in the most part with moss and dead leaves.

"We do not maintain this path as we should," Clotilde said. "There is always so much else to do, and few of the sisters come out here anymore for prayer."

Perdita kept her gaze straight ahead to see what their destination might be. She could see they were approaching the hillside through an unremarkable expanse of tree trunks, bushes, and undergrowth. Suddenly, amid the trunks, she could see the outline of a brick building with the familiar Gothic tracery, quatrefoils, and arches of all ecclesiastical buildings in Ste. Odile.

"This is the Reliquary Chapel," Clotilde said. "It is my favorite spot on these grounds."

There were three limestone steps which Clotilde ascended. She pulled open the small but heavy door and they entered. The vestibule of the chapel was dimly lighted and simpler in architecture and decoration than the main chapel. As Perdita's eyes became accustomed to the darkness, she could see she was in a small, demurely decorated church which might comfortably seat a hundred people. There were only six stained glass windows, three on the north wall, and three on the south. In the apse, she could make out three altars: the main altar and two glass-fronted smaller ones, at angles to it on either side. Behind the glass fronts of the side altars, Perdita could see masses of brilliant color: reds, aquas, golds, and blues in arrangements which did not quite make sense to her in the dim light.

"Let me show you what we have here," Clotilde said, making the sign of the cross and walking down the central aisle toward the front of the church, nodding for Perdita to follow. Perdita kept her eyes fixed on the left altar as she approached it. A sense of uneasy familiarity and apprehensiveness grew in her as she slowly recognized what she was seeing behind the glass.

"These are the precious relics given to Sister Maria Phillipa by the Holy Father more than one hundred years ago for safekeeping," Clotilde murmured. "On the left we have St. Aurelia, and on the right, St. Eulalia Falco, both martyrs of the second century."

Perdita felt a sense of apprehension pass through her at Sister Clotilde's words. Perdita studied the altars as best she could in the shadows. She could see that the side altars were actually ornate glass-sided caskets. The corpses lay, dessicated and grotesque, dressed in rich fabrics and brocades with gold foil embossing, on beds of silk. Dried, stretched scraps of gray flesh still clung in spots to the skeletons, and all exposed areas of the faces, feet, hands, and arms were covered with a film of milky gauze.

On the rear wall of the left altar enclosure, written in gold letters and surrounded by a golden wreath of palm fronds, were the words: "Corpus Sanctae Aureliae Martyris." Perdita noticed an inconspicuous alcove between the crypt altar and the main altar, in which stood a tall monument carved of white marble. The top half of this consisted of columns and tracery framing a very old painting of a female saint in ecstasy. The bottom half formed a pedestal consisting of another glass-fronted chamber, holding a collection of bones bound within a jeweled gauze cloth, surmounted by a skull wearing a gold tiara. Above this ossuary were carved the words: "Berencis In Pace." Perdita saw there was a similar alcove and monument on the opposite side of the main altar. Perdita said nothing for several minutes.

"Do you find it unsettling?" Clotilde finally asked, genuflecting in front of the main altar and making the sign of the cross again.

After a few moments of studying each tableau, the grotesque, contorted figures seemed to Perdita to melt into their gorgeous surroundings of plush fabrics, luscious colors, and the plentiful evidence of the impeccable skill of the ancient goldsmiths who had adorned them.

"A bit, yes. I can understand the sisters' avoidance of the chapel. It is really quite fascinating, though, to me." Perdita also genuflected before the main altar and made the sign of the cross.

"We have Mass here on certain holy days," Clotilde said, "and on the feast days of these saints interred here. To me it is a great source of inspiration and reaffirmation of my vocation to come here and be in the presence of these holy martyrs, who actually had the honor, the *gift,* of suffering and death for our Lord!" Clotilde sat in the front pew. "You yourself considered the sisterhood, did you not?"

"Yes. With the Ursulines in New Orleans. Unfortunately, I was unable to finish my novitiate." Perdita's injured right hand was beginning to throb.

"No, not unfortunately. Not everyone is meant for this life." Clotilde frowned a bit, then smiled. "Your work is out in the world. God has something else in mind for you. Perhaps you will be a wife and mother someday."

"Perhaps. Odder things have happened." Perdita smiled weakly and sat on the pew next to Clotilde.

"You left a young man behind in Boston," Clotilde said flatly.

"Yes." Perdita was surprised by this statement. "You are well informed, Sister."

"You were considering marriage?"

"Considering, yes. But I thought better of it. I knew little happiness with the gentleman before—how much could I have expected after being bound to him in marriage? He had needs and expectations of me which I could not fulfill."

"So, you got away from him by coming here?" Clotilde smiled slightly.

"Well, that isn't the only reason. I wanted a new life. I needed independence in order to live a creative life."

"And are you so certain that independence is a good thing? Do we not depend upon our Lord for everything?" Sister Clotilde's tone was far from accusatory, but Perdita found herself becoming uneasy.

"Of course. I don't mean it like that. I mean self-reliance—creatively and personally."

"If not spiritually. Spoken like a true Bostonian. You've read Emerson, I take it?" Clotilde smiled.

"A little. Hardly enough to be influenced by him. I'd much rather read Shakespeare or Keats or Byron."

"Oh, dear," Clotilde said, with what could have been mock concern.

"And Thomas Aquinas, or St. Thomas More."

Clotilde laughed. "A well-rounded reader, then. I understand your parents were in holy orders in England before they married?"

Perdita shifted on her pew awkwardly. She felt herself blushing. "Yes. They had the difficulty of being Anglo-Catholics, the disgrace of leaving holy orders to marry, and the embarrassment of having a child who could not succeed where they had failed. I had no vocation either, to their great disappointment."

"Ah."

"Nor could I even marry and provide them with grandchildren whom they could mold, who could…pay their debt to the church for them." Perdita's voice was quivering.

"So, you have felt a burden upon yourself. The expectations of others." Clotilde raised her eyebrows sympathetically.

"It may seem like I am running away. I suppose in some ways I am. But I still feel I can do good work here. I am here for more than just selfish reasons."

"Certainly." Clotilde smiled magnanimously.

"I can teach these girls about the things that have inspired wonder in me. Open up to them the world I love. I know I can contribute something here. I can tell you, Mother Superior, my father's punishments were much harsher than a rosary. And longer lasting, like his anger. I spent many an hour terrified—" Perdita stopped herself short, considering the propriety of giving sister such personal and secret information. "Forgive me for that," she said. "But I learned from it all. I learned the importance of patience and love, the importance of creating beautiful things!"

"Of course." Clotilde brushed away a tear from Perdita's cheek. "I have no doubt of it. You will not need to prove yourself to us here. God has placed you among us."

"Yes. One can make something beautiful, even if... if *beauty* is just an idea, not a fact of one's life. If one can convey even just the *idea* of beauty, of perfectibility, or empathy to some other being— That is important. Essential to a full life. I think that is why I am here. And I am glad to be here. I had some misgivings the night I arrived and the next day, but everyone has been so kind to me. I believe in the basic goodness of people, I *must* believe it, I find. I am inclined to think the best of everyone I meet. A hopeful and positive outlook is essential, in spite of life's trials, and an important intangible I hope to convey to my students. In spite of our suffering, God's world is full of good. Children, I think, need to have that fact reinforced as they face reverses, disappointments, and pain. I *know* this is true, and I think that is also a part of why I am here." Perdita bit her lip a moment to prevent herself from sobbing.

"I do not question God's plans." Clotilde's smile was broader now. "It was a part of God's plan to take to Himself the young woman who had your position before you. She died of peritonitis, God love her. I think you will bring much richness to the lives of these poor girls. I think Anatolia has taken a liking to you. And I think you can help Sister Solana, too. She is a young woman yet to be molded, it seems. She wants to do good, she is brimming with the desire for it, and I have much affection for her. But she needs the influence of a more mature woman. Not a Mother Superior, but an equal. I am hoping you will take her under your wing. I am counting upon you to do so."

"Yes. I like her very much." The pain in Perdita's hand had become sharper now.

"She is much impressed with you and your charity toward Mrs. Chardin."

"To be honest, I am not sure—"

"She will follow your lead. You see, already you have touched three lives. Some would say you now have responsibility for those lives."

"Yes. I feel I do, for better or worse."

"For better, I am sure." Clotilde nodded. "I am certain you will not disappoint them."

8

Sister Solana cut a length of bandage from a roll and wrapped it around a folded pad of linen she had placed over the cut on Perdita's palm.

"We should have cleaned this better when it first happened," she mumbled. "It doesn't look good."

"Oh, it is healing slowly," Perdita said. "I still cannot hold my hammer. My stone has sat undisturbed for three days now. At least it has given us an opportunity to plan our term. Otherwise, I would have been tempted to spend these days in a creative 'idleness,' as Mother Superior might say."

Solana smiled politely, if disapprovingly, at this statement. "I saw Mrs. Chardin today. She is so ashamed that she is the cause of your injury." Solana tied the bandage in place, then refreshed the tea in Perdita's cup from a flowered teapot.

"I am lucky to be in your charge," Perdita said. "You are taking excellent care of me."

Solana smiled. "I can't very well teach medieval and modern art history, aesthetic theory, *and* drawing, watercolor, and plein-air sketching, can I? I *must* insure your health!"

"Yes, you must."

"Something else occurred to me," Solana said thoughtfully. "Have you ever tried your hand at weaving? Have you used a loom?"

"No, but I have always been interested in learning."

"Well, I've found an old loom in the cellar. The sisters used to use it, but no more. I learned the skill as a child. There's no end to the pretty things the girls could make with it!"

"Well, then I think we should ask Mother Superior if we can include it in our teaching plan." Perdita smiled.

"Oh, I'm so glad you feel that way!"

Perdita picked up her cup and saucer with some difficulty and moved to the bentwood chair near one of the four windows in the sparse room.

"How do you like the classroom?" Solana asked.

Perdita looked around herself approvingly. "It will suit me nicely," she said. "Plenty of northern light for when we start painting."

"Mother Superior made certain we got this room at the end of the building just for that purpose: the light."

"I am anxious to begin," Perdita said. She took a sip from her cup. "You started to tell me about your meeting with Mr. Bastide last evening."

"Oh, my word yes…where did I leave it?"

"The sitting room." Perdita adjusted the bandage on her hand a bit.

"I didn't see much of the place from the outside," Solana continued. "It was dark. A great, rambling place, and, from what I could tell, a hodgepodge of styles architecturally. I had the oddest feeling on entering: a sense of loss, of apprehension, of separation from…everything important to me. That's the only way I can describe it. Anyway, the sitting room is enormous. There are all sorts of mounted animals on the walls such as I have never seen before. Hyenas, some sort of wild dog, and some sort of great red ape from the East Indies, he said—"

"An ourang-outan?" Perdita asked.

"Possibly. Probably. A snow leopard from the Himalayas and a whole mounted baboon. It nearly frightened my supper out of me. It was difficult, I can tell you, to have that great hideous brute staring down at me all evening! And, oh, the books! There are books everywhere."

"What about the man himself?"

"The man himself." Solana thought for a moment. "It is a shock to see him at first—"

"A shock?"

"Yes, poor soul. He has some sort of deforming condition and he hides his face under bits of wax. I suppose you would call them prosthetics—is that the word?"

"Yes."

"It is unsettling and strange at first, I can tell you. Like talking to one of the cadavers in the Reliquary Chapel, I guess. Yet, he quickly put me at my ease. He explained about his condition and how he has spent the last several years at Berne receiving treatment." Solana thought for a moment. "I do not think I have known a more gracious and accommodating host. He made every deference and anticipated every need. I wanted for no refreshment, nor were there any awkward gaps in the conversation. He was able to speak with authority on any subject that arose during the evening."

"What about his wooden figures? Do you think they were by Sluter?"

"I do not know, but I doubt it." Solana frowned slightly. "What is more, I think he doubts it too. I believe he just wanted companionship for the evening. I don't think our examination of the figures occupied more than three minutes."

"I am sorry you didn't get to see more of the house. I'm dying with curiosity about it." Perdita smiled a girlish, conspiratorial smile.

"Well, I will get my chance. He asked me back. If Mother Superior gives her permission, I am most eager to return."

"Ask for a tour next time."

"I will. And look at what he gave me." Solana reached into the folds of her habit and withdrew a heavy gold disc.

"What is it?"

"A gift," Solana said guiltily. "I shouldn't have accepted it, but look. It is Roman. A gold *aureus*."

Perdita took the heavy coin from Solana's palm. It was brilliant and glittering. "This is an exceptional gift. Two millennia means nothing to gold. This could be newly made."

Solana took the coin and returned it to her habit. "Mr. Bastide has, in spite of himself—of his appearance—a true charm about him," she said thoughtfully. "An active mind to say the very least, and I found myself responding to him…intellectually, *and* as a…. I think he would have an especial appeal to women."

Perdita laughed. "You say that as if you are not one yourself!"

Solana blushed. "In a real sense, I am not. Not allowed to be. Not *supposed* to be. Now don't tempt me to be naughty!"

"Am I tempting you to be naughty by telling you that you are as much a woman as I?"

"You know what I mean!" Solana blushed again. "I will never have a husband, not an earthly one, and no children will come from my body. I will have no children but the ones I teach; I mean—"

"What do you mean, about his being of interest to women. I mean, if he is repulsive?" Perdita asked.

"I mean…" Solana went silent for a long moment. "I mean, he *listened* to me. As few conversationalists have done. I…I am having difficulty putting it into words. I felt there was a melding, a union of minds, I suppose. I have rarely felt that I was so *interesting* to someone else. And I am not sure men notice the absence of that sensation the way women do."

"So, now you are comfortable calling yourself a woman!" Perdita teased. "I don't have to call you *Mister* Solana?" Both of them burst into laughter for a few moments.

"I tried to define my feelings in the carriage on the way home," Solana continued at length. "I suppose I would call my response to him, my reaction to him gratitude, for want of a less obsequious word. It was a sort of...," she looked pained to say it, "*dignity* I felt in being given his attentions."

"Oh my." Perdita sat back in her chair and thought for a moment.

"Is it wrong to put it that way?"

"No." Perdita thought for a moment. "Not wrong. You've granted him much power, though. This man you have only just met can bestow dignity upon you?"

"Oh, I know it's a wretched way to put it, but, in a real way it is true. A person who will make your mind and your opinions legitimate by listening to you, by taking seriously anything you have to say, when you are so unused to that legitimization elsewhere in life; that is a gift, don't you agree?"

"But, he has not *made* these things legitimate, you see?" Perdita insisted. "They already were, regardless of how the world has previously regarded them."

"But how are you to know that except through the kindness of a sympathetic and engaged listener?" Solana asked adamantly.

Perdita smiled. She loved the sincerity and brightness of Solana's face, and the forthrightness, the artlessness of her eyes. "Do you know, Solana, I do not know how to respond to that. For all I know, I think you are right!"

Solana smiled and glanced out of the window. "Time for prayers soon." She stood. Perdita stood also.

"Yes, I should get back to the rectory," Perdita said. "I have a letter to write."

"You may be getting an invitation to Jardin Noir soon, too," Solana said as she handed Perdita her notebook and pencil. "I told him about you. All about you. He seemed fascinated."

Letter from Perdita Badon-Reed to Moira Keane Parnell

August 20
Ste. Odile

My dear Moira,

In answer to the most pressing question in your recent letter: yes, my hand is healing well. It had been inflamed for four days and very tender, but I think in another day or two, it will be well enough for me to hold my hammer again. Secondly: no, my block for the Havilland piece has not yet arrived. Mr. Dufresne at the packet office can find no evidence it was ever shipped, and my letter to the quarry has not been answered. In the meantime, Sister Solana and I have completed that portion of our lesson plans which required the closest cooperation. The idea is for me to have drawing and watercolor assignments which echo Sister's lectures in art history. This is intended to give the girls a greater insight into technique and methods of the great milestones of art. How can we do this, you may ask, given only the mediums of pencil, charcoal, and watercolor with which to work? Originally, we had intended to actually make figures and objects out of clay and wood, as Cro-Magnon Man or the Neanderthals may have done in prehistoric times. But this was considered to be too avant garde and potentially distracting for the girls by Uncle Tancred and Sister Clotilde. We then had to revise our plan and settle for merely representing objects of prehistory with acceptable modern media such as those mentioned above. Similarly, our plan to show the girls the use of the ancient loom in the cellar was rejected. Mother Superior and Uncle have approved our reconsidered efforts and now we have only to wait until Monday for the beginning of the term. I am more than a little nervous as the date approaches, but still anxious to get the first day behind me.

I meet a few more of the girls each day as they return to school in greater and greater numbers. They add an energy, I would call it, an essence to the place that is palpable. The grounds have a different feel now than they did when I first saw them, when they were more deserted, almost gloomy. The population appears to be split nearly in half as regards the girls' heritage: half are the daughters of former slaves and freedmen, and half are children of the Fox, Sac, Tamaroa, and infrequently, Osage tribes. I have been told there are fewer of the Indian girls each year in the Mississippi valley, as these peoples are slowly displaced from their ancient homelands by our government. In general, these displacements have passed by Ste. Odile, as has so much else in this advancing century, but the tide of change cannot be entirely avoided and denied, even here.

Let me tell you that, yes, the drawing of the angel which I found on my desk in my classroom was done by the child Anatolia, of whom I told you. It was a refinement of one she had done in the choir loft the day I met her. Solana told me she had seen her bring it in. Yet, when I saw the child on the grounds, and thanked her, she seemed almost pained, and ran away.

You asked if I had begun to read *Moby Dick*. I have, and I find it, as you and Solana have said, a revelation. On reflection, I am not surprised it has been poorly received. It is too great a work to be understood well by the mass of readers, I think. You will be surprised to hear me say this, but I have no doubt that you agree since, as I remember, you do not always share my hopeful opinion of our fellow creatures.

You asked about Mr. Robert. I would say he has been attentive, but not overly so. It could be that, like myself and Solana, he merely craves the company of a like spirit with whom to share his thoughts. And no, I have not considered what my response would be if his attentions strove to take on a more personal tenor. I do not seek attentions of that sort, and would, of course, tell him so immediately, if he offered them.

I have conveyed your regards to Marie Delaporte Chardin, and she was much moved. She has promised to remember you in her prayers. I spent nearly four hours with her yesterday. She showed me several poppets she has made to pass the time. They were similar, she said, to some she had made with her slain daughter. Then she told me the story of her life from earliest childhood up until this past spring. She remains guarded about certain elements of her crime and events leading up to it. She repeats that the well being of her family is at stake, though she wishes to give me her journal as I accompany her to the gallows on de Castres Island on the day after tomorrow.

Oh Moira! That horrible event is only two days away! I have barely slept in half a week thinking of it, dreading it. Am I a coward to say I wish nothing more than to be as far away from the morbid spectacle on that day as I can possibly be? Marie depends upon me so. In spite of Solana's kind overtures, Marie has not responded to her, I think, perhaps, because she bears the habit. I feel Marie has come to believe that the church and its minions have misunderstood and condemned her. All except Uncle Tancred, whom I think she regards as a kindly *pater familias*. So she has placed all of her expectations of human and female contact and understanding upon me. It is a burden I bear uneasily and with dread. She inspires great sorrow and compassion in me, but how can I accompany her to her death? How can I watch her die?

A packet left the landing this morning for de Castres, loaded with timbers with which the scaffold will be built. And this afternoon, when the breeze off of the river was right, I could hear the sounds of the crosscut saw, and of nails being driven home. I will close now.

Much love,
Perdita

Later

Moira: I must add this addendum. It is now nine p.m. and I have just returned from the jail. Something extraordinary has happened. As I arrived at the jail, the office was empty, but I heard sounds of activity in the back, in the vicinity of Marie's cell. I walked back to find Sheriff Aubuchon and the doctor tending to a large wound on Marie's left calf. Marie was on the floor, languid and glassy-eyed, lying in a pool of her own blood. Dr. Duclos, who is something of a newcomer here, too, having only been in practice in town for three years, was questioning Marie about the nature of her injury.

"She'll have nothing to say about it," Aubuchon said. Apparently some sort of animal, perhaps a marten or badger, had come in through the bars of the window and attacked her, disappearing when she screamed, the sheriff surmised.

I washed Marie's face as the men attended to her, checking her gingerly for unseen injuries. She scarcely took notice of me, but seemed to be in a state of shock, or lost in thought, a thousand miles away. All the while I wondered: how can so much misfortune and suffering befall such a frail and pathetic little being?

"Marie," I asked, "you did not do this to yourself?"

She shook her head weakly, never looking at me.

"No, it was an animal," Duclos said. "There are marks of teeth and claws here. I treated a man who was attacked by a wolverine at Mackinac a few years ago. Wounds were very much like this."

"Surely there are no wolverines this far south," I said. "What kind of creature would come into the middle of a town to attack—"

"My mother...," Marie interrupted. Her voice was weak and far away, "my mother told me to expect it. She had expected it herself. But there is madness in my family, perhaps my mother was mad, too."

"Marie," I said, "expect what? What did this?"

"I had fallen asleep," Marie said, "an hour or two ago, I have no way of telling time. I had horrible dreams and awoke with a start. I thought I would record my dream, of a dark form devouring my family, in my journal. I was on my stomach on the cot. I reached down with my left arm to retrieve the journal on the floor under me. I did not feel the book, but I felt something else. I could not tell what it was I was touching at first, but suddenly, suddenly I knew: it was *teeth!*"

I felt a shudder pass through me.

Marie looked at the ceiling of her cell, at the wall opposite, and the barred window. The sill bore a number of small, bloody footprints. "*Le Vorace*," she said weakly. "Mine."

I still do not know what to make of this. I think poor Marie created the wounds herself, or was attacked by some creature as mentioned above, and concocted the rest in her mind.

This is all for tonight.

Always,
Perdita

9

From the Journal of Prosper Redon

August 19, 1882, aboard the *Egeria*

I am told we are nearly midway across the Atlantic. As one day runs into the next upon the face of featureless waters, and I have not made daily entries into this journal, I have lost count of how many of the nine days predicted for our crossing have passed.

The seasickness that troubled me yesterday, and the day before, has subsided with the rough seas. I was able to eat a little this morning, although I have had no desire for food since. Perdita told me once—in her instructive way, which I made the mistake of calling didactic—that naturalists call the ocean the mother of all life. She and Moira seemed to feel a romantic connection to these deeps which I have never quite understood. It is a barrier full of dangers and terrors which must needs, against all trepidations, be faced by the voyager. I will be glad and grateful to set foot upon dry earth at Lisbon again, and soon after, Marseilles.

We have not seen a fishing boat for two days or more as we approach mid-ocean. We did see a magnificent brigantine this morning, which made me think of our sloop, the *Hera*, on the day Father sold her. I wonder if she is serving Mr. Mene's pleasure as she served ours, or I should say my family's, since I was never at my ease upon the void of the sea. It is silly, I think, how an image or smell, perhaps, or a sound, can trigger such memories and incite such melancholy! But, so many things have that effect upon me these days.

My sleeplessness continues, and my appetite had been poor even before I set foot upon this ship. This pattern must needs remain unaltered for many months to come, I think. The greatest grief is still ahead and to be faced in the sitting rooms and hallways of home. It is one to which I will be doubly susceptible, owing to my inexcusable and extended absence from my family, and the condoling with them which should have been my first and immediate duty.

I am surprised, a little, that the ship is so empty. Those few passengers I have met are business people, industrialists on their holidays, and idle travelers of the upper class. Mr. Mineer, the first mate, told me the return trip will be much different. The wealthy go from the New World to the Old for their pleasure. The poor come from the Old World to the New for survival or opportunity. The ship, he assured me, will be much more full upon my return to Boston next month. What do those intervening weeks hold?

There will certainly be many recriminations from my family for my long absence, to be sure. My duties to my clients, to the law, and the difficulties in my personal life scarcely justify an absence of so many months, in light of such a monumental family tragedy. My family knows my highly strung nature and the debilitating effect melancholia has upon me. Still, how can my actions be justified? I have no inkling of what I will say to them or how I will explain myself.

I have too much time to think about these things. I try to fill my time with reading on the decks, but the rolling of the ship brings on my sea sickness. I nap or write letters in my cabin. The closeness of my quarters reminds me of

Perdita's dislike of enclosed places, and I think of how I will never again have the opportunity to comfort and assure her through that fear or any other. Then my mind is off, thinking a thousand thoughts of her and what I could have done to prompt her abandonment of me. Certain looks, certain phrases spoken, which meant nothing at the time, are now full of meaning, of clews of what was to come. If only I had been more sensitive to them! But I must needs put these thoughts out of my mind, as no good, nothing of a constructive nature, can come from them. I am ashamed to admit that this jilting by a fiancée has occupied so much more predominant a position in my mind than the savage murder of my poor sister. My dear Claire!

Would my family understand this, if they knew it? I think I understand it. I can scarcely believe that Claire is dead. How many times has the whole notion seemed impossible? How *could* it be true? How could my playmate, my confidante, my confederate of a thousand schemes and mischiefs of so many golden summers, my sister three years my junior, be dead? It still does not seem possible. Yet, it is true. I must live the rest of my life without her. We all must.

Together we explored the battlements of Carcassonne, chased each other through the ancient streets of Toulouse when we accompanied Father on business trips, and we searched for the lost treasure of the Cathars in our own back garden. How could the energy and warmth which she carried always within her go out of the world? Our faith seeks to give us solace in the face of such a tragedy, but thinking on the manner of her death, the pain, the terror, the violation, how can those memories, those experiences, be recompensed by knowledge that she is now at peace? Who could have foreseen that those happy children and those loving parents would come to such ruin, such catastrophe?

The ship is starting to pitch and roll again. How much rougher will the seas be upon my return, closer to cold weather? How much easier a passage it would have been to have postponed my trip until spring? But that would have been impossible. I do not know what my presence can do to elucidate the mystery of Claire's death that my brother, my father or the police have not already accomplished. But this is my mother's wish.

10

By four in the morning, Perdita had given up trying to sleep. She lay in bed listening to rain falling most of the night and, for the last half hour or so, she could hear Uncle Tancred moving about the rectory. The night had begun too humid and hot to sleep, but the rain had cooled her room to a more comfortable temperature. On any other night, she might have slept well.

She arose, washed her face, and dressed quickly. She found Tancred in the front parlor, arising from the kneeler and crossing himself.

"Good morning, Uncle," Perdita said.

"Mornin', girl," Tancred said weakly.

"Did you sleep?"

"No."

"Nor did I. Have you eaten?" Perdita said, suppressing a yawn.

"There were zome kippers and a bit of cake. I've made coffee, if you've a taste for it at this hour." He looked pale and very tired.

"No. I don't have any stomach for anything. I saw her last night, Uncle. She can scarcely stand upon her injured leg. She'll need a crutch, or to be carried. She said she was attacked by *Le Vorace*. Do you know what she was saying?"

"'The Ravenous.' A local hobgoblin or zuperstition,

I would zay. It were probably a rabid cat or raccoon, or zum zuch thing."

"I should walk over," Perdita said. "Are you coming?"

"In a bit. Go ahead. Aubuchon is expecting you."

Perdita did not possess a black hat and shawl. The darkest hat she owned was dark brown, and her darkest shawl was burgundy. She retrieved these from her room. She pinned the hat on and wrapped the shawl around her shoulders. As she passed through the front parlor to the vestibule, she turned to speak to Tancred. He was back on the kneeler saying his rosary. Perdita selected an umbrella from the umbrella stand and stepped outside.

The rain had tapered off in the last twenty minutes or so, but was still falling hard enough for Perdita to open the umbrella. The streets were completely deserted, except for two cats chasing each other. The street lamps' small flames flickered intermittently along Mal Ardents and Constantinople streets, and more prominently along Bucephalus Street, where the merchants paid to maintain them.

Her footsteps resounded on the wet, empty pavement, causing first the blacksmith's dog across the street, then two or three other dogs off in the darkness, to bark. Perdita could feel a pang of dread beginning to clench her stomach as she crossed over to Bucephalus Street and neared the jail.

It appeared all the rooms in the jail were lighted. As she pushed open the front door, she saw Aubuchon sitting at his desk filling out and signing forms.

"Good morning, Sheriff."

"Good morning, Miss," Aubuchon said, glancing up at her briefly. "You're here just when you said you'd be. It is good of you to do this. To stand with her like this."

"I quickly found I had a…responsibility toward her. I was just trying to do good by her, since it was lacking in the other women hereabouts. Is she awake?"

"Of course. She has been up all night. I'll let you in." He rose and picked up a ring of keys from his desk. "Miss," he said, pausing at the door to the corridor, "an execution is always a bad business whatever the circumstances. This one will be the worst, I can tell you."

"You have a necessary but unenviable responsibility, Sheriff."

"Yes. I should tell you also, that we found a journal she had been hiding in her bed. She said she had intended it for you. The judge ordered me to confiscate it for the time being, until he can examine it."

"In case the contents might exonerate her?"

"No. Too late for that. She confessed and a sentence has been passed which must be carried out." Aubuchon opened the hallway door and stepped aside for Perdita to precede him.

Marie was kneeling beside her cot, lost in prayer. She was rocking slightly from side to side. Her bandaged calf and ankle protruded from under her shift. She didn't seem to notice as Aubuchon opened her cell door. Perdita stepped into the cell and sat silently at the foot of Marie's cot. After a moment she spoke.

"May I pray with you, Marie?" she said. Marie seemed suddenly aware she was not alone.

"Miss Perdita!" She lifted herself awkwardly and painfully onto the cot next to Perdita. She threw her arms around Perdita, buried her face in her shoulder, and began to sob quietly.

"The day has finally come, Miss Perdita. Finally come."

"Yes, Marie. It has come."

"And you have seen me through to it."

"I have done nothing. Would you like me to pray with you?" Perdita said softly.

"I have prayed all night. I have talked to God and to my dear Michee, and to my husband, my Louis. In just a few hours I will be with them again."

"Yes. They are waiting for you, I am sure. There was a time when I wasn't sure, but I am now. It is the only way anything makes any sense in the world." Perdita stroked Marie's face gently.

"But—Miss Perdita. There is so much pain in this life. People who try to live righteously suffer along with the wicked. God allows such evil to move about on earth. This God who loves us, who gave us His only begotten Son. What sense does it make?"

"We have to understand His purpose." Perdita tried to smile. "In the face of trials and sorrows, we must prove ourselves worthy."

"Worthy to join a capricious and cruel God who torments us?" Marie looked earnestly into Perdita's eyes, as though she expected an ultimate and unassailable answer from her friend.

"No, Marie, no. You must not think of God as capricious and cruel. There is a purpose to these things."

"Purpose!" Marie buried her face in Perdita's shoulder again.

"Yes, a purpose, and in a few hours you will see that purpose revealed to you, whatever it may be. You will be free of suffering and rejoined with your daughter and husband. You will see the overriding good of all of this, unknown as it is to us now. Nothing is more important than that!" Perdita held Marie's face in her hands and looked at her intently. "Now your faith must be stronger than ever. This is *not* the time to question God's purpose for you, a few hours before its completion. You must keep your faith now, not lose it. This is the last and best advice I can give to you as your friend."

Marie embraced Perdita tightly. There was a sound

of footsteps in the hallway. Perdita saw Uncle Tancred approaching, carrying his valise, with his stole around his neck.

"Father is here to hear your confession," Perdita said.

"Dear Father Condell," Marie whispered. "I *must* keep my faith now. It would hurt him so if I didn't."

"Good morning, dear girl," Tancred said, entering the cell.

"Good morning Father." Marie smiled and stood to greet him. Suddenly, violently, she moved toward him and embraced him, bursting into tears. Tancred returned her embrace: Perdita knew that under different circumstances this would have surprised her, but this morning it did not. Marie sobbed for many minutes, and Tancred did not relax his hold upon her.

"Yes, my dear, yes," he murmured again and again. Soon the crags and wrinkles of his cheeks were glistening with tears.

"I must not pity myself," Marie muttered. "It is wrong to pity myself. Will I be in heaven today, Father?"

"Yes, yes. Zertainly, yes."

"But I have committed such a great crime. How can God forgive me for it? How can just making a confession and doing penance atone for a murder?" Marie grasped Tancred's hand tightly.

"Our Lord understands your zuffering, my girl. He understands why you did what you did—better than you."

"But how can I be forgiven?"

"You've been making penance for many months. You *must* make a good confession now. Remember *everything*. Our Lord has granted me the blessing of acting as 'is agent upon earth, to convey 'is forgiveness of your zins. I tell you, Marie, you 'ave been forgiven!"

"But I am so afraid!"

"Yes, of course you are afraid. But for the zake of

your dear daughter and husband and all of those departed with whom you shall zoon be rejoined, you must 'ide your fear from the crowd, the 'arpies, and preserve your family's honor. There will be a further moment of pain, then peace and comfort forever!"

"Yes, I must hide it. I mustn't be hysterical…sobbing or terrified. I mustn't be a spectacle for them."

Perdita dabbed at her eyes with her handkerchief, one left on her bed by Mrs. Moon a few days before to replace the one she'd ruined when she cut her hand. "I will wait in the office while you hear confession, Uncle," she said, leaving the cell.

She returned to the office where Aubuchon still sat at his desk reading through his stack of papers: court papers and orders for execution, Perdita imagined. Perdita sat in an oak chair against the wall to the left of Aubuchon. She produced her miniature copy of *Brown's Concordance* from her bag, opened it to a random page, and read.

Tancred remained in the cell for a long time. Occasionally Perdita could hear Marie sob, and then try to cut short her sobbing and control her emotions. This attempted preservation of dignity upset Perdita more than if Marie had wept uncontrollably.

Soon Perdita could hear conversation and footsteps on the street outside. People were already beginning to make their way toward the landing to board the packet for de Castres Island. Perdita glanced at Aubuchon just as he glanced at her. He seemed embarrassed at the sounds of excitement outside.

After a moment, Perdita spoke: "I cannot understand how good people can revel in a tragedy like this. I hope Marie won't be going over on the packet?"

"No," Aubuchon said. "We'll take her in the skiff, along with Father. There is room for you, if—"

"Thank you, yes; I think she is counting on my going across with her."

"Is Hypolitte coming?"

"No, he has the propriety to stay away. I wish to God I had that choice."

"Yes," Aubuchon said. "It's too bad you have gotten involved like this. But you were trying to do good, as you said. *Aucun acte de la bonte ne disparait unpunished.*"

Perdita understood little French, but she could make out what he meant. "Yes, very true." She sighed. It was a lesson she had learned from her father at an early age.

The front door of the jail began to swing open slowly as if someone were having difficulty getting through it. Perdita rose and opened the door. Mrs. Moon stood in the doorway, carrying a large basket covered with a linen cloth. She also held a pot of steaming coffee and carried a bottle of wine under her arm.

"Wasn't sure what she'd want to drink," Mrs. Moon said. She crossed the room and sat the basket on Aubuchon's desk. "She said she just wanted tarts for breakfast," she continued. "Because you like them, I think, Mr. Aubuchon. But I forgot to ask her about her drink. Wasn't sure if she'd want coffee or something stronger."

"None of it will go to waste," Aubuchon said, rising. "I'll see if Father is finished back there yet." He turned to open the hallway door just as Tancred opened it from the inside. Tancred's eyes were red. He removed his stole and folded it, then returned it carefully to his valise.

"Do you think she'll eat, Father?" Mrs. Moon asked.

"I don't know," Tancred said. He sat in the chair Perdita had vacated. Perdita took the coffee pot and bottle of wine and followed Mrs. Moon down the corridor to Marie's cell.

Marie sat on the edge of her cot, staring vacantly at a spot on the floor. She looked tiny and frail, holding her injured leg stiffly in front of her.

"I brought the tarts," Mrs. Moon said. "I didn't know if you'd prefer coffee or wine. You said you sometimes have wine early of a morning. So I brought both coffee cups and wine glasses, just in case."

Marie seemed not to hear. She continued to stare at the floor. Her nose was running, but she did not seem to notice. Perdita sat the coffee pot and wine bottle carefully upon the floor, then knelt down beside her.

"Marie," she said gently, "Mrs. Moon has brought refreshment, if you want it. Could you eat a little?"

Marie lifted her gaze slowly to meet Perdita's. "I asked for tarts," she said slowly, remembering. "Mrs. Moon was kind enough to ask if I wanted breakfast, and I thought, what a silly thing to ask. Who would have a stomach for food three hours before they are to die? Tarts were all I could think of when she asked me. But she was kind enough to ask. She didn't think it a silly question at all. People eat every day, and this is like any other day." She held out her hand to Mrs. Moon, who placed a tart in it.

"You must have been up so early to make these," Marie continued. She cupped the tart in her hand and stared at it like a naturalist examining an unfamiliar specimen. "You must have awakened your whole family, making them."

"None of us slept well," Mrs. Moon said quietly. "Will you have coffee?"

"I'll have some wine," Marie said. She took a small bite from the tart, then placed it on her cot. Mrs. Moon removed a corkscrew and a wineglass from her basket. She opened the bottle and poured a little wine into the glass.

"I think I will have some of that," Perdita said.

"And I believe I will too," Mrs. Moon agreed.

"They've taken my journal, Miss Badon-Reed. Perdita," Marie said.

"Yes. Aubuchon told me," Perdita said.

"I don't know if you'll ever see it now. The sheriff's

top right-hand desk drawer sticks. He has to wiggle it open. I heard him put it in there." Marie looked at Perdita evenly, as though she wanted to be certain Perdita understood her.

"I see."

Marie took the glass of wine from Mrs. Moon and drained it. Perdita and Mrs. Moon sipped theirs.

"More?" Mrs. Moon asked.

"No," Marie said. "I have to have all of my faculties. Thank you for all your kindness to me, Mrs. Moon."

"It was nothing," Mrs. Moon said. "A few tarts here and there. I wanted to do more. *Wanted to*. I am ashamed of myself that I didn't."

"I understand you," Marie said soothingly.

"I wanted to do more. My husband has his position, I had to think of that. And the children."

"I understand," Marie smiled.

Perdita noticed Marie's jaw was quivering a bit, as though she were cold.

"Would you like a shawl or blanket, Marie?" Perdita asked.

"No. I am quite warm." She looked at Perdita for a long moment. The quivering became more pronounced. Marie's eyes filled with tears again. "I am so afraid. I don't know how I can face this. I don't think I can, bravely. I am going to look weak and frightened up there."

Perdita embraced her. Marie's small body was bony, rigid and quivering under her shift, and egested an odor which implied she hadn't bathed in several days.

"It is natural that it weigh upon you," Perdita said. "Try to put it out of your mind. The anticipation will torture you."

"Aubuchon said the condemned is allowed to make final remarks," Marie said weakly. "I do not think I could say anything. I thought of something to say, but I do not think I could get through it."

"You do not have to say anything if you fear that you—"

"What would they care, anyway? Do you know they have sold tickets for the closest positions to the scaffold? If I don't say anything, will those people feel they haven't gotten their money's worth?"

"Please," Perdita said, pushing Marie away so as to look into her eyes. "Do not continue in this way. You must not fill your mind with these bitter thoughts. Please. Think about your child, your husband. Michee and Louis. Think of nothing but them. Be brave for them, and strong. For them."

"Yes. I will. For them."

"The crowd does not matter," Perdita went on. "Whether they are there or not, what will happen today is still a private thing. The court, the crowd, nothing can change that. They can take your life, but they cannot take away the manner you choose for yourself, unless you allow them to. No matter what kind of spectacle they try to make of it, all that will remain of today is what you will leave behind. The manner of your death."

"Yes, the manner," Mrs. Moon said.

"The manner, how you accept it," Perdita continued. "This is the last thing you will leave behind. You must consider what you want it to be. That must be your goal. The thing no one can take from you."

Marie embraced Perdita again.

"I know you are afraid," Perdita murmured. "But you must jealously guard what no one can take from you."

"Yes, I will." Marie wiped her eyes and nose on her forearm and stood erect. "I must bathe," she said. "I am hurt. Will you help me?"

"I'll get a basin," Mrs. Moon said, leaving the cell. Marie slipped off her shift and stood before Perdita naked: tiny, scarred, nearly emaciated, and shivering. Soon Mrs. Moon returned with a basin of steaming water and two cloths.

"Mr. Aubuchon was heating water on the stovetop," Mrs. Moon said. "He said you told him you would want to wash."

"Yes." Marie nodded. "I have gotten out of the habit lately."

Marie stood between the two of them. Perdita wet her cloth in the water and began to gently wash Marie's face. Perdita and Mrs. Moon carefully cleansed around the red and swollen cuts on Marie's wrist, the injuries to her leg, and the many bruises and scabs left from her moments of hysteria and struggling in the preceding weeks. Her arms and legs were amazingly thin, and Perdita felt nothing but a few strands of muscle upon the tiny bones.

"There is a comfort only women can provide," Marie said peacefully, "and a coldness only they can master, I think. I have come to think much about the nature of women since all of this has happened. I cannot thank both of you enough for being with me this morning."

"I am glad to be able to do it," Mrs. Moon said earnestly.

"Yes, we are glad to be with you," Perdita said.

A clean shift lay folded at the foot of Marie's cot. Perdita opened it and helped Marie slip it over her head. Marie seemed refreshed. She had stopped trembling.

At seven A.M., the steam packet *Seraphim* sounded its whistle. The boat had been moored at the landing for two hours. It was now ready to start taking on passengers. The sounds of the townspeople walking past the jail were louder now. Marie sat on the edge of her cot, kneading her hands together, and rocking forward and back. She had begun to tremble again. Mrs. Moon picked up her basket of tarts and returned to the office to deliver them to Sheriff Aubuchon and Tancred.

"You must get my journal, Perdita," Marie said. "Somehow you must."

"Yes. I will." Perdita moved to the wall next to the window and leaned against it. "Marie," she said, "will you tell me one thing? What is *Le Vorace*?"

Marie shook her head. "Euphrosine will answer everything."

"Euphrosine?"

"Yes. A time may come when you will need to seek her out. She is a *traiteur*, a wildcrafter. If that time comes, she will tell you what you want to know." Marie touched Perdita's hand. "She will tell you."

"Where is she?"

"South. Two miles or so, up Saline Creek in the salt marsh."

Footsteps could be heard in the hallway. Aubuchon approached the cell, then pushed the door open wider. "It is time for us to go, Marie," he said.

Marie stepped into leather slippers which were under her cot, and dutifully limped into the hallway. Aubuchon preceded her into the office and Perdita followed them. Aubuchon stopped at his desk. A pair of iron manacles lay on the desktop.

"Marie," he said, turning toward her, "I will leave your ankles free because of your leg."

"Her wrist is injured also," Perdita said suddenly.

"I must put the manacles on," Aubuchon said firmly.

Marie held out her small wrists in front of her. She was trembling noticeably again and murmuring something to herself. Aubuchon fastened the manacles, and they nearly slipped off Marie's wrists as she lowered them. Perdita glanced at Aubuchon's desk. The right-hand drawer was pushed closed, but didn't appear to have a lock on it.

"Where are Uncle Tancred and Mrs. Moon?" Perdita asked.

"I suppose they have decided to take the packet," Aubuchon said. "It is leaving soon."

Marie continued to mumble. "What are you saying, Marie?" Aubuchon asked.

Marie's voice was flat and without inflection. "It is the manner they cannot take from me. It is the manner."

Aubuchon did not understand.

"How will she walk?" Perdita asked.

"Dr. Duclos has brought a crutch," Aubuchon said. The crutch was leaning against the wall under the front window. Aubuchon retrieved it and helped Marie place it under her right arm. Aubuchon opened the front door and Marie hobbled toward it. Perdita held her arm for the first few steps, until Marie seemed to master the use of the crutch.

As they stepped outside, the steam whistle of the *Seraphim* sounded again. The packet was leaving for the island. A dark red trap hitched to a gray gelding stood waiting in front of the jail. Aubuchon helped Perdita up into the seat. Marie attempted to step up, but the step was wet from the rain and she couldn't get her footing. Aubuchon took her crutch and handed it to Perdita.

"Let me try this," he said. He grasped Marie by the waist and lifted her easily into the trap. He found a blanket under the seat, unfolded it, and placed it across the women's laps.

"Thank you, Sheriff," Perdita said.

"*Merci beaux coup,*" Marie nodded.

Aubuchon nodded. He patted the horse's flank and, walking forward, grasped its bridle. He began to walk it toward the landing. It was still raining lightly. Fortunately, Perdita thought, the streets were empty.

"Everyone has gone already," Marie said weakly. Her eyes were full of tears, and her jaw was quivering.

"Yes," Perdita said.

"I wonder what it will be like?" Marie said quietly. "I wonder if it will hurt?"

"Oh, Marie..." Perdita put her hands on Marie's.

"I heard the executioner in the office yesterday," Marie sniffed. "Talking to the sheriff. He said the noose will only require five or six coils since I am a woman and so small. He had to weigh me and pre-stretch the rope he is to use. He was concerned about how little I weigh. He said it could be a problem."

Perdita could think of nothing to say. She grasped Marie's hands more tightly. She was trying desperately not to cry, to be strong for Marie. At Bosphorus Street, Aubuchon turned north. In a few blocks they had reached the landing. Standing at the water's edge was Aristide, the man who had met Perdita on the landing the night she had arrived at Ste. Odile.

Aubuchon led the horse to Aristide, who took the bridle from him. Aristide gave the horse a carrot.

"It was two dollars, wasn't it, Aristide?" Aubuchon asked.

"One will do," Aristide said.

Aubuchon took a silver dollar from his vest pocket and gave it to Aristide. Aristide looked at Marie. "Goodbye to you, Marie Chardin," he said. "May God love you."

Holding Marie's crutch, Perdita stepped down from the trap as Aubuchon came back to Marie.

"Do you think you can get down on your own, or should I lift you?" Aubuchon asked.

"Please, lift me."

Aubuchon lifted her down as easily as he had put her in. She winced a little as her feet touched the ground. Perdita helped Marie position her crutch under her right arm. Aristide began to lead the horse back onto the street.

"Here is the skiff," Aubuchon said, indicating a long boat tied to a cottonwood sapling on the riverbank. "It's got muddy overnight, so let me help you." He took Marie's left arm and helped her toward the boat. Perdita lifted her skirt from the ground a few inches and followed. At the water's edge, Aubuchon stopped and looked at Marie.

"Marie," he said, "I need a promise from you. I need an oath you will stay in your seat and not get up."

Marie said nothing for a moment. "I promise you I will not jump in the river," she said quietly. "If I would kill myself, I would never see my family. How could I see them from Hell?"

"All right then. Miss Perdita, will you get in first?"

Perdita stepped uncertainly through the mud and climbed carefully into the boat. Aubuchon lifted Marie into the boat, and Perdita helped her to the rear seat. Once Marie was seated and her crutch stowed on the floor, Perdita sat next to her. Aubuchon untied the boat from the sapling and lifted the bow a little off of the mud. He pushed the boat off into the river and jumped in. He seated himself on the middle seat and grasped the oars. In a moment, he had the boat turned around and out into the channel and heading downstream.

It was a damp, humid morning. The current in the channel was apparent, but not overpowering. Aubuchon guided the skiff toward the middle of the channel where the current took it. The skiff drifted effortlessly and slowly away from the landing toward the southern edge of de Castres Island, where the channel rejoined the main body of the river. Aubuchon turned around on his seat to see downriver and guide the skiff as it drifted with the oars.

The two women said nothing for a long time. Marie held Perdita's hand tightly and looked out across the river and back toward Ste. Odile, the only home she had ever known, as it slowly disappeared behind the bushes and huge cottonwood trees on the bank. A beautiful white egret flew over them from the east and landed on a snag a few feet from the western bank.

"I never saw very much of the world," Marie said at length. "I read, for myself, and Michee, to try to understand what life would be like in other places. But you cannot really know that without living it, can you?"

"I have always thought if you know fifty people reasonably well, that you have the world. Or a good sampling of it. People are the same everywhere." Perdita smiled.

"I have known fifty people well," Marie said.

"Then you have known most of the human natures there are to know. The rest is just a changing of landscape."

After ten minutes of drifting, the boat had nearly reached the southern tip of de Castres Island. Through stands of maples, sycamores, and cottonwoods, the *Seraphim* became visible moored at the landing. Alongside it was another packet, the *Western Empire*. As Aubuchon guided the skiff past the landing, dozens of small boats and rafts could be seen tied up both upstream and downstream from the packets. The riverbank was full of people, talking, laughing and gossiping. Most of them were making their way up a path that led into the trees. Several people noticed as the skiff drifted past. They stopped and watched silently until Aubuchon had guided the boat out of their sight.

At the southernmost tip of the island, Aubuchon put in to the riverbank. There was a small clearing cut into the bushes and a narrow, but well-worn path that led up a small hill. As the bow of the boat ran onto the sandy bank, Aubuchon stood, stepped out, and pulled it securely out of the water.

Perdita retrieved the crutch from the bottom of the boat and stood while holding Marie's arm. Marie winced and touched her injured leg. "It always hurts when I first put weight on it," she said.

Perdita handed the crutch to Aubuchon and helped Marie toward the front of the boat. Perdita could feel Marie trembling violently. At the bow, Aubuchon lifted Marie onto the bank.

"Thank you," she said.

Aubuchon helped Marie situate the crutch under her right arm and began to guide her up the path.

"You should try to ignore what people will say," Aubuchon said. "Being in a crowd changes people. You don't know what you might hear."

"Yes, Mr. Aubuchon," Marie said weakly.

"Marie," Aubuchon went on, "you know how sorry I am for this. I wish I could pack you in the skiff and send you downriver a hundred miles."

"You've been very kind to me, in spite of how poorly I have behaved," Marie said. "This is your duty. God will remember your kindness to me."

As they walked up the hillside through the undergrowth, they began to hear the sounds of the crowd. There was a jumble of voices and music from a violin and accordion playing haunting airs unfamiliar to Perdita, which she imagined to be traditional French tunes and ballads.

Walking behind Marie and Aubuchon, Perdita could see Marie was shaking slightly. Marie began to moan in a discordant, forlorn voice, quietly at first, then louder until it became a protracted, garbled wail, an expression beyond words of helplessness, terror, and despair. She stopped and let the crutch fall to the ground.

"Marie," Aubuchon said, "we have to go on."

But Marie seemed insensible to everything around her. Perdita put her arm around Marie and tried to get her attention.

"Marie, Marie," Perdita said insistently. Marie shook her head, never looking at anything, wailing unintelligibly. Perdita grasped her by the shoulders.

"MARIE! Look at me!"

Marie stopped wailing and looked at Perdita. "*Je souhaite que J'aie ete plus courageaux,*" Marie said weakly. Perdita embraced her.

"But you *have* been brave. Very brave," Aubuchon said.

"There is not much left for you to do to see this through to the end," Perdita said. "But this is the time when you must not fail. Do not force Mr. Aubuchon to carry you, or to drag you. Is that a spectacle you want? Would that kind of end honor your Michee and Louis?"

"No," Marie said. For a moment she seemed to be choking. Suddenly she leaned over into the weeds and vomited. Perdita stroked her back.

"You must not fall into pieces now," Perdita said.

"Yes," Marie said, her voice a little stronger. "The manner is what they cannot take from me."

"Yes, the manner," Perdita said. She picked up the crutch and helped Marie position it under her arm.

"I will do it honorably," Marie said, smiling weakly at Perdita, then Aubuchon. "There will be no more of that. No more hysteria. I will do it honorably."

Aubuchon grasped Marie's left arm gently and they continued up the path. Within a few hundred feet they had reached the top of the hill and the clearing known as Montpelier Field.

The three had emerged from the trees behind the scaffold, a massive structure of roughly sawn oak beams. Thirteen stairs led up to the platform. There were many hundreds of people in the field, more than Ste. Odile alone could provide. Three other packets and scores of other boats, rafts, and skiffs moored on the opposite side of the island had come from two adjoining counties and ten or fifteen nearby towns, bringing all manner of onlookers: the sympathetic, the outraged seeking justice, the morbidly curious, and those who sought a profit from the aggregation of so many people.

At first, no one seemed to notice Marie had arrived. But soon a general murmur of recognition swept through the crowd. Tancred, Mrs. Moon, and two of Aubuchon's deputies stood beneath the scaffold. Tancred approached Marie with a pained smile. He blessed her as she made the sign of the cross, then embraced her. Mrs. Moon then embraced Marie and kissed her on the cheek.

A light rain continued to fall. Montpelier Field had become a muddy morass. Two rows of chairs for dignitaries and representatives of the court and local government were placed on planks near the scaffold. An area immediately behind the chairs was roped off for ticketholders. Beyond this area were massed hundreds more onlookers and vendors of roasted corn, cider, cakes, breads, fruits, buttermilk, and coffee. There were children chasing each other and playing other games at the edge of the field. Deputies and many other men whom Perdita had never seen before, formed a barricade between the crowd and the small group which had formed around Marie.

"There the murderer is!" someone in the crowd called. Others began a chant: "Murderer, murderer!"

On the scaffold, Perdita could see a stocky man in a swallowtail coat and stovepipe hat whom she took to be Mr. Arliss, the executioner. There was also a priest, whom Perdita knew must be Father Vannier, Tancred's peripatetic assistant, there to preside over the spiritual protocol of the execution in Tancred's place, since he had declined. Dr. Duclos was also there, as was another deputy, sworn in for the occasion.

Aubuchon still held Marie's arm. He leaned toward her. "You should say your farewells now, Marie," Perdita heard him whisper. Marie nodded. Tancred lifted her manacled hands in his and mumbled a prayer with her.

"Ye'll be in heaven with yer family thiz day!" he murmured.

Marie nodded. "Thank you, Father," she said softly.

Mrs. Moon stepped up and embraced Marie again. "Mrs. Moon," Marie said flatly, almost insipidly, "I meant to ask you earlier. What are you making for dinner tonight?"

Mrs. Moon dissolved into tears. "Lord, I don't know,

child. Bess is making it…dumplings, I think."

"That sounds lovely." Marie turned toward Perdita. "You have been a great friend and comfort to me in these last weeks," she said. Her voice was trembling and her jaw quivering, as if she were freezing. Perdita embraced her.

"It has been a great privilege to have been your companion and friend," Perdita said.

"Just a few minutes more," Marie said, almost painfully. "For a few more minutes I must guard, must maintain the manner of my death." Marie seemed unable to look directly into Perdita's eyes. Marie's whole face was quivering in an attempt to hold back her tears.

"Hang her! Hang her!" several voices shouted. The command was repeated by a group of children who had run up to within a few feet of the scaffold.

"You are the bravest woman I have known," Perdita whispered. "You defy what is happening here today, with your dignity."

Marie nodded her head in desperate agreement. "Yes, I do defy it." She began to breathe in short, panicked breaths. She closed her eyes in concentration, and in a moment, her breathing had returned to normal. Aubuchon gently grasped Marie's arm again to guide her to the steps. For a second she met Perdita's gaze with a last desperate and terrified glance. Then she became resolute and focused upon the task of climbing the wet stairs with the crutch.

Aubuchon helped her to slowly negotiate one stair at a time. By the fourth or fifth stair, some of the crowd were becoming impatient

"Carry her, Sheriff!" A voice called out from the sodden crowd. A large wave of laughter arose and other voices called: "Carry her! Carry her!"

After several more minutes, Marie and Aubuchon reached the platform. She seemed exhausted by the effort. Aubuchon allowed her to rest for a moment. Soon she resumed making her way toward the group of men who were waiting for her. After a step or two, the crutch slipped out from under her on the wet boards. Aubuchon lost his grip on her and she fell forward onto the platform. Perdita gasped. A wave of laughter passed through the crowd, mostly toward the back, but seemed to immediately lose momentum and stop. Aubuchon helped Marie stand and they made their way to the center of the platform.

Father Vannier moved toward Marie and spoke a few words to her. She nodded. Vannier then approached the front of the scaffold.

"Any death," Vannier said, in a loud, strong voice, "is a tragedy. The death of the innocent child, Michee Chardin, was a tragedy indeed. And now the death of her mother, ordered by our law, redoubles our grief and sense of loss. What do we know of the pain which led this good mother —and we all knew her as such—to have felt the compulsion to commit this crime? Only our Lord God knows all there is to know about these events and how they came to be. Yet the law is clear and must be satisfied. For the great purpose of preserving, in peace and safety, our property, our life, our civil and sacred rights and privileges, we are bound by love and duty to each individual and the whole community to support the order of society. In civil society, the wicked would walk on every side, and the cry of the oppressed would be in vain; the foundations would be destroyed, confusion and misery would prevail, if capital punishment were never executed. Therefore, it is our sad responsibility to obey the law and carry out the sentence which has been passed upon our dear sister in Christ, Marie Delaporte Chardin."

A murmur of agreement passed through the crowd and many heads nodded their approval of Vannier's words. Perdita noticed a particularly animated woman in the front row. She was portly and pink-skinned, dressed in a stylish and expensive dark blue dress and holding an ivory-handled umbrella over her head. It seemed she was being attended by two more plainly dressed women who sat behind her.

"I would ask you all to rise and pray together," Vannier continued.

Those spectators who were seated rose. The portly woman stood with some difficulty. Her attendants helped her, each grasping an arm from behind.

"Lord God," Vannier continued, "we pray that You will today accept the soul of Your servant, our sister, Marie Delaporte Chardin, into the glory of Your mercy and divine presence. She has repented of her sin and made a good and true confession. She has been granted your forgiveness and begs—we all beg—for mercy." He made the sign of the cross, as did most of the spectators. "In the name of the Father, and of the Son, and of the Holy Ghost...Our Father which art in heaven, hallowed be thy name..."

The crowd mumbled along with Vannier, and made the sign of the cross at the prayer's end. Vannier then stepped back and spoke to Marie again as the spectators took their seats. To Perdita's horror, Marie stepped forward to the front of the platform. She had decided to speak. Marie cleared her throat and looked out over the crowd.

"Most of you have known me all of my life," she said in a voice that was weak and quavering.

"Speak up! Speak up!" several people called from the crowd.

"My voice," Marie said more resolutely, "is not strong. I am not as strong now as I once was."

Perdita felt Uncle Tancred put his arm around her shoulder. "I don't know if she can do this," he whispered.

"I pray she can," Perdita said tearfully. "I had wished she wouldn't, but it seems she must. I pray she can."

"You have known me all my life," Marie continued. "I once considered all of you to be my friends. But now, few of you think of yourselves as such. Nor will you be friend to my family and loved ones whom I must leave behind. For that reason, I must weigh my words."

Marie looked tiny and waif-like on the platform. It seemed to Perdita that Marie's voice was transforming, growing stronger, and she became aware of a feeling within herself which, after a moment, she identified as admiration for the condemned woman, where she had felt only what she would call pity before.

"Since the earliest days," Marie continued, "women have carried an especial burden in this village, as we all know. And we know, too, that any woman who carries this heavy mantle here, does it alone, forsaken by her sisters. It is a fact of our lives, a filthy tradition. I chose not to abandon my child to it. There has always been a price to pay for upsetting the scheme of things here, for threatening our livelihoods and prosperity. More than one poor soul has paid the price with beatings or even death for the sin of too much outrage, of saying too much—"

A restlessness began to overtake the crowd. The portly woman in front stood with some difficulty.

"Sheriff!" she bellowed. "Surely she has had her say. We've heard enough of this."

Aubuchon held out his hand to still the crowd.

"I knew," Marie continued, her voice cracking, "I knew that by ending my child's life I was ending my own. I knew when I did it, that some day I would stand before you like this, humiliated and terrified. But I did it anyway. Any one of you could be in my place today." Marie was now shouting defiantly.

Perdita found herself amazed and enthralled by the transformation, and puzzled by Marie's declarations. "Uncle, what does she mean?" Perdita asked.

"I would that I could tell you, girl," Tancred shouted above the growing din. "Like many another newcomer, zertain zecrets are kept from me."

"And in future times," Marie went on, "if you find the necessary courage and love within you, some of you *will* be in my place here!"

Many people in the crowd began to shout and hiss and whistle. Aubuchon held up his hands for silence, which was many minutes in coming. The portly woman sat.

"The last words I have to say on this earth," Marie continued, "are thanks. Thanks to Father Condell, Mrs. Moon, and Sheriff Aubuchon for their kindnesses. Thanks to my dear family for their love. Thanks to our Lord for the blessings and years of happiness He has given me in this life, and thanks to Miss Perdita Badon-Reed, who came here with a heart full of Christian charity and gave comfort, friendship, and love to a soul without hope. God bless her."

Perdita sobbed violently for many moments. Tancred embraced her tightly. A well-dressed man sitting next to the portly woman stood and addressed Aubuchon. Perdita later learned he was Judge Antoine Bessier, who had condemned Marie.

"Sheriff," he said, "you may carry out the sentence."

Aubuchon guided Marie back to the center of the trap door on the platform. Mr. Arliss placed a white hood over Marie's head. He then placed the noose, which was hanging behind her, around her neck and adjusted it so its coils were on the left side of her head. As he was doing this, the deputy produced a length of leather cord and tied it tightly around Marie's knees. Aubuchon removed a document from his vest pocket and read: "Marie Delaporte Chardin, you have confessed to the crime of murdering your daughter, Michee Chardin, on the evening of May 3, 1882, and you have been condemned by the laws of this sovereign state to be hanged by the neck until you are dead, on this, the twenty-second day of August, 1882. You have had your say. Do you have anything else to add?"

The white hood twitched slightly from side to side.

"Then sentence must be carried out," Aubuchon said.

Mr. Arliss grasped a wooden lever alongside the trap door. All of the murmuring and grumbling of the crowd stopped. Firmly and quickly, Arliss pulled the lever backward. The trap dropped open about a third of the way. Marie jerked downward a few inches, her fall partially blocked by the door. Her body started to slide through the opening as the trap broke free and opened fully. Perdita and many others in the crowd gasped in horror.

"It broke her fall!" Aubuchon said.

"It's the rain," Arliss said. "The rain swelled it. And her weight."

Marie could be heard gurgling and gasping for breath. Dr. Duclos, Mr. Arliss, Aubuchon, and the deputy rushed down the platform stairs. Duclos ran under the platform. He could just reach Marie's wrist as she swung above him.

"She's still alive," he said.

Judge Bessier stood and approached Duclos. Marie's fingers began to move, and her struggle for breath became more pronounced. Aubuchon looked at her helplessly.

Perdita was too horrified to say anything for many moments. She looked at Uncle Tancred and said, "The sentence has been carried out." She suddenly began to make her way under the platform. "The sentence has been carried out!" she screamed. "The sentence has been carried out! Cut her down! Cut her down!"

A few voices in the crowd could be heard calling, "Cut her down! Cut her down!"

The portly woman stood again. "This woman has no say here," she said.

Aubuchon intercepted Perdita. "She must hang for a quarter hour, miss," he said. "It's the law."

He motioned for Tancred, who came immediately

to remove Perdita. Bessier conferred with Arliss and Aubuchon for a few moments. Aubuchon then waved to each of the deputies, who had been containing the crowd, to approach him. The six men joined the rest under the scaffold. In a moment they formed a circle, at Aubuchon's instruction, around Mr. Arliss, who stood directly under Marie. Marie had begun to twitch and jerk and gurgle more audibly. Then, partially hidden from general view, Arliss's arms could be seen reaching up to grasp Marie's legs. Perdita gasped as Arliss jerked down suddenly and powerfully on Marie's body. A constricted groan was heard under the white hood. The deputies stepped away and resumed their former positions.

Dr. Duclos reached up to touch Marie's wrist. "She is dead," he said quietly.

11

"It wasn't there," Hypolitte said, as he finished his last bite of cassoulet. "Marie's journal was gone."

"I didn't intend for you to steal it when I told you where it was." Perdita sipped her Burgundy. She was beginning to feel she'd had one glass too many. A week after the execution, she still found that she had little appetite.

"It was the judge who was stealing it, in my opinion. Marie wanted you to have it, not Judge Bessier. I had stopped in to see Aubuchon for a moment, he stepped outside to help restrain a prisoner, and I saw my opportunity. Unfortunately, it was all for nothing."

"I suppose Aubuchon had given it to Bessier already," Perdita said.

"I don't think so. Bessier didn't have it when he left after the execution, according to Villiers, the deputy, and Bessier has been at the other end of the county since."

"Perhaps Aubuchon moved it to a safer place until the judge returns." Perdita looked out the window to the street a floor below them. It was full of carts and wagons drawn by oxen and horses, as it seemed to be every day. "This town is so prosperous," she said, "for such a small, out-of-the-way place."

"A fact not lost on the inhabitants."

"I have enjoyed luncheon. It is a nice change to have it away from the school. I am feeling a bit light-headed, though. Perhaps the wine was a bad idea. I won't have too much more."

"How has your first week gone?" Hypolitte dabbed at the corners of his mouth with his napkin.

"Well. Most of the girls are well behaved. Lillian enjoys tormenting Anatolia, so we had to separate them. Anatolia seems completely unable to defend herself." Perdita sipped her wine. "The sisters have been so wonderful to me."

"I am glad to hear it." Hypolitte smiled remotely. "I have wondered if you've had second thoughts about coming here. I mean, so much has happened."

"Yes, it has." Perdita nodded and her eyes filled with tears. "It was horrible! Marie was so terrified. She tried so desperately to be brave. Just seeing her hanging there like that!" Perdita used her napkin to against her tears. "And I do not understand the town turning out like vultures…I didn't know how I would be able to start teaching this week. But, it is a good thing the term started. It has kept my mind occupied."

"Yes."

"No one came to the burial. A few of her family, Uncle, Mrs. Moon, and myself."

"Yes. I would have come. I had to leave for St. Louis."

"I knew you had business."

"A manufacturer of blowpipe assaying equipment," Hypolitte said quickly. "He didn't have time to come down to Ste. Odile to meet me, so I had to go up to meet him on his way east."

"Your work must be very interesting."

"It was, at first. Pretty dull now. Predictable."

"You are interested enough to keep doing it." Perdita smiled.

"I don't know that I would quite categorize my longevity that way."

"Tell me something interesting about your work. Something most people do not know." Perdita pushed her wine glass away.

Hypolitte thought for a moment. "Well, we retrieve almost enough precious metals, and other metals, as a byproduct of mining lead, to make payroll."

"Really?" Perdita was surprised. "Why not mine for those metals instead of lead? Have another gold rush?"

"For the quantities involved, lead is much more lucrative. There are trace amounts of gold. Some silver, but not as much as in other areas, other veins. Mostly we find copper and zinc."

"Tell me something else. Something else people do not know." Perdita smiled broadly at him. Then, suspecting it may have looked like a silly smile, attempted to wipe it from her face.

"I can tell you something about my employer and the mines. There is an old headframe a mile north of town. A very old tunnel. Braced and supported in the old way. Played out. Yet, a team of mules is still kept there to raise and lower the cage at a moment's notice."

"Why is that?"

"Because my employer uses one of the tunnels, drift tunnel four to be exact, to store some of his many treasures of art and antiquities."

"Really? But why?"

"It is perfect for that use. He owns far too many objects to permanently display them all. Those drifts are dry and cool. I'd never seen them before two months ago, soon after Bastide returned from France. He sent a request that Mr. Strauss, the engineer, and myself do a survey of the tunnel, and make a report to Mr. Morisot."

"And what did you report?"

"There is an adequate salt level to keep moisture low, no parasites that could damage the objects. But Strauss found the opening to the tunnel is now supported by one ancient elm post bracing an old lintel. We now use a system of bracing walls and ceilings called square sets: interlocking beams in sort of a square honeycomb to prevent collapse of a tunnel. Number four was dug long before that system was in use. We saw evidence of old worm damage on the elm post, so we ordered it be treated with coal tar and naphtha to prevent any new destruction."

"One old post supports the whole thing?"

"Yes. The tunnel opening. It is such an old drift that there was probably some shifting during the 1811 earthquake that no expert eye has seen before now. We recommended the opening be reinforced with at least four new beams and square sets installed."

"Has that been done yet?"

"No. I would know if it had."

Perdita looked out of the window again. "I wonder if Solana knows of the cache of art works? She has been to see Bastide twice more this week. She is cataloguing his medieval collections."

"Perhaps we could arrange a tour. For the two of you."

"No," Perdita said quickly. "I think I could never go down there."

"We would just need permission and the padlock key from Mr. Morisot."

"No. I do not think I could do it."

"Ah." Hypolitte suddenly understood. "It is your dislike of enclosed places."

"Yes. It is silly, I know. But you remember the difficulty I had in the jail that day?"

"Yes, I remember. It's a shame. It would be something to see."

"I thought you had seen it already?"

"Not much. Most of it is locked away in a chamber

toward the back of the drift. I saw a few Greek marbles, and a stele, Babylonian, I think, or Assyrian."

"Still," Perdita said, "even if I had no difficulty with going down there, it would be a presumption. I do not even know Mr. Bastide."

"Have you always had this fear of enclosures?"

Perdita shook her head. "No. I know the exact moment it came upon me."

Hypolitte looked at her expectantly, but said nothing. For a few moments, Perdita was silent, too. When she had gathered her thoughts, she spoke.

"The day of my First Communion was a warm day. We came home after church. There were a lot of rabbits that year, and my father had set several wooden box traps in our back garden, and as we approached from the street, we noticed one of the traps was sprung. I asked my father if I could open the door of the trap. He said yes, if I was ready to dispatch what was inside. I did not know what he meant by this, so I agreed. I tilted the trap on end and slid the door open. Inside was a young rabbit, no more than a month or two old. My father said it would grow with time and destroy our gardens, and he should kill it, but since it was young and it was my special day, I could let it go. My parents went into the house. I thought to myself, this day *is* a special day. I should be able to keep this little rabbit as a pet. So I disobeyed my father. With stones and bits of old planks and bricks I built a little pen against the far side of the house, an area rarely seen by my parents. I dumped the rabbit into it, found a small bowl for water and a few vegetables to sustain it, and I went into the house.

"My aunt had come to visit, and a neighbor lady. A very old woman who lived alone, blind in one eye, I remember. She had been a nanny to me for a while. They were there for cake to celebrate my receiving the sacrament for the first time. My mother had her first matched pair of dogs then.

Lap dogs. I always thought that on a list of all the things my mother loved, I would appear second or third, depending upon whether one counted the dogs as one or as two individuals."

Hypolitte smiled.

"My mother doted upon the dogs," Perdita continued, "as she does to this day—the ones she has now, I mean. She talked about the dogs with our guests, had them perform tricks she had taught them, fed them cake which made them sick, and started a trend which I first noticed on that day: I have always been a peripheral figure, even at events held in my honor!"

Hypolitte smiled again, sympathetically. "I believe I recognize that situation."

"The next morning," Perdita continued, "my father noticed a crow behaving oddly near the far side of the house. It was fluttering around, diving at the ground, as if it were attacking something, and then perching on the fence momentarily before diving again. My father walked over to chase the crow away, and discovered my humble rabbit warren. He said nothing, but reached down and grasped my pet, and with a twist, broke its neck. I cried out. He dropped the dead animal on the ground and roughly caught me by the arm. He dragged me to the coal chute on the opposite side of the house. He unlatched it, opened it, and forced me into it. 'Honor thy father and thy mother,' he said. 'This will teach you to do as you are told.'"

Perdita touched the corners of her eyes with her handkerchief. "I shouldn't drink wine in the afternoons." She took a few moments to compose herself.

"The coal bin was about eight feet square," she went on, "and empty at that time of the year. He left me in there for the better part of two days. I thought I would die in there. I was certain of it."

"Didn't your mother object?"

"Not very much, if at all. He passed food to me through the coal chute. I was too terrified to eat much of it. Later I was punished for wasting the food. The time in the bin did have the desired effect. I never disobeyed him again. Until now."

"He wanted you to marry?"

"Yes, since I failed to find a vocation in the church, he wanted me to marry Prosper. He was adamant about it." Perdita suddenly felt she had told Hypolitte too much.

"So, by leaving, you defied both Prosper—"

"And my father. That is essentially true, though I have never put it in those words." Perdita noticed that Hypolitte's eyes were fixed upon her. She felt embarrassed and looked away.

"Thank you for luncheon," she said awkwardly. "Sister Patrice and Sister Rose Agnes do the best they can with meals at school. They haven't much to work with."

"When do you have to be back?"

"Not until two."

Hypolitte looked at his pocket watch. "It isn't one yet," he said.

"Where is your office?" Perdita asked suddenly.

"On Gentian Street. A short walk."

"Could we walk there?"

"If you like." Hypolitte seemed surprised by the suggestion. He left three silver dollars on the table and stood to help Perdita up. "Shall we go now?"

It was a fifteen-minute walk south on Bosphorus Street, and west on Rouen to Gentian and Hypolitte's office. It was a clapboard building of two stories in need of paint, with many windows all around on the upper floor. They climbed an exterior staircase, and Hypolitte pushed open an unlocked, weathered wooden door with an etched glass window. Perdita stepped in at Hypolitte's invitation.

"This is where I spend my days," Hypolitte said, closing the door. The room was flooded with light. It was partially a laboratory, with many slate-topped tables and benches covered with ore samples, flasks, burners, brass scales, and bottles of chemicals, and partially an office, with two large desks, oak filing cabinets, and shelves full of books.

"And what do you *do* here?" Perdita asked, after several moments of unimpressed silence.

"Generally, what I please. I have an assistant. It is all I can do to keep him busy. To put it simply, we test the quality of the ore samples to assure the drifts we are cutting continue to be profitable. We test the purity of the ores by assaying. We have a significant amount of antimony in the ores, so we use the wet method of blowpipe assaying—"

"I don't have much of a mind for science or numbers, I'm afraid. What is that?" Perdita nodded toward the back of the room. She was still feeling the effect of the wine and was having a difficult time thinking of anything else but hiding the fact.

"You mean my fishing gear? I keep it on hand in case—"

"No, I mean *that*." Perdita indicated a large chart pinned to a wall between two bookcases.

"That is the tunnel I was telling you about. I told Karl to put this away. Here, I'll show you." He moved to the chart and flattened out its sagging middle against the wall. "This is the main shaft coming down from the headframe." Hypolitte pointed to a large square on the chart. "These are drifts one, two, three, and that's four, where the objects are stored."

"And what is this?" Perdita asked, pointing to a small square and bar.

"That is the post at the entrance to drift four."

"The over-worked support beam."

"The very one."

"And what are these jackstraws here?"

"Rubbish. Old beams and supports stacked just beyond the opening there. It all needs to be cleared away."

Perdita felt suddenly tired, and leaned against Hypolitte's desk. She removed her handkerchief from her sleeve and patted at the perspiration on her cheeks and forehead. "So, you do what you please here?" she asked, feeling her head clear a little.

"Yes."

"And you have a difficult time keeping your assistant, Karl, busy?"

"Yes."

"What do you do with your apparently plentiful free time, besides fishing?"

"I do fish, and disappear for a day or two at a time, when our load allows it. I also follow my own interests, investigations."

"What would those be?"

"Well, I am interested in the *history* of science. Alchemy, rudimentary natural history, navigation, the engineering marvels of the ancients. Chemistry is not my field, but I am very interested in its development since classical times."

"Ah." Perdita wanted to seem interested, even though, at that moment, she wished she were sitting in the shade of one of the cypresses at the seminary or napping on the sofa back at the rectory.

"For example." Hypolitte walked to a nearby table and removed a small porcelain pot with a metal lid from a shelf above it. He removed the lid. "Have you ever heard of Greek Fire?"

"Yes. It was a weapon of war. In the Byzantine Empire, wasn't it?"

"Yes. Virtually unquenchable by water. Some even say that water ignited it."

"Is that Greek Fire?"Perdita indicated the pot Hypolitte held.

"I don't know. No one knows its exact composition. It was, as you can imagine, a closely guarded secret. This is a mixture of sulfur, naphtha, quicklime, and a little sodium. This may or may not be right. I have been playing with proportions of the components for months. Watch this."

Hypolitte set the pot on the desk top. He then pulled a straw bristle from a broom leaning against the near bookcase. Dipping the straw into the nondescript viscous liquid, which left a tiny bead on the tip of the strand, he produced a match from his vest pocket and ignited it with his thumbnail. He touched the flame to the small bead of liquid. A large flame flared at the contact, producing a cloud of black, foul-smelling smoke. Perdita gasped minutely.

"My word," she said. "What a flame it produces!"

"And watch." He submerged the flame in a half-empty glass of water on his desk. The tip of the strand bubbled briskly until he withdrew it, and the flame reignited.

"What a catastrophe that would be for a wooden warship," Perdita said.

Hypolitte returned the straw to the water glass. It bubbled for a few moments and then went out.

"And you are paid to explore these diversions?" Perdita asked.

"I am paid for my knowledge and experience, not for hours worked or even productivity." Hypolitte smiled.

"Apparently." Perdita smiled also.

"If my idleness has put a smile on your face this week, that alone makes it well worthwhile."

Perdita went silent again for a moment, reminded of the cause of her melancholy. She felt suddenly dizzy and almost sick to her stomach. "Poor Marie. It was such an awful thing to see! I pray I never see anything like that again ...then, when she didn't die straight away!" Perdita buried her face in her handkerchief for a few seconds. Hypolitte raised his hand to touch her shoulder, but quickly withdrew it.

"You have been very attentive," Perdita said. "I thank you for that. It has been a difficult week, but as I said, I am grateful for the occupation, the distraction, of teaching."

"I am sure Solana has been understanding."

"She has done her best. She seems to have had a difficult few days also."

"Oh?"

"She's been distracted, tired, even a bit irritable."

"That doesn't sound much like her."

"No. She has not been herself this week."

12

Solana had never seen such a collection of rare, medieval books. There were bestiaries, Bibles, treatises on natural science and alchemy, rudimentary atlases, Books of Hours, and histories. All were gorgeously illuminated, undeniably genuine, and in improbably good condition. Most were Irish in origin, but some were known by her host to be English, French, or Italian. The leather bindings were generally not cracked, and the upper corners of the pages unsoiled by centuries of moistened fingers. Most looked as though they had never been in circulation.

Antique books were not Solana's area of specialty. Her interest was that of the well-informed amateur, as Bastide knew. Still, he was most anxious that she catalogue all of his medieval collections, and Mother Superior felt, given his generosity in the past, that the sisters should show him every deference.

On her first visit, Solana had been excited by the prospect of being involved in such a project. Now, on her third visit, she was beginning to feel some discomfort and apprehensiveness at being there. The cataloguing was proving to be a daunting undertaking: too much for one person to accomplish in any reasonable amount of time. Bastide had said he wanted the catalogue in preparation for donating much of his collection to the Carthesian Library in St. Louis by the end of the year. But Solana had come to realize that the books alone could not be adequately listed and described in that length of time, much less the art objects, which included statues, enamelware, icons, jewelry, tapestries, and paintings.

And Bastide himself complicated the task. He kept her distracted with comments and observations, offers of refreshment, and questions about her upbringing, her life in the convent and her sisters in Christ. She would frequently agree to sit and talk with him, as he wished, in the library or a sitting room, for an hour or more at a time. He would pose a question and sit in rapt attention watching her answer, his yellow eyes darting across her features and up and down her body from behind his expressionless wax face. And every few minutes he would moisten his eyes with drops of a saline liquid from a small bottle he kept always at his side. She felt she was becoming accustomed to his startling appearance, although there were still moments when the sight of him unnerved her.

It seemed that no opinion she expressed was without merit to him. In fact, he often appeared to credit her with insights and levels of understanding she did not truthfully feel she could claim. Still, the attention flattered her. He had read *Moby Dick; The Vindication of the Rights of Women; Eve of St. Agnes; Nana; Madame Bovary,* and *Carmilla*, and many other works read by her before and after taking the veil, but little known, and even forbidden to the sisters who comprised her daily society. His insights into the works were layered and complex, and she felt their discussions had broadened her appreciation of them, and his as well. He seemed to discover new levels of meaning and relevance as they talked, which only seemed to compound his excitement and curiosity, as well as it did hers.

In spite of this, Solana's sense of unease was growing. The time she was spending at Jardin Noir was detracting from the time she should be spending in preparation for her classes. Twice in the previous week, she had felt she had disappointed Perdita in her preparedness, and she had felt ashamed for that. Perdita was one person whose good opinion she wished ardently to maintain. After all, these discussions, these visits, this validation, although dressed in the guise of work for a valued patron, were actually luxuries, weren't they?

And she was tired. Her sleep had been fitful and nightmare-haunted for several nights. Dreams of doomed heretics in a mountaintop fortress brought immediately to mind her readings of the history of the Albigensian Crusade and the annihilation of the Cathars, the *Bonnes Hommes*. But each night, before hundreds of the heretics were burned alive in the meadow below their citadel of Montsegur, she would awaken feeling paralyzed, gasping for breath, and oppressed by an unsettling kind of torment.

Her body felt alive and sensitized in a way that almost frightened her. Her limbs were weak, her thighs and stomach overheated and tingling. And her mind was full of thoughts, passions, and obsessions which she could not countenance, which shamed her, which she must not allow.

And as soon as she would awaken in her darkened garret, she would sense a presence in the room with her, a palpable being just out of sight, which would disappear as her mind cleared. Then, ashamed and disoriented by the unambiguous, blood-flushed language of her body, she would dress herself from head to foot, with habit and veil, and say her rosary until dawn.

She could not determine which of the weaknesses of character and faith that she bore would allow this state of sin to repeat itself each night. She knew herself to be far too worldly, far too attuned to the sensuality of the world to be a worthy bride of Christ. Was her vocation a true one?

She had felt her vocation since she had been a child of seven or eight. At first she did not perceive certain elements of her nature to be impediments to her goal, but her mother, her great aunt and her parish priest recognized her failings as she grew, and warned her of their potential destructiveness. They advised her that her love of pretty clothes and deferential young men, and the beautiful ornaments that adorned the fine houses and museums of the world, would not count a straw toward her salvation. And the temptations were everywhere. She had only her faith and vocation to fight them, and only herself to blame if she failed to resist.

But these new sensations were beyond anything with which she had struggled before. They held an allure that was almost sickening, and a profanity that was breathtaking, and seemed from moment to moment almost powerful enough to eclipse everything else in her life. She could well understand both how people could succumb to these feelings, and how lost she would be if she ever allowed herself to do so.

A clock on one of the study mantels struck eleven, reminding Solana of how tired she was. She gathered her notes and papers from across the tabletop, and began to return them to her leather portfolio. The study door swung slowly open, revealing Bastide in the doorway holding a silver tray upon which he carried a crystal decanter and two crystal wineglasses.

"You have worked late tonight," he said in his garbled, wet tone from under his prosthesis. He entered the room and placed the tray upon the table. "I have sent Tertius off to bed, and thought I could attend to you myself, Sister."

"Well, thank you, but I really must be going. I have prepared nothing for class tomorrow. It is *so* late! I shouldn't drink anything."

"It is Madeira," Bastide said. "It isn't like drinking. It isn't even French." He filled both glasses and placed one in front of Solana. He then took an awkward, audible sip from his glass.

"I have my prayers to say," Solana protested, "and my lesson to review. I am rather tired. I admire the saints and hermits who could deny the needs of the body, of the heart, and give all to God."

"Do you think," Bastide said thoughtfully, "that they may have actually denied the needs of their souls?"

"Why, no." Solana was puzzled. She sipped the wine. "They acted for the benefit of their souls."

"Through self-denial?"

"Yes."

"Do you think God finds a soul more complete and desirable which has had few comforts, joys, and pleasures?"

"Well, I am sure that even the saints had some comforts—"

"Homely ones, though, certainly, and they were ashamed, probably, of even those. How could they be certain God found the abasement of their bodies, their human needs, their…selves, to be pleasurable? Isn't God taking pleasure in their suffering?"

"One hardly thinks of God as requiring 'pleasure.'"

"But we so often hear of this or that thing being pleasing to God—"

"No, no, not at all. God is not taking pleasure in suffering." Solana sounded alarmed. "It is the *self* that one must control. This is the reason for self-denial. We all have plenty of incentive to be naughty. To control those impulses, in spite of our natures, is what God finds pleasurable. I mean pleasing."

"Oh yes." Bastide appeared to smile under his prosthesis. His elongated, yellow teeth could be partially seen. "The *self*. That which must be escaped, transcended, if one is to thrive in Holy Orders, if one is to get closer to God. Knowledge of the self, the fact of the self, is our greatest sorrow, I have read. The self, that which defines us as an entity, an individual, is the same force which keeps us from perfect union with the Trinity."

"Yes, that is it," Solana agreed enthusiastically. "Unless the self is lost, perfect union with the Trinity cannot be."

"And has such union ever been achieved?"

"Of course. I mean, I assume so. I don't know for *certain*," Solana puzzled. "Perhaps at the moment when Our Lord ascended into heaven. And some of the saints must have achieved it."

"So it is very rare?"

"Certainly. If it were easily done, how would one gain grace?"

"Will you achieve it?"

"My life is dedicated to the effort. I have many sins and weaknesses to atone for."

"Including the sin of existing at all?"

"I suppose so, if original sin is what you mean. Yes, we must atone for that."

"These questions, this search, have long occupied my thoughts. The *problem* of it. 'You have seen strange things, the awful hand of death, new shapes of woe, uncounted sufferings, and all you have seen is God.'"

"No," Solana said emphatically. "No, that is... Sophocles, I believe. He spoke of Zeus, not *our* God! Not *God!*"

"I think I understand it—and you—better now." Bastide's tone was a bit conciliatory. "Thank you for clarifying it for me."

"Thank you for the wine," Solana said. She took another sip, then placed the glass on the table.

"Will you allow me to convey you home?" Bastide asked. "I had no intention that you stay so late."

"Oh, no, thank you," Solana smiled a tired smile. "I am keen to walk. I enjoy it. It is under two miles, I think. The walk will give me a little time for reflection. And prayer."

"Until you can come again, then." Bastide placed his glass upon the table. "I will see you out."

Solana promised to return early the following week to finish her work on the bestiaries and books of herbal cures. Bastide led the way out of the study and into the hallway. He easily swung open the massive oak vestibule doors and the equally substantial front door. As Solana passed him and stepped over the threshold, she resisted an urge to look at his face, his eyes. She could feel his gaze upon her. He touched her elbow as she passed. She flinched. She stepped out into the damp curtain of the humid night air.

The darkness was alive with sounds from all directions at once. The chirruping and burring of tree frogs and the calls of whippoorwills surrounded her, and the hooting of a few owls could be heard occasionally in the middle and then far distance. Her feet crunched on the drive of crushed limestone gravel, which shone like an almost spectral, silvery band in the full moonlight. Bastide closed the front door slowly as she walked away, shutting off the light, the security of artifice, and she felt a small sense of abandonment, and the dread of having to cross a wild and fearful expanse of sounds and unseen movements of night things until she should reach the light and artifice of her home again.

Solana tried to direct her thoughts toward tomorrow's ancient art history lesson. She was to discuss the formality and tradition of Ancient Egyptian art. Perdita had prepared reed pens and a serviceable ink from crushed pokeberries to allow the girls, against the doubts and suspicions of Mother Superior and Father Condell, regarding the seriousness and necessity of such an assignment, to experiment with the tools of the ancient scribes. She tried to remember her readings from Champollion and Belzoni, and the few monographs she had read on the Egyptian traditional style. She wondered how severely Mother Superior would disapprove of the mess the girls would inevitably make with the pokeberry ink. But surely even that would not compare with the results of the next project: to make mud clay tablets and write and impress seals on them in the manner of the ancient Mesopotamians.

Solana's mind wandered. The burring of the frogs and the rhythmic crunch of her feet on the gravel slowly began to mesmerize her. She had been rejuvenated a bit by stepping out into the night air, but now she remembered how tired she was. If only she could sleep well tonight. If only her prayers tonight would be strong enough to keep away the nightmares, the undeniable feeling of presence, and the sensual thoughts that accompany those things. She would start praying now.

"Hail Mary, full of grace, the Lord is with thee," she mumbled. "Blessed art thou among women and blessed is the fruit of thy womb—"

A rustling in the undergrowth a few feet to her left startled her. She stopped and looked in the direction of the sound. In a moment, she heard it again. Suddenly, a form burst from the bushes onto the road in front of her. She was relieved to recognize it.

"Raccoon," she said. She took another step, and another commotion from the same area to her left startled her again. This time the noise was more distressed, and violent, and was accompanied by an odd chittering sound unlike anything else she had heard in the dark woods. Suddenly a form larger than the raccoon crashed through the underbrush onto the road, followed by a second, identical creature. The creatures moved in an oddly liquid, somehow obscene, motion, in a way she had never witnessed in an animal before. The forelegs seemed to be impossibly long, more like arms than legs, the paws prehensile.

The first creature stopped short in the moonlit road and turned on the second one. Solana could see few specific characteristics of either creature. She could see the first creature's needle-like teeth and flashing yellow eyes in the moonlight. The second creature leapt upon the first, and the two rolled over in the dust growling and chittering and screeching in pain.

In the gloom, Solana could not distinguish one animal from the other. After a few seconds of struggling, one of the creatures grasped the other by the throat and shook its head violently, like a terrier killing a rat. In a moment, the wounded animal was dead. Immediately the attacker ripped through the skin and fur of its victim and began to noisily devour it, snapping its bones and gulping its blood. Solana gasped and stepped into the undergrowth to give the animal a wide berth in the road. She scurried past it and down the hill. The predator did not seem to notice her.

13

Stone dust stuck to the perspiration on Perdita's face, neck, and arms, forming an uncomfortable film on her skin. Her eyes burned from the grit, and she could scarcely find a clean spot on her apron to wipe the dust and sweat away from her eyelashes and nose.

"A very lady-like profession you've chosen!"

Perdita was startled to hear Uncle Tancred's voice behind her. "Sweating like a field hand and twice as dirty."

"Uncle, you surprised me."

"Are you making progress?"

"Yes, I am." Perdita stroked the stone, a forearm she had been shaping all morning. "Since the cut on my hand is better, I am trying to make up for lost time. The other stone for my commission has still not appeared. I have written to the Havilland about the delay."

"Mrs. Moon zaid you wanted to zpeak to me."

"Yes." Perdita untied her apron, and wiped her face with the underside. "I've had something on my mind for a week or so, and I wanted to discuss it with you."

Tancred settled himself purposefully on the anvil and folded his hands tightly together, as if he were bracing himself for bad news. "Very well," he said.

"Last week at school, and the week before in town, at the butcher's, I overheard talk that I am making free with your hospitality, and the church's, by living here."

"Who zaid that?"

"Two Sisters who didn't really mean anything malicious by it, I'm certain; they were making a joke, and a couple of old women in town."

"Tongues will wag."

"Yes, I know, but there is some truth to it. This house is, according to the archdiocese, a rectory. A home for a priest, not a boarding house."

" 'Tiz also my home. You are my family and my guest."

"But it is subsidized by the church, the parish, and archdiocese. I know you have not asked permission of the archbishop for me to live here."

" 'E's ill."

"Yes, but if he weren't, I think he would deem it appropriate for me to find my own room somewhere, don't you?"

" 'Ow can I know what 'is Eminence would zay until 'e zayz it?"

"But in Bonne Terre, there was a similar situation a few years ago, and His Eminence ordered the priest's house guest to move out. Sister Clotilde told me."

"That wasn't a relative, just a friend of the family. And there was more to that ztory than you know—"

"Still, I think the situation is adequately similar."

"Well, where would you want to go?" Tancred asked irritably.

"I have an appointment in an hour with Mrs. Zell at Tranquille House on Rouen Street. It is just a few dollars a week, meals included. Nothing I can't afford."

"But your ztudio iz 'ere . . ." Tancred's resolve was beginning to fade.

"I'll still see you every day. I'll be here to work every chance I get. We can still have suppers together a few times a week."

"The moving. 'Tisn't necessary," Tancred grumbled.

"I'll still see you every day." Perdita lay her apron across the marble block, then put her arm around Tancred. She had become more comfortable in doing so.

"That 'ouse," Tancred said, "is owned by Mrs. Morisot. Most boarding 'ouses in town are. You won't like 'er."

Mrs. Zell looked as though she were perpetually in the midst of bestowing a kiss, a perfunctory kiss to the forehead of a grandfather, perhaps, not a passionate kiss to a lover. Her skin was pale and drawn, her nearly black hair pulled back tightly. Her dress was a deep wine color and looked to Perdita to be extremely uncomfortable in the heat.

"I can offer you *lemonade*, Miss Badon-Reed," Mrs. Zell said. Her tone sounded oddly ironic. "We have *ice*." She seemed to emphasize one word—the subject or some other noun or verb—of every sentence.

"Thank you, Mrs. Zell. That would be lovely and greatly appreciated in this heat."

Mrs. Zell rang a bell which sat on a table near her. In a moment a young girl in an apron entered through the pantry door carrying a wooden tray with a single glass of lemonade on it. She offered the glass to Perdita.

"You aren't having any, Mrs. Zell?" Perdita asked, taking the glass and nodding thanks to the serving girl.

"No. I have had a *glass* this morning. Too many acids upset the *liver* and *kidneys*."

"Yes, I have noticed that." Perdita agreed.

"There are five *boarding houses* in Ste. Odile, Miss Badon-Reed, and Mrs. Morisot *owns* four of them. She *provides* comfortable, well-appointed *rooms* for her boarders, along with good *meals*. And at a very reasonable *price*. She could easily charge an inflated *rate* if she chose to, owning most establishments as she does. But she is a *Christian* woman."

"Of course."

"Her wish is to provide comfortable *accommodations* to those who need them, for as long as they need them, not to make herself *rich*. Or more rich than she *is*."

"Yes, I am glad to know that."

"In short, here you will have a comfortable and secure *lodging*, and healthful *meals*, characterized generally, by generous *servings*. Of course, Mrs. Morisot expects a certain decorum from her *guests*, as do I. You may entertain young men in the *parlor*, but never in your room. I ask that you be in the *house* by nine P.M. I ask that you waste no *food*: only help yourself to as much of *anything* as you will eat. As the niece of our parish *priest*, I am sure you will observe all Holy Days of Obligation and *hear* mass on Sundays."

"Certainly."

"Let me speak bluntly, Miss."

"Please do."

"You are Father Condell's *niece*, therefore, your character reference is implicit."

"Yes."

"But, you are of a, shall we say, *artistic* temperament. I do not intend to insult you by calling you such, but I believe in speaking plainly. You are…*artistic*."

"I admit that I am. And I take no offense at the description."

"Indeed?" Mrs. Zell seemed a bit surprised to hear this. "Because of your *connection* to Father Condell, we are almost obliged to offer you *lodging*. But I have had unpleasant experiences with *artists* in the past, with nonconformists."

"Oh, I doubt that I qualify as a nonconformist."

"Excuse me, but you are a lady who seeks a career as a *stone carver*. You are nearing *middle age* and have never been *married*."

"Yes, Mrs. Zell, I see your point. I do hope to achieve some small recognition as an artist, but aside from that, I have not the slightest desire to attract attention to myself."

Mrs. Zell considered this statement for a moment. "Well, I am glad to hear it, Miss Badon-Reed. On behalf of Mrs. Morisot, I am glad to welcome you to *Tranquille House*."

"Thank you." Perdita smiled.

"Board is due on Monday mornings. You may leave *mail* to post on the pier mirror at the front *door*. It is picked up every day. Do you *bring* a large wardrobe with you? Your room has a bureau and a small *closet*."

"No. I have but two dresses. I had three, but one was ruined. I wear the ruined one to carve in. I could hardly cut a dash in what I have left."

"In that case, you may wish—"

The front door could be heard opening suddenly. Several sets of heavy footsteps resounded on the vestibule floor, then in the hallway. "Ah," Mrs. Zell said, "you will have an unusual *opportunity*, Perdita. Mrs. Morisot is here to look over the books." Mrs. Zell arose and entered the hall way.

"Good afternoon, Ma'am," she said.

"Is she here, then?" a gruff female voice answered.

"Yes. Just here, in the dining room."

"Will she do for us?"

"Yes, I think *she* will. Admirably."

"I will leave that to you, as always. She is your responsibility."

"Yes," Mrs. Zell answered.

She stepped aside to allow a large woman, dressed flamboyantly in yellow, to enter the room. It was the portly woman Perdita had encountered at Marie's execution. Perdita's first thought was that Mrs. Morisot looked formidable and humorless. Her second was that yellow did not suit Mrs. Morisot. The two women who had served as the large woman's attendants at the execution entered the room. All three were flushed with the heat.

"Miss Badon-Reed," Mrs. Morisot said.

"Good afternoon, Ma'am," Perdita nodded, trying to hide her surprise.

"I am glad to meet you under more cheerful circumstances than those of our first encounter."

"Yes."

"A tragic day. And an unfortunate one for the village. Such notoriety…to draw *that* kind of attention to ourselves."

"Mrs. Chardin was a tragic figure," Perdita said curtly. "And a victim, I think."

"Surely her dead child was the victim, as was the reputation of our community here."

"The community?"

"We are fortunate to have the blessings we have been given here. We have a prosperity unheard of in most parts of the country. Yet nothing is guaranteed or assured in life. It could all vanish in a trice. It has happened elsewhere. It has happened in my own life, but will not again, if I have any hand in it. Prosperity, I find, is most valued by those who have known the lack of it."

"That applies to everything, does it not? Only by comparison and contrast—"

"Yes, yes," Mrs. Morisot said huffily. "I contrast my life now with the one to which I was born. There were eight children in my family. My father was a subsistence farmer in Georgia. When I was eleven, he was beaten to death by a man to whom he owed $22.00. A large land owner. The man was acquitted of murder and a year later my mother died of consumption on a poor farm. When I was seventeen, I met Mr. Morisot, a man of color, but prosperous: Mr. Bastide's key man. And he was kind. I saw my opportunity, and I married him. Are you shocked?"

"That you seized an opportunity, or that you married a man of color? Although I suppose they amount to the same thing."

"The latter."

"No. I am from Massachusetts. Such a thing is not unheard of there, nor in New Orleans, where I was in school."

"We had to go to the West Indies to be married. I have been criticized, perhaps hated, for forming this union. I expected no less. Hated or not, it does not matter to me, because I am respected. I will keep that respect, regardless. So, as the town goes, so goes Mr. Bastide. As Bastide goes, so goes my household. That is the root of my concern for the reputation of Ste. Odile."

"Yes, certainly. Of course. Still, Mrs. Chardin became my friend."

"And you saw her situation only from her perspective. I understand that. After you have been here for a few years, reconsider your opinion. You may come to a different one."

"Perhaps," Perdita said irritably.

"Welcome to my house."

14

Letter from Prosper Redon to Moira Keane Parnell, from aboard the Egeria

August 27, 1882

My dear Moira,

I have been ill for many days. I can scarce attribute my condition to seasickness, but I must needs call it something. It is a digestive distress which I can compare to nothing else I have felt before. I have such pain in my stomach and such a revulsion to food, that my strength has been much compromised. The ship's physician has forbidden me fresh fruit and vegetables, and has instead insisted my diet be restricted to cheese, eggs, milk, certain breads of a less coarse variety, and meat freshly prepared and only lightly seasoned.

At Lisbon yesterday, upon seeing the picturesque fortress Torre de Belem in the bay, I had much anticipated sight-seeing during our eight-hour stop in that port. The weather was fine after three days of choppy, unsettled seas, and my spirits rose mightily at the prospect of a brisk walking tour with the sun in my face.

Unfortunately, I became violently ill again as we made port. I got back into bed and stayed there until half past ten. My poor steward, what I have put him through! I must leave him the most generous gratuity I can afford when we reach Marseilles.

By about one in the afternoon, I was recovered enough to leave the secure port of my cabin, and trek, unsteadily, out into the city. I only ventured as far as a small English restaurant on the Avanida da India. In spite of the strong breezes which blew inland from the bay, the heat was excessive, or so it seemed to me, and my reserve of strength which had been much taxed in the last week, was soon depleted. I knew I must needs rest from the sun and the humidity, and so I stepped into the first inviting door I encountered.

I did not make a note of the establishment's name. It was nearly empty and very dark inside. Fortunately, as I have said, it was an English place. The proprietor was a Mr. Hemmings from Cornwall, a one-time sailor from a family of innkeepers, who preferred the warm breezes of Lisbon to the chilly gusts of Tintagel or Land's End.

As I had been fluctuating between feeling very ill and having no appetite to being hungry, I thought I would try a little meal. It was English roast beef—I know you would have approved! I ate slowly to test the waters, as they say. The first few bites presented no difficulty, but after the fifth or sixth bite, I was again suddenly and violently ill.

Mr. Hemmings and his wife Rosa, a native, were at a loss as to what to do for me. Rosa suggested taking me to an infirmary nearby, but I refused, asking only that Hemmings assist me in getting back to the ship. He graciously did so, and that is where I find myself now—back in bed.

Later

I am told it took a day to reach Gibraltar from Lisbon, and that we will be at Majorca tomorrow. I slept for many hours. I have been so ill and have slept so much, I am not even certain of what day it is as I sit at my desk and write this. We made Gibraltar this afternoon. The British military is much in evidence, both at Algecieras and in the ships in the bay. I did not venture off the ship today. I sat on deck for an hour or so, watching the activities of dock workers and merchants on the pier and docks. I saw a man with several of the Barbary apes native to this promontory—the only apes indigenous to Europe—tethered to him. The beasts performed small tricks for the amusement of onlookers, until one of the brutes abruptly attacked another, leaving its ear and scalp bloodied before the trainer could separate them. All for now. I will write more later.

Morning

I have done little for two days but rest and adhere strictly to my very bland diet. I am glad to report that I feel much improved. Today we find ourselves at the port of Palma on the island of Majorca, some ninety miles from the Spanish mainland. I am happy to anticipate seeing some of the sights the city has to offer and, for a few hours, to be forgetful of the concerns of illness or family tragedy, or personal loss.

Evening

Moira, you must see this city. It is something of a resort or spa for Germans, French, and English, all of whom are in some evidence here. The city itself is pristine and charming, beloved of Chopin and George Sand, I am told. The waters of the bay are a pale, clear blue in the shallows, deepening to indigo out in the depths. An old fortress attended by quaint windmills caps a hill on the western end of the bay, and the city is dominated by the Castel de Bellever, situated upon a high prominence to the northwest.

The ship berthed on a quay very near the Paseo

Maritimo Ronda, a beautiful roadway that borders the bay. This, according to my Baedeker, connected to the Paseo Sagrera, and it appeared to be a short walk east to the cathedral. And so it was. I made this walk, feeling I had much energy in reserve, and that I might indeed be well enough to see the sights.

The Gothic church itself is smallish by French standards. The interior is very dark, especially when contrasted with the absolute sunbathed brightness of the streets without. Still, it was cool and quiet inside. The only sounds to be heard were the shufflings of several old women sweeping the centuries-smoothed stones of the floor. I decided to stay and rest long enough to say a rosary. I prayed for an end to the suffering of my family, for my lost Perdita, for you, Moira, for the soul of my dear Claire, and for myself, that I might find a strength which I do not feel that I yet possess, to recover from these losses and give my family the succor it needs and expects from me.

After my visit to the cathedral, I was distinctly hungry; not vaguely or slightly hungry, interspersed with nausea, as I have been so frequently lately, but undeniably *hungry*. A few doors west of the cathedral, on the Paseo Sagrera, I found a small café nearly full of patrons, from which emanated the most enticing cooking aromas. I took a table under a canopy on the street. The temperature was pleasant, the breezes refreshing, and I felt a sense of well being wash over me which I haven't felt in months.

I decided to try a local lobster stew, renowned across the Mediterranean. It was comprised of lobster pieces, onion, peppers, garlic, and a peculiar liqueur made from herbs. I knew, of course, this would be a trial to my constitution, but I was feeling so much better, that I decided to take the risk. It was delicious.

Afterward, I retraced my steps west along the bay, and decided to climb the citadel to the Castel de Bellever above the city. All along the avenue I passed many shops and street vendors selling goods ranging from carvings in olive wood, to iron work, to embroidery, glassware, pottery, shoes, and gloves.

As I approached the Calle Espartero to begin to make my ascent to the castle, the folly of having had such a rich and spicy luncheon became apparent to me. I stopped to steady myself against a palm tree. Just then a very elderly man driving a cart pulled by two donkeys and loaded with newly-made wooden chairs, noticed the distress in which I found myself, and stopped to see if he could be of some assistance.

His name was Jorge. He spoke flawless English, having been pressed into service in the Royal Navy as a boy. Within one or two minutes of having met him, I learned he had eleven children, eight surviving, and that he had been married for forty-eight years. He helped me onto the cart. Although little more than five feet tall, he was amazingly strong, and I have little doubt he could have lifted me with relative ease onto my seat.

At first, and you will be amazed at this, Moira, my intention was to continue up to the castle. But Jorge dissuaded me, and offered to sit with me in the shade for a few moments before returning me to the ship.

Being so free with the details of his personal life, I found that he was equally interested in the details of mine. I told him of my childhood, of my emigration to America, my education, my engagement to and abandonment by Perdita, and of Claire and the circumstances of her death. In this last subject, he seemed excessively interested, almost morbidly so. I soon began to weigh my gratefulness for his kindness against my growing indignation at his fascination with so private and inappropriate a subject.

"Please excuse me for this curiosity and these painful questions," he apologized. "I was most surprised to hear of the circumstances of your dear sister's death, and in the south of France, too. Surprised, because it almost seemed as though you were describing the death of my own mother."

I was curious. I thought the facts of Claire's murder to be so peculiar and strange as to find no parallel in the chronicles of such things.

"Yes," Jorge said, "more than fifty years ago, after my father's death, and after my youngest sister married, my mother went into service at Marseilles. But she soon found a better situation somewhere to the northwest, in the mountains. I never knew where. I was still at sea then. My mother had been a tutor, a well-educated woman for her class, but had given up the work when she married. My father was not passionate on the subject, but he disapproved of education for women, and did not want her to pursue her former career. But after he died, she needed an occupation. In middle age, she thought that the only work likely to be available to her was nanny or housekeeper. She took a position as a housekeeper in Marseilles, and very soon, in her letters to me, expressed dissatisfaction with her choice of occupation. As a young woman she had taught mathematics and history, and as an unhappy housekeeper, she was grateful to receive an offer from a minor French noble to become tutor to his two small sons. The few letters I received from her after that were brief and preoccupied, but gave no real hint of her state of mind, her thoughts and fears. But the letters she wrote to my sister were different. She described nightmares and unreasonable terrors which made sleep impossible. Within a year of taking the new position, she was dead. Murdered. They found her in much the same condition as that which you have described for your sister. And there were even stories of similar things on this island more than three hundred years ago, in the days of Rodrigo II, but nothing since."

They call this hemisphere the Old World, Moira. For hundreds of generations, these lands have been occupied, going back to dim prehistory. Within no more than a thousand miles or so of where I sit tonight, grain was first cultivated, early societies were built, laws were made, indeed, the *idea* of law was first conceived. We know there has always been a surfeit of struggle, conflict, religious superstition, and bloodshed. I have often thought that when the dark burden of this crabbed, exhausted history became too much, God revealed to us the New World. In that way, man was allowed an opportunity for a fresh start and, hopefully, to leave the old, long familiar ways behind. Alas, human nature does not change, and must needs express itself, regardless of the current of ideology in favor at any moment in time. Our recent civil war has demonstrated this to anyone who may harbor a fragment of doubt upon the subject. Still, we would hope most of the old ways have been left behind, that the burden which history has placed upon these regions so long inhabited, might be left here.

We must count among these the fears and terrors of old superstitions. Who knows if these played a role in the deaths of Claire and of Jorge's mother, and others of whom we have heard in the last half year? Certain allusions just under the surface in the letters I have received from my brother Michel and my mother have implied as much without being explicit, and Jorge seems to believe there were elements of his mother's death which must have originated in some region beyond the rational world. But Jorge is a man of the Old World, the old beliefs. He was certain it was fate that he and I should meet, that I hear his story. But there is a generous portion of irrationality in old beliefs. The sleep of reason begets monsters, they say. The monsters of that irrationality are as much a part of this European landscape and its bloody history as are parasites to a stray dog. If this be true, let us hope these monsters, these parasites, if they can be made flesh by collective belief, or if they just remain an unsettling phantasm of the ignorant, have found no means of crossing the wide barrier of the ocean, nor the philosophical chasm separating the Old World from the New.

Yours,
Prosper

15

The afternoon light coming through the north-facing windows of the classroom was diffuse, and yet the child seemed to glow as if illuminated by some impossible and invisible beam of sunlight. Perdita's gaze continued to be drawn to her, and as she meandered between the concentric benches, checking the progress of each girl's drawing and making passing suggestions and criticisms, she found her eyes regularly drawn to Anatolia.

The child worked earnestly and vigorously on her drawing, frowning her concentration onto the coarse paper on the table before her. The subject was a plaster cast of the hawk god Horus, molded from an original found by Belzoni in upper Egypt in 1811, Solana had told them.

"You must draw only what you see, Elinor," Perdita said, looking at the girl's drawing, "not what you *know*. Your Horus's tail is sticking up and fanned out like a turkey's, not like the figure's in front of you, which is pointing downward."

"Do you want me to change it, Miss Badon-Reed?" Elinor asked tiredly.

"No. Just note what I have said, and remember it next time. Girls, I am only interested in seeing you represent the object before you. Only in that way may I objectively comment upon how you have rendered what *I* see. I cannot comment upon how well you represent what is in your imagination."

"Yes, Miss," several of the girls said in unison.

"Master the objects of the real world first," Perdita continued. "Then there will be time to give free expression to the landscape within."

Perdita had, by this time, moved behind Anatolia, who took no notice of her. She looked at Anatolia's drawing. The image of Horus appeared complete, drawn on a small scale in the center of the paper. Above this was a larger representation of the hawk's eye, with tears streaming from it. On each side of the central figure were angels with beams of light emanating from their heads. At the bottom of the page were several figures, most of which were indistinct. One, however, appeared to be a representation of Perdita herself. Written on the right edge of the drawing were these words: "In a land of light which knew nothing but darkness, sad, sad to be ignorant of God's love."

"Anatolia," Perdita said patiently, "here you are again. Didn't I just tell you to draw only what is there?"

Across the room, where she had been moved so as to be away from Anatolia, Lillian sniggered. She was full-blooded Fox with a very broad face. "She is so *odd*," Lillian said. "Seeing angels and the Elysian Fields!" Some of the other girls laughed.

"Lillian!" Perdita reprimanded. "I have told you about the rudeness of speaking out in class. We can function very well without your uncalled-for comments, thank you. Particularly if they are at someone else's expense. Do you understand?"

"Yes, Miss," Lillian mumbled. "I am sorry, Miss."

"Very well." Perdita nodded. "Now, Anatolia, what do you have to say for yourself? Why have you not drawn only the object as we all see it, as I have asked you to do?"

Anatolia was silent for a moment. Her eyes were fixed upon her drawing. She slowly raised her eyes to meet

Perdita's.

"But, Miss, I did see it this way. Everything was there, I saw it all."

"Anatolia—"

Several of the girls sniggered again.

"Class!" Perdita said sternly, and all were silent. "Anatolia, we have had this talk before. The very first day I met you, you were drawing Heavenly hosts. You are always putting angels and saints in your drawings, and bits of theology, philosophy, and poetry as well."

"No, Miss," Anatolia insisted. "It was all there. Only for a moment. If I didn't put it down just as it was, who would ever know it had happened?"

"Now you must listen to me, child," Perdita began.

Just then the classroom door opened. Sister Solana entered looking tired and ill.

"Give me your drawing, Anatolia," Perdita said. Anatolia complied. "Now draw it again. This time, only as it appears—nothing extra. Everyone else, change seats and draw the Horus from another perspective. Sister and I will be just outside, so no tomfoolery!"

Perdita approached Solana with a look of concern upon her face. She took the young sister by the arm and led her into the hallway, closing the classroom door behind them. Perdita could immediately hear giggling and sniggering coming through the glass.

"Perdita, I am so sorry to have missed class this morning; I was just so exhausted."

"Please," assured Perdita, "think nothing of it. Are you better now? More rested?"

"No, I am not. Class will be finished in ten minutes. Please, meet me in the Reliquary Chapel—a private place where we can talk."

"Of course. I'll be there in fifteen minutes' time."

Solana touched Perdita's hand and walked unsteadily away, toward the dining hall.

In a quarter hour, Perdita was pulling open the massive door of the Reliquary Chapel. She found Solana in the last pew on the right side, kneeling, saying her rosary, a relic inherited from her grandmother. As Perdita approached her, the rosary dropped from Solana's hand, into the pew in front of her.

"Solana?" Perdita called.

The young nun was startled.

"I drifted off," she said, in a weak, embarrassed voice. Perdita touched Solana's face and sat down next to her.

"You have seemed so tired lately."

"Yes. I cannot sleep. I have given up on sleeping draughts. Nothing works."

"What is it? Is there something on your mind? Is something troubling you?"As Solana sat back in her pew, Perdita could see there were tears in her eyes.

"Do you ever feel a sense that you are profoundly and utterly alone?" Solana pressed at the corners of her eye with her handkerchief. "Do you ever fear confronting those things in life that expose that aloneness, that no amount of society or love or friendship can allay?"

"I am not sure I know what you mean."

"I am not sure I do either." Solana dabbed at her eyes again. "But I *am* afraid," she said resolutely, as though she were keeping a promise to have said the words out loud. "So afraid of…what, I do not know. I have never felt this before. Never. Nothing like it, and I know no one can help me."

"But you cannot describe what frightens you?"

"I cannot really say. Am I frightened of myself, of the night, of aloneness, of darkness…of sleep itself?" She grasped Perdita's hand. "I cannot rest or sleep. I have such a sense of dread, such terrible dreams."

"But nightmares aren't real. I know they *can* be terrifying."

"This is worse than just nightmares. I have always managed to detach myself from nightmares. Even in my sleep, I could always maintain a distance from a bad dream. I always *knew* it was just a dream. These aren't like that."

"No?"

"No. In this state, I know I am doomed, and that I am too weak to resist. If I were only stronger ..."

"What kind of doom?"

"Death, ultimately. A horrible death by fire. Have you read of the Cathars?"

"No."

"They were an heretical sect of Christians that thrived in Provence in the Middle Ages. They practiced true poverty, true goodness. They were called the *bonne hommes*, the good men. In 1244, more than 200 of them were burned at the stake at Montsegur."

"Montsegur? That is where my former fiancee's sister lived, I believe. But I do not understand."

"I feel a connection to their suffering. *My* death by fire is in some way connected to theirs. And there is something more."

"What is it?"

"At certain times of the night, on certain nights, I feel *surrounded by something*. A presence. On those nights, at the edge of sleep, I am not alone in my room. I have somehow allowed something to invade my room, my boundary."

"*You* have allowed—?"

"Yes. I have no doubt that this is true. I sense it more each night. Why do my prayers not deliver me from these terrors? It can only be because of my weaknesses, because my prayers are not pleasing to God."

"You are blaming yourself for your terrors?"

"Isn't it clear? Clear as green tea when you think

about it. I can be so silly and worldly. I say the wrong things. Inappropriate things. I admire the wrong things. I have been so taken in by Mr. Bastide's home and treasures, and his interest in me. It is pride, I know. I was proud to have been singled out, to be the focus of his attentions. I know all this has to do with him. I know it is some sort of punishment."

"Why must it have to do with him?"

"Because I feel it *must*. And he is in my dreams. Barely recognizable, but I know it to be him. And there is something more, too." Solana applied her handkerchief to her tears again. She gathered her thoughts for a few moments, and seemed hesitant to speak. "It is of a physical nature," she said meekly. "I have told no one. I am too ashamed even to mention it in confession. I couldn't say it to Father Condell."

"A physical nature?"

"Yes. Sometimes my body is…it is almost on fire."

"Oh." Perdita understood.

"There is terror and foreboding and a sense of doom, as I have told you, but also…anticipation. I will rouse myself from my horrible visions in the middle of the night, and along with the terror, there is a hunger. I do not know how to describe it."

"Yes. I understand."

"I am hungering for something unholy, something repugnant to God. I know I will be breached, violated."

"And yet you want it to happen?" Perdita embraced Solana. "But these feelings are normal, don't you see? I have them from time to time. They aren't sinful, or a sign of weakness."

"Oh, but they are. I can feel they are. And I know the difference between what you describe and what I am experiencing. It isn't the same thing. You are speaking of normal human desires. I am speaking of something evil. Incomparably evil. Something that wishes to destroy me."

Perdita did not know how to respond. "Very well," she said. "Is there something I can do to help you? Would you like for me to stay with you for a few nights?"

"No. Mother Superior would not allow it. And I feel it would be dangerous for you."

"Solana, forgive me. I know you are in earnest, but how could it be dangerous for me?"

Solana grasped Perdita's hand tightly. "Because this is more than dreaming, more than silly night fears or imagination. There is something real, something substantive, living, aware, watching, something that occupies some vile and horrible dimension within this plane, which I feel my weakness has brought into being, or at least, drawn to me. What I dread in myself has taken form. I cannot subject you, my dearest friend, to physical danger. I can only face this alone, and if I cannot fight it on those terms, I feel, I *know* it will kill me."

16

The day was less hot than the previous few days had been. Although summer still hung heavily on the parched trees and dying grass like the stones carried by the prideful in Dante's *Inferno*, Perdita found herself thinking of autumn and the changing of the seasons. Although Solana's distress had not improved, and she appeared to Perdita to be in a severe physical as well as emotional decline, Perdita had found herself revived a bit in the last few days.

She had completed her move into Tranquille House and had found Mrs. Zell to be somewhat less of a busybody than she had expected. Even when Hypolitte had visited her yesterday to deliver a bottle of claret, which he called a house-warming gift, and they had sat in the front parlor tasting the wine and talking of Solana, *Moby Dick*, and the relative merits of Houdon versus Canova, Mrs. Zell had seemed quite affable and scarcely disapproving at all, as Perdita had imagined she would be. In fact, after an hour or so, Perdita had rather wished that Mrs. Zell had given some sign of disapproval that could have been used to end the visit. Perdita had wanted to work on her Beatrice that day, but did not want to appear rude or unappreciative to her guest.

So, she had resolved to work on the statue in the afternoon instead. Her classes were finished for the day. She had encouraged Solana to return to her garret to rest mid-way through the afternoon session. Perdita would have a cup of tea with Uncle Tancred and Mrs. Moon, get a few hours' work done on the stone, and check on Solana later, on her way back to her own rooms.

She turned north from Endymion Street onto Constantinople. A breeze blowing across town from the river carried with it sounds of activity on the landing, and the occasional sound of bells and whistles of steamboats either stopping at Ste. Odile, or, more typically, passing it by, both on the western and eastern side of de Castres Island. A whistle sounded and abruptly stopped. There was a brief high-pitched whine, like the sound of steam escaping, followed instantly by a resounding, reverberating boom. Perdita stopped, puzzled and startled by the sounds.

Other people on the street stopped also. In a moment, a wave of recognition seemed to pass over everyone in Perdita's sight, and they all began to run toward the landing.

"Boiler explosion," a man said.

"Must be the *Julia Cerre,*"Perdita heard someone say.

She found herself moving toward the landing with a crowd that was growing by the second. By the time she reached Bosphorus Street, the crowd had grown to perhaps two hundred, and nearly everyone, it seemed to Perdita, had a sense of purpose and seemed to know what would be needed of them. Many of the men were carrying ropes, tow sacks, life preservers, grappling hooks, and oars or paddles. At the entrance to the channel at the north end of de Castres Island, the *Julia Cerre* could be seen, on fire and listing to the starboard side, with her aft slowly swinging about as she drifted helplessly in the current.

The boat was turning into its own smoke drift and scattered bits of flotsam eddied in the current alongside her. There were thirty or forty survivors bobbing in the water, or trying to swim toward crates, timbers, or barrels floating past. An at least equal number of dead or injured crew and passengers could be seen drifting with the current, or coming to rest against snags.

The crowd moved to the water's edge and several men began to load skiffs tied to saplings nearby with the equipment they carried. The pounding of horse's hooves approached from behind and Sheriff Aubuchon and Deputy Villiers rode up quickly amid the crowd and dismounted.

"Water rescue only!" Aubuchon shouted. "The *Julia* has two hundred barrels of coal oil aboard. Give her wide berth. She could explode at any time unless she sinks first!"

Aubuchon and Villiers began to help the men who were loading a large skiff near to them. They climbed into the boat and, with eight or ten others, were pushed free of the bank.

Perdita and the crowd watched speechlessly as the *Julia Cerre* drifted completely about in the channel, and with her bow now pointed upstream, came to rest against a huge sycamore snag thirty feet from the bank of de Castres Island opposite the landing.

"She ain't gonna sink now," Perdita heard an old man say behind her. "Better clear off the landing. It ain't safe."

The fire had become enormous, and forty-foot-high flames quickly ignited branches overhanging the bank. As the small flotilla of skiffs made its way toward bobbing groups of survivors in the water, another high-pitched whine was heard coming from the midst of the flames. Suddenly the entire landing was engulfed in the flash and concussion of a massive explosion, as a billow of flame climbed high above the tree level surrounding the *Julia Cerre*.

A bloom of shattered wood and splinters sprayed out from the explosion. A few were blown with such force that they nearly reached the landing and the onlookers who had remained transfixed watching the conflagration.

"Don't approach the boat!" Aubuchon called to the other skiffs in the flotilla. "Let her burn out. The fire is too fierce!"

"I will give a bounty of fifty dollars to anyone who finds my parcel!" a woman called.

Perdita recognized the voice. She turned to see Mrs. Morisot and her two attendants approaching the landing.

"Mr. Baker!" Mrs. Morisot called to a young man returning his skiff to the landing. Two adolescent boys in the skiff were tending to three severely burned men whom they had pulled from the water. "Mr. Baker, I will give you fifty dollars if you recover a parcel or crate addressed to me with a blue banner emblazoned upon it."

"Might have sunk by now," Baker called back.

"It is a cork-lined package meant to float if the worst happens. It contains some very valuable and old lace from Flanders. It was meant to be on this boat."

Perdita was aghast. "This is no time to worry about lace, Mrs. Morisot!"

Mrs. Morisot looked at her indignantly. "Miss Badon-Reed," she said through her teeth, "I have not sought your opinion. There are boats aplenty on the water for rescue. If I wish to engage this young man to recover my valuable parcel, that is my affair!"

"Baker!" Hypolitte called, emerging from the crowd behind Mrs. Morisot. "Let's get these three off, then help the sheriff up at those riffles."

He moved past Perdita and caught a rope tossed to him from one of the boys in the skiff. Hypolitte dragged the boat up onto the bank. He, Baker, and the boys lifted two of the burned men from the bottom of the boat.

"Clear this space," Perdita heard herself saying to the crowd. "We will lay the victims here. Mrs. Morisot, could you and your ladies find us blankets and sheets for bandages, as many as you can carry, and perhaps butter or some sort of burn salve?"

Mrs. Morisot glared venomously at Perdita, then turned silently and, followed by her attendants, rushed off toward Bosphorus Street.

"We need Dr. Duclos," Perdita said.

"I saw him at Maupin's," a boy said. He was holding a muddy puppy.

"Fetch him. And we need the attendants at the mine infirmary." The boy ran off. "And the doctor there, if there is one," Perdita called after him.

Hypolitte and Baker lay the burned man they carried at Perdita's feet. She knelt and began to unbutton the man's shirt. He had a gash across his left chest and a burn along the left side of his face and neck.

"Can you hear me, sir?" Perdita asked.

"Yes, Miss. I think I am half deaf from the explosion, but I can hear you. God bless you."

"What is your name?"

"Halbert Moncrieffe."

"Can you move all of your limbs, Mr. Moncrieffe?"

"Yes, Miss."

The two youths from the skiff lay the second man alongside Moncrieffe, followed closely by Hypolitte and Baker with the third.

"What do you need?" Hypolitte asked Perdita.

"I have sent for blankets and bandages. Duclos is coming. I need to wash these wounds. I need clean water and towels. And a pair of sharp shears, too."

"I'll send someone." Hypolitte looked at her intently for a moment.

"I'll get those *things*," a woman's voice said. It was Mrs. Zell.

Baker and the two youths returned to the skiff. Hypolitte joined them, and after they had climbed into the boat, he pushed them away from the bank and jumped in.

Soon, many other skiffs and small boats began to return to the landing with the injured, who were then laid out in rows along the cobblestones. Within a half-hour, some forty-four victims had been recovered. Mrs. Morisot's attendants quickly returned with blankets, burn salve, and sheets, which, at Perdita's instruction, they began to tear into bandages. Mrs. Zell and two of her daughters soon appeared with two buckets of warm water, towels, and a large pair of shears.

"We need to cut away clothing wherever necessary and wash these wounds," Perdita said. She took the shears from Mrs. Zell, and the two women knelt beside Moncrieffe. Perdita cut away his shirt and left trouser leg while Mrs. Zell began to gently wash the gash on his side.

Dr. Duclos and two infirmary attendants arrived on horseback and were quickly directed toward Perdita by one of Mrs. Zell's daughters.

"You have organized this?" Duclos asked Perdita. He was out of breath.

"Yes, such as it it."

"Excellent. Obviously, we need to stop bleeding, wash wounds, and check for compound fractures—they may not even be felt by a victim in distress, and we must guard against infection."

"Yes. I helped with a ferry disaster on the Charles. We'll need splinting material, too. I'll send some of the boys."

"Keep those with serious burns in this area," Duclos said, "and others, we'll put over there."

"We are placing the dead near the street," Perdita said.

"I have arranged with Aristide for a wagon," Duclos said. "Listen carefully for a heartbeat, check pulse, and wet your hand and feel for breath before putting them there."

"Of course."

Over the next three-quarters of an hour, as the hulk

of the *Julia Cerre* burned and slowly collapsed in upon itself on the riverbank opposite, some fifty-three injured were recovered and twenty-two dead. Many townswomen, children, and young men who did not go out on the boats were helping with the injured and with removing and placing the dead. Some worked under Perdita's direction, some under Duclos's, some independently. Mrs. Moon had come from the rectory with her daughter Bess to wash wounds, and Uncle Tancred knelt among the dead and dying, delivering blessings, and last rites.

Perdita and Mrs. Zell continued to cut away clothing from wounds and wash them. Both women helped Duclos with splinting of the three compound fractures that were found. When no more survivors could be found, Hypolitte, Baker, and Aubuchon continued to search the banks, eddies, snags, and overhangs for the dead.

After another hour, all of the seriously injured had been attended to, and had begun to be moved to the mine infirmary. Perdita and Mrs. Zell had attempted to help loading into the wagons the victims who could not stand, but Duclos pressed many of the men into service who were coming in from the river search.

Perdita was exhausted, covered with mud, insect bites, and blood. She tried to brush a strand of hair away from her forehead with her wrist, but it was plastered to her skin with sweat. Mrs. Zell wiped her hands on her apron and pushed aside the strand of hair.

"Thank you," Perdita said. Mrs. Zell smiled. Perdita looked down at her dress, at the hours-old bloodstains across the bodice and skirt. "I think I have made an enemy of your employer, our Mrs. Morisot, by ranking the saving of lives above the recovery of her Belgian lace! And, I've ruined another dress," she said tiredly. "I have only one outfit left now."

"Did you *hear* that?" Mrs. Zell frowned.

"What?"

"Sounds like a *child.*"

"I don't hear it."

"I am accustomed to listening for whimpering *babies* in the night…I hear a *child.*" Mrs. Zell moved away from the noise of the landing toward the riverbank and some overhanging willow trees. Perdita followed.

"Yes, now I can hear it," Perdita said. "But I cannot tell just where it is coming from."

"It sounds to be in the *water.* Under these *branches.*"

Hypolitte and Baker, along with his two boys, were returning to the shore. Hypolitte noticed the women's interest in the overhanging branches. "What is it?" he called.

"We hear a child in here," Perdita answered.

"We'll try to get closer," Hypolitte said.

"Can't get under there with those snags in the way," Baker said.

"Maybe I can climb out onto them," Hypolitte mumbled, studying the floating mass of logs and branches. "They won't support your weight from this side. It's just a mat of branches and weeds. You'd have to get downstream, where the women are."

"I can get in from this side," Perdita said.

"No, Perdita," Hypolitte said. "There is an eddy here, and it's very deep. It's too dangerous."

Perdita tried to crawl up the riverbank, but it had eroded away to a drop-off of ten feet or more, straight down into the water.

"I am going to have to wade in there," she said.

"No," Baker insisted. "It's too deep, maybe fifteen feet."

Perdita moved back to where Mrs. Zell still stood and waded into the water. A few feet out, she stepped onto a partially submerged log, steadying herself by holding onto overhanging branches. Mrs. Zell followed her. After a few steps, Perdita stopped and stared into the shaded slough from where the sound had seemed to come. She saw a spot of color in the muddy water. After a few moments, she recognized a green bonnet fringed with hair.

"There is a body here. A woman!" she cried. A slight movement in a branch overhanging the dead woman caught Perdita's attention. As her eyes accustomed to the deep shade, she could make out a child wrapped in swaddling hanging from a strap looped over the branch. The child, an infant no more than a month old, was submerged in the water nearly to its shoulders.

"Oh my God!" Perdita whispered. "A child is hung on the branch!" she shouted to Hypolitte.

"Sweet *Jesus!"* Mrs. Zell exclaimed.

"The poor woman must have just secured it there trying to reach the bank through this eddy before her strength gave out!" Perdita said, as she started to reach the baby. "Twenty feet from the bank!"

"Can you reach it?" Hypolitte asked.

"I don't know."

Perdita shifted her grasp to a branch closer to the now-wailing child. She stepped out further onto a fork of the snag. It sank a bit under her weight. Reaching as far as she could into the gloom, her fingers barely touched the strap of the swaddling. Tentatively, she worked her fingers under the strap, and after several tugs, pulled it free. The child dipped briefly under the water, and Perdita pulled it quickly out, its eyes open, gasping for air and coughing. Perdita swung her parcel back behind her toward Mrs. Zell, who caught it.

"Quickly, do you have it? I'm losing my footing." Perdita could hear panic in her own voice.

"Yes." Mrs. Zell held the child to her breast and stepped carefully backward toward the bank. Perdita found she could not right herself. As she tried to gain her balance, the fork of the snag upon which she was standing sank deeper into the eddy. Suddenly the fork gave way altogether with a muffled pop, and Perdita fell into the dark water.

She felt her hands and face pass through a billow of water-inflated organdy and silk, and felt also the cold face of the dead woman as the momentum of her fall carried her past the body. Perdita sank quickly, and she flailed frantically for a branch to grasp as she felt a deep undercurrent and the weight of her skirts pulling her down. The branches she touched were moss-covered and slick, and she couldn't hold onto them. The dim, green-brown light that filtered down to her quickly seemed to be impossibly distant and as weak as the last few moments of twilight.

She heard a muffled splash above her and saw a riot of dim bubbles surrounding a figure descending toward her, which blocked out the twilight. It was not until a hand grasped her wrist that she could make out that it was Hypolitte. He pulled her toward himself, and she felt an arm around her waist. Quickly the gloomy light brightened as he lifted her toward the surface.

In a few seconds, they had broken through and both gasped for breath. Each grabbed a dry branch of the snag and held on, to regain their strength.

"Thank God!" Baker called from the skiff. "I thought you were both lost!"

"We're all right," Hypolitte said. "You are all right?"

"Yes," Perdita said, smiling. "Thank you. Thank you for my life. I ...had no strength left. I do not swim."

Hypolitte smiled at her warmly. "That was quickly apparent."

"I'll get above you on the bank with a rope and bring you up that way," Baker called. "Just rest yourselves. I will be right there."

Hypolitte lifted Perdita up further on the snag. He smiled at her again. "We could have lost you. What a loss to Ste. Odile that would be." Perdita could make out a slight quiver of emotion in his voice. "I am touched and amazed at what you have done here today," he continued, "and at what you did for Marie."

"Oh—" Perdita did not know what to say. Hypolitte's gaze seemed to turn serious and intent. Suddenly, he pulled her toward him and kissed her. Immediately she pulled away, still speechless.

"I'm sorry," he said.

17

Letter from Moira Keane Parnell to Perdita Badon-Reed

Moira Keane Parnell
14 Newgrange Circle
Boston, Massachusetts
September 10, 1882

My dearest Perdita,

Yes! What did I tell you? I knew you should be wary of your Mr. Hypolitte Robert. He seemed too attentive by half to have had no romantic designs upon you. And, if I may say it, one is never too far off of the mark to assume romantic designs in any man who fixes one's gaze for more than a second or two.

So, now what will you do? With whom shall you conspire and commiserate? Mr. Robert has placed you in an uncomfortable position, placed a stress upon your friendship, while your Sister Solana continues in her most peculiar malaise. Has she improved at all? You say sleeping draughts are of no avail, that she fears sleep itself. I have known the sensation of feeling a presence in my sleeping chamber at night, as have most people, I would wager. I even saw it from time to time amongst my injured charges during the war. But what you describe in the young Sister sounds for all the world like a mania beyond any in my experience. There are men of medicine now who are making a study of these dark regions, these illnesses of the inner land of the soul. Perhaps a consultation with this sort of doctor would be just the thing for her, if Mother Superior and the bishop would permit it.

But my Lord, what an adventure you had with the rescue effort of the *Julia Cerre*! I wish I could have been there with you and that we could have worked side by side to aid the injured, just as we did during the Charles disaster. But I am horrified to think of how close I came to losing my dear friend in the muddy waters of the Mississippi! I thank God Mr. Robert was on hand to rescue you from the depths. The giddy excitement of the moment, coupled with the thrilling day's events, must have overwhelmed his emotions and led to his effrontery. In that sense, I almost think one might understand and forgive him. Still, I am convinced it was only a matter of time before he made his intentions and interest known. At any rate, I am certain he is mortified now, poor man. He may have lost a valuable friendship, too, by his rashness. One wonders if your association with him can move on from this. *Consummatum est* ? I wonder. It is never wise, is it, to give in to the passion of the moment? "By these passions do we diminish ourselves."

And I would have so loved to have been at your side for the luncheon given in your honor by the Ladies Sodality of the Holy Mandillion to recognize your work during the rescue effort and the saving of that child, poor little thing! It was fortunate that the dead mother could be identified and her family in Cincinnati contacted. I am hopeful the little waif won't have to be orphaned for long.

As I mentioned in my last, Prosper is not well. I did not know much then. He arrived very ill at Marseilles. He was met by his brother Michel, who greeted the sight of him with such alarm that he spirited him immediately to a hospital.

He has lost much weight and complains that his clothes no longer fit him properly. It is so like him, I think you will agree, to be more concerned about the expense of refitting his wardrobe, which he can well afford, than he is about a prudent and realistic evaluation of his own health. His doctors are insisting on a period of observation, and a strictly controlled diet, perhaps in a sanatorium, until his strength is restored. He is being given doses of a purple loosestrife mixture to which he seems to be responding well. I pray for him daily, as I do for his entire family, blighted as they are with tragedy and loss.

The new girl your mother has engaged may well be hopeless. She comes at a bargain, but in some areas one certainly is not well advised to seek out a bargain. Her name is Bridget Connolly, and she is not two weeks off of the boat. I myself had to take her to the market to teach her how to buy vegetables, and later to the butcher to show her how to buy beef. I could scarcely digest the stringy, tough, gristle-bound roast she served on my last visit for supper. I would never have thought that such inseverable, undivideable ligamentations existed in any beast created by God for the mastication of human molars and incisors. I doubt a Bengal tiger could have done other than to have abandoned that overcooked carcass in frustration after an hour's profitless gnawing!

But your parents, as you know, having been raised on English cuisine, scarcely know a good meal from a bad one. I'll be sunk if they wouldn't as soon have a kidney pie as Chateaubriand, or bread pudding instead of crème brulée. Do you remember Christmas dinner two years ago? It was the last time our families dined together. Mary prepared a beautiful sirloin of beef, and when asked if he preferred the Burgundy or a Bordeaux with it, your father replied: "Lemonade."

I have heard that Wagner's *Tristan and Isolde* is to be performed here this winter, though I have heard nothing about where. The prospect of hearing this controversial piece alone should be enough to tempt you to come back home, if only for a visit. Wagner himself said that one should hope for a mediocre performance of this work, because an excellent performance would drive people insane!

I will close for now, but as he has requested, I have enclosed a letter to you from Prosper, written, I gather, during his convalescence.

Adieu,
Moira

Letter from Prosper Redon to Perdita Badon-Reed

August 1882
Marseilles

My dearest Perdie,

Perhaps ten times I have sat down to write you this letter. As Moira has informed me of your progress across the country and your new career as a teacher, I find myself amazed at what you have done, no less than by the secrecy with which you initiated it all. Always when I began to write to you, I would find some excuse to delay: my letters will go astray unless she is settled at an address; I should wait until I have accepted this development and am no longer pained by it; her escape from our promised life together was an unambiguous act—she does not want to hear from me. Etcetera.

But as I recover my strength here (the Marquand Sanatorium; Moira has told you of my illness), I have much time on my hands to think of you and our many happy hours together (at least they seemed so to me), and muse about what it was that I must have done to have warranted this abandonment. And now I find myself at the moment when I must needs express to you how I feel.

Firstly, I should ask you, what was my deficiency? Was I not gentlemanly enough? Did I not always put your needs and wishes ahead of mine, when my health allowed it? It seems to me that if the answer to all of these questions is yes, then I would still be at your side, attending to your every need. Therefore, I have failed in some way.

I think back to our picnic on the Fourth of July last year. Do you remember? How infernally hot it was! Other couples had rented boats and were punting around the lagoon. Knowing my aversion to boats and the water, you asked me if we could rent a boat, too. I'd had too much of Moira's nearly-spoiled roast beef and was feeling rather sick. That, coupled with the heat, had me quite queer. I had to decline. I will always remember how you looked at me then: disgusted, put out, angry for a moment; then even worse, completely indifferent. It was as if at that instant I ceased to exist, and all memory of me, along with any affection you might have ever felt, evaporated like dew on a flagstone. But, I must ask you, what would you have had me do in such a circumstance? Would you rather I had hidden my illness, paddled us to the middle of the lagoon, then stranded us there with my incapacity? No, I think your response was but an expression of a disdain which must have been growing over some extended period of time. Thinking back, I can recall some dozen or so moments when I should have recognized these signs, but I foolishly never assembled all of these bits of evidence into a cohesive and predictable verdict. If you would have but told me of your concerns, you know I would have moved mountains to have pleased you, to have set things right. Or, did you not want to take any constructive step which might have salvaged our union?

Forgive me if this last sounds excessively accusatory. Remember, I do not blame you for our dissolution, but rather, myself. To what other conclusion can I come? With no word of parting or explanation from you, there can be no other conclusion, I think. Surely my years of single-minded devotion to you warrant some sort of an explanation, just for the sake of politeness and good form, if nothing else?

I am sorry, but I am not strong. I must rest now. I have enclosed my return address. I may be here another three weeks, should you choose to write. The sanatorium will forward any mail I receive here on to my father's house, if you should miss me here. I await your response. I deserve it.

Yours,
Prosper

18

Perdita heard the back door of the rectory close. She looked up to see Mrs. Moon approaching her across the drive, carrying a folded piece of paper in her hand. The weather had turned hot again, but breezy. Perdita had risen early and walked to the rectory, to her lean-to, to work on the *Beatrice* before the heat became oppressive. To disturb Uncle Tancred's already fitful sleep as little as possible, she had been rasping the arms of the figure rather than shaping the gown with her hammer and points. Sweat mixed with marble dust stung her eyes. She wiped her face with the underside of her apron.

"I hope I have not disturbed you, Mrs. Moon," Perdita said.

"No, Miss, not at all."

"Nor Uncle—?"

"He's been awake since two this morning, or so he says. He can't get a night's rest anymore."

"No."

"A message came for you just now. From the convent. Sister Solana." She held out the note to Perdita who took it and unfolded it. It read:

> The worst has happened and I am in despair. I must get out and make a small trip. You may be my only friend now. Will you meet me at the boat dock at

the end of Rouen Street at nine A.M.? I depend upon you, and upon the mercy of Our Lord. Yours, S.

Perdita read the note a second time.

"I recognize bad news when I see it," Mrs. Moon said.

"Hmmm?"

"On your face. I hope the young sister is all right."

"I am not sure. I don't know what to think. What time is it, Mrs. Moon?"

Mrs. Moon glanced at a watch she kept pinned to her blouse. "Half past eight."

"Barely enough time to clean myself up. Is Uncle about in the house?"

"In the study, writing his sermon."

"Good," Perdita said, as she began to walk toward the rectory. Mrs. Moon followed her. "I would like to keep him in the dark until I know what this is about."

"Certainly, Miss Perdita."

The walk south along Constantinople Street seemed much longer than usual. Mrs. Duchamp wanted to chat about the weather, and Claude Boulle needed a sympathetic ear to complain about the recent drop in prices for green hides in St. Louis and the diminishing bounty that wolf pelts were bringing. Perdita tried to be polite; since the wreck of the *Julia Cerre*, she had felt more accepted by the townspeople at large and did not want to compromise in any way her growing inclusion in the community. With these delays and the near disaster of almost being overrun by several stray wine barrels that tumbled from a passing flatbed wagon whose rear axle suddenly broke, Perdita arrived at the small dock at the foot of Rouen Street at about ten past nine.

As she approached the dilapidated, weathered oak structure, she recognized Urbain, the eldest son of the dray-man, Aristide. Urbain held a rope tied to a large skiff at rest against the upriver side of the dock. Next to him stood a young woman in a faded, pale blue walking outfit that seemed to Perdita to be about fifteen years out of date. As Perdita's footsteps resounded off of the pink granite cobblestones, the young woman turned to face her. Perdita was astonished to recognize Sister Solana.

"My word...Solana! I had to look twice to recognize you in that get-up. Where on earth did you get that outfit, and why are you wearing—"

"I am sorry for all of this," Solana said. Her face was pale and drawn, her eyes red and swollen with recent tears. "I am sorry for all of this drama and mystery."

Perdita was overwhelmed with emotion at the sight of her friend. She embraced Solana, who began to sob quietly.

"I will tell you all," Solana said, glancing meaningfully at Urbain. "Soon, not just now. Please, Urbain, may we get under way?"

Urbain nodded. First Solana, then Perdita climbed into the skiff and sat on the rear seat. Urbain then stepped into the boat and, taking his place on the middle seat, he pushed them away from the dock with an oar. Soon the current was carrying them slowly downstream.

Perdita did not know what to say. All of the questions she wanted to ask, she assumed Solana would only want to answer in private, when they were out of earshot of Urbain. Perdita put her hand on Solana's, who watched the bank slide past silently with a tragic half-smile on her face that Perdita could barely see in profile.

"Are you all right?" Perdita thought the question insipid as soon as she asked it. Solana's eyes welled with tears, as she shook her head no.

After a few minutes' floating, they were past the southern tip of de Castres Island and in the confluence of both channels that flowed past it. Perdita had forgotten how wide the river was, having not seen its true, undivided width since she had arrived in Ste. Odile.

Perdita decided to remain silent, to wait for Solana to speak as she needed to. Perdita thought of her trip downstream with Marie on the day of her execution. This trip had the same tragic feel, she thought. After some five minutes, Perdita's resolution to silence was impossible to keep.

"Won't you tell me where we are going?" she asked at length. Solana looked at Perdita. After a long moment, she spoke.

"We are going to see *Meres des Sicles*."

"What?"

"The Mother of the Centuries," Urbain said. "The *traiteur.* The wildcrafter, Euphrosine."

"Euphrosine." Perdita recognized the name. "Marie told me about her on the day she died. She said there may come a time when I would want to see her too."

"Heaven forbid," Solana said.

"My father and I have taken many people, many young ladies to see Euphrosine," Urbain said. "She has been out here since before my father was born. No one remembers a time before Euphrosine."

"A wildcrafter?" Perdita was puzzled. She turned to Solana. "Why on earth would you need — ?"

"Euphrosine come up from the Atchafalaya, from Louisiana, I've heard," Urbain interrupted. "But I don't know when. She always been here, it seems. One thing or another brings people to her. Mostly young ladies, though. Philtres, poultices, spells. My father told me she can go into a trance and see the future, or speak to the dead. So they say. I never seen it myself, though."

Solana stared silently at the riverbank. Several egrets waded in the shallows, stabbing into the sluggish water for the silvery, muscular fish which they swallowed whole, spines splayed, struggling. Beyond a small point of marshy land the western bank opened into the mouth of a creek.

"That is Saline Creek," Urbain said, guiding the skiff toward it. "They used to get a lot of salt out of here. Still do get some. I'm putting you ashore at the foot of the path. Follow it for a mile or so. I will wait for you." He smiled. "And stay out of the poison ivy—three long leaves..." He pointed to a tangled mass of the plant overhanging the bank, "Or you will regret it."

The bow of the skiff ran up onto a black, muddy bank, stinking and scattered with opened mussel shells. Numerous flies and mosquitoes rose from the shells and swarmed around the women as they stood, uncertainly, to step out of the boat. Perdita and Solana swatted futilely at the pests.

"You smell too good!" Urbain laughed. "I don't have that problem. I will wait for you."

The women started up the path. Within some twenty or thirty feet, they had lost sight of the bank, and within another fifty, surrounded by undergrowth and enormous sycamores and cottonwoods, they were out of earshot of the river and Urbain.

"Please," Perdita said, "tell me what this is about."

Solana could only meet Perdita's gaze for an instant. She looked at the ground and her eyes filled with tears. "I am sorry for this mystery. I didn't want to say it aloud until we were alone, or write it in a note this morning that someone else might read. Oh, Perdita! I depend upon your friendship so. I depend upon you now. Who else could help me?"

"Please, dear, what is it?"

"I believe, I truly believe, that I am...pregnant!"

Perdita was speechless for many moments. "But surely," she said at length, "surely that is impossible! How could it be? You are Sister Solana, a bride of Christ. I know how sacred, how important that vow is to you. Surely you haven't…I *know* you. I *know* you haven't—"

"No, my intention has been to honor my vows. That is my life. My life is nothing without that. This involves no mere infidelity to my vows. It is connected somehow to my fears, my terrors in the night, the fearsome and dreadful dreams I have been having. I *feel* it is."

"What makes you think you are pregnant?"

"I've been very ill. My time of the month is long past. I have prayed for that uncleanness to end, that connection to carnality, the flesh, but not like this. And, somehow, I just *know* it to be true, in the way women must have known these things for thousands of years."

"You must be mistaken. You have been so ill lately, that could affect your cycle."

"No. I am not mistaken. If you should ever experience this yourself, God forbid, then you will understand. Somehow, you just know."

"What has this to do with Euphrosine?"

"Oh, Perdita, can't you see? She can verify what I fear—and put an end to it."

Perdita was shocked by the suggestion. "Put an end to it? Solana, dearest, you need to see the doctor. You must see a real doctor and find a reasonable explanation for all of this. This old woman cannot help you. Let's go back to town and consult with Dr. Duclos."

"There is nothing a doctor can tell me. I cannot bear the shame of anyone else in town knowing about it. After what you endured with Marie, I am so very sorry to include you in this, but you are my closest friend."

"I will help you gladly, but we must see a doctor. Duclos will say nothing and pass no judgment."

"No. I am adamant. I have prayed over this every night for nearly a week. Will you come with me?"

"Of course, of course. If I cannot dissuade you."

Solana turned away to continue along the path.

Perdita grasped her arm, Solana stopped to face her.

"You have changed so much in such a short time," Perdita said. "You were so joyful, so full of vivacity when I first knew you. There seems to be so little of that left in you now."

Solana smiled slightly. She thought for a moment, then spoke softly: "Neither poppy nor mandragora nor all the drowsy syrups of the world shall ever medicine thee to that sweet sleep which thou owe'dst yesterday."

"Is your life as irretrievable as that now?" Perdita asked.

"Yes." Solana nodded sadly and turned toward the path again. "Yes, I fear it is. Nothing is the same. It never can be again."

A few hundred feet along, Saline Creek spread out to a dank marshy basin dotted with dead tree trunks and areas of malformed cedars, cypresses, and oaks. On the north edge of the basin, the path ended at the door of a rough shack of cedar shakes and rough-hewn boards which seemed to form a connective growth between two enormous oaks on either end of it.

A huge, wild-looking dog tied to a low-hanging branch began to bark savagely at the two women. Perdita hesitated a moment at the sight of the animal. Solana continued undeterred, as if she were in a trance.

The door of the shack, hung with rabbit and raccoon pelts, slowly opened. An old woman in a tattered cotton shift stepped out into the sunshine.

"*Soyez tranquille, Potiphar,*" she shouted at the dog in a surprisingly strong voice. The animal immediately went silent. The old woman glanced at Perdita and Solana. She nodded and waved them toward her as she turned and stepped back into the shack.

"Euphrosine—" Perdita whispered.

Solana, then Perdita, followed Euphrosine into the

shack. As her eyes slowly became accustomed to the darkness inside, Perdita could see there was only one room, ventilated by two windows which were covered with curtains of a gauzy, dark fabric. The walls were almost completely covered with shelves that overflowed with bottles, flasks, crocks, sprigs of herbs, dried leaves, animal bones, and a smattering of old books and papers. An iron stove was situated against the western wall alongside a high oak table. Euphrosine sat in a large walnut chair piled with pillows and an old quilt, near a crude fireplace. Perdita and Solana sat on a pine bench against the front wall. Euphrosine picked up a large clay pipe which had been resting on the hearth, and puffed it back into ignition.

Euphrosine looked incredibly old to Perdita, and of a racial heritage impossible to pinpoint, as if all of the streams of humanity were mixed in her. In spite of the heat of the day, the old woman wore a shawl across her shoulders and a cap festooned with feathers, mussel shells and dried flowers. After a moment, Euphrosine looked deeply into Solana's eyes. She arose from her chair and approached Solana. She stroked Solana's face and stomach with her gnarled hands, and smelled her hair and breath. She entangled a few strands of Solana's hair in her fingers and felt its texture. She smelled her neck, breasts, and lap.

"I saw you in a dream two nights ago," the old woman said. "I knew you would come today. I know why you are here. You should have come before now." Her accent was odd, peculiar to Provence or the Albi, Perdita thought, very much like Prosper's. "Trust what your flesh tells you," Euphrosine continued. "What you fear is true."

Solana buried her face in her hands and began to sob. Perdita embraced her. "We should go to see Dr. Duclos," Perdita whispered. Solana shook her head.

"Duclos will not understand this," Euphrosine said. Perdita was surprised the old woman had heard her. "If I were not needed here," Euphrosine continued, "I would not stay. I would leave it all to the doctors. But, you have come, girl, as others have come, and for the same reason."

"My friend is distraught," Perdita said. "I am sure your poultices and salves are of benefit, great benefit, but my friend needs…what she believes is impossible. It is *impossible*," Perdita insisted. "She has never been with a man, I am certain of it. She needs a medical examination, not folk remedies!"

"Her woes, her fears, are not all in her mind, her imagination, and you give her little credit for thinking so." Euphrosine puffed at her pipe. "You will know this for yourself soon. I would have prevented this curse on her and countless others if I could, but to have done so would cost me my life. I can help her now, though. It was best for her to come to me, as it will be for you. You have faith, still, as do many, yet no belief. What is faith without belief? If you have faith that you have been redeemed, saved in a miraculous way, how is it that you cannot believe in the forces of *L'adversaire* that would steal that redemption, whether by design or by accident? Is not conflict in every aspect of life and nature, of heaven and earth?"

"This has nothing to do with *L'adversaire!*" Perdita exclaimed. "It is…the climate of guilt in which she has been raised. She thinks her calamity is of her own doing!"

"Yes, I am betrayed by my weakness," Solana sobbed.

"No!" Euphrosine said firmly. "You will not believe me when I say it, but this is not because of weakness. You absolve the malefactor by thinking so."

"Do you have what I have come for?" Solana asked.

"Yes," Euphrosine said, retrieving a yellow cloth parcel tied with twine from the hearth. "Here is the art of Galen: mug wort, aristolochium, and colocynth. There are also instructions for their use."

"Will they work?"

"Usually, but not always. In a week's time, you will know."

"If they do not work—"

"Come back."

"What do I owe you for this?"

"Have you anything with which to pay me?"

"Only two dollars. And my grandmother's rosary."

"Pay me nothing. Come back in seven or eight days, and let me look at you again."

19

Letter from Moira Keane Parnell to Perdita Badon-Reed

Moira Keane Parnell
14 Newgrange Circle
Boston, Massachusetts
September 17, 1882

My dear Perdita,

We continue to see signs the autumn is close upon us. The days are becoming shorter, or so it seems to me, and there is a touch more chill in the evening air. Your parents are well, though they have had to let their girl Bridget go. The poor thing just could not be taught. She ruined one too many roasts of beef, and she broke a kitchen canister, leaving your mother with an incomplete set, and the final straw came last Sunday as she was helping to serve dinner. She stumbled into the large Chinese vase that stood next to the silver cupboard, knocking it from its base. What a crash it made! We found shards as far away as the front parlor fireplace. I stopped counting the pieces at two hundred. Poor Bridget. She was sacked on the spot. She wept pitifully for twenty minutes. I know she has sisters and a mother back in Galway whom she was supporting. I may have an idea or two of new situations for her, though I must admit to some reservations about recommending her to anyone.

I look in on your parents at least once a week. I am certain your mother means to write to you sometime soon. She has followed your adventures with growing interest, and the concern in her face when I related the story of the steamboat rescue and our near loss of you was genuine and of some duration. But I think she has many emotions and thoughts to reconcile before she may put pen to paper. Your father, of course, remains inscrutable. Always taciturn, he is more so now. He may not have five words to say during one of my visits. Whether he is this way with everyone, I cannot say. Perhaps it is just me. As you know, I have never felt that he particularly likes me. But many people, I am told, carry that impression home from his parlor.

How does your *Beatrice Cenci* progress? Have you finished *Moby Dick*? I am anxious to discuss this with you. I am so sad to read of the continuing difficulties of your Sister Solana. Has she seen a doctor yet? Has she determined the reason for her unsettled digestion and insomnia?

I had a letter from Prosper the day before yesterday. He will be leaving the sanatorium tomorrow, if his recovery has progressed as expected. He says he never received an answer from you to his letter—did you receive it? His brother Michel was able to stay with him for three or four days during his convalescence. Michel had come and gone several times as his business had allowed, to be with his brother at Marseilles. (Michel is now a banker at Carcassonne, if I failed to mention it before. His opportunity was such that he elected to leave his position at Toulouse, and explore a new situation a few months ago.) And I am sorry to report that Michel has brought more sad news with him on his most recent visit. The troubles of the Redon family are not yet at an end. Prosper's father has suffered a stroke. Michel had been reporting their father had all but abandoned sleep and rest. He had lost much weight, as his appetite had dwindled to nothing since the spring. Four days ago, Mrs. Redon discovered him insensible on the floor of the conservatory, with his tongue nearly bitten through in the fall he had taken, apparently. The doctors fear he may never regain the use of his right hand and leg, and they anticipate a permanent paralysis on the right side of his face. He is still in a hospital at Toulouse, of course, and his condition has only worsened. They have a great difficulty in feeding him, as you may have imagined, and there is some debate as to whether the old gentleman's condition is due solely to his physical infirmity, or whether his state is not at least partially compounded by a lack of *desire* to recover, by his recent melancholia.

Prosper's mother's health is suffering now, too although she has greater religious faith than her husband and has always been a more active person with her hobbies and charity work. Prosper also mentioned that Mr. Guibord, Claire's husband, has been completely cleared by the police in the crime. You remember he was out of the country at the time of Claire's death, but was still suspected by the prefect of perhaps having structured a conspiracy to have his wife killed in his absence, giving him an unassailable alibi. I would as soon suspect the prefect himself of killing the poor woman as Mr. Guibord, judging from the stories of his many kindnesses to the family as told by Prosper and related in Michel's letters. I'll be sunk if the police do not invent artificial webs of accusation and implication to incite confessions from the innocent when they are against a stone wall in an investigation. And they appear to be against a wall in this one.

Michel has said that police records show a precedent for murders like Claire's in that part of the country, but oddly they seem to come in cycles of some fifteen or twenty years. The records only go back a decade or two into the previous century. Before that time, the accounts are more anecdotal, except in a case or two in which a vagabond or hapless village idiot were brought up on charges which were, in all but one case, dropped. There was one sad incident in the 1740s in which a feckless half-wit named Gaston deVian was lynched by a mob in a place called Montsegur following the murder of a young governess under circumstances very similar to Claire's. The poor man was almost certainly innocent, because it had been a sexual assault and deVian was physically incapable of such an attack, if you follow my meaning.

As a lawyer familiar with the investigation of crimes, Prosper has been promised an interview with Mr. Vautrollier, the commissary of police for the area, to discuss the facts of the case and the progress of the investigation so far.

This brings you up to the mark on your parents and Prosper. Of myself there is little to say. I went to a lecture at Hesperus Hall two nights ago with Miss Principia Stoddard. You remember her from our charitable work and our efforts at aid during the Charles ferry disaster? The lecture was given by Professor McKay who, as you know, has written such interesting monographs on Brunelleschi and Leonardo. His subject was "The Golden Mean," and I'll be sunk if Principia did not expect the talk to consist of advice on investments! Such is the quality of my society since you have been gone.

Yours,
Moira

20

Hypolitte spun his empty tea cup nervously between his hands on the tabletop. Perdita allowed him his discomfort for many minutes. She drained her wine glass and signaled to the waiter for another.

"Thank you for agreeing to lunch with me, Miss Ba-…Perdita," Hypolitte said at last.

"I could at least do that much. But I find myself in a difficult position. A man whose friendship I value first saves my life, and then moments later forces his affections upon me." Perdita's tone seemed to affect more sternness than it actually carried. "You have shown me much friendship and courtesy since I have been here. With the business about Marie and the *Julia Cerre*, we have been thrown together, and have worked well, in harmony, I think."

"Yes, we have."

"In spite of what it pains me to call your effrontery, I do not think you to be a rash and certainly not a boorish man."

"I would hope not." Hypolitte smiled. "I apologize."

"And I gladly accept your apology, with the understanding that I am not in Ste. Odile seeking a romantic attachment. It is not my wish to hurt or offend, and different circumstances might have produced a different result, but this period of my life must be devoted to my purpose, my work." She sipped from her fresh glass of wine. "It seems everything has conspired to keep me from my purpose since I have been here. I cannot take the time to be involved—"

"I understand." Hypolitte cut her off delicately. "I will not do anything so rash again. I won't try your patience by attempting to explain why it happened. I was caught up in the moment, overwrought with excitement, and so admiring of your work with the victims, that—" He went silent.

"No further explanation is necessary, Hypolitte. I think we may set the matter aside and not mention it again."

"Very well. Thank you." He shifted uncomfortably on his chair. Perdita drained her wine glass.

"He never fills it up enough," she complained, signaling to the waiter.

"Did you see Sister Solana this morning?"

"Yes, she was terribly sick. She vomited twice while I was there. She needs to be taken away from here." The waiter refilled her glass and she drank deeply from it. "We need to put her on a packet and take her to St. Louis."

"Has Dr. Duclos seen her?"

"Yes. He examined her superficially. Mother Superior had to insist upon it. Of course the other sisters are greatly affected by all of this. And Mother Superior, Sister Clotilde, has been very patient and kind toward Solana, and has tried to discourage my friend's delusion that her imagined sinfulness is the cause of all of her suffering. The doctor told me in confidence he thinks she is having a false pregnancy brought on by hysteria and exhaustion. She is so deprived of sleep that the doctor's sleeping draughts will work on her now, but she will only sleep in the daytime while someone sits with her. I sat with her for five hours yesterday."

"Did she rest?"

"But barely. She rolled about fitfully, mumbled things about death by fire and assault, carnal assault, and woke up screaming twice."

"Who is with her now?"

"Sister Patrice."

"She is very reliable. Solana is in good hands, then."

"Yes, I trust Sister Patrice."

"In that case, I wanted to take you on a small excursion, if you are agreeable."

"Excursion? To where?"

"A surprise destination. One you had some reservations about seeing before, if I remember correctly, but one you will be glad to have visited, once you are there, I think. Will you come? My trap is outside."

"Hmmm. Should I trust you, I wonder?" Perdita said with mock concern. "I suppose you are harmless, as you have told me. How could I refuse?"

Some quarter mile north of the landing, Bosphorus Street turned from a well-maintained cobblestone thoroughfare to a dirt road. The scrub, stunted trees that typified the forests surrounding Ste. Odile to the west and north soon gave way to giant sycamores and oaks. At the foot of the high bluffs, Constantinople Street merged with Bosphorus and became one rutted, dusty lane.

The day was breezy and cool once again, and cloudy enough that Perdita did not bother to open her parasol to keep the sun at bay. Perdita noticed that Hypolitte was skillfully steering the mare pulling the trap to avoid most of the ruts in the road.

"Look there," Hypolitte nodded toward the tops of the bluffs. "There is Bastide's house. There is Jardin Noir."

Perdita followed his gaze to the summit. She could see what appeared to be a tower, or high wall with an oriel window, abutted by an archway that appeared to be of Romanesque design. "I can't see much," she said. "Looks like a mixture of architecture."

"Yes. It was built and added onto over nearly two hundred years by Bastide's family."

"Why is it called Jardin Noir?"

"The Black Garden? As I understand it, there has always been an abundance of black oak, black cherry, and black walnut trees, and many flowering plants with darker-hued blossoms. And I am told there is deadly nightshade."

"Belladonna?"

"Yes, *also* known as black cherry. It was cultivated there in the early days as a medicine. Thus the name, Jardin Noir."

Just below the mansion, the bluff jutted to an outcropping that overhung the road in a half arch and created a sheer drop from the top of the bluff to the river, some three hundred feet below.

"The village was founded here in 1689," Hypolitte said, "by de Castres, a Father Moussat and Mr. Bastide's ancestor. The region was part of a land grant given by Louis XIV, but the spot was chosen by de Castres, who was said to be a heretic searching for a remote but accessible spot to settle, to avoid possible persecution."

"And he had a priest with him?"

"Yes. Moussat was a Jesuit, a radical, but there is some doubt he knew of his companion's heresy. But we know Bastide knew. He turned out to be a heretic, too."

"Of what stripe?"

"A Cathar."

"Cathar?" Perdita recognized the word. "Solana mentioned the Cathars. She said she dreams of them. How odd! But I thought they were annihilated in the Middle Ages."

"For the most part. Pockets survived, apparently, in Languedoc and Spain, but disappeared from the notice of society and the church. Bastide, de Castres, and Moussat headed a mixed company of twenty-four Frenchmen and Michigamea Indians. They departed from Quebec under the patronage of Frontenac and Talon, the governor and intendant of Canada. They arrived here in September and built a stockade. Within a month, they were being intermittently raided by bands of Fox and Sioux. Before their defenses could be repaired and reinforced, they were attacked by a party of Osage. Moussat and de Castres were killed, tortured to death, as were most of the party. Bastide survived with only minor injuries. A young Mr. Renault also survived, the son of an iron founder in Paris, who had come to look for metals to mine. They made their way back to Quebec, and ten years later, with a newly issued grant in hand, established the permanent settlement. Renault knew there was an abundance of lead to be found here. He and Bastide recognized that this was where their fortunes would be made."

"They were right, apparently."

"It was in the late summer of 1699 that the first stone was laid at Jardin Noir."

"What happened to Renault?"

"He disappeared after a year or so, leaving Bastide and his heirs as sole owners of the mining operations that developed, as well as salt and lime production."

"How do you come to know all of this?"

"As you know, I spend my time as I like. The company has a large library, and archives."

Beyond the stone overhang, the road was shaded within an arch of tall trees.

"This is the second time in a week that I have been taken on a mysterious tour of the area," Perdita said.

"Oh?"

"Yes. I went with Solana a few days ago to see Euphrosine in the salt marsh. Oh." She stopped herself. "I suppose she would rather I hadn't told you that. I shouldn't drink wine in the early afternoon."

"Well, I know she didn't go there for the usual reason, for Galen's Sisters. She *didn't* go for Galen's Sisters?"

"What?"

"Abortive herbs. Young women go there looking

for abortive herbs, as I understand."

"Yes, that's it. You know about those?"

"I know it is a secret tradition hereabouts, as Aubuchon says. Solana? It is the most absurd thing I have ever heard. She somehow believes she is pregnant, then? By some arcane miracle?"

"Yes. But you must not let on to her that you know."

"Of course not. I have heard about those herbs. They are a secret that everybody knows."

"Well, it seems the herbs didn't work. She feels her condition is unchanged."

"I hope Duclos can get her to St. Louis."

"So do I." Perdita looked up at the thinning clouds above them and down at the dust covered weeds along the road. "So tell me: where are we going?"

"Are you familiar with the work of Polydorus of Rhodes?"

"Yes, certainly. He was one of three sculptors of ancient Greece to carve the magnificent *Laocoon* group now at the Vatican. Laocoon was the priest who warned the Trojans against accepting the gift of the Trojan horse. He and his sons were killed by serpents sent by the gods to silence them. The statue influenced Bernini and others."

"Very astute, Miss Badon-Reed. Very informative. Would you believe me if I were to tell you that you can see an example of Polydorus's work not a mile from where you sit at this moment? Right here in this backwater of a village?"

Perdita was speechless for a moment. "Here?"

"Yes. It is the infant Hercules killing the snakes sent by the goddess to kill him, to be exact. Bastide is a great one for cataloguing his possessions. I came across it on a list, also in the company archives, two days ago."

"Polydorus of Rhodes!" Perdita marveled. "But where is the statue?"

"In drift four. Remember the old shaft I told you about and the played-out drifts where Bastide stores his treasures?"

"It is underground? I don't know that I can go underground," Perdita said ruefully.

"I know you are fearful of enclosed places, but I thought you might be willing to test yourself for the opportunity to see a statue that might deserve a place in one of the great museums of Europe."

"Well, yes." The worry in her voice was apparent. "I would not be able to resist, I know. I mean, I would scarcely be able to contain myself, knowing that the statue is here, regardless of *where* it is. I *have* to see it!"

Hypolitte smiled. "It's worth the attempt. We will see how you do." The bluffs fell away suddenly into a natural limestone basin. Hypolitte turned the mare onto a gravel-covered road that was surprisingly well maintained. As the forest dwindled to scrub growth and a sloping glade, Perdita could see a skeletal framework of iron and timber jutting above the tree line ahead of them.

"That is the headframe,"Hypolitte said. "Inadequate for today's needs, but it serves its current purpose quite well."

Perdita nodded and smiled weakly. She realized that she was clutching her seat tightly. She wished she had been able to have one more glass of wine at the café. At the edge of the glade was an iron gate which was standing open. The headframe, which appeared to be about forty-feet high, towered over several brick and clapboard buildings, including a low barn with an attached pen, where five or six mules could be seen grazing. As the trap approached the headframe, a boy ran out of the barn to meet them. They stopped under the headframe and the boy grasped the mare's bridle.

"Good afternoon, François," Hypolitte said.

"Good afternoon, Mr. Robert," the boy said respectfully. "Mr. Behr said you were coming, so everything is ready."

"Is there a team hitched to the cage?"

"Yes, sir. I just did that. You can go down now."

Hypolitte jumped out of the trap and came around to Perdita's side to help her down. She looked pale.

"Will you be all right?" he asked.

"I don't know. How far down do we have to go?"

"It is less than eighty feet down."

"Oh."

Hypolitte took her arm and started to lead her toward the headframe. "We will get into the cage," he said in a reassuring tone, "and Mr. Behr's team of mules will lower us. That's the old way of doing it. We have steam engines in the active shafts now."

"How will Mr. Behr know when we want to come up? How can we contact him from eighty feet down?"

"I will throw a switch at the bottom of the shaft telling him we are ready."

"What if he should leave the area? Will he stay near the switch?"

"Yes, he will. If you are too uneasy about this, we could postpone . . ."

"No, I will never forgive myself if I let these silly fears spoil such an opportunity."

"Very well. Here is Mr. Behr now."

A short, sinewy man with a broad smile approached them. Beyond him, Perdita could see two large mules hitched to a series of ropes which she followed back over her head to a confluence of pulleys suspended from a wood and iron framework behind her. The ropes hung from the pulleys and attached to the top of a wooden cage some four feet square and seven feet high, which was visible within a clapboard shack that sheltered it.

"Mr. Robert!" Behr beamed and held out his hand. Hypolitte took it.

"This is Miss Badon-Reed," Hypolitte said. Behr doffed his straw hat and nodded to Perdita.

"Miss," he said. "So you are going to see our treasures?"

"So I am told. It is a pleasure to meet you, Mr. Behr."

"I have heard a deal about you, Miss," Behr said, "that the ladies honored you for your work in the rescue, and saving that infant like you did."

Perdita blushed a little. "Thank you. Who told you this, if I might ask?"

"It's common knowledge by now, but most of it came from Mr. Robert, here. He is the one. Sings your praises to the sky!" Behr laughed as Hypolitte reddened, too.

Perdita glanced suspiciously at the mules.

"Are two mules enough to lower us?" she asked. Behr laughed again.

"Don't think I would shortchange you on mules, do you?" he said. "Two are more than enough. Mule is about the strongest four-legged creature you ever seen, Miss. One alone can haul two-ton ore cars underground for twelve hour a day. I give you two so's you'd feel more safer."

"Oh." Perdita smiled. "Well, thank you."

"I suppose we are ready," Hypolitte said. He took Perdita's arm and led her back toward the cage. He opened the cage door and stepped in first. She followed him tentatively. Hypolitte closed the door and latched it.

"All right, then," Behr said, releasing an iron safety clutch that held the suspended ropes immobile. "You'll be on your way in a minute. Throw the switch when you are finished. I'll be right here."

Within a few seconds, the cage started to descend. Cool air immediately began to engulf Perdita, and she found the change of temperature somewhat comforting.

"He tries to lower the cage at a rate of about a foot every three seconds or so," Hypolitte said. "Is it slow enough for you?"

"Yes," Perdita said, a little nervously. "I am sure I will be fine. That boy, François, who hitched the mules, does he know what he's about? Does Mr. Behr check after him?"

"He has hitched the team a thousand times, I am sure."

"Will there be lights burning below?"

"Yes. There are Davey's lamps on the walls. Behr has already lighted the ones we need."

After a few minutes' smooth descent, the cage settled lightly on a wooden platform at the bottom of the shaft. Hypolitte unlatched and swung open the cage door. Perdita stepped out ahead of him and off the platform onto a neat wooden walkway that followed the tunnels to the left in the dim illumination of the Davey's lamps, and to the right into utter darkness. Hypolitte stepped down from the platform.

"Do you wish to proceed?" he asked.

Perdita looked up the shaft at the dim daylight filtering down from eighty feet above. Then she looked at the rough limestone walls surrounding them, and then down the lighted tunnel. "Yes, I do," she said at last.

Hypolitte preceded her on the wooden walkway into the lighted tunnel. "These planks are laid over the tracks that used to carry the ore cars," he said. "We can remove these and still use a car to transport heavy statues and such, if need be."

Perdita nodded. She found that she was wringing her hands. "How far is it?" she asked.

"Just a few hundred feet."

Perdita focused her attention down on the walkway, watching her own feet stepping on the oak planks.

"I know you are feeling uneasy," Hypolitte said. "But I am certain that once you get to the drift and see all we have to show you, you will forget your fears and be glad you have come."

"Yes," Perdita said nervously, never looking up from the walkway, "I have had few chances to see Classical sculpture and none to see anything by such like as Polydorus. A rarity, to be sure. I would never rest knowing the statue is here if I missed the chance to see it because of ...because of —"

"I admire your determination. We are not far now, and the area is very well lighted, if that helps you."

"Yes, it will." Peripherally, Perdita could see a dark hole open in the wall to her right, but she kept her gaze downwards.

"That is drift one," Hypolitte said, "and drift two is here, opposite. And just ahead—here we are, drifts three and four."

Perdita raised her eyes to see the tunnel fork ahead of them into two smaller drift tunnels. A network of oil soaked beams festooned with burning lamps supported the entrance to the drifts.

"They have started to reinforce this," Hypolitte said, slapping a single warped beam that supported the ceiling on the right-hand side of the passageway that led to drift four. The beam was buttressed by a framework of new, much smaller beams that extended across the ceiling and connected to a small beam that supported the left-hand side of the structure. "Hmmm, this won't hold," Hypolitte said, examining the construction. "Must be temporary. These beams are pine and not nearly thick enough, and very dry. I'll have to talk to the engineer about this."

Perdita looked skittishly at the framework as Hypolitte examined it. After a moment, she looked beyond him, further into the drift. Some thirty feet along she could see an iron grate with a heavy, padlocked gate. Beyond the gate was the portion of the drift that served as the storage chamber, brightly illuminated with dozens of Davey's lamps. Perdita's gaze was soon transfixed by what she could see on shelves and tables within the chamber. There were bronze satyrs and nymphs, gilt candlesticks, heavily framed Restoration-era English and Dutch portraits, carved limestone saints, and numerous marbles of Roman statesmen and Greek gods. Perdita walked toward the gate speechlessly. As she walked, her eyes fixed on the art objects, she felt her foot strike a barrier in the floor, nearly tripping her.

"Oh, be careful!" Hypolitte said, steadying her. "It's an iron staple set in the floor as an anchor in the old days." He withdrew a tarnished key from his vest pocket and unlocked the padlock. The gate sagged precariously as Hypolitte opened it, and Perdita thought it might fall out of its framework. Hypolitte blocked the gate open with one of the new beams left on the tunnel floor by the workmen, then stood aside and smiled at Perdita.

"Please," he said, waving her into the chamber. She entered slowly, looking from left to right to left again.

"It is all so wonderful," she said reverently.

Hypolitte thought he could see her eyes moistening.

"I can scarcely believe that one man can own such treasures," Perdita went on, "and that they exist in this small town, in this out-of-the-way place."

Hypolitte started to speak, but did not.

"Solana must see this," Perdita continued. "She *must*! Once she is recovered, we must—"

"I have already talked with Mr. Morisot. Whenever she is well and has Sister Clotilde's permission."

"Oh yes. Yes. She has described beautiful things to me in Bastide's house, but nothing like this. This must be where he keeps his greatest treasures!" Perdita stepped past tables laden with objects, passing her hand over silver salt cellars, Roman votive figures, and Baroque crucifixes and monstrances as she went. "To own these things," she said, "to own so many wonderful things, that you cannot keep them all around you, that you have to store them in a tunnel rather than display them so the world may enjoy them, is just incomprehensible to me. Bastide should build a museum, in St. Louis, perhaps. It would rival anything in New York or Boston."

"Morisot has advised that," Hypolitte said. "So did I, in a letter I wrote to him last year."

"And what was his response?"

"I don't know what his response was to Morisot. I don't know if he ever received my letter. I sent it to his residence in France, at Montsegur. That was his fourteenth year there, away from Ste. Odile. I received no response then, or since he has been back."

"Perhaps he is developing a philanthropic bent," Perdita said. "Solana told me he is donating many of his old books and manuscripts to a Jesuit library in St. Louis."

"Yes. Perhaps these things will see the light of day yet. Look here." Hypolitte pulled a linen cloth off a large object sitting on the plank floor, away from the tables. Beneath was a considerably larger-than-life-size marble of the infant Hercules strangling two huge and truculent snakes. The bodies of the serpents entangled with each other and coiled fantastically around the infant's chubby arms and legs. The highly polished surface of the statue nearly glowed in a blue-gray patina, highlighted here and there with age stains in shades of yellow or brown which had ingrained themselves into the details of the form over the course of nearly two and a half millennia. Even though the statue was more than half of Perdita's height, she knelt down to see it better. She began to run her hands over the voluptuous stone.

"Polydorus of Rhodes," she said reverently.

"And it was found on Rhodes," Hypolitte said, "about a century ago. Workmen were clearing away debris after a fire caused by an earthquake when they found it. The German consul bought it, and it resided in his baronial home near Nuremberg until twenty years ago when the family fell upon hard times and Bastide bought it."

"To think one man can own something like this!" Perdita repeated. She looked around her. "All of this."

"At least it has been safe for the last twenty years," Hypolitte said. "I look at it that way. Does anyone really *own* these objects? Or do people merely pay for the privilege to safeguard them for a small part of their long lives?"

"Yes," Perdita said quietly, "but one also buys the right to do with them what one wishes: to destroy them, or hide them away from the enjoyment of the rest of the world." Perdita was smiling, though her eyes were still glistening with tears. At length she spoke again: "Yes, Hypolitte, Solana should see this."

The day had become cloudy during the hour that Perdita and Hypolitte had spent underground, and now rain clouds were heading toward them from the west. "If we are lucky, we will get back to town before the rain comes," Hypolitte said as he guided the mare south onto the dirt road again. Perdita felt relaxed and a little tired after the stimulation of the afternoon. She thought the rocking of the trap on the ruts of the road might even put her to sleep if she'd had any means to rest her head. After a few drowsy moments, she roused herself.

"Thank you for thinking of me, for sharing all of this with me today." She glanced briefly at Hypolitte.

"I am glad you enjoyed it." Hypolitte sounded awkward and a bit insipid.

"It was overwhelming. It has exhausted me."

Within a few moments, the trap had reached the rock overhang in the road. Perdita had not spoken for many minutes. Her thoughts were far away, on Rhodes and in Alexandria and Byzantium, when she realized Hypolitte was slowing the trap. He stopped directly under the stone overhang. She became aware of voices down the slope of the riverbank that dropped off nearly perpendicularly, to their left.

"What is it?" she asked groggily.

"Some skiff men down there. It looks like they've found something in the river. A body."

"Oh no."

Hypolitte tied off the reins and climbed out of the trap. Perdita followed him.

"Hello," Hypolitte called to two men, who were wading out of the water between their bobbing skiffs. They were pulling a drab, sodden figure into the bank behind them. As Perdita stumbled down the wet slope, losing her footing every few steps, she kept her eyes fixed upon the drowned victim, fixed in disbelief and dread recognition. She recognized a faded blue dress that was some fifteen years out of date. Perdita began to gasp for breath as she fell backwards onto the ground and knew it would be many minutes before she would be able to stand again.

"Oh my God," she sobbed. "It's Solana!"

21

Doctor Duclos had decided to keep Perdita sedated for the better part of two days. She slept fitfully in her sweltering room, Mrs. Zell checking in on her every few hours. Uncle Tancred and Mrs. Moon sat with her through the first afternoon and night. Mrs. Moon left mid-morning of the second day to take care of some responsibilities left undone at the rectory. By mid-afternoon, Perdita was conscious but weak. Uncle Tancred left her to the attentions of Hypolitte, who, under the circumstances, had been given permission by Mrs. Zell to sit at Perdita's bedside.

"Would you like some water or lemonade," Hypolitte asked, "or better yet, some food? Mrs. Zell has left some broth here, and a peach."

"Thank you," Perdita said weakly. "I don't want anything. What day is it?"

"It is Wednesday. Father Condell has just left to finish his sermon. How do you feel?"

"Sick. Hot. Very weak."

"I think the rest did you some good, but you are bound to be unsteady for a while. Don't try to get up for a few minutes."

"Solana is dead. Really dead?"

"Yes."

"Has her family been contacted?"

"Yes. A wire was sent."

"Will she be buried here? On the convent grounds?"

"No." Hypolitte shook his head. "Her family must take her home."

"Why?"

"It was a suicide." Hypolitte touched Perdita's hand as he said it. Her eyes filled with tears, but she said nothing. "As we feared," Hypolitte continued. "She left a note for you. Aubuchon has it, but he allowed me to copy it out for you." Hypolitte retrieved a folded paper from his vest pocket and handed it to her. "I've spoken to Duclos and the coroner. The fall broke her back and she drowned. She jumped from the bluff at Jardin Noir."

Perdita drew a handkerchief from the sleeve of her nightgown and held it to her eyes for many minutes. At length she composed herself enough to open the letter. She read:

> My dearest friend and sister, Perdita,
>
> My weakness and frailty have been my undoing. I feel God no longer wants me in His presence, for He has forgotten me. Euphrosine's cures have failed, and I have no other recourse. At this moment, I feel I could face an eternity of damnation, but not the next few months. Thus, I have done what I have done. Thank you for your friendship. Forgive me. Pray for me.
>
> Yours, S.

"She was little more than a girl," Perdita said tearfully. "How could she have thought herself pregnant? I know it was impossible."

"Completely." Hypolitte nodded.

"I failed her in some way. She was so full of life when I came here. She changed so much, and so quickly."

"You didn't fail her. No, you were her steadfast friend. I think perhaps no amount of condolence can save some who are lost to melancholy and mania. I think, for the most part, their fates are inevitable. But, like you, I would have never thought of her as such a person until recently."

"That is a rather Calvinistic sentiment, coming from you."

"I am not talking about God's will, but about her medical, temperamental, or even phrenological makeup, if you want to call it that."

"No." Perdita looked out of her window, held open by a stick Mrs. Zell had jammed under the sash. "No. It was religion. She was raised to think of herself as innately a sinner, somehow loved by God, yet disgusting to Him. She thought her most natural impulses to be shameful and wrong."Perdita looked at Hypolitte as though a revelation had just struck her. "You spoke of mania a moment ago. Mania. She must have had some sort of mental disease all along, or at least a tendency for one, even when she seemed so vivacious and happy. The idea of sinfulness has always been hidden in her soul. With the condemnation and death of Marie, this tendency, by degrees, became a preoccupation, a dread fear. Then she became a victim of her suggestive nature."

"Yes, I suppose you are right."

"Everyone has nightmares. I told her of Marie's and, in some way, she connected these to Bastide and to—how would she say it?—to the unwelcome knowledge of his allure. Add to this her sensual nature, which was at odds with her piety and vocation. This gave her, I think, a self-loathing that was abetted, if not created, by religion."

"Yes, I am sure you are right. What other explanation can there be?"

"None. Yet where would she have been—where would I be—without faith? It is...a paradox." Perdita thought for a moment, and as she considered expanding upon her hypothesis, there was a gentle knock upon the door. "Yes?" Perdita said. Mrs. Zell opened the door and stepped in.

"How are you *feeling*, Miss Perdita?" Mrs. Zell asked.

"Still weak, but better, thank you."

"I see you haven't *eaten* anything. Still no appetite? Perhaps you would be more *comfortable* out on the veranda. It is actually cooler *outside* now, than inside."

"I think there is rain coming," Hypolitte said. "It will be October soon. How much longer can the heat last?"

"Yes," Mrs. Zell said.

Perdita thought she sensed some disapproval in Mrs. Zell's manner, and wondered if she thought it no longer appropriate for Hypolitte to continue to sit in Perdita's room.

Mrs. Zell continued: "Sister Clotilde sent a boy to ask if you might be back in class by Friday."

"Yes, I think I will be able to go back Friday. I will send Sister a note. And I *would* like to try the veranda."

Hypolitte retrieved a Japanese robe from the foot of the bed and handed it to Perdita. He then rose and stepped out into the hallway.

"Mrs. Morisot is in the *parlor*," Mrs. Zell said, as she helped Perdita to put on the robe. "She is concerned for your *well being*."

"*Is* she?" Perdita seemed genuinely puzzled.

"Yes, of course."

"Oh, well, that is very kind of her."

"She would have come up to see you, but she doesn't manage *stairs* very well anymore. She will join you on the veranda for a few moments, if you have no *objections*?"

"Certainly not."

Troubled by the heat, Mrs. Morisot had already moved out onto the veranda, and Perdita, steadied by Hypolitte down the stairs and out the front door, found her seated on a large, wicker-work chair, her two attendant ladies flanking her like porcelain Chinese dogs guarding a doorway.

"Miss Badon-Reed." Mrs. Morisot nodded.

"Very kind of you to inquire after me, ma'am," Perdita said. Hypolitte guided her to the large swing at the end of the veranda. She sat, and Hypolitte sat a respectful distance from her.

"Might we have some lemonade, Mrs. Zell?" Mrs. Morisot asked. "Will you have some lemonade, Miss Badon-Reed?"

"Yes, thank you. Suddenly, it sounds refreshing."

Mrs. Zell disappeared through the front door.

"So, how are you today, if I might ask?" Mrs. Morisot smiled at Perdita.

"Better, thank you. A little stronger. I'm glad to get out of my room, for a change of scene. I felt as though the walls were closing in upon me."

"Does your room not suit your needs?"

"Perfectly well. I have something of an aversion to close and confined spaces. I just needed some fresh air, I think."

"The air is fresh, but not moving much," Hypolitte said. "I wish we could stir up a breeze."

"A breeze would be heavenly," Mrs. Morisot mumbled. She opened an ivory and silk fan suspended from a strap around her thick wrist and began to fan herself. "Such a tragedy about the young sister," she said, "and another friend of yours, too."

"Yes," Hypolitte agreed. "She will be greatly missed."

"Such vivacity, such forthrightness, they say," Mrs. Morisot sniffed. She raised her chin so that the breezes from her fan might reach within the creases of her neck. "And quite a scholar of all types of medieval lore too, if I remember correctly."

"Yes," Perdita said. "All of that is true. I will miss her very much. I miss her terribly."

"Another of your dear friends, as I said. Both gone

in such a short period of time, one upon the other. What you must think of our little village here!"

"It is a portion more melodrama than I would have ever expected, or wanted."

"Yes, just so, poor dear."

Mrs. Zell backed out onto the veranda through the front door carrying a tray with three glasses of lemonade. She offered one to Mrs. Morisot, then one to Perdita, and finally to Hypolitte. Perdita thought it odd and more than a little rude that none was brought for Mrs. Morisot's companions.

"As you know, Miss Badon-Reed," Mrs. Morisot continued, "I am very much concerned with our little village: with its prosperity, with how it is perceived by the greater world beyond the circumscription of the river, the bluffs, and the miles of unattractive scrub forest that surround us." She smiled as though this last statement was meant to be humorous or clever.

"Yes, I remember you saying so on the occasion of our first meeting," Perdita said, slightly puzzled.

"You know, interestingly, the *reason* much of the surrounding forests is stunted is that—" Hypolitte interrupted offhandedly.

"Surely you understand me, Miss?" Mrs. Morisot insisted.

"Understand you, ma'am? I assure you that I do not."

"The young sister's death," Mrs. Morisot continued, "has been such a shock to us all—a suicide too! What temporary discomfort can be worth damnation for eternity? All of this has added such a component of overwrought emotion to our little mix here."

"I assure you, ma'am, that what Solana suffered was a great deal more than discomfort."

"Certainly it was. That was an unfortunate choice

of words."

"She was in despair. She was in the grip of a mania and saw no way out of it. All of her hope was gone."

"These are the situations," Mrs. Morisot commiserated, "that test one's faith. Our faith must be strong enough to get us through."

"I hardly feel worthy to judge the strength of Solana's faith!" Perdita felt herself becoming angry. "You and I have not been tested in such a way as to have the latitude to judge her."

"Just so."

"And what does her death have to do with the town and its fortunes?"

"Prosperity is such a fragile thing, isn't it?" Mrs. Morisot sipped her lemonade. "We have to keep in mind on which side our bread is buttered."

"I am afraid I am not following you, Mrs. Morisot."

Mrs. Morisot handed her lemonade to one of her ladies and, repositioning herself in her chair, she looked Perdita squarely in the eye. "We must be grateful for what we have here," she said, "and remember to whom we owe our prosperity. Most everyone in Ste. Odile does, I think; particularly the true natives, those who can trace their connection to this place back several generations. Rumors always start to fly when something like this happens. My ladies have heard them already. I mean, when you consider *where* the young sister was found, the spot at which she chose to end her life. Coincidence, pure and simple. She merely sought the highest promontory near town."

Perdita furrowed her brow. "I still do not . . ."

"I have heard of a journal," Mrs. Morisot continued, "a journal you were to receive from Marie Chardin. One of Mrs. Moon's daughters is sometimes in my employ, and is a friend of Miss Portia here, and the girl mentioned, quite inadvertently, that there was a journal—the ravings and accusations of a despondent woman, I am sure, which you were to receive from her."

"There was a journal, yes," Perdita said, "a diary. It disappeared. It was stolen. I never got it, and I can't imagine how Mrs. Moon's daughter even knew of it."

"Disappeared?" Mrs. Morisot repeated suspiciously.

"Yes. Sheriff Aubuchon was keeping it to give to the judge."

"Bessier? Why didn't Bessier just take it on the day of the execution?"

"I don't know," Perdita said irritably. "Perhaps he didn't want to come all the way back to town to get it. He went downriver on one of the packets after the execution."

"And how do *you* know the journal disappeared?" Mrs. Morisot asked.

"Well, ma'am, if you must know—"

"I told her," Hypolitte said. "I looked for it myself and couldn't find it. Aubuchon mentioned to me a day or so after Marie's execution that it was gone, stolen, apparently. I didn't mention it to Mrs. Moon, though."

"Do you think Mrs. Moon could have taken it?" Mrs. Morisot continued.

"No," Hypolitte said. "After her visit to Marie on the morning of the execution, I am certain she was never in Aubuchon's office alone before I looked for it myself. Disregarding her lack of opportunity, she is scrupulously honest. I could no more imagine Mrs. Moon stealing anything than I could imagine Father Condell having a leg of lamb for his Friday night dinner."

"Yet her daughter knew of it," Mrs. Morisot said gravely. "People are not always what they seem. Wherever that journal is, it must be found and its contents reviewed."

"But why?" Hypolitte asked.

"Of what concern are the ravings of a despondent woman?" Perdita asked sardonically.

"To be plain, Miss Badon-Reed," Mrs. Morisot said in an admonishing tone, "I think you are a person of great passion, and I think your passion could, in certain circumstances—such as the deaths of your friends—affect your reason and judgment. I feel the journal may contain accusations and assumptions which must be questioned by more dispassionate, level heads, not championed by the bereaved, emotionally distracted compatriots of the dead. You have no history here, no vested interest."

"Why, Mrs. Morisot," Perdita said, exasperated, "do you see me as such a threat?"

"Miss Badon-Reed! Miss Perdita!" A child's voice called from the street. It was Anatolia, accompanied by Sister Patrice, walking briskly toward Tranquille House. Perdita stood, smiling, and seemed to lose her balance slightly. Hypolitte steadied her.

"Anatolia, Sister Patrice," Perdita called. Anatolia began to run toward the veranda. She was carrying a large, folded sheet of paper.

"Don't run, Anatolia," Sister Patrice called after her. "You know you do not look where you are going. You could fall." Patrice attempted a smile for Perdita, but her face was pale and swollen, as though she had been crying minutes before. "I am sorry for this unannounced visit, Perdita," Patrice said. "She made you this drawing, and nothing would do but for her to deliver it."

Anatolia ran up the veranda stairs, her drawing held aloft, and hugged Perdita with such exuberance that she nearly lost her footing again.

"Thank you for visiting me, Anatolia, and thank you for your gift."

"When are you coming back to school, Miss?" Anatolia asked excitedly.

"The day after tomorrow; very soon. I have missed you all. Sister Patrice," Perdita took both of Patrice's hands as she climbed the stairs, "how kind of you to visit."

"I can see you are better," Patrice said. "Thank God for that. Hello, Mrs. Morisot, ladies, Mr. Robert."

"How are you, Sister?" Perdita asked. "You look tired."

"I think we are all exhausted." Patrice's voice was weak. "We have prayed continuously. It is so terrible, so confusing...a *suicide!*"

"Yes," Perdita agreed, "so confusing."

"And we pray," Patrice repeated. "For women in orders, grief must have a limit. Prayer must answer all questions, heal all ills. To give free expression to grief when we have the solace of prayer, would be to—"

"Deny the solace of prayer?" Perdita said, touching Patrice's cheek.

"I brought you this, Miss Perdita," Anatolia interrupted. "I was praying yesterday and I saw these things. I knew I was meant to show them to you."

"I did not ask Mother Superior's permission to come this morning," Patrice said. "I fear she might consider this gift to be blasphemous."

Anatolia offered Perdita the drawing. Perdita smiled and opened it.

The drawing was a riot of color, both chalk and gouache. In the uppermost left-hand corner was a brilliant light with a large hand reaching through it. On the ground below were two angels, arms raised as if in celebration. Between the angels, scattered about, were the tattered remnants of a faded blue dress, and rising through the air toward heaven was a joyous nun, whose round face undeniably represented Solana's. Written along the right side of the ascending figure were the words: "To Heaven, to Heaven, God gladly takes her. The angels rejoice that so much of love and goodness is not forgotten after one sin!"

22

"Now while Macy, the mate, was standing up in his boat's bow, and with all the reckless energy of his tribe was venting his wild exclamations upon the whale,and essaying to get a fair chance for his poised lance, lo! a broad white shadow arose from the sea; by its quick, fanning motion, temporarily taking breath out of the oarsmen. Next instant, the luckless mate, so full of furious life, was smitten bodily into the air, and making a long arc in his descent, fell into the sea at a distance of about fifty yards."

"So full of furious life," Perdita repeated, closing the book, "and in the next instant, dead." She mumbled the words.

"Excuse me?" Hypolitte said, folding his newspaper onto his lap. The afternoon light had grown poor in the front parlor of Tranquille House. Hypolitte had agreed to occupy himself quietly while Perdita rested, after an arduous first day back to class, and she read a little before they went out to walk and have some supper at Herve's.

"How is it, I wonder, that death is always something of a surprise?" Perdita asked, almost rhetorically. "Even when it is expected, but certainly when it isn't. I greet news of death with a degree of sadness, usually. But there is always something more. I have never attempted to categorize it before now, but in thinking about it tonight, I would call it 'surprise.' A whaler arises from his netting in the morning, thinking this is a day like any other, not knowing he will be dead within two hours."

"Ah," Hypolitte said knowingly, "you are taking *Moby Dick* to heart."

"And as someone dies, or struggles not to die," Perdita went on gravely, "others eat their suppers or brush their horses, or sweep their floors in perfect indifference."

"It must be so." Hypolitte suppressed a slight smile, which Perdita did not see. He had grown fond of her occasional philosophizing. "We must have pity and commiseration, certainly, but the world would cease to move forward if humanity fell apart at each small, tragic loss."

"But doesn't the loneliness of it terrify you?"

"No. Well, perhaps sometimes."

"There is so much we must suffer alone in this life, and no amount of commiseration from our fellow creatures, or God Himself, can allay that. Death is one of those things. If two hundred people go down with a ship, that mass of death is comprised of two hundred individual, lonely endings. Uncle's sermon yesterday was on this subject. He referred to Solana and Marie, in a less direct way. He said he thinks death is a gift from God. He said our knowledge of it drives us to achievement, to accomplishment. Without that knowledge, that fearful presence looming before us, we would languish in idleness and dissipation."

"I think that is true."

"But how can Solana's death, or Marie's, be a gift?"

"Of course, they can't be."

"No."

"But your uncle's basic idea is true, I think. Why achieve anything unless we see some boundary, or limit to our opportunity to do so? *Et In Arcadia Ego*. It is a vital fact, an irreplaceable knowledge."

"Perhaps," Perdita conceded. "I was sitting on Moira's sofa having just heard of the death of my fiancee's sister, when, for some reason it struck me that I was hard upon my middle age. I felt panic at having accomplished nothing significant by this point in my life, having not had the confidence in myself to pursue any real and serious commissions. Within three days of that moment, I had secured the Havilland Library work, and thus, I am here now and we are having this conversation. Have you never felt that sense of urgency?"

"Yes, I have. It is easy, perhaps even necessary, to distract oneself from these sobering thoughts through hobbies, reading, lectures. Any form of distraction. Even human connections, I am starting to think, fill that need. It may not have to be creative or scientific, or political expression. Maybe the affection, or…love of others gives that same sense of …of—" He stopped for a moment. "Consider someone like me, for example," he went on, "who has no avenue of creative expression as you have. You are fortunate."

Perdita closed her book. "Am I fortunate? I've started to think what a burden it all is."

"Burden?"

"Yes, burden. Are you ready to go? I am feeling hungry suddenly."

"Yes, of course." Hypolitte stood and extended his hand to her. She took it and stood.

"Mrs. Zell!" Perdita called toward the back of the house.

"Yes?"

"I am going out to dinner now."

"Very well. You are *missing* a good vegetable soup tonight."

The evening was cool. Uncharacteristically odorless breezes from the river carried with them the sounds of tree frogs and whippoorwills, invisible in the blackness of the woods and undergrowth, just beyond the weak glimmer of the town's dim and intermittent oil lights that dotted the sidewalks. Rouen Street was all but deserted as Perdita and Hypolitte walked eastward to connect to Bosphorus Street and Herve's.

"It's getting cooler," Hypolitte said after a long silence.

"Yes."

"In December, maybe late November, the ice will come. That spells the death of many of these steamboats."

"I can well imagine."

"Shipping and commerce slows to a crawl, and we'll be lucky to get mail delivery once or twice a week."

"Still," Perdita said dreamily, "it isn't *so* bad being cut off from the world, is it?"

"More than we already are, you mean?"

"Yes."

"No, it isn't terribly difficult. The world barely notices Ste. Odile in fair weather, and we are all but forgotten in winter."

"I came here to be cut off from the world, to absorb myself in work." Perdita smiled.

"I'm glad you did," Hypolitte said awkwardly. He added quickly, "You will finish your work soon, and I have no doubt the world will know your name."

"The world may not count my Havilland Library commission amongst my accomplishments," Perdita said somberly. "I doubt my *Heloise and Abelard* will ever see the light of day. I checked at Vizir this afternoon. Still no response from the man in Tennessee. I have all but given up on ever receiving that block."

In a few minutes' time, Perdita and Hypolitte found themselves at the front step of Herve's. They were greeted in the vestibule of the restaurant by Herve himself, and were shown to Hypolitte's usual table in a corner overlooking the street. Herve, a thin, swarthy man, held Perdita's chair as she sat, and then lighted the candle in the simple brass candlestick in the center of their table.

"A slow night, Herve?" Hypolitte asked, looking around the moderately-sized dining room. There was only one other occupied table out of perhaps twenty.

"It is a little late," Herve said. "We were rather busy two hours ago." He looked at Perdita expectantly.

"I'll have the Bordeaux tonight," she said. "And leave the bottle, if you would." Herve smiled and glanced at Hypolitte, who nodded his approval. "We'll share that," Hypolitte said.

Herve removed two wine glasses from a nearby shelf and placed one in front of Perdita and one in front of Hypolitte. He then nodded in a courtly manner and disappeared into the kitchen.

"Has your appetite returned yet?" Hypolitte asked.

"A little." Perdita glanced down at her slightly threadbare outfit. "My dress has gotten looser on me. I cannot change into a more appropriate one, because it is the only one I have left."

"I have been meaning to mention it to you." Hypolitte furrowed his brow slyly. "If you would allow me, I would like to make a gift to you of a new dress, since your wardrobe has been so depleted. I would have made a surprise of it, but I learned from my mother to make no assumptions about a woman's size in clothes or her taste in them, when giving gifts."

"Oh, no, I couldn't possibly."

"Surely the town owes you one dress, at the very least, considering the circumstances under which the others were ruined and relegated to stone-carving costumes."

"The town, perhaps, but not Hypolitte Robert."

"But I am acting as the town's emissary—"

Herve returned from the kitchen with a bottle of wine. He filled Perdita's glass, then Hypolitte's, then placed the bottle on the table between them and disappeared back into the kitchen. Perdita drained half her glass, and Hypolitte refilled it.

"Well, you could think of it as a peace offering," Hypolitte said, "for my effrontery, as you call it."

"As *I* call it?" Perdita smiled and drank another half glass of wine. This time Hypolitte did not refill it. After a moment Perdita refilled her glass herself. "What would *you* call it?"

"An act of …nature. Ill-advised, yes, but not—"

"It seems the sincerity of your apology is fading away like daffodils in the summer heat."

"No, no, not at all." Hypolitte laughed. He realized that as recently as two weeks before, he would have felt awkward teasing her in this way. "It was sincere, at the time. Most sincere. Painfully sincere."

"Well, as long as it was most and painfully sincere. 'Most' and 'painful' are acceptable. Especially 'painful'." They both laughed.

"I don't think I've ever seen you quite this way before," Hypolitte said. "You seem happy this evening, Perdita. Finally. Even a little frivolous."

"Thank you for being such a pleasant and faithful distraction."

"I am nothing, if not a distraction. A faithful, painful distraction!" They both laughed again. Perdita finished her glass and refilled it.

"You know," she said, "when you said my name just now, it reminded me that Prosper used to call me Perdie. I had forgotten."

"I think I will continue to call you Perdita."

"Yes. I never really liked Perdie. Or Prosper, for that matter!" They both burst into laughter. The laughter seemed to build upon itself for several moments, increasing each time their eyes met.

"No!" Perdita touched her fingers to her lips. She felt a little dizzy. "No. That is not fair. Nor true. I did care for him, in my way. I did. But not enough. Not in the way he wanted."

"I can't blame him for that." Hypolitte seemed embarrassed as soon as he spoke. He took an awkward sip of wine. "You said earlier," he continued, "that your work, your vocation, is a burden. Did you really mean to call it that?"

"Yes," Perdita said quickly. "It is a life sentence of dissatisfaction, of unease. To be satisfied with one's own work is to invite complacency and to die as an artist."

"To die?" Hypolitte seemed a little amused by this, Perdita thought.

"Yes. To be satisfied with one's own work is so… what is the word?"

"Bourgeois?"

"Yes, that is it! Bourgeois. And pedestrian. There is a smugness to it that I hope will never settle upon me."

"You *want* to be dissatisfied?"

"Yes. Once you are satisfied, you lose objectivity, the ability to be self critical. That is the moment I cease to be an artist and become a craftsperson, a maker of decorative *things*."

"I would think the ability to be either would be a great blessing, to spend one's time in some creative or productive way."

"What it is," Perdita said after some thought, "is a responsibility one can scarcely choose to ignore. If one does ignore this responsibility, at the end of one's life there could be the feeling that life has been wasted. On the other hand, if one sacrifices all and devotes one's life to this and fails, isn't that life also wasted?"

"No. At least the effort was made. If you spend your

time that way, if you did the best you could do, what would be the worst you could say about yourself?"

"That I was untalented. That would be the worst realization of all."

Herve re-emerged from the kitchen and seemed to glide to their table side, silently and formally, almost as if he were mimicking himself. He looked at Hypolitte expectantly.

"Have you decided?" Herve asked. Hypolitte looked at Perdita.

"The turtle soup, Herve, as always. I do not feel adventurous tonight," she said.

"Neither do I," Hypolitte said. "I will have the catfish." Herve nodded and withdrew back into the kitchen.

The meal was, as Perdita and Hypolitte expected, competent, palatable, but uninspired. An altogether functional catfish, Hypolitte noted. An exceedingly practical turtle soup, Perdita responded; no unnecessary subtleties or surprises, with no taint of sentiment or disingenuousness. They laughed loud enough to attract Herve's attention and suspicion. Hypolitte compensated by leaving a larger than usual gratuity.

They had intended, after the meal, to have a leisurely walk back to Tranquille House. The breezes of earlier in the evening had picked up intensity and changed direction. They were coming from the west, now, and had the smell of rain in them. Having brought no umbrella, Perdita thought they had best walk at a brisker pace. As they crossed Bosphorus Street, Perdita stumbled a little stepping off of the curb. Hypolitte grasped her arm and steadied her.

"Soon you will be limiting me to one glass of wine on our outings," she said, embarrassed. Hypolitte smiled and said nothing. After a few minutes, he slowed his pace and stopped. Perdita was a few steps beyond him before she realized this.

"No," Hypolitte said, "I don't think I could limit

you to one glass of wine, if you wanted more, or limit you in any other way, at least without much difficulty."

Perdita was puzzled for a moment.

"I wouldn't limit you at all," he continued. "I could not limit or dominate you or restrict you in any way. To do any of that would be to change you, and I can't think of anything that would be more offensive to me than that."

"Hypolitte—?" Perdita was confused.

"I know you've said you want no attachments, and I am trying to respect that. But I have been in this little town for nearly fifteen years, and there has been no one like you here before. Should I ignore the fact you are here now, or act upon it? If I keep a respectful distance and suppress these feelings, let this moment pass, will I ever find your like again?"

Perdita's head was spinning. "Hypolitte, I understand." She put a hand on his shoulder to steady herself. "And I, by no means, want to discourage, completely discourage your feelings. I am…confused, too." She stumbled. "I am not well. Please, I want to get back to my room and off my feet."

"Of course." Hypolitte took her arm again.

On Rouen Street, as they neared Tranquille House, they noticed a young woman approaching them from the opposite direction. It was Mrs. Moon's daughter, Bess. The girl waved when she recognized Perdita.

"Miss Badon-Reed," she called. She quickened her pace toward Perdita and Hypolitte, and closed the distance in a few seconds. "I have messages for you, Miss," she continued.

"Good evening, Bess," Perdita said.

"Good evening, Miss. Father Condell asked me to tell you he will be gone for a few days, or maybe weeks, he isn't sure."

"Oh?"

"Yes, he is leaving for St. Louis tonight."

"Whatever for?"

"I don't know, Miss. Mother says it is very urgent business with the archdiocese. With the archbishop ill, he has arranged to see someone else, some other bishop or monsignor, or someone."

"Do you know what this is about?"

"No, Miss. He has told neither Mother nor I. It is something very serious, though. There have been several telegrams back and forth."

Perdita and Hypolitte looked at each other, puzzled, for a moment.

"Also," Bess continued,"this came for you this evening." Bess handed Perdita a letter written on a single sheet of heavy, expensive paper, folded and sealed in the old-fashioned way, with a wax imprint. "It is from Jardin Noir," Bess went on, "from Mr. Bastide."

23

Mrs. Morisot attempted to compose herself, moving toward her customary chair on the veranda of Tranquille House. Perdita sat calmly on the swing, enjoying the last of her morning coffee. Her head hurt a little; the effect, she had come to recognize, of too much wine the night before.

"Is what Mrs. Zell tells me true?" Mrs. Morisot said, sitting heavily. She adjusted herself to a comfortable position with the help of her attendant ladies.

"Hmmm?"Perdita mumbled. "Excuse me, ma'am?"

"Is it true that you have received an invitation to Jardin Noir?"

"Yes."

"And you have refused it?"

"That is not entirely accurate. I have postponed it."

"Postponed it? For what reason, if I might ask?"

"My mind and my life are very occupied just now. I have just lost my closest friend here. I am curious—I have always been curious—to meet Mr. Bastide, but at this moment in my life, I am distracted and tired, and doubt I would make a favorable impression."

Mrs. Morisot's expression softened. "Oh, I see," she said. "Well, if that is the case, perhaps he will not take offense. You will want to put your best foot forward when you meet him." Mrs. Morisot attempted to adjust her position in her chair. Her ladies moved to assist her, but she waved them away. "Did you respond? Did you notify him?"

"I did," Perdita said. She retrieved the invitation, folded on a wicker table near the swing, and handed it to Mrs. Morisot. Perdita smiled as Mrs. Morisot, as she expected, eagerly took the paper and opened it. "I did respond," Perdita continued, "although as you can see for yourself, he did not require it."

Mrs. Morisot read aloud:

My dear Miss Perdita Badon-Reed,

I am Orien Bastide. How deep must your sorrow be to have lost your dearest friend in Ste. Odile. She spoke of you often, in the most beatified of terms, as she carried out her scholarly services to me most excellently. Long before this tragedy I set myself the agreeable task of making your acquaintance, since Sister spoke of you as an admirable scholar, an uneffacing conversationalist, a promising artist, and a true friend. Any one of these high qualities would be to me an irresistible inducement to warrant self-introduction, but all of them together put this event in the region of inevitability. When your period of grieving is at an end, and you are ready to rejoin kindred and, I hope, engaging society, please send me a message at Jardin Noir so that I may arrange a supper in your honor as a means of making my formal introduction.

With anticipation,
O. Bastide

Mrs. Morisot refolded the paper and dropped it into her lap.

"And you *did* respond, you say?" she said.

"Yes," Perdita nodded. "It is a most gracious invitation, but I told him the time is not right, just yet."

Mrs. Morisot looked perturbed but said nothing for a few moments. She appeared to Perdita to be weighing her words.

Finally she said, "I am certain you will not fail to accept his offer when the time is right. Decorum and good manners demand it, as I am sure you know. I am certain also you know it is a great honor to be noticed in this way. There isn't a personage of greater consequence than Mr. Bastide within three hundred miles of here in any direction."

"I have no doubt of that," Perdita said.

"And please do not doubt this fact, either." Mrs. Morisot stood with some difficulty and help from her attendant ladies. Bastide's letter fell from her lap as she stood, then dropped onto the floor, fluttering near to Perdita's feet. She picked it up. "Our great benefactor," Mrs. Morisot continued, "must receive all deference due to him from any young lady who counts herself among my guests. I can countenance nothing less."

Mrs. Morisot made her way ponderously to the stairs, descended them carefully, with her ladies solicitously in tow, and climbed into her carriage which had been waiting at the curb. Her ladies stepped into the carriage after her.

Perdita refolded Bastide's letter and returned it to the wicker table at her side. She thought it must be about nine o'clock. She was expecting Sister Patrice and Anatolia at any time. Anatolia had another gift for Perdita, and was anxious to deliver it, according to a note written by an unfamiliar hand and sent from the convent earlier that morning.

Perdita finished her coffee. Some of the trees lining the street were just beginning to change color, and the occasionally chilly breezes that had come and gone over the last few hours had blown some of the leaves onto the ground to be scattered and rifled through by squirrels and rabbits that were, according to Hypolitte, in unusual abundance this year.

Soon Perdita could hear Anatolia's excited voice, coming from the direction of Constantinople Street. Perdita stood and glanced up the street and saw Anatolia approaching, carrying a small picnic basket. She was accompanied, not by Sister Patrice, but by a tall, buxom nun whom Perdita had never seen before. When Anatolia saw Perdita, she smiled and ran toward her, nearly dropping the basket twice.

Anatolia ran up the veranda steps and threw her arms around Perdita. Perdita embraced her for a few moments, then gently removed the child's arms from around her waist.

"Anatolia!" she said. "How good of you to come this morning."

The child smiled and embraced Perdita again.

"There is no containing that one when she gets her mind set on something, I've found," the tall nun said as she climbed the stairs. She smiled and extended her hand to Perdita, who took it. "I am Sister Elizabeth," the nun said.

"Good morning," Perdita said. "I expected Sister Patrice. She usually brings Anatolia."

"I only arrived yesterday morning. It must have been God's will, because Sister Patrice left yesterday. God must have intended that I replace her." Her tone was friendly, almost jovial.

"She left?"

"Yes, perhaps for good."

"Was there some emergency that called her away?"

"No. Well, yes, of a sort. We think she means to leave the sisterhood."

"Leave it?" Perdita was baffled.

"Yes." Elizabeth nodded. "Mother Superior is mum, but we hear Patrice had been undergoing some crisis of faith, starting with an execution that happened recently, I have heard. And then the death of Sister Solana—your dear friend, as Anatolia describes her—was the straw that broke the camel's back. I mean, there was talk of the eternal loss of her soul, with it being a suicide, you know."

"I had a dream she would leave," Anatolia said. "She will be happier now."

"So I have stepped into her duties," Elizabeth continued. "Both in the kitchen, and in bringing Anatolia to see you."

"I wish Sister had said goodbye." Perdita gently pulled Anatolia's arms from around her again, and looked down at Anatolia, who was smiling up at her. "If we could turn all of the affection in you lately into steam, we could send a locomotive to Chicago and back, I'll wager!" she said. Anatolia laughed.

"You are the main topic of conversation for this one," Elizabeth said. "You and visions she has. Visions are what you would call them, I suppose. What an imagination. I never quite know what to do with a child like that. Imaginative ones. Especially the imaginative ones."

"Yes," Perdita said. "I guess it is imagination."

"No!" Anatolia protested. "The things I see are real!"

"We made bread this morning," Elizabeth continued, "and nothing would do but to bring you a loaf. Once she fixes her bead on something, there's no shifting it, it seems. A bit headstrong, if you ask me. Headstrong children have me at a disadvantage. Sometimes I think I would have been better off working with the poor or the aged, instead of with the Sisters of Perpetua, but—"

"I made it!" Anatolia exclaimed.

"And we packed butter and peach preserves," Elizabeth said. "And milk and cider, since we didn't know your preference."

"What a wonderful gift!" Perdita stooped and kissed Anatolia on the cheek. "Take it to the stone bench in the back. We'll have it in the grove, if you can stay a while?"

"I *can!*" Anatolia disappeared around the corner of

the house.

"Oh," Elizabeth said. "I really can't stay. I am preparing lunch now back at— "

"I can return her," Perdita said. "Would that be all right?"

"I suppose so," Elizabeth said. Her brows knitted over her eyes. which were deep brown and full of benevolence. "Mother Superior seems to give this child more leeway than she does the others. The imaginative ones need it the least, if you ask me, need more of a routine, more structure. It is better for them. But, our Lord didn't put me in charge of the school, and He knows best."

Perdita extended her hand and Sister Elizabeth took it. "I am glad we have met, and I am certain we will be great friends," she said.

"Oh, yes, I am certain we will." Elizabeth nodded. "From what I hear, we may be cut from the same fabric. Thank you for seeing her back home." She smiled and turned, retracing her steps back toward the school.

Perdita followed a brick-lined gravel path, surrounded on both sides by boxwoods, roses, lilies, and ivy, to the rear of Tranquille House. The path ended at a grassy area overhung by a grove of fruit trees and dogwoods. At the center of this was a weathered stone bench upon which Anatolia was arranging the contents of her basket, spread on a large napkin she was using as her tablecloth.

"So many good things," Perdita said. "Sister had to go back. I will be taking you home."

"I *know*." Anatolia smiled, never looking up.

Perdita sat on the edge of the bench opposite Anatolia. The child had cut several slices of her bread in thick, crooked slices, and placed a small crock of butter and another of peach preserves close to Perdita. She then, with some difficulty, removed the corks from a jug of cider and another of milk that she had placed on the ground in front of the bench.

"Oh dear," Anatolia said. "I forgot to bring beakers to drink from. Could we get something from inside, Miss Perdita?"

"We could drink right from the jugs, I think. None of the Sisters are here to question our manners."

"As long as we don't make a habit of it," Anatolia said seriously. "The milk is fresh this morning, and the cider was just put in the cellar yesterday."

"It should be delicious, then. Everything looks delicious. This is such a wonderful surprise, Anatolia."

"I thought you needed a surprise," Anatolia said earnestly. "I thought you needed someone to do some kind thing, because your heart is heavy." She spread some soft butter on a slice of bread with a dull knife, tearing the bread. "Oh," she frowned, "this one will be mine."

"I can prepare my own, if you like," Perdita said. "So, my heart is heavy?"

"Yes. I can feel it is." Anatolia spoke in the same matter-of-fact way, with no trace of doubt or uncertainty, that Perdita had noted many times before.

"Well, I think you are right, Anatolia. It is very kind of you to notice, and to feel something should be done about it. It says very much to me about the kind of person you are."

"The lady they hanged was your friend, and Sister Solana was your friend. I have only had one friend since I have been here."

"Only one?"

"Her name was Precious and she had a harelip. She had big spots on her skin, too, so the girls didn't like her. But she was nice, and she was my friend. She didn't think I was odd because I see things other people don't see. She did at first think I was odd, I mean, but she believed me and got used to it. She didn't make fun of me."Anatolia carefully spread butter on another slice of bread and gave it to Perdita. Perdita scooped some peach preserves out of the crock with a spoon and spread it on the bread.

"What happened to Precious?" Perdita asked.

Anatolia sat still for a moment. Her eyes filled with tears.

"She died," Anatolia said in a quavering voice. "She got measles and died." Anatolia burst into sobs for a few moments and then stopped abruptly. "I don't think any of the other girls would have come to the funeral if the sisters hadn't made them. Her family didn't want her. Nobody cared but me. It's sad, I think, to die and leave only one person in the whole world who misses you. So I haven't had a friend; I have been alone until you came here." Anatolia looked at Perdita timidly. "Can I say that you are my friend, even though you are my teacher?"

A slight but undeniable sense of discomfort passed through Perdita for which she could not account at first. After a moment she wondered if the short history of her life in Ste. Odile had dissuaded her from actively seeking connections which she would call friendships.

"Of course you can, Anatolia. You know, to be very honest with you, before I came here, I wasn't sure I could ever make a friendship with—"

"A child?" Anatolia interrupted, smiling. She dried her eyes on her sleeves.

"Yes. I was a little uncomfortable with children. Before I met you."

"Because of Precious, I knew how sad you would be that your friends died. That is why I wanted to surprise you and do a nice thing for you."

"But you already made me the picture of Sister Solana. In Heaven."

"Yes. I *needed* to make that picture for you."

Perdita took a bite of her bread. It was coarse and

yeasty, but palatable. "Anatolia," she said, "have you always seen things that others do not see? Have you always had visions?"

"Yes. When I was very little, I saw God in the top of a tall tree."

"You saw God?"

"Yes. My mother told me it must be the sun, but He told me His name, and my grandmother knew it was true. She believed I could see things, because she could too."

"She could?"

"Yes. When I was three, I think, she got a fever. I got the fever too. She died and I lived. That was when the rest of her sight went into me. We shared it, you see? When I die it will go into my daughter or my granddaughter. My grandmother called it her sight. She was the wise woman of her tribe, the Tamaroa. My mother didn't like the old ways, my grandmother's ways. My mother didn't have the sight, and she didn't look very much like an Indian either. I think she said her father was a white man. She didn't talk about him very much. I think my mother did start to believe I had the sight, and she thought it was a bad thing, and people wouldn't want to be around us if I saw things other people didn't see. That is when she left me here. I haven't seen her again."

"Oh," Perdita said sadly. "I am sorry. What about your father?"

"He was born a slave, but freed before the war, in Louisiana, I think. Just before my mother brought me here, he went to New York to find work. He never sent for us. My mother thought he didn't want an Indian wife and a mixed daughter and that he'd never come back. I don't know. I can see him sometimes, in dreams or in a vision. I think he is still alive, and I think *he* will come back. But I know my mother never will."

"Of course, you miss them."

"Yes. I miss my father the most. My mother wasn't happy that I was born, I think, but my father was. When I was little he would sit me on top of his head so I could touch angels I saw in the branches. And at night I would tell him what I had seen that day, and he would write it in a book."

"I think he loves you," Perdita said, "and that he is very proud of you."

"Yes. That is why I think he will come back for me. After he left, my mother started to punish me when I saw things. She burned the backs of my legs with candles when I had a vision. I would show you, but it doesn't look very nice." Anatolia took a large bite from her bread and a sip from the milk jug.

"My God," Perdita whispered.

"You don't think your father is proud of you," Anatolia said with her mouth full of food, never looking at Perdita.

"I don't?" Perdita was surprised by the child's statement.

"I don't think so. I feel coldness there, and that you feel you are not loved."

"Really, Anatolia. Your visions might be wrong, you know. I wouldn't say I felt—"

"Mother Superior said I can be intrusive sometimes. I am sorry if I am."

"Oh, no, Anatolia, that isn't what I meant." Perdita took a sip of her cider. She didn't speak for a moment. Anatolia looked at Perdita intently.

"You have done things that were unexpected," Anatolia said. "Some things have made him sad."

"Him?"

"But you are his gift from God. He knows he has not been worthy. He is sorry for that."

"Anatolia, really—!"

"But you are his gift, his and mine, here for a purpose different from the one you think of. I have seen it. And you *are* loved."

24

Moira had chosen O'Connell's for its incomparable brisket: it was salty but tender and it suited her very well. She was surprised at how empty the restaurant was for a Saturday night. It was still early, though, and the theater crowds would surely fill the place in another two hours. She had reserved a table near a large window framed in green velvet drapes, overlooking D'onston Street three stories below. The traffic of hackneys and carriages was just starting to taper off as a light rain began to fall. Moira was glad she'd had the presence of mind to bring her umbrella.

The circumstances of her being at O'Connell's on a damp Saturday night were still something of a mystery. Two days before she had received a note from Perdita's father. She withdrew it from her handbag and glanced at it:

> Moira,
>
> Would gladly buy your dinner on Saturday, at the restaurant of your choice, if you would agree to meet with me to discuss my daughter's circumstances. Please respond by midday on Friday.
>
> Edward B-R

Moira drank from a glass of claret in front of her. She thought she would switch to a Burgundy with her meal, when the time came. She had felt little but uneasiness in the presence of Edward Badon-Reed in all of the years she had known him. In fact, she couldn't remember a time when she had any impression other than that he had a distinct dislike of her. But she knew many others who felt the same way. He was not an effusive or warm man. He and his wife seemed to manage a tense coexistence with little pretense of affection or camaraderie. If they had any conversation at dinner or in the evenings, Edward's part of it usually consisted of terse, general responses to his wife's comments about her health, the weather, the state of morals in modern society, the decline of civility and good taste, or Perdita's abandonment of her parents as they approach old age. The majority of Mrs. Badon-Reed's most cheerful and unconditionally affectionate comments were usually lavished upon her lap dogs.

Since receiving his note, Moira wondered if perhaps she had misinterpreted Edward's responses to any discussion of Perdita's actions which she'd had with him and his wife. He had always seemed inscrutable, emotionless, and uninvolved. But perhaps, Moira thought, her established opinion of him had colored these perceptions. Could not his somber, mute expressions have also conveyed anguish or concern if Moira had been disposed to see those things on his face? Moira thought of an engraving of Rembrandt's *Bathsheba* she had seen last year. She remembered commenting then to Perdita that the artist's genius had formed a countenance in his subject in which the viewer could read a vast range of emotions or thoughts, each with equal validity, and each changing, depending upon the mood or predilection of the viewer at the time. She wondered, if she could revisit those moments when Edward seemed inscrutable, if he would still seem so, regarding him as she did now, in a slightly different light.

At eight o'clock precisely, Moira saw Edward appear in the vestibule. His umbrella and mackintosh were dripping. He checked these, and scanning the dining room, spotted Moira at her window table. With something nearly passing for a smile, he raised his hand in greeting and made his way toward her. He was a bit above average height and at sixty, just starting to look his age.

"Moira," he said, nodding in an almost courtly way, "it's such a disagreeable night, I wouldn't have blamed you for staying home." He sat opposite her.

"It isn't *too* dreadful. I said I would be here, and I hate to not keep my word," Moira said.

"Yes, I have noticed that about you." Edward nodded. "If Moira says she'll do it, she'll do it. You have always been that way." He still carried the slightest trace of his Kentish accent, Moira noticed.

"Dependable, but not always agreeable, the nurse called me when I was working with the veterans." Moira smiled.

"Dependable is meat and pudding. Agreeable is a soufflé with nothing to it, in my book."

Moira was puzzled by this apparent compliment. "Yes, I agree," she said. "Though we can all do with a little civility."

"What is that you are drinking?" Edward asked.

"It's claret. Quite good on a chilly night."

"Yes, the English like claret." Edward frowned. "I don't know wines. I'd like some orange juice or lemonade, but I'm not likely to get it at this time o' year. Suppose I'll have tea. No, coffee. I'll have coffee." He signaled a waiter he saw across the room. "Coffee, if you please," he called to the waiter who nodded and disappeared into the kitchen. Edward looked around the dining room. "Never been here before. You say the brisket is good?"

"Yes, very good. I've never had a bad piece of beef here."

"Well, that says something then. I'll try it." The

waiter emerged from the kitchen with a steaming cup of coffee on a saucer, which he placed in front of Edward. "It's the brisket for us," Edward said. "Does it come in well done?"

"No sir, it's all the same," the waiter noted.

"If there *is* a well-done piece, that's what I want. Burnt. Very well done."

"Yes, sir." The waiter smiled and disappeared again.

"So," Edward said seriously, "what can you tell me about my daughter? Is she well? Is Tancred taking good care of her? Is she staying clear of men?"

Moira tried to suppress a smile. "It is her intention to stay clear of men. There is one who seems to be pursuing her, *is* pursuing her, but she is discouraging him."

"Is he a gentleman? I assume he's not a lout. She wouldn't have anything to do with a lout."

"He is a gentleman. He is not pressing the issue. Perdita has moved out of the care of her uncle. She moved out of the rectory some time ago and is on her own now."

Edward frowned. "But she has never lived alone in her life."

"She thought it inappropriate to live as a permanent guest of her Uncle Tancred. Her room is in a boarding house nearby."

"Well, there is no love lost between Tancred and us now, as you may have guessed." Edward took a large gulp of his coffee. "But it might be better for him if she lives elsewhere. His health isn't what it was before his service in Providence. We were once close, the lot of us. I'm sure he did his best for his niece."

"His service in Providence?"

"Hmmm? Oh, I'm daft. You wouldn't know about that, would you? I forgot we kept it from Perdita. Father Tancred Condell once performed a very special service for Holy Mother Church."

"What service was that?" Moira asked.

"The service of exorcist."

"Oh my." Moira was intrigued.

"Yes." Edward nodded. "He filled that role for about eighteen years. Worked on many a case. When Perdita was a girl he was called to a possession in Providence. It was a child, a lad of seven or eight, and the most heinous defilement of a human soul Tancred had ever seen, I heard. He and his assistant fought the demon for nigh onto ten weeks, and it drained every ounce of strength out of him. He had broken ribs, three broken fingers, bruises, cuts, and worst of all, the memory of things too vile and foul to remember. Tancred developed a congestion of the heart and just as he had met his last ounce of strength, the demon was purged."

"Then he was successful."

"He was. But at a cost. The child's heart burst at the last moment, and he dropped dead in a pool of blood."

"My God."

"Tancred's health was never the same. It aged him terribly. He gave up the role of exorcist and asked to be moved west. That is how he came to be in Ste. Odile." Edward finished his coffee. "I asked you about my daughter's health. Has she been well?"

"I suppose her health is fair," Moira said. "I told you about the deaths of her friends, a Mrs. Chardin and Sister Solana. These have affected her most seriously, and I have started to have misgivings about how these things might be weighing upon her."

"Yes?"

"Yes. She very quickly had come to feel great affection for those women, and their violent deaths have… *changed* her. I have sensed it. As you know, she has a great capacity for empathy and compassion."

"Yes. She was always rescuing stray dogs and injured alley cats."

"And rabbits too, as I remember." Moira immediately regretted making this statement. Edward's face flushed for a moment, and he turned his gaze to the tabletop. Moira thought to apologize to him, but the words didn't come. After a moment, she continued. "Her involvement in the tragic events in Ste. Odile have been a mighty distraction to her purpose for being there. Her sculpture."

"Yes," Edward acknowledged sheepishly. "The rock carving."

"I'll be sunk if I can imagine how she has accomplished as much as she has, with all that has happened to her there."

"She can be very driven when she is of a mind to be." Edward thought for a moment. "In a roundabout way," he added. "She was timid, and I put the fear of God into her, but she still managed to do a thing, if she set her mind to it, regardless of what she was told. I had to be firm with her—firmer than I wanted to be—to get a point through."

The waiter refilled Edward's coffee cup and he took a sip, holding the cup in his hands as if to warm them. He frowned down into the dark liquid.

"I don't know what my daughter might have told you about me, Moira," he said gravely. "I have no notion of what your opinion of me might be. Thinking back on it now, it seems I was harsh with her. I beat her, even locked her in the cellar once when she defied me, as you seem to know. It is how I was raised, and I thought that, as with our Lord, to be feared is to be respected and loved." Edward continued to stare into his cup. He seemed unable to raise his eyes to meet Moira's. "But nowadays," he continued, "as her mother and I get older, I feel I showed her too much of my anger and not enough, not nearly enough of my love. Do you understand me, Moira?"

"Yes." Moira nodded, astonished by Edward's forthrightness. In years of acquaintance with him, going back to her childhood, she'd not had as much of his conversation as she'd had in the last five minutes. "Yes, Edward, I believe I do understand you."

Edward began to arrange and rearrange the silverware in an awkward, self-conscious manner. "Do you think," he said quietly, never looking at Moira, "do you think my daughter understands that, too?"

Moira thought for a moment. She knew the truth was not, after all, the answer Edward was seeking. She also knew if the seeds of conciliation and reassessment of her upbringing were to be planted in Perdita's brain, Moira would have to take it upon herself to plant them there.

"Yes, Edward, I am sure she does," Moira said.

Edward smiled slightly, but a bit disingenuously, it seemed to Moira, almost as if he were relieved to hear a comforting answer he knew to be untrue.

"When I heard you tell my wife," he raised his eyes to Moira's, "about my daughter's near drowning in saving that infant, such a stab of fear went through me. To have come so close to losing her! I couldn't sleep for three or four nights afterwards. I have wanted to mend my fences with her for years, but have not known how to go about it. If she had died…the only child I will ever have—!" He seemed unable to speak for a few moments. "I want her to know me in a different way," he continued. "I have done such a poor job of expressing my affection to her, of expressing *anything* to her but disapproval. I thought she would get this nonsense about being an artist out of her system in a month and come home."

"So did I." Moira nodded. "It seems the town has swallowed her up, its drama, its tragedies. I wonder how easily now she could extricate herself. She is showing me more than I ever knew she had in her nature."

"I was unhappy at first that she rejected Prosper," Edward continued. "I think it odd that any middle-aged woman would decline an offer of marriage and the prospect of a comfortable life with an honorable man, but that is beside the point, I suppose. If she wishes to live as an old maid in her father's house, that is what she will do. If she wishes to carve rocks for the rest of her life, then she should do *that*." He reached into his waistcoat and withdrew a large leather wallet. "But I know I must have her here. I know it now."

"She has this idea fixed in her head for the time being," Moira said, "and as you yourself have remarked, once she gets an idea—"

"Yes, yes," Edward said a bit impatiently. "Whether she will come or no—and I cannot insist, I realize—I want her to have this." He placed the wallet in front of Moira on the table. "I have been saving this for her since the time of her First Communion, without her mother's knowledge. It is $944.00. I don't know if she will accept it if she knows it is from me, so I do not want her to know, just yet. In time I will make things right with her, if she will come home, if *you* can convince her. Even if she won't, this will make her life less of a struggle."

Moira was speechless for a moment. "Yes, it would help her greatly. She is living very modestly. I know her wardrobe has been much distressed by her activities, by some unfortunate luck there. But you should tell her, give it yourself."

"No, not yet. Not until I have had time to consider how I will rebuild the ties that bound us together when she was small. The end is not far away for me, and however many years I have left may hardly be time enough to retie those bonds. Someday I will tell her that the money came from me. Tell her whatever you like. Say it was an inheritance from some forgotten aunt or some sort of annuity. You will see she gets it?"

Moira looked at the wallet on the table, then at Edward, who looked back at her expectantly. "Yes, I will," she said. "And I think perhaps nothing will do but that I deliver it myself!"

25

"I came as soon as I got Mrs. Zell's message!" Mrs. Morisot was pink-faced and out of breath. Her attendant ladies helped her sit on the camelback sofa facing Perdita, who sat in her favorite armchair, near the parlor's marble fireplace.

"Really, ma'am," Perdita frowned, "I can assure you and Mrs. Zell that this is not a situation which requires neither your attention, nor your supervision. I am perfectly able to wait by myself for Mr. Bastide's carriage, and, having seen it arrive at the curb, as it is not yet dark, exit the house and climb inside." Perdita was a little surprised at herself, at her defiant, acerbic tone.

"Of course, Miss Badon-Reed, of course." Mrs. Morisot forced a smile. "I did not know, I was not informed, that you had finally agreed to accept Mr. Bastide's invitation."

"I did not know you required to be informed of that," Perdita said suspiciously.

"I consider myself, we all should in Ste. Odile, to be Mr. Bastide's humble servant." Mrs. Morisot smiled. "As my tenant, my guest, I feel you represent me and that I am somewhat responsible for you."

"I will not embarrass you," Perdita said peevishly.

"Of course not. It is only that you have postponed this meeting once, and I—"

"I think I am ready to do myself justice, to Mr. Bastide. It is time I met him."

Mrs. Morisot mopped her face with her handkerchief. "With this cooler weather, I cannot imagine why I am so hot all of the time," she fretted.

Perdita noticed Mrs. Morisot's two attendant ladies glance at each other furtively and smile. Perdita suppressed a smile herself.

"You must consider, my dear," Mrs. Morisot continued, "whether you will be warm enough later this evening, with just that light shawl."

"Thank you for your concern, ma'am. I think the shawl will be more than adequate."

"The paisley clashes a bit, don't you think, with your dress?" Mrs. Morisot raised an eyebrow.

"Yes, it does," Perdita agreed. "But it cannot be helped. This is the only dress I have left that has not been ruined."

"Ah, yes." Mrs. Morisot nodded. "Mrs. Zell told me of your wardrobe situation."

"*Did* she?"

"Yes. Depending upon how this evening goes, we may find a means to remedy that."

Perdita started to respond indignantly to this remark, but decided to let it pass. The sound of horse's hooves on the pavement drew Mrs. Morisot's attention to the window.

"It's he," she said with a barely repressed excitement. "It's Tertius with the Rockaway! He's hitched the chestnut geldings, too. That says something. Off you go, my dear!"

Perdita rose with a deliberate, antagonistic slowness, and made her way casually into the entry hall. Mrs. Morisot attempted to rise, but soon thought the better of it.

"I hope you have a pleasant and…demure evening, Miss Perdita," she called.

"Thank you, ma'am. I wish the same for you."

Perdita reached for the doorknob just as it was opened from the outside. Perdita had seen Tertius twice before, but never when standing. She was surprised by how tall he was.

"Miss Badon-Reed?" Tertius nodded in a courtly manner.

"Yes," Perdita said.

"I am Tertius, and I am at your service." He was well-dressed in swallowtails and a top hat, and his voice seemed to reverberate across the veranda.

"Thank you, Tertius," Perdita said, accepting his arm down the front stairs. "I believe you were the first native of this village I ever saw, the evening I arrived. You and Aristide. You were at the landing to retrieve a large crate from Herter Brothers in New York."

"Ah, yes," Tertius remembered. "That would have been the new entry table. A beautiful piece of work, it is."

"I am eager to see it."

"In fact, Miss, I am not a native of Ste. Odile. I am from Port au Prince, in Haiti."

"That explains your accent. It sounds like an exotic place to be from."

Tertius smiled. "In some regions," he said. "My part of it was considerably more on the squalid side. Watch your step, please."

Tertius opened the door of the Rockaway and Perdita climbed inside. As she situated herself on the maroon leather seat, Tertius continued to hold the door open. Perdita looked at him quizzically. He appeared to have something to say.

"Miss Badon-Reed," he said at length, "if you would forgive my presumption—"

"Yes?"

"If I may suggest…I have been in the service of Mr. Bastide for many years, since I was sixteen, in fact. As you can imagine, I am very familiar with his ways, his habits."

"I am certain you are, Tertius."

"I owe very much to him. My entire family does, as my employment with him has raised our fortunes. He can be very generous."

"Yes, I think you and Mrs. Morisot are very much in agreement, in that estimation."

"As are many of us in this village," Tertius continued. "Mr. Bastide enjoys nothing so much as companionship and lively conversation, especially with young women."

"Yes." Perdita was beginning to feel apprehensive.

"Yes. My concern is for appearances, reputation. Both his and yours. Resentments often arise in a small village, when one is singled out for favor by a powerful man."

"I am sorry, Tertius," Perdita said, with a trace of impatience in her voice, "I am not following you, I am afraid."

"Sometimes, after an evening's conversation, Mr. Bastide's sense of generosity overcomes him, particularly with young ladies. At the end of the evening he may offer you a gift. A Roman *aureus* is most usual."

"Yes, he gave one to my friend, Sister Solana. I think she was a little ashamed of herself for accepting it."

"Precisely. It has always been my opinion that this is improper, that to offer a gift and for it to be accepted, that both of these things are inappropriate."

"Inappropriate?" This seemed like a harsh assessment to Perdita. The action could be said to be in bad taste, perhaps, but, she thought to herself, does that universally imply impropriety?

"Yes, at least until one knows and understands Mr. Bastide better."

"I see," Perdita said cautiously. "Thank you for your advice, Tertius. I will certainly consider your remarks, should circumstances warrant it this evening."

"Miss." Tertius nodded and closed the carriage door.

Tertius drove the carriage west to Gentian Street, then north until, passing Endymion, it became Thermopylae Street. Perdita watched the town flow past her window on her right. The carriage passed by a small hill and thicket of forest which she knew to be the rear aspect of the Reliquary Chapel, the convent and the Seminary of St. Perpetua Flavia. Further on, she saw the rear of the Church of the Holy Mandillion and the rectory, empty now, except for Mrs. Moon. Uncle Tancred still had not returned from his sudden and mysterious trip to St. Louis, nor had either Perdita nor Mrs. Moon heard any word from him yet regarding how long he might be away, or explaining his precipitate disappearance in the first place.

The pace of the chestnut geldings slowed a bit as Thermopylae Street wound its way up the hill overlooking Ste. Odile. The road threaded through a thick hardwood forest of oak, walnut, and hickory. The light from the setting sun, more obvious at this elevation, stabbed through the foliage which, as the autumn progressed, was starting to turn shades of yellow and orange.

At the summit of the hill, as Thermopylae Street gave way to a wide gravel drive, the foliage opened to a vast, intermittently tended lawn and dreary gardens, all cast in the penumbra of fading day, like an interior in one of Gerome's Orientalist paintings, Perdita thought.

Dominating the lawn to the right was a huge, fantastically gnarled oak tree. Many of its lower branches drooped to the ground then arced up again like the massive necks of an unmoving Hydra. The tree reminded Perdita of hundreds of grotesque live oaks she had seen in New Orleans in her time with the Ursulines. Beyond the oak tree were more dark gardens and a maze of hedges radiating from an ornate, wooden observation tower topped by a copper onion dome. And between the expanses of dark gardens, and the trees on either side of the drive, arose the fantastic and imposing hermitage known for two hundred years as Jardin Noir.

The gravel drive formed a circle around a lichen- and moss-covered centerpiece: a dry stone fountain in which carved demons and griffins and other mythic creatures battled to dominate a fanciful escarpment. As the Rockaway circled the drive approaching the large front door, Perdita was able to see the house more fully. It was a massive, rambling structure, built almost entirely of dressed limestone, embellished here and there, as in two oriel windows visible on the front and side of the building, in Gothic, arched cast iron. It was an odd mixture of styles: buttresses flanked Romanesque towers and round arches; clerestory windows and rosettes topped lintels and columns that were almost Classical, or even Egyptian, in places. Perdita perceived that the enormous house had all the signs of generations of owners with imagination and refinement, who followed the ebb and flow of two centuries of changing taste and many tangents of intellectual and aesthetic obsessions.

As the carriage rounded the drive and stopped at the iron-hinged, double front door, Perdita could see a long conservatory built of brick in a Gothic or Jacobean style at the northwestern edge of the lawn, in front of yet another maze of gardens. The roof of this building was entirely glazed in glass panes set in iron and bronze frameworks and panels. Tertius stepped lightly to the ground, and opened the carriage door for Perdita. She stepped out.

"This is all very impressive," she said, trying to not sound awestruck. "Mr. Bastide is quite a horticulturist, it would seem."

"Yes," Tertius nodded. "But there are few things under the sun which are not of interest to Mr. Bastide."

Tertius preceded Perdita to the front door and dragged it open with some effort. He did the same with the inner vestibule door which opened on a large entry hall. As she crossed the threshold, Perdita had an odd sensation of loss and dread, as if she were about to give up some sacred and private part of herself that could never be recovered. She tried to put this feeling out of her mind.

The entry hall was a wide, roughly pentagonal space lined in dark wainscoting, off of which radiated several rooms and hallways. A large, round table, made of rich woods of various hues, dominated the space and was piled with books, papers, pieces of bone and rocks, all surrounding a silver vase at the table's center, which held many varieties of wilted flowers and wild plants.

"That is the table from Herter Brothers," Tertius said. "Not much of it is visible now, unfortunately."

Beyond the table was a large, oak staircase that rose to a landing featuring a window that must have been twenty feet high. The fading daylight illuminated medieval scenes of battle, siege, and immolation of prisoners of war, depicted in stained and painted glass across the expanse of the window.

Several dark niches in the entry hall on either side of the staircase were populated by life-sized stone statues from antiquity. A pharaonic figure and ibis-headed god represented Egypt, marble figures of Eros and Psyche bespoke the Classical world, and bearded, winged bulls of basalt recalled Nineveh and the court of Assurnasirpal.

"Mr. Bastide is out in the conservatory, I believe," Tertius said. "He asks that you wait either in the parlor or the library. Which do you prefer, Miss?"

"The library, thank you."

Tertius nodded and directed Perdita to a large pocket door to her right. He pulled the door open revealing a vast, paneled room. Bookshelves, in two tiers in some places, covered most of the high walls, except at an over-sized limestone fireplace and a ceiling-high oriel window that overlooked the front lawn and the gnarled oak tree Perdita had seen as she drove in. As she entered the room, Tertius withdrew, closing the pocket door.

The room was scattered with desks and work tables, all of which were buried under books, charts, fossils, and bones of creatures of all sizes and descriptions. Ornate glass display cases formed a barrier between the main expanse of the floor and the book shelves; these contained specimens of mounted birds and fish, seashells, and small antiquities. One walnut-trimmed case contained the fearsome, enormous skull of a crocodile, and another, a selection of heavy-browed, prognathous skulls of anthropoid apes. Perdita walked spellbound toward the lit fireplace at the opposite end of the room. She stopped at a table she passed to glance over some volumes, dog-eared and smudged, stacked together in front of a brass and wooden orrery, which illustrated the movements of the planets around the sun, and under a painted bronze of Mephistopheles. The smallest volume was *The City of God* by St. Augustine, a larger one was Francis Barrett's *Magus*, and the largest was Collin de Plancy's *Dictionnaire Infernal*. Perdita pulled this book from under the other two and opened it. The page revealed held an engraving of the bat-winged, three-headed demon Asmodeus, the personification of rage and lust. She closed the book and replaced the other two upon it, as she had found them.

A large painting above the fireplace attracted her attention. She approached it slowly. It depicted a dark and brooding sky hanging like a shroud, over a desolate beach. Ruins of ancient buildings, blasted remnants of a long dead civilization, were scattered along the low horizon line, and ran into the subdued, fatigued surf. Human bones could be seen here and there, being slowly buried by sand and waves. At the center of it all, his giant form dramatically lighted by an unseen setting sun, sat the hideous, yet somehow pitiable figure of a Cyclops. A brass plaque affixed to the bottom of the picture's massive frame read: *Polyphemus in Solitude, by Elihu Vedder.*

"Are you familiar with Mr. Vedder's work?"

The voice startled Perdita. She turned quickly to see her host opening the pocket door across the room. Perdita was a little disquieted at the figure she saw. Orien Bastide was of above average height. He was dressed in a black frock coat, tie, and trousers, and was unusually, if not morbidly, thin. His hands were knotted and gnarled like old roots of trees and the skin was very pale and splotched. His face was covered from the upper lip to his forehead with a wax prosthesis, or mask, which gave him a lifeless, mannequin-like appearance. His hair was gray, long, and somewhat disheveled.

"Mr. Bastide," Perdita said awkwardly.

"Miss Badon-Reed."

Bastide approached her in an animated way and extended his hand. Perdita fought the impulse to back away from him and look at the floor. Instead, she shook his hand, which felt unnaturally warm, yet somehow unliving.

"How do you do?" she said.

"Arc you familiar with Vedder's work?" Bastide repeated. His voice was wet sounding and slightly garbled.

"Yes, I am," Perdita responded. "I have seen it in New York. He is a creator of haunting images."

"Yes, a 'Prophet of Mystery,' if I may employ the grandiose phrase of the art dealer from whom I bought the picture. I hope to get a few more of his works when I next travel east. They suit me mightily."

"Your home and collections are astounding, Mr. Bastide." Perdita avoided a direct and penetrating gaze from his oddly round, watery eyes.

"I have the whole world here, or at least as much of it as I want," Bastide said. "I am not unlike other persons of means these days, I think." He seemed to be smiling. His teeth were unusually elongated and discolored. "I flatter myself," he continued, "that I have collected art all, or most, should I say, of my life, and independent of trends and fashions. Does that sound high-toned? And although I think this century will be known as the age of the gentleman naturalist, again may I truthfully say there was never a time when I was not interested in all of creation and all wonders that engage the human intellect."

Perdita looked at him furtively. "Then you are in disagreement with the views of Father Lallemant?"

"You amaze me, Miss Perdita, if I may so address you. Few lay people in this day and time recall the ravings of Father Lallemant. No, I do not believe that the study and enjoyment of nature is an impediment or distraction to knowledge of God. Quite the opposite, if the two must be connected."

"Must they not be?"

"Perhaps."

His eyes seemed to her to dart all across her form, from head to foot, from side to side. This gave her some sense of unease and made her wish momentarily that there were some barrier, a screen or piece of furniture, between them.

"Won't you sit?" He motioned toward a threadbare, overstuffed chair near the fireplace. Perdita sat. Bastide sat opposite her, in a similar chair. "If you will pardon me..." Bastide picked up a clear glass bottle with a glass tube resting in it, from a cluttered table near him. Putting a finger over one end of the tube, he captured some of the liquid within it. This he raised to his eyes, head tilted back, and dropped a small amount of the solution first in his right, then his left eye.

"An unpleasant display, I know," Bastide apologized.

"No, not at all," Perdita responded insincerely.

"Solana, our dear Solana, told you about my degenerative condition?"

"Yes, a little."

"I can only blink with great difficulty. My eyes, you see, must be held open with wires. I must therefore use the saline solution."

"Yes, I understand. Is there any hope for your condition?"

"Only the grave." He smiled unpleasantly.

Perdita forced a small laugh. A nearly hidden door between two bookcases opened. Tertius appeared carrying a silver tray which held a wine decanter and two crystal glasses.

"Will you have some Bordeaux?" Bastide asked. "I have heard you are a great lover of wines."

"You have *heard?"* Perdita said, a little offended by the statement. "Oh, I suppose you mean Solana mentioned it?"

"Yes." Bastide nodded. Tertius placed the tray on a large ivory-inlaid Damascus table. He filled the two glasses, then gave one first to Perdita, then to Bastide.

"Dinner will be ready very soon," Tertius said. He placed the wine decanter on the table, and with the empty tray in hand, disappeared through the same door through which he had entered.

"Dear Sister Solana," Bastide said, taking an audible sip of his wine. "How deep must your sorrow be to have lost her."

"Yes," Perdita nodded, "her Sisters, Mother Superior, myself. We all miss her terribly."

"And have you discovered the source of her great distress?" Bastide took another audible sip followed by a pronounced, guttural gulp.

"Yes. It was a private matter." Perdita took a long drink of her wine, half emptying her glass. She thought for a moment, considering whether she had the right or the courage to ask her host a question which had been on her mind since Solana's death. "I have wanted to ask you, though, if we should meet, why is it, do you think, Mr. Bastide, that she came here to your doorstep to end her life?"

Bastide looked into the fire for a few moments. His watery, yellow eyes glistened in the firelight behind his wax mask. "I have myself wondered at that. I had become her friend during the course of her excellent service to me. Perhaps she was seeking my counsel, or perhaps nothing more than the highest promontory in the region from which to—"

"Yes, possibly," Perdita interrupted. "May I ask, did Sheriff Aubuchon ever question you at all about the incident?"

"No, he did not."

"That seems odd, doesn't it, since she jumped from your property, from your escarpment?"

"There is no unassailable proof of that." Bastide smiled. It was a grotesque gesture intended, it seemed to Perdita, to convey benevolence. "She could have gone into the water anywhere and merely ended up below my escarpment."

"No, the coroner said her body fell from a great height and carried bits of twigs broken off trees just above where she was found. He also said she was partially impaled upon a snag at the point of impact in the river. He seems certain she jumped from here."

Bastide's gaze left Perdita and returned to the fire. "It is unfortunate that we will never know. I cannot explain the workings of her mind at that moment. I was rather hoping you could." He rose from his chair and refilled Perdita's glass. "As her friend," he continued, "you, of course, want to know all you can about her end." He returned to his chair and sat.

"Yes," Perdita said, sipping from her glass. "I don't want to seem impertinent."

"Of course not."

"Not to a man of such consequence, the great benefactor of Ste. Odile."

"I assumed no impertinence, I assure you, Miss Badon-Reed."

"Perdita."

"Perdita. Although trivial compared to the sense of loss that you and the Sisters have felt, my sense of…," he paused to find the right word, "…of remorse at the death of Sister Solana has been deeply felt and beyond consolation."

At that moment, the hidden door opened again and Tertius reappeared. "Dinner is served," he said.

"Thank you, Tertius." Bastide nodded, rising. Tertius withdrew through the hidden door. Perdita rose from her chair gripping her wine glass. Bastide directed her toward the pocket door. He preceded her and pulled the door open.

They crossed the entry hallway diagonally and entered the arched door of the dining room. The room was large, but much smaller than the library. A bronze and crystal chandelier overhung the long, heavily carved dining table. A massive chair at the head of the table, its back to the wide, blazing marble fireplace, appeared to be Bastide's. Bastide held the chair to the right of this for Perdita.

"Thank you," she said, sitting.

Bastide seated himself as Tertius appeared through the butler's pantry with a single bowl of soup. This he placed before Perdita. He then silently withdrew.

"Aren't you having anything?"

"No. There isn't much of my appetite left these days. I will join you in the main course, though. It's duck, one of Tertius's specialties."

"He cooks and cares for you, too?"

"Yes, he is invaluable. Keeping up with this large house is too much for one person, though. I didn't want servants underfoot everywhere, so our housekeeping is somewhat casual. I keep gardeners and grooms, but no house servants."

"I am very impressed with Tertius." Perdita tasted her soup. "Onion. Most flavorful," she said. The thought suddenly struck her that it might be very unpleasant to watch and hear Bastide eat.

"I understand you have seen my collections underground," Bastide said. He dropped more saline solution into his eyes from a bottle on the dining table.

"Yes, thank you for giving your permission."

"Mr. Morisot did that, but he speaks for me."

"The sight of everything left me speechless. The young *Hercules* by Polydorous is magnificent."

"I am very proud of it. I have not yet thought of a suitable disposition for it, however. I am most concerned that it be well displayed. Mr. Hypolitte Robert accompanied you underground, then?"

"He convinced me to overcome my uneasiness and see the collection."

"Uneasiness?"

"Yes. I have a silly fear of enclosed places. I am glad I let him convince me."

"Mr. Morisot speaks highly of him. I have been most satisfied with his years of service to me. A man of many interests, too, which speaks of intellect."

"Yet, you have never met him." Perdita finished her soup. She took another drink of wine and Bastide immediately refilled her glass from a decanter left on the table by Tertius.

"Have I not?" Bastide said thoughtfully. "I thought I had remembered meeting him, but after so many years, the mind plays tricks. I must make a point of meeting him."

Tertius soon served his duck, accompanied by a small salad, during which conversation drifted like a mote of dust across the table and back, covering subjects ephemeral, superficial, and polite. As she feared, the sight and sound of Bastide eating proved an unpleasant distraction to Perdita, and lessened her interest in her own food.

"You and Mr. Robert have become fast friends, then?" Bastide asked, applying his linen napkin to the edges of his mouth. He seemed to be consciously avoiding his wax prosthesis.

"We are friends," Perdita agreed. "Kindred spirits are hard to come by in a small town."

"Or anywhere." Bastide's eyes were darting across her face.

"You seem to lead a life of reading, study, and seclusion," Perdita said, avoiding his gaze. She identified at that moment a sensation which she had been feeling all evening, and of which Solana had spoken many times: the simultaneous stimulation and repulsion of Bastide's company.

"Yes, I have a need for very much privacy, but value an exclusive and stimulating companionship on occasion. Either here or in my ancestral home back at Montsegur, this companionship is a most rare commodity."

"Montsegur?" Perdita asked, incredulous that she now had a second connection to that tiny place. "A friend of mine, a former fiancée, in fact, had a sister who lived at Montsegur! What a remarkable coincidence. Did you know her? Claire Guibord was her name."

"I have not heard the name before."

"That is very odd, Mr. Bastide. I'm certain you would have heard of her in such a small village. She was murdered, horribly murdered, last spring. Surely you knew of that?"

"No, I did not. Perhaps it happened after I came back to Ste. Odile. I live a life very disconnected from the rest of the day-to-day world." Bastide shifted in his chair and faced the fire. "Would you say, Perdita, that isolation and loneliness are as much the wages of original sin, if there is such a thing, as suffering and damnation? After Eden, we are separated from God, and from each other, because the lifelong quest for individual salvation inevitably isolates us one from another, as we must each look after our own souls."

"Made all the more tragic, I would think, for its futility," Perdita said, emptying her wine glass.

"Futility?"

"Is anything more inevitable in us than our own weakness? God's grace is everywhere, the good He has made is everywhere, if we are strong enough to recognize the fact and admit thcsc things into our hearts. But that strength, history has shown us, is rare. Isn't our moral weakness incurable?" Perdita felt herself becoming dizzy. "Therefore, if what you say is true, isn't it inevitable, an inescapable component of our own natures that we be, that we suffer, alone?"

"Yes."

"The connections we make to other persons," Perdita continued slowly, weighing her words, so that the wine would not lead her to misspeak, "to kindred souls, as I have said, are precious and fragile, and to be prized. All will end eventually in physical separation, or death."

"Miss Perdita, are you feeling well?"

"The brevity of this life is an injustice." Perdita suddenly felt a little surprised by her own vociferousness.

"Yes," Bastide agreed. "There is scarcely enough time to learn what the world is about, and it is over."

"What control is it, Mr. Bastide, that you exert over this town?" Perdita could scarcely believe she had asked the question. She thought of the nervous deference Mrs. Morisot and others showed to this strange man, of Uncle Tancred's admonition, of the decline Solana suffered after she came into his circle of influence.

Bastide smiled his grotesque smile.

"None, Miss Perdita, I assure you. I am as removed

from the affairs of this hamlet as it is possible to be."

"No...no, I don't understand it yet," Perdita's head was spinning, "but you are the fixed point. The life of this place, its very sense of itself ebbs and flows...around you."

Bastide looked at Perdita steadily. She returned his gaze, fighting every urge to look away. Bastide reached into his waistcoat pocket and withdrew a large gold coin. He offered it to her.

"I do not know when I have enjoyed a conversation so much," he said. "Won't you accept this small gift as a memento of the pleasant evening we have passed?"

Perdita looked at the coin, but made no move to accept it. "What is it you buy with this little gift, I wonder?"

26

"The commission for the Havilland Library is lost," Perdita said dispassionately. "Even if the stonc was found and delivered today, I could scarcely get the figures even roughed out in time, much less finished. No, I wrote to the director this morning withdrawing from the project."

"Surely he can't blame you for that," Hypolitte said, seating himself on the anvil, upwind from the stone dust from Perdita's rasp. "If he would have advanced you enough to purchase another block—"

"Their funds are limited, and I would have had to travel to Tennessee, since Vermont would be out of the question; a trip I could not afford. As it is, I have had more time to give to my *Beatrice Cenci.*"

As Perdita rasped at the arm of her figure, Hypolitte regarded it from his point of vantage. Several of the proportions seemed wrong: the distance from the elbow to the wrist appeared too long to him, and the distance from elbow to shoulder too short. The head was turned at an angle which would have been impossible to accomplish, as was the left foot, which, Hypolitte imagined, would have to be broken to complete the angle described in the statue. As for the general lifelessness of the face and its lack of expression, he knew he should reserve judgment until Perdita considered the work to be finished.

"If I had known," Perdita continued, "the other block

would never turn up, I would have carved the *Heloise and Abelard* in this block and saved my *Beatrice* for some future one."

"Would the director accept this statue instead?" Hypolitte asked.

"No. They have a *Lucrecia Borgia* already. This would be too much of the same, I am afraid. The director is a student of Abelard's theology and was keen on the double figure."

"Too bad." Hypolitte stood. "So, Mrs. Morisot was unhappy with your report of your dinner with Mr. Bastide?"

"Yes. That may be an understatement, in fact."

"Do you feel you were an unappreciative guest?"

"Not at all." Perdita stopped her rasping and stood straight. "He incites a lively conversation. He expects it, from what Solana told me. I was hardly a gadfly. I had a bit too much to drink a bit too quickly, but I don't think my tongue was loosened to the point of impertinence. He even offered me a gold coin as a token of his gratitude for the evening's companionship."

"That seems a bit…inappropriate, doesn't it? What kind of coin was it?"

"A Roman *aureus*. Gold. An antique of some value, I would think. I refused it."

"Yes." Hypolitte's interest seemed piqued. "I wish he would offer one to me. I have a small collection of coins. That would be a valuable addition."

"He called it a memento. As though I would have any difficulty in remembering my first meeting with Mr. Orien Bastide." Perdita wiped her brow. "It will be too cold to work out here soon. I'll have to get this stone moved into the old stable."

"Well, you've had one more meeting than I." Hypolitte smiled.

"He said he would remedy that. I think it would

make an interesting evening: Bastide, you, and me." Perdita rested against her block. "The house is almost beyond description," she continued.

"I've been on the grounds, but never actually inside."

"It's a vast, rambling place, filled with curios, specimens, art, antiques, and books." Perdita noted the excitement in her own voice, and something else: she felt a certain thrill at sharing her experience with Hypolitte, at the knowledge he would have appreciated it in the same way she had. It occurred to her she would have enjoyed the visit more if Hypolitte had been a part of it, and the thought that Bastide might include him in a future evening's diversion pleased her in a way that she would have found excessively troubling just a month before. She still found it somewhat troubling, but it seemed she had little difficulty in assuaging her doubts. She had not come to Ste. Odile to form an attachment. She had only come to work, to execute her commission, and to see once and for all if she could establish herself as an artist.She had not sought Hypolitte's friendship at first, but she had come to value it, and even depend upon it. She had always feared that friendships with the opposite sex carried with them the danger of deeper emotional entanglement. Would Moira believe it, when Perdita told her, that her apprehensions on that score seemed to be fading?

"I think you would be very interested in his collections," Perdita continued. "Everything from skulls and fossils to Assyrian statues, and I only saw a few rooms on the first floor."

"Bastide has not been keen to share his bounties with me up to now," Hypolitte said. "An incentive to do so might be my friendship with you."

"I wonder if he will offer you a coin?" Perdita laughed. After a moment, Hypolitte laughed also.

"I would take it, if he did. You should have taken it

for me. You know my interest in the ancients," Hypolitte chided.

"Yes, I remember the Greek Fire you showed me."

"What I showed you *may* be Greek Fire," Hypolitte corrected her. "I don't know for certain it is."

"And how did you develop such interests?" Perdita asked, as she resumed her rasping.

"My mother, I suppose. She taught me the Classics back in Quebec."

"Quebec?"

"Yes. She was a private tutor for several well-to-do families. She taught Homer, Sappho, Virgil, and Ovid in English, French, Greek, and Latin. She supported us alone and educated me after my father died."

"Oh?"

"He owned a publishing house, but lost all his money investing in a new, higher-speed press that didn't work. One November night, his building burned to the ground, with him inside."

"Oh my."

"His friends, and my mother's family, suspected arson and suicide, but I never believed that. His debts were considerable, and my mother and I were left with very little. Yet she seemed determined I should want for nothing I had known when our family was whole, as much as that was possible."

"That is when she began to teach?"

"Yes. She had a good Parisian education, and she was adamant that I would have a good education, too. We lost our house and took rooms on Caussade Street. They were a little shabby, but were not far from the elegant homes of her employers. She sent me to the Jesuits for preparatory school, then to the Jesuit university in St. Louis."

"Which is how you came to be in this part of the country, I suppose?"

"Yes."

"All of that Jesuit education," Perdita smiled, "yet you are not a Catholic now."

"No, it is a great irony, I think, that the Fathers taught me to question, to doubt, and it was they who set me on a path which led away from Holy Mother Church. 'The Jesuits have tried to combine God and the world, and have gained only the contempt of both!' as Pascal said."

"I think you may have found that path on your own, eventually." Perdita smiled and looked at Hypolitte for a long moment. "But I hope I never do."

"No?"

"No. For all of my questions on dogma, and the counter-influence of my parents, I need the church. I take a great comfort in it."

Hypolitte seemed incredulous. "Still? Even after all that has happened just since you have been here?"

"Yes. I think all would be chaos otherwise. For me, at least."

Hypolitte stood and dusted himself off. "You know, Perdita, I am a little surprised to hear you say that. What comfort has the church, or its representatives, been to you after the deaths of Marie and Solana?"

"I think representatives do not always represent. I think there is forgiveness in the heart of God, and love for lost souls like Marie and Solana. Mother Superior, the bishop, Father Vannier, and even Uncle Tancred interpret the will of God and the church as humans who are full of fallibility, according to their own natures. I have had my doubts, certainly—you have seen them. But I have not strayed too far from the path."

Hypolitte stepped over to Perdita and brushed a strand of hair from her forehead. "And that path has given you comfort through all of this?" he asked.

Perdita felt a small chill in her spine. She avoided

Hypolitte's gaze for a moment, but soon met it, and found she could not look away.

"Not just that," she said. "There was you, also."

Hypolitte slowly grasped Perdita's shoulders and drew her to him. He kissed her gently at first, but with a growing passion. She offered no resistance. She felt herself responding to him. Her body became flushed and her knees weak. After a moment, she pushed away.

"No," she said.

"Why?" He did not release his grasp on her.

"I can't. I cannot do this."

"I've heard you say this before." Hypolitte tried to capture her gaze, but she turned her face away from him. "I have tried to understand you," he went on, "and to honor your wishes. I've tried to be a gentleman, to give you the time and latitude you needed. But I cannot make myself understand how this would be wrong, how it would be the thing that ruins your prospects and your career."

"But it would." A tear came to Perdita's eye. Hypolitte released her.

"Why?"

"I know myself. Knowing you has frightened me. I know how I could respond to you, I knew it from that first day at the jail, the day we met. I am afraid of you—"

"Afraid?"

"Yes, afraid of what a connection to you would mean. How could I stay focused on my purpose if I allowed myself to do this? It *isn't* that I don't want to do it: it's that I *do!"* Perdita stopped short, shocked by the implications of what she had said. "I do, but I can't. I can't think about you when I should be teaching, I can't wish I were driving with you instead of carving my stone. In ten or twenty years' time, I want a body of work to look back on, not just memories."

Hypolitte went silent for a moment. "I don't understand how one prevents the other. I would never allow myself to get in your way, to be an impediment. I wouldn't want you to have nothing but memories of me to show for your time, even though that may be the thing you would value most. If your career should falter, if you do not accomplish the reputation you seek, then you have thrown away my regard for you, my great affection, for nothing."

"'If I should falter, if I should not accomplish…'" Perdita repeated his words. "You have little to say about what I am doing here when you watch me working. I have sensed you do not think very highly of this piece, or perhaps even of my ability."

"Perdita, this is nonsense."

"No, I haven't imagined it. I sensed it in Moira, too, from time to time."

"I have thought no such thing. I am no critic."

"Yes, you are. You are full of observations and opinions."

"Not of your work."

"And why should my work be the one forbidden area? Are you afraid to own to an opinion on that subject?"

"That is a silly way to put it."

"That is surely what you must expect," Perdita said, wiping the stone dust from her forehead with her apron, "since I am a woman. I won't be patronized or humored for the sake of your romantic designs upon me!"

"Perdita," Hypolitte said helplessly, "this is a rather offensive accusation you are making. I do not think you believe what you are saying."

"I do believe it." She removed her apron and draped it across her *Beatrice*. "And I won't be distracted by it anymore, because there is nothing, *nothing* more important than this!" She grasped the arm of her statue. "I wish you every happiness and good health."

She turned and walked toward the rectory. Hypolitte watched speechlessly as she disappeared through the kitchen door.

27

Letter from Michel Redon to Moira Keane Parnell

October 30, 1882

My dear Miss Parnell,

Prosper, my brother, has asked me to write to you on his behalf. I must begin by begging your indulgence on my skill in the use of this English language. What mastery of it such as I have acquired, came at somewhat later an age. I did not begin its study before the age of fifteen, and have not the mastery of it as I would have if I had begun its study at a younger age. And what little I have learned has been used hardly at all in the last twenty years, as we, in this small city, have little contact, if any, with persons of the English speaking.

My brother is very ill, and remains so, as you have known him to be, I think, from his letters to you. Having arrived at home after his release from the sanatorium at Marseilles, his condition collapsed and he fell very sick once again. He has lost very much of weight and can take little food, and thereby is quite weak. His appearance, should you see him today, would, I am sure, shock and distress you as it has me. Two days ago such an effluence proceeded from him, whose filthy nature I need not describe, that I feared for his life and thought it not likely he would survive such a violent paroxysm. He is, as you know, of a delicate constitution, most especially in regards his stomach and bowels. These areas have plagued him for as long as I can remember.

He has very much upon his mind. The murder of our sister, Claire, has changed him in a way profound. Also the loss of his fiancée, your friend, Miss Badon-Reed, and the declining health of our parents. All taken together, these can account, I think, for his weakened condition, or I should say his susceptibility to sickness.

Our parents show no sign of improvement, and we must soon, most certainly, lose one, if not both of them. What calamities have overshadowed our family in the last few months!

The investigation into the death of our sister has not progressed. A Monsieur Vatrollier is the commissary of police for this district. He and his clerk were among the first officials of police at the scene of the murder, and it was he who wrote the *process-verbal* for the prefecture. As Prosper is an attorney, Mr. Vatrollier has agreed to share his knowledge of the facts of the case with him when my brother's health and strength will allow him to attend upon the commissary at his office. For myself, I have left these matters to the officials. With the poor health of my parents, and my professional responsibilities, I have been depending upon my brother to take charge of this affair and direct it toward a just end. And this thing I am certain he will do, as he does in his criminal practice in America, when his health is restored.

It was my brother's intention and his hope, to return to Boston by Christmas. He very much dreads ocean travel, and especially in the time of winter. But these delays in the execution of his business here, which have found their source in his illness, may keep him with us until the holiday. And this may be a hidden blessing because I would be very much surprised if this winter does not prove to be the last for both of our parents.

Prosper wonders, also, if you have any news at all of Miss Badon-Reed? I think his concern for her, as well as his love, are genuine and most deeply felt. Are you still in regular congress with her? Will she provide any small part of good news or encouragement which I may impart to my brother and so elevate his spirits? And here I have revealed the purpose of my letter: the hope you will write quickly any news of her that might rally soul and body, and bring him back to himself once again.

Yours sincerely,
Michel Redon

Letter from Moira Keane Parnell to Michel Redon

Boston
November 15, 1882

Dear Michel,

Many thanks to you for your letter informing me of the condition of your brother and my dear friend. It is true your family has suffered many disasters and that all of these have been severely felt by Prosper, perhaps more than anyone. Yes, he has a fragile constitution, and I have no doubt that these sad events, going back as far as the loss of your family fortune, have exacted a heavy toll on his health. I can only hope you are mistaken about the prospects for the longevity of your parents, as their loss, under these circumstances, will add enormously to the burden which you and your brother must carry.

I have heard from Perdita some weeks ago, although her letters are getting fewer and more infrequent, as they say. As I assume Prosper has told you, she has suffered the loss of two newly-made friends since August, and has been very much distracted from her efforts to complete one statue on commission, and another on her own. I cannot give you any news of encouragement from her to convey to Prosper. She seems convinced she could have no future with him. I am doubly pained to tell him this, because I feel responsible in certain measure for Prosper's suffering on her account. It was I who introduced them and encouraged the pairing over the last few years. She professes no concern for any attachments, yet she has shown some begrudging interest in a young man from Ste. Odile who seems very much to want to be her suitor. She has resisted him up to now, but I have a sense that her resolve is evaporating. I am sorry to tell you this, but there it is.

I have been amazed also to learn from Perdita of a remarkable coincidence. It seems the eccentric scion of an ancient French family, a Monsieur Orien Bastide, who has an estate at Ste. Odile, also maintains an ancestral home at Montsegur, very close to your town of Carcassonne, I am led to understand. It is the village, if I remember aright, where your sister Claire lived! How remote is the likelihood of this conjunction, I wonder, that two small villages nearly unknown outside of their region, separated by thousands of miles, can claim residence of an individual possibly known to your family and now an acquaintance of my friend Perdita? I say possibly, because Bastide has told Perdita he did not know Claire Guibord. This seems unlikely, in a village as small as Montsegur, unless he did not know her under her married name. A small world, as the saying goes.

In one of his letters to me before he became ill, Prosper mentioned that he wished to travel to Ste. Odile at some point, to see Perdita face to face and resolve their differences personally. Although I feel this is almost certainly a mistake, especially in light of her possible growing attachment to the young man I mentioned earlier, I also know that if Prosper has set a course of action, once his initial, irresolute shilly-shallying has been overcome, that he will not rest in his mind until he has done it.

As it turns out, I will be planning a trip there very soon myself. Perdita's father has entrusted me with a small windfall that he wishes me to convey, and I was planning to undertake the journey to the Mississippi in the spring. If Prosper is still of a mind to make the trip, I will wait for his return here, to Boston, so we may travel together.

Sincerely,
M.K.P.

28

The two letters sat on the pier mirror in the hallway most of the morning. They had arrived sometime before Perdita had arisen. She noticed them as she left for school: one was from Hypolitte and the other from Bastide. She picked up Hypolitte's letter to open it, but hesitated. She wasn't sure she wanted to read what it had to say, at least not now as she was hurrying out the door. She decided to leave both to be read when she came home at midday, when she could peruse them at leisure.

Drawing and art-history classes were uneventful that morning, as they had been since Solana's death. Perdita knew her effort and application in teaching her classes was wanting, that little was being accomplished, but she had no notion of what to do about it. She felt she had lost what skill she had for conveying information and inspiring insight in her girls. The measure of this was the growing sense of listlessness and distraction she felt in her classes. All the girls now seemed restless and bored most of the time. Except Anatolia, who was, as always, never at a loss for inspiration and industry.

This in spite of the fact the child was obviously not herself today. Two girls, Louise and Bertha, had taken ill in the morning with sore throats and mild fevers, and were now in the care of Sister Consolata and Sister Elizabeth in the school's small isolation infirmary where children feared to be infectious were quarantined. Anatolia was palc and perspiring, and Perdita noticed a slight grimace on her face when she swallowed.

"Anatolia," Perdita said, walking to the child's side, "are you well?"

"Yes, Miss,"Anatolia answered with a faint smile. Perdita touched the child's forehead.

"You have a bit of a fever."

"I am all right, Miss. I just want to finish my drawing."

"I will take your drawing," Perdita said. "I will take good care of it. Go and see Sister Consolata."

Anatolia rolled her drawing and gave it to Perdita. She rose slowly from her work table and made her way unsteadily out of the room.

At midday, though Perdita was not hungry, she wrapped herself in her shawl to walk home for a bit of bread or fruit, something to put in her stomach, and perhaps a glass of wine, as had become her habit. The day was chilly, and breezes from the north and west scattered leaves across the streets and sidewalks. Two days earlier she had walked home for her lunch. She ate only an apple, but had three glasses of wine. She hadn't felt incapacitated, but in class that afternoon she dropped a plaster cast the girls were to draw, and she stumbled in the hallway, in front of Sister Clotilde. The Mother Superior looked into Perdita's eyes, smelled her breath disapprovingly, and sent her home for the day. Yesterday Perdita stayed at school for her lunch, but today she wanted a glass of wine again. One glass only would do. She would not allow herself to have a second.

By the time Perdita reached Tranquille House, Mrs. Zell had returned from the market with two large catfish she meant to serve for dinner and was occupied with instructing her daughter in their preparation. She scarcely noticed Perdita come into the kitchen. There were two scones left from breakfast under a glass cake plate lid on the counter. Perdita took these and found a suitable glass in the cupboard.

In the dining room she found a bottle of wine she had opened yesterday. She filled her glass. She then returned down the hallway and retrieved her two letters from the pier mirror. In the parlor, she sat in her favorite chair near the hearth and placed her glass on the table next to her. She left the letters in the chair beside her while she slowly ate the scones. She finished the wine quickly and fought an urge to refill her glass. After a few minutes, this urge subsided, and she turned her attention to her letters.

Bastide's was written on the same heavy, expensive paper as his first note had been. She tore it a little, breaking its wax seal. It read:

> My dear Miss Perdita,
>
> I very much enjoyed our recent meeting and am most anxious to repeat that pleasure. Thinking on it afterwards, it was ungracious of me to have failed to show to you the rest of my house and collections then, since I perceived in you such an active interest in such things. At a moment's notice, whenever the mood may strike you, I will send Tertius to collect you for a more complete tour and a supper, I hope, to surpass the first.
>
> O. Bastide

Perdita felt a small thrill pass through her. She could not define it as dread or anticipation at the thought of seeing Bastide again at Jardin Noir. She remembered her excitement of a few days before at the prospect of having Hypolitte share her next visit to the mansion. No one of her acquaintance, except Moira, would appreciate the peculiarities and treasures of Jardin Noir more than Hypolitte. In the mornings, in class, as the girls drew their still lifes and plaster casts of hands, feet and eyes, Perdita found her mind wandering toward thoughts of her first sight of him: of his subduing layabouts with an axe handle at the jail; of rescuing survivors and pulling her from the river after the wreck of the *Julia Cerre*; of scores of lively conversations and comfortable hours of no talk at all, sitting on the veranda or enjoying a late supper. She tried to resist thoughts of him, to bar him from her mind, and she reviled her own weakness, and the man himself, for her failure. Her eyes misted a little and she rested her head in her hand, tired and angry at the dreaded fact that she missed him.

"This ruins everything," she whispered to herself. She dried her eyes on her sleeve and opened Hypolitte's letter.

My dear Perdita,

Since all has escaped from Pandora's box, there is no longer any reason to hold anything back. I have intruded into your life, it is true, but in no more or less a way than you have intruded into mine. I do not really believe you think I have patronized you or that I undervalue your talent or ambitions. That is not what your anger, your dismissal of me, was about. No, it was rather the intrusion itself. Surely there is some reason you came to Ste. Odile, more even than the establishment of your reputation as a sculptress. I have felt it nearly from the day we met. I have dreamt that you have a mission to fulfill here. There is the creative one, certainly, but there is more. I think of the lives you have affected, from Marie's to Solana's, to the infant you saved from the river. How different would these months have been for them if you had never come here. I think of myself, also.

I came to this town soon after I took my degree in St. Louis. I had some qualms about coming to such an out-of-the-way place, a backwater. Mr. Morisot, however, was determined to persuade me, and he offered a salary I would have expected to earn at the end of my career, not at the beginning. So I came into the situation with much optimism, and not a little idealism, as young people do. As they say: "It's all ahead of you then."

The work at Bastide's mines was interesting, even rewarding, at first. My skills and knowledge were valued, and as I said, I was well paid. Then, as now, society here was limited. Having been encouraged by my mother to embrace a wide spectrum of interests and preoccupations, I found this tendency to be frustrated by my residence here. What satisfaction is there in a passion felt in solitude? Any excitement or enthusiasm wants a companion, or like-minded spirit to share its rewards. None were to be found in the town. Eventually, your Uncle Tancred arrived. He seemed a beaten man then, nearly destroyed in body and spirit, in need of a fresh start. He seemed also to be an intellectual with traces of what I saw as a liberality of spirit, which had been smashed by some catastrophe which he would never discuss. We found some common ground and a certain camaraderie, but there was an irascibility about him, a general conservatism which greatly limited our friendship.

Of course, I was missing more than mere friendship. Over the years, I became acquainted with several young women in the district. Most were pleasant enough, even appealing to the eye, and all were seeking marriage. They were the daughters of tradesmen, farmers, and miners; none of whom, I am sure, had ever travelled more than thirty miles from this village. Their interest in the world was as circumscribed as their experience of it. Still, you will be surprised to learn that I became engaged. Her name was Jeanne-Marie Dufresne. She was the youngest daughter of Edmund Dufresne of Vizir Packet Lines, with whom you have dealt in your efforts to recover your lost block of marble.

She was a lively, pretty girl of above average intelligence and a favorite of her parents. She was sufficiently educated to have filled some of the duties which are now yours at St. Perpetua's. She had an innate wit and curiosity that made her an engaging, if not completely satisfactory, conversationalist (it sounds so uncharitable and patronizing to say it like that). But I had lived alone for many years, and she seemed as good a prospect for a partner in life as I was likely to find in my limited contact with the world at large. In my way I loved her, though not as much as I knew she hoped for.

On a Sunday a few months after our engagement became official, she began to complain of an acute pain in her lower abdomen. This continued with varying severity for several days. Dr. Duclos diagnosed acute appendicitis. He had performed abdominal surgery twice, both ovarian extractions to cure hysteria, but never an appendectomy. Fearing the organ would burst and spread its toxins, Duclos undertook the surgery. Soon afterward, Jeanne-Marie experienced a new swelling and tenderness in the area of the liver, then fever, chills, and a loss of breath. Duclos suspected peritonitis, a frequent effect of appendectomy. She died within a week.

My fiancée was gone. With her loss, I felt more alone than I had before I had known her. I mourned her for many months, then fell into an extended period of melancholy. The village offered no other prospects to me for a helpmate, friend, and wife. Until you arrived.

Father Tancred had spoken of you with his particular species of begrudging pride before he knew you were coming here. When he received that news, he was greatly taxed to suppress his excitement. As was I. I felt I had come to know you from his descriptions. I dreamt of you before I ever met you, and in the dream you were coming to Ste. Odile for no other reason than to find me. I tried not to expect too much: that way lies disappointment. But when we met, and I saw your beauty and elegance, and first heard the workings of your mind, and became acquainted with your sense of taste and your aesthetic, from that day on, you were the predominant subject of my thoughts, and the object of an ever-growing regard, and, if I may tell you, love.

You remain so. There has not been a span of ten minutes' time in the last two months when I have not thought of you. This separation, this misunderstanding, has been terrible for me. Please believe I had no thought of questioning your ability or your chances for success. Believe also, as I suspect you really do, that I would never patronize you, and that I anticipate your future renown with the utmost pride and sense of satisfaction.

May we talk? Cannot we discuss these difficulties face to face? How else will I convince you that far from being an impediment to your success, I hope to be its most ardent witness. I want nothing but your happiness. Your companionship assures mine. Cannot we put this unpleasant country behind us?

Love,
Hypolitte

Perdita refolded the letter and returned it to its envelope. She smiled slightly, though there were tears in her eyes. The dining room clock struck one. Her afternoon class would be starting soon. She dabbed her eyes and rose from her chair. On her way out the front door, she returned the two letters to the pier mirror, where she knew they would not be disturbed.

She walked briskly up Constantinople Street toward St. Perpetua's. Her mind felt clearer than it had all morning, and her spirits slightly improved. As she approached the brick and ironwork wall at the seminary, and neared the front gate, she could see that the girls were being directed out of the school to the lawn by Sister Clotilde, Sister Rose Agnes, and several other nuns. The girls were agitated and talking excitedly, milling around the statue of St. Perpetua. Perdita's brisk pace up the avenue of cypresses toward the school building built quickly to a run. Sister Clotilde noticed Perdita approaching and walked quickly to meet her.

"We cannot enter the building, Perdita. We must evacuate!" Clotilde said excitedly.

"What is it, Sister, what is the matter?"

"Diphtheria!"

29

"We have seen these symptoms before," Sister Clotilde said, as she watched the girls move past her in single file toward the convent. "Louise and Bertha have developed a discoloration in their throats and a wracking cough."

"And Anatolia?" Perdita asked.

"She is not as advanced in the disease as the other two. No one else is showing the symptoms yet. Those three are quarantined and in the care of Sister Consolata and Sister Elizabeth. Both have some experience with infectious disease."

"Where is Dr. Duclos?"

"On Kaskaskia Island with Dr. McWhorter of the mine infirmary. There was a report of yellow fever there, and they left last night."

"One of them must be recalled," Perdita said urgently, touching each girl on the shoulder as they passed. "These girls will die without medical aid."

"The doctors were wired an hour ago," Clotilde said. "They cannot come. This is up to us, and God."

"But they will *die!*" Perdita did not try to modulate the panic in her voice.

"Half of the children die who contract the disease. Many live. There is nothing we can do but make them comfortable and put our faith in God."

"There must be *something* we can do," Perdita insisted.

"We have chlorodyne, which has been given but has had no effect as yet. We will have to scrub down every room in the school and dormitory with carbolic soap and burn sulfur candles. For now, we must keep the girls calm and put forward a hopeful and reassuring demeanor for them."

"Of course."

"We will situate them in the convent as best we can until we are certain the contagion has been scoured away."

"Yes, Sister. May I see the girls? May I see Anatolia?"

"I don't think—"

"I have had some experience in medical emergencies, Sister, as you know." Perdita's voice began to quiver, then quickly became strong and resolute. "I can be of assistance, I am sure. I feel…I feel I *must* care for Anatolia. I must take personal charge of her care and perhaps keep her condition from advancing as far as the other girls."

"And how would you do that, Perdita?" Clotilde asked patiently. "How could you possibly have that effect?"

"My presence will comfort and assure her, perhaps even enough to help her body resist the contagion. An assured and confident state of mind has been known, or suspected, of accomplishing this. And it will allow the Sisters to concentrate on the other girls. Please, Sister."

Sister Clotilde smiled sympathetically at Perdita, but the concern on her face was obvious. "In the past five years," she said, "only three of our girls have died. We have been fortunate and blessed. I can't bear the thought of losing any of them. Very well. May God be with you."

Perdita smiled gratefully. She entered the school through the main door and turned left down the corridor toward the offices and infirmary. The infirmary was a small room with only one window and space enough for four beds. Bertha and Louise were in the two beds at the north end of the room. Sisters Consolata and Elizabeth were gently wiping their faces with damp cloths. Anatolia was at the opposite end of the room in a bed almost against the wall. The nuns seemed surprised to see Perdita.

"Miss Perdita, why are you here?"Sister Elizabeth asked incredulously. "There is contagion. You will be exposed to it."

"I am here to look after Anatolia. I mean, to help you in any way I can. I can care for Anatolia while you nurse Louise and Bertha."

"Well, you are here," Elizabeth said in a resigned tone. "I suppose it's too late to shield you now. God bless you."

Louise and Bertha were damp from perspiration and racked with painful-sounding coughs. They winced and grimaced with each cough, and the nuns made ineffectual efforts to cover the girls' mouths with a linen when a cough seemed imminent. Perdita moved to Anatolia's bedside. The child's eyes were closed, but they opened as soon as Perdita touched her arm.

"Miss Perdita!" Anatolia said weakly, with a slight smile. The effort triggered a bout of coughing that lasted for a few seconds.

"Don't speak, just rest," Perdita murmured. "I will keep you as comfortable as I can. I will get a cool cloth for your head. Would that make you feel better?"

Anatolia smiled again and nodded her head.

"Close your eyes, child, and rest," Perdita said. "I won't leave you."

Anatolia's eyes closed slowly, and she grasped Perdita's hand.

"Perdita," Elizabeth said, "you should see this."

Perdita crossed the room and joined Sister Elizabeth at Louise's bedside.

"Open your mouth again, Louise," Elizabeth urged gently. The child opened her mouth with some difficulty.

Elizabeth produced a small mirror from the folds of her habit and held it near the child's face. Reflected light illuminated the mouth and throat. Perdita glanced inside and could see an odd, grayish film at the back of the mouth extending back as far as was visible into the throat. Elizabeth took Perdita's arm and led her into the corridor.

"This is a bad sign," Elizabeth said. "I have seen this before in children with this disease."

"What is it?" Perdita asked.

"It is a membrane that forms in the throat. As the infection advances, it could suffocate her. Bertha has it, too. If it does not suffocate them, its toxins could stop their hearts."

Perdita gasped audibly. She felt a moment of panic, but calmed herself as quickly as she could. "Is there nothing that can be done?"

"We can give them more chlorodyne for the cough, though I am not certain it helps. They are experimenting with inoculation in Europe, I have heard, by extracting blood serum from deliberately infected horses, but we have nothing like that in this country. We must keep them as comfortable as possible and pray that Dr. Duclos returns soon, though God knows there is little he can do either, I fear."

"Is there anything you need from me now?"

"Sister Consolata and I will stay with Bertha and Louise. Just sit with Anatolia, reassure her, as you intended. Avoid her cough."

The two women reentered the infirmary. Bertha had begun to cough again, tears streaming from her eyes as her body shook with each paroxysm. She sat up in her bed, and Consolata held her against her breast, comforting her and mumbling a Hail Mary.

Through the afternoon, the girls rested fitfully or not at all. Perdita paced the room or sat for a few moments at a time, exasperated by a growing feeling of helplessness. In the evening, Louise's breathing became more labored, and

Bertha's fever rose. Perdita watched for these symptoms in Anatolia and noticed her breaths were becoming shallower and more difficult, though her fever had not risen since the afternoon. Anatolia dropped off to sleep from time to time, only to be roused awake by a coughing spasm. By midnight she had drifted off again and, in her sleep, kicked off the sheet covering her onto the floor. Perdita picked up the sheet to re-cover her, and as she gently lifted the child's foot to place it again on her mattress before replacing the sheet, she noticed ridges and scars partially visible at the sides of the child's thighs, which appeared to continue to the backs of the legs.

"Her mother's punishment," Perdita whispered to herself, "for seeing angels!"

Perdita intended to stay awake all night, but dozed infrequently when Anatolia seemed to be resting and the other girls' coughing had subsided. By ten in the morning, Bertha was lying still in her bed, her complexion sallow and waxen. Louise's breathing had become labored: at times she seemed to be choking; when done, she would struggle for breath. Consolata, who had been resting in a chair in a corner, roused herself.

"I think I dozed off," she said. She rose and touched Bertha's arm. Her face went blank as she lightly grasped the child's wrist, feeling for a pulse. Her eyes filled with tears and she made the sign of the cross. "She's gone!" Consolata said.

Elizabeth and Perdita approached Bertha's bed. Elizabeth touched the child's cheek and throat. She made the sign of the cross. "It must have been her heart," she noted quietly but emotionlessly.

By early afternoon Bertha's body had been removed to an unused classroom and covered with a linen sheet to await examination by Dr. Duclos. Perdita left Anatolia's side only long enough to walk to the kitchen and cut herself a bit of cheese which she quickly ate. As she walked back down the corridor toward the sick room, it occurred to her there was no priest at hand who could have given Bertha last rights, nor was it likely there would be one for the other two girls, if needed. Father Vannier had left for Montreal a week ago to see to his ailing father, and Uncle Tancred had still sent no word from St. Louis regarding his mission there or when he might return. Perdita felt if Uncle Tancred knew that Vannier was absent, he would end his business and speed his return. She knew he would have been appalled to think the entire village was without the services of a priest and the benefits of the holy sacraments. Perdita missed him, and she was beginning to fear for his safety. What could have taken him away so suddenly? Why had he made no attempt to explain himself or contact her or Mrs. Moon, who, he must know, were anxious to hear any word from him?

She wondered, also, if Hypolitte knew what was happening at the seminary. If so, did he have any thought of helping or any apprehension of the danger he would surely know she was now exposed to? She half expected some word of concern from him to have been received within the last day or so, but none had come.

Back in the infirmary, Perdita pressed a damp cloth to Anatolia's perspiring face. Anatolia's coughing had been building in intensity since morning. When the coughing subsided and the child seemed to be resting, Perdita realized how exhausted she was. She sat in a chair beside Anatolia's bed, and rested her head against the wall.

Perdita was startled awake by Consolata's frantic exclamations. "She can't breathe! She can't breathe, she is suffocating!"

Perdita jumped to her feet. Consolata was holding Louise's hand and weeping bitterly. Elizabeth held the child's mouth open and was depressing her tongue with her fingers to try and open her airway.

"We need to get air into her," Elizabeth said grimly. As Perdita arrived at the bedside, Louise's face had turned a ghastly, pallid blue. The child had a look of terror in her eyes, but in a moment they lost all expression and she went limp. Consolata held Louise's lifeless hand against her cheek as her weeping became more forlorn and nearly convulsive. Elizabeth closed Louise's eyes and embraced Consolata.

"Sister, Sister," Elizabeth said. "Pray for the poor child. Calm yourself. We could do nothing. It was inevitable."

At the same moment, Perdita and Elizabeth looked across the room at Anatolia. Her breathing had become noticeably more shallow and operose in the last hour. Perdita rushed to her side and began to again feel the sense of panic and desperation growing within herself that she had struggled to overcome before. She grasped Anatolia's hand and squeezed it. The child glanced at her and smiled weakly.

"No," Perdita said under her breath, "it cannot be inevitable. We have to save this child." She turned away from Anatolia to hide the concern on her face. Footsteps could be heard running up the corridor. Sister Elizabeth looked out of the infirmary door.

"Sister Rose Agnes," she said, "stop where you are. Don't come any closer. What is it?"

"Dr. Duclos is on his way back. Mother Superior sent me to tell you. He should be back by about seven tonight."

"Thank you, Sister. Thank you for the news. His return, I hope, will not come too late."

Perdita looked at Anatolia for a long moment. Her feeling of panic seemed to evaporate, and she felt a sense of calm wash over her.

"Sister Consolata," she said, "does the infirmary have a small funnel?"

"No," Consolata sniffed, just beginning to regain her composure. "We had a glass one, but I dropped it yesterday."

"Very well," Perdita mumbled stoically. "Sister Elizabeth, are there any small kegs in the pantry?"

"Yes, one for vinegar."

"Does it have a spigot?"

"No." Elizabeth was puzzled.

"In that case, Sister Elizabeth, in the cellar of the convent is an old loom. Solana and I intended to use it in a class lesson until Mother Superior stopped our efforts."

"Yes?"

"Would you go to the cellar, please, and remove the yarn bobbin from the shuttle and bring it to me? And as you pass through the kitchen, stoke up the stove and put on a pail of water to boil, if you will."

"What is this about, Miss Perdita, if I may ask?"

"Please, Sister, time is precious. Will you fetch the bobbin? If there is any yarn left on it, remove it, and on your way back through the kitchen, put the small end of the bobbin in the boiling water and bring it here."

"All right, Miss, as you say." Elizabeth rushed from the room.

"Sister Consolata," Perdita continued, "does the infirmary have a lancet?"

"Yes, we do have one," Consolata answered and dabbed at her eyes, "for pustules and splinters."

"Could I have it, please? Quickly!"

Consolata left the room for a few moments and returned with the instrument.

"Is it clean, Sister?"

"Yes, I boil it after every use."

"Good. I have one more thing to ask of you."

"What is it?" Consolata's eyes were red and swollen.

"Go to the kitchen and get me a piece of ice about the size of a large walnut."

"Yes, Miss. We got ice this morning." Consolata

scurried out of the room, seeming grateful to have been given a duty to perform.

Perdita pulled her chair closer to Anatolia's bedside. She stroked the child's feverish cheeks. Anatolia seemed to be barely conscious. Her eyes fluttered open and shut. She began to cough a rasping cough, grimacing in pain each time. After the coughing subsided, she gasped for breath. Her breathing had become more constricted in just the last few minutes.

Elizabeth and Consolata returned from their errands at the same time. Consolata gave Perdita a balled-up linen napkin. Perdita unwrapped the chunk of ice within it. Elizabeth placed a small pail of steaming water she had been carrying on the cabinet which also held the lamp. In the pail bobbed a thin wooden cone. She removed it by its thick end to hand to Perdita. It was some ten inches long, tapering from a diameter of about three-quarters-inch on the thick end to no more than a quarter-inch on the small end. Perdita carefully took the bobbin by its thick end and held it to her eye looking toward the lamp.

"Good, it's clear," she said. "Consolata, would you push this cabinet to Anatolia's bedside, please? I will need more light, and both of you need to have your hands free." She dropped the bobbin back into the water.

"Perdita," Elizabeth said warily, "what are you going to do?"

"I saw a doctor do this once," Perdita mumbled, as if to herself. "I assisted him in the disaster on the Charles. In Boston. One of the victims was a boy of about twelve. He had a piece of debris lodged in his throat. He was suffocating."

Elizabeth was aghast. "You can't be serious! You can't risk this! We must wait for the doctor."

"If I do not risk it, she won't last another twenty minutes. We have no choice, Sister, if we want to save her, and we *will* save her. I won't let this child die!" Perdita moved to Anatolia's bedside and bent over her. "Anatolia," she murmured, "can you hear me?"

Anatolia's eyes flickered open and she looked at Perdita.

"I have to do something now that will be unpleasant," Perdita continued. "I know you believe I do this only because I must. I must do this to save your life. Do you understand?"

Anatolia nodded.

"Think of the angels who visit you. They are with you now. I don't know if you can see them, but I can see them, and so can Sister Elizabeth and Sister Consolata. I see they are protecting you and helping me to do what I must do."

Anatolia looked deeply into Perdita's eyes and smiled.

"And now, child," Perdita continued, "you will feel cold on your throat. I need to make a spot on your throat very cold. Then you must lie as still as you can. The Sisters will help you to lie still."

Elizabeth moved to the side of the bed, opposite Perdita, and crossed herself. At Perdita's direction, Consolata moved to the head of the bed behind Anatolia. Perdita touched Anatolia's small suprasternal notch, just above the clavicle. At a finger's width above the notch, she applied the chunk of ice. The child did not flinch or react in any way.

"Sister Consolata," Perdita whispered, "would you grasp her under the chin? Hold her chin up and her head still. Sister Elizabeth, would you hold her shoulders?"

The nuns complied. Holding the ice in place, Perdita moved her chair a bit closer to the cabinet so that the bobbin would be within easy reach. After four or five minutes, she removed the ice and quickly dabbed Anatolia's skin dry with the linen napkin. Perdita dipped the lancet blade into the steaming pot of water and shook off the drops. Leaning down to within a few inches of Anatolia's throat, with a quick stroke, she slit an incision in the child's skin about an inch long. Anatolia flinched slightly and grimaced. Tears seeped into the corners of her tightly closed eyes, but she held her body rigid and still. Sister Consolata gasped and lost her grip for a moment.

"Sister!" Perdita admonished. Consolata resumed her position. "That is the worst of it, Anatolia," Perdita continued. "You are a brave girl!"

Perdita spread the incision slightly with the index and middle fingers of her left hand. There was little blood. Behind a small red band of muscle, she could see the translucent, ribbed trachea. She slipped the lancet into the wound and cut a tiny slit between two of the ribs. She quickly removed the bobbin from the water and inserted the small end into the slit and held it still.

"Breathe, Anatolia," she urged, "breathe, now." Anatolia's chest began to rise and fall in a regular, unencumbered way. Consolata yelped for joy. Elizabeth looked at Perdita with astonishment and admiration.

"God be praised!" Elizabeth said. "Let me get another linen to hold under the wound."

"I'll get one!"Consolata said excitedly, and scurried out of the room.

"We'll have to hold the bobbin in that position until the doctor arrives," Elizabeth noted dispassionately.

Perdita's eyes were damp. She was exhausted and trembling slightly. She wiped her eyes on her sleeves and felt the sense of tension and excitement that had gripped her slowly drain out of her body.

"Yes, Sister," she said weakly. "I know. I won't be going anywhere."

30

Mrs. Zell embraced Perdita. "Dr. Duclos just sent *word*. He thinks *Anatolia* is out of *danger*. She is breathing easily now, and her *fever* is broken."

"Thank God!" Perdita smiled and returned Mrs. Zell's embrace. "Thank God. Sister Elizabeth tells me it will take two or three more days to scrub down the classrooms. The girls will be idle for a while longer."

"I don't *envy* the sisters. Did you *rest*?"

"Yes, I slept well. I feel quite refreshed. Otherwise, I wouldn't have accepted Mr. Bastide's open invitation for tonight. I think one should have all her faculties when visiting Orien Bastide."

"I wouldn't *know,* dear. That must be Tertius with the *carriage* now."

"Yes, I think it is. I will try not to disturb you on my return tonight."

Mrs. Zell smiled at Perdita affectionately and returned to the kitchen. Perdita opened the front door in advance of Tertius' knock.

"Beautiful evening tonight, Miss," Tertius said, as he buttoned his black velvet jacket. "Getting chilly, though."

"Hello, Tertius. Yes, it is beautiful tonight. It will be cold. Winter is just over the next hill."

"Yes," Tertius said, opening the door of the Rockaway and helping Perdita climb in. "The house is draughty in the winter, from what I remember, but less so than the chateau at Montsegur. But that house is about six hundred years old."

"I suppose at that age you have to allow it some failings."

Tertius started to close the carriage door, but stopped. "If I may presume, Miss, do you recall my admonition on your first visit regarding Mr. Bastide and his gifts?"

"I do. Thank you, Tertius."

"Certainly, Miss. Forgive me for bringing it up again." He closed the door.

Perdita settled into her seat, looking forward to the carriage ride through town along Endymion Street and on to Thermopylae. Along those dimly lighted streets, on that chilly evening, Ste. Odile showed few signs of life. Most activity was moving indoors for the winter, she thought. Somewhere in the dusk, Hypolitte was having his supper about now, at Herve's, probably. She smiled to remember their last dinner there, and the suspicion with which Herve seemed to regard their whispers and laughter that night.

As she watched the dimming landscape outside the carriage window, she decided she would send Hypolitte a note the next morning, agreeing to meet him and discuss their differences. Most of the afternoon, she had been turning over in her mind what to say to him, and trying to decide, most importantly, what it was she really wanted of him. But this seemed to be a question she could not answer with any finality. Any given morning, he might seem like a distraction, and the time they spent together wasted. By evening, though, she might be thinking of his laugh, his discourses on arcane or little-known subjects, how his hair curled around the backs of his ears, or how his suits fit him. She often felt as though her reading of *Moby Dick* in the parlor should be scented by his subtle eau de cologne, or that he should appear at her side from time to time to refill her wineglass.

The sight of the moss-covered fountain and the massive oak tree roused her from her reverie, and she could scarcely believe they had so quickly traversed the two miles to Jardin Noir. Tertius stopped the carriage at the front door, and before he could perform his prescribed duty, Perdita had opened the door herself and stepped out. Tertius preceded her to the front door and pulled it open. As he did this, the inner door at the far end of the vestibule simultaneously opened, revealing Bastide, eyes and teeth glistening behind his wax prosthesis, in a smile of welcome.

"Miss Perdita," he said, "how good it is to see you again!"

"Thank you, Monsieur Bastide. It was very gracious of you to extend such a liberal and open invitation."

"Come in, come in. If I may, I will leave your hat and wrap here." He took these items as Perdita proffered them, and placed them on an enormous Gothic-style hall tree of walnut and marble that stood against the northwestern wall of the vestibule. He then waved her grandiloquently into the entry hall. Perdita remembered the sense of loss and dread that had overcome her on her first visit as she crossed the wide threshold. She felt some small sense of these again.

"Word has reached me," Bastide continued, "of your work with the diphtheria victims at the seminary, and how you undoubtedly saved a child's life."

"Thank you,"Perdita said a little awkwardly. "I thank God Anatolia's life was spared. I am full of regret that we failed to save the other two girls."

"Yes, it is a tragic loss, yet you did your best, I am certain."

"One hopes so."

"Hardly a new month arrives without some report of your exploits, of your compassion, heroism, even."

Perdita blushed. "Unforeseen responsibilities have come my way in Ste. Odile. One can do no less for God or our brethren than to meet these as best we can. Fortunately, or coincidentally, I have had the experience to help in certain circumstances."

"And this child, Anatolia, I have heard she has become a special charge of yours."

"You hear a lot, sir. I wasn't aware that any such connection between me and one of my students was apparent."

"Tertius has many old friends in the town, and he has been most interested, as I have been, in your progress here."

"Yes," Perdita admitted, "I must say I have developed a special rapprochement to Anatolia. She is a beautiful and caring child. She is also an unsettlingly talented artist and writer, for her age. And she is…a visionary. She has wonderful visions of heavenly hosts, of the inner workings of the soul. It seems, often to the discomfiture of those around her, that all things are transparent to her."

"Indeed?" Bastide's interest seemed more than a little piqued.

"Yes. In spite of myself, I have been drawn to her. She is truly unique in my experience."

"Why do you say 'in spite of myself'?"

"I had planned on maintaining more detachment from my students—had expected to—given my admitted disinterest in children, or perhaps I should say inexperience with them before taking this position. Anatolia, it seems, has changed that."

"I am fascinated. I would welcome the opportunity to meet this visionary child some day."

Perdita was appalled at the thought of introducing the sensitive Anatolia to the monstrous figure before her. "Perhaps, some day," she said.

"My plan this evening," Bastide digressed, "is to show you the rest of Jardin Noir, as I failed to do on your last visit, then offer you some refreshment in the study upstairs before dinner is served."

"Excellent." Perdita smiled, and followed Bastide through a small door to the left of the larger one she knew to be to the library. The door opened on a small, dimly lighted adytum which seemed to be an anteroom to a larger chamber visible through an archway. The anteroom was poorly maintained and contained only one decorative element: displayed on the northwestern wall and lighted inadequately from above were twenty or thirty yellowing and dusty plaster death masks. Some were public figures. Perdita thought she recognized Beethoven, Napoleon, Robespierre, Liszt, and Goethe, but most appeared to be women, young to middle-aged, and anonymous. One mask, low on the wall and off to the right, was concealed, perhaps inadvertently, under a sheet, that also partially draped over a chair situated under it.

"My word!" Perdita gasped. "How did you come by these?"

Bastide regarded the masks silently for a moment. "There are many ways," he said. "A mask made of any notable personage will be copied, probably many times, and these maybe had, if not the originals, for the right price, if one knows where to seek them out. Some may be found in curiosity shops, and others...acquaintance with and influence over coroners, doctors, undertakers, and even artists can be beneficial."

Perdita found this statement to be cryptic in the extreme, but decided not to question her host further.

"History," Bastide continued, "is, I think, more accessible than most realize. And history is made by individuals. It is critical to me to remember the essence of those individuals, and their humanness. An artist can only interpret a nature, a personality within the strictures of his talents and biases. But these masks are not an interpretation. These are truly the souls themselves; them! Through these mementos, their actual faces, I may truly remember them."

Bastide led Perdita through the archway into a long gallery, the ceiling of which was entirely made of intricate ironwork framing that supported glazing of translucent panes of white glass. The ceiling provided, even this late in the day, ample natural light to illuminate the room. Filling the one-hundred-foot length of this gallery were glass cases both large and small, containing fully articulated skeletons of every manner of creature. There were ourang-outans and chimpanzees, wolves, a lion, an elephant displayed next to its brown-boned counterpart, which Perdita took to be a mastodon; fish, an ostrich, a walrus, and two nearly twenty-foot long whales. Lower cases lining the walls displayed the skeletons of birds, ranging from the tiny and delicate to a large golden eagle, and vast collections of mounted beetles, spiders, and butterflies. On shelves near the archway were some two dozen jars, murky and dust-covered, holding preserved and monstrous specimens of fish, amphibians, reptiles, and the malformed, embryonic remains of a lamb, a dog, a pig, and two human infants.

Perdita's emotions ranged from awestruck to appalled as she walked slowly around the room, agape, from one case to another. It was hard for her to conceive of an individual, a private citizen, owning such scientific and aesthetic treasures as Bastide possessed.

"There is truly no area of investigation or study which is beyond the limit of your interest, it seems," Perdita said. "It is just as Tertius told me on my first visit."

"I see. And is that all Tertius told you?"

Perdita was surprised by the question. "As far as I remember, yes."

"Some of these specimens were once part of the collections of Peter the Great in St. Petersburg," Bastide continued. "Some are from the inventories of museums and universities to which I have given large cash endowments; still others collected on commission by professional hunters, whalers, fishermen, and native peoples around the world. We live in an age of great discovery, of a rapidly growing understanding of history and nature. For he who is hungry to *know*, there has never been a more exciting time to live. I am glad to have survived to see it all."

"To have survived?"

"Yes. Perhaps that was the wrong word to use. Please, if you will follow me through this corridor." Bastide led Perdita through another anteroom and into a short corridor. At the end of this was a double door made of oak set in a wall of smooth limestone. Bastide opened the doors and revealed a large room that reminded Perdita of the ambulatory in a cloister, but with Tudor windows replacing the arches between each tall pilaster. The room was filled with statues of stone, bronze, and wood from antiquity, as well as fragments of Roman mosaics and gladiatorial weapons; Egyptian stele, canopic jars, and three mummies in their sarcophagi enclosed in glass cases; meso-American daggers, crockery, and jade masks; bronze Chinese basins and porcelain objects; and gold-clad musical instruments, cylinder seals, and cuneiform tablets from the kingdoms of the Tigris and the Euphrates.

The statues were placed before each pilaster separating the windows, and ranged through history from Sumerian deities in basalt to a larger-than-life Moses in limestone holding the tablets of the Law, which could have been snatched from the façade of some northern European cathedral. Perdita walked amidst the objects, running her fingertips along expanses of formed marble, granite, limestone, bronze, and wood, smoothed, in many cases, by centuries of tactile admiration. She said little. Occasionally, she would make some passing, appreciative remark, or ask some question relating to the provenance of a piece, or the history of the culture that produced it. Feeling overwhelmed by all that her senses were recording, she wanted to subdue her responses somewhat. To truthfully express what she was feeling might seem pedestrian or provincial to her host.

Bastide then led his guest through a sitting room and a rear parlor to what he called the "small conservatory" attached to the northeastern end of the house. Here were housed palms and many exotic species of flowers, as well as several over-sized cages inhabited by many types of live tropical birds. Another expanse of lawn could be seen from the conservatory windows, as well as more dark gardens and hedges, and a panorama of cliffs, river, and countryside stretching many miles to the northeast.

From the rear parlor, Bastide ascended a servant's staircase to the second floor. At the top of this, Perdita found herself in a large common area populated by all manner of mounted animals. A complete snow leopard, hyena, and ourang-outan all gazed at her lifelessly, as well as the heads of a rhinoceros, a Cape buffalo, a lion, and several species of antelope which she could not identify. Interspersed among the mounted heads were many heavily framed paintings in the Mannerist style and other works, portraits, and religious scenes that seemed to date from the early Renaissance.

The focal point of the area was a double pocket door framed in a Tudor arch of dark wood. Bastide parted these and pushed them open. The room revealed was large, if not as large as the library downstairs. There were more bookshelves here, though the volumes had the look of greater antiquity than those in the library. To the right of the doorway stood an almost life-sized flayed human figure in aging plaster with one arm outstretched: muscles, tendons, and some bone were visible.

"This is an *ecorche* by the great Houdon," Bastide said. "I rescued it from a cellar in Paris."

At the far end of the room an oriel window looked out to the northeast, affording a view of the bluffs above the river, and the forests and plains beyond. A long work table stood before the bookshelves on the left side of the room. This was cluttered with scrolls, parchments, stacks of papers, and very old books. At the far end of the table, surveying all with menace, was the hideous gray figure of a mounted Hamadryas baboon.

"This is where Solana did her work for you," Perdita said. "This is where she was cataloguing your medieval volumes. I recognize it from her descriptions."

"Just so."

In a sitting area just to the right of the baboon, a decanter and two glasses had been placed on a table between two leather chairs.

"Please sit, Perdita, if I may so address you."

"Certainly." She sat in the chair furthest from the baboon. Bastide poured a glass of the pale liquid and offered it to her. She drank.

"It is a Pouilly Fume I have recently discovered," Bastide said, pouring himself a glass. He sat and sipped the wine.

"A bit of a bite," Perdita noted, "but very rich. I like it."

"Yes, I like it, too. If you will pardon me." He set his glass on the table and, finding a vial and hollow glass rod on the tabletop, he placed a few drops in each eye. Some of the liquid appeared to miss its target and run off under Bastide's wax prosthesis. "You are a native of Boston, are you not?" he asked, dabbing at the overflow with a napkin.

"Yes."

"You must miss its cultural distractions?"

"I do. My friend Moira and I attended many lectures, museums, painting exhibits, and musical programs together. I think it is the musical programs I miss the most."

"Yes." Bastide dropped more fluid in each eye. Again most of it seemed to miss its mark and run off under the wax. "Only two years ago," he continued, "I found myself in Boston in November. I only stayed a month and didn't hazard the journey here before returning to Europe. I was fortunate enough to hear a performance of Mozart's *Requiem* —"

"Yes," Perdita nodded. "I missed that performance, but I know the one."

"Sluggish *Confutatis*, but a satisfying *Lacrymosa*. Those two elements must be right in that work, if nothing else."

"Yes. Monsieur Bastide, you appear to be having some difficulty. Please feel at ease and remove the wax, if you wish."

Bastide looked at her, his eyes glistening. "If you would so indulge me. It is sometimes difficult to manage with this on my face."

Perdita felt a sense of trepidation pass through her. "You should be comfortable. Please."

Bastide returned the glass dropper to the vial. With both hands he grasped the lower part of his prosthesis, and with a twitch, popped it off his jaw. The skin revealed was drawn and pale, and appeared to be very thin. Its pallor was shocking, especially when contrasted with the cracked redness of the lips and especially gums, which were almost the color of arterial blood, and shriveled away from the base of the teeth, making them look elongated and rapacious. He then grasped the upper part of his prosthesis and carefully removed it from his face. Perdita was noticeably unnerved by what she saw. Bastide's eyes, which had never left hers, gave the illusion of being unnaturally large and appeared grotesquely round from the barely visible wires that held them open. The cheeks and nose were bony and tightly covered with dry skin the color of the long-blind eye of Perdita's childhood nanny. The absence of the mask seemed to make his long, gray hair seem wilder, more feral.

Perdita felt conflicting compulsions to look at him and to look away. She shivered for a few seconds but quickly gained control of her emotions before her host, livid and corpse-like in the gathering dusk, could notice.

"I apologize if I make you uncomfortable, Perdita."

"No, not at all."

"It is a condition unknown to medical science. After years of their attentions, my physicians in Berne have had little success in treating me."

"Please, do not apologize! I am abashed at the thought that you feel you must do so."

"An uneasy response is only natural." Bastide smiled wetly. His voice had much less of its usual garbled quality with his wax removed. "Will you have more of the wine?"

"Yes, I think I will." Perdita held out her glass to him, and he refilled it. She drank. "Thank you for showing me your home. I can well understand why you feel little need to leave it when you are in this country."

"Yes, my home at Montsegur is much the same as this. Perhaps more so, if you can imagine it."

"Only with some difficulty."

Bastide smiled. "Your friend, Mr. Robert, would approve?"

"Yes, I am certain he would."

"Then he must surely accompany you on your next visit, if you would arrange it."

"Thank you." Perdita nodded.

Bastide sipped audibly from his glass. "It is my understanding that Mr. Robert was nearly lost to the priesthood."

"Lost? He considered it briefly, yes. I was a novice myself, with the Ursulines in New Orleans. I had a change of heart."

"Do you ever regret it?"

"No, never."

"It is so unnatural, don't you find, for a lively young woman like Sister Solana, for example, to have her spirit, her love of life, and finally her sexuality cauterized by her vocation?"

"That is a rather brutal way to put it. I found her spirit to be intact and her love of life very great."

"Really? I found her to be ashamed of those things." Bastide looked at Perdita with an intensity that froze her for a moment. She looked away.

"I suppose a vocation is what you make of it," Perdita said awkwardly. "It can be a way of expressing an appreciation and love for God's creation. But the greatest mistake one can make is to convince oneself that a calling from God is there, when it isn't."

"But how is one to know? Why would God allow the devout, but conflicted, individual to misinterpret his search for Him as a vocation?" Bastide's look of intensity seemed to suddenly melt into a deep, genuine need, a demand, for understanding. "Many people have I known in a long life," he went on, "who have felt that God has…has wounded them, pierced their hearts with a certain knowledge of His apparent beneficence, yet kept them at a distance, kept them unsure of His designs for them, so their lives are consumed with an incessant, yet ultimately unsatisfied longing for Him. Their lives are given over to this, and they know no peace."

"Well, I have known such people," Perdita admitted. "Solana was one. I was one myself, as were both of my parents. I would have to say this is an example of the nature of free will. It is a burden as well as a blessing. When I began to doubt my vocation, I knew that the cloistered life, far from being God's will for me, was instead only a choice, one possible option. My faith has been in crisis, from time to time, but I believe now that God directed me, through prayer and contemplation, to examine my life and gain a measure of self-knowledge that I would not have had otherwise. Not everyone is fortunate enough to come to this understanding, I know—"

"Prayer!" Bastide said disdainfully.

"Yes, prayer."

"What in this life provides less of a dividend than prayer? If Mr. Morisot's management of my investments were no more fruitful than those of prayer, he would be back on his island cutting sugar cane, rather than living the life he has richly earned."

"Its benefits are sometimes less tangible, more far reaching, but very real, in my opinion," Perdita said defensively, taking a nervous sip of her wine. She was startled by his vehemence. "Even if they are not immediately apparent to us."

"Yes, yes, the mystery of God's plan," Bastide said derisively. "A mystery which includes revealing Himself and His dictates to different cultures around the world, in innately contradictory ways, insuring conflict, warfare, and suffering throughout history. You speak of His plan, what of *our* plans? If we have free will and choose a certain course, why are those plans frustrated, sometimes so cruelly?"

"We are tested, certainly, as was Job."

"You are a perfect example, Perdita, if I may say so. You planned a course of action for your life and came here to follow it, and have had your time and energies distracted by the tragedies and problems which have surrounded you since you came to this village."

"My selfish ambitions have not been served as yet, but *good*, the cause of *good* was served by those distractions."

"*Good*?" Bastide repeated, as if hearing the word for the first time. "You say the word, Miss, as though it were a solid, substantive entity, an object of devotion, or a boulder blocking the road which one must circumvent. I once took that Dualist view, that good and evil were separate, warring forces in the world: the Manichean, Catharist view. But now I say, good must not oppose evil, or triumph over it. The completed soul—the one most likely to find balance and peace—is the one that recognizes this and unifies his good and evil selves, masters them, becoming a higher order of being by the accomplishment. One aspect must not be banished, nor the other, they must be reconciled into one."

Perdita considered his words for a moment. She remembered similar discussions she'd had with Hypolitte over too many glasses of wine. Hypolitte's arguments often contained some of the points Bastide was making now, but with less vehemence and always with the hint in them, almost the hope, that his direst views of the human condition would be proved wrong.

"Until very recently," Perdita said at length, "my resentment for the distractions you mention was rather high. It still is, much of the time. But now sometimes I have moments of clarity. I do believe in *good* as a force initiated by God. I depend upon it, I find. So much so, that I cannot admit of the free movement of evil in the world. There have to be things that God, who loves us, would not allow to be. Sometimes we are tragically mistaken in our interpretation of why we must suffer. But the reason cannot be that God wills us to suffer. Surely that isn't possible. Surely that isn't his purpose. Thanks to our Mr. Robert, I see how my distractions have served a larger good. Anatolia would not be alive now if I had never come to Ste. Odile. And the other things that have happened…it all must have some purpose, as Hypolitte suggested." She smiled slightly as she thought of his letter and of seeing him again. She would apologize to him and make their peace. Perhaps she would even make him a peace offering of some sort. A surprise. "Mr. Bastide, if I may ask—"

"Anything."

"On my last visit, I rather brusquely refused your offer of a keepsake, of an old Roman coin."

"Yes."

"This is not for myself, you understand, but if you will forgive my very bad taste in revisiting the subject, I would be grateful to be able to make a gift of the coin to Mr. Robert, who would greatly value it."

Bastide's ghastly face remained nearly expressionless. There was perhaps a quickening of the distended orbits of the eyes, or a twinge at the corner of the mouth, barely perceptible in their brevity. He reached into his waistcoat pocket and produced the heavy golden disc.

"Of course," he said.

The dinner Tertius served, which Perdita regarded as exceptional, was a rack of lamb on a bed of garden vegetables, lightly but unexpectedly accented with what must have been spices from Tertius' own country. The taste surprised her, but she grew to an enthusiastic appreciation of it by the meal's end. Also surprising to her was the fact that she seemed to have little taste for wine during the meal and during the after supper conversation. One glass seemed enough for her, and she sipped it through discussions of humane treatment of mental illness; the evolution of certain English moths, and lesser known scandals of Roman and later Papal history. Perdita felt elevated by the discussion, but cautious, in case Bastide's excessive interest and engrossment in her opinions and observations should be some sly form of flattery. As one hour bled into another, she decided that no flattery was intended by her host, but that he was genuinely entranced by the workings of her mind. She could well understand how Solana had been gratified, in spite of her misgivings, by this quality in Bastide.

The conversation eventually moved into the great library, and Perdita was tempted to sample a slightly sweet port that Bastide offered.

"It is a Conseca that is barely available in Europe and unknown in this country," Bastide explained.

"When will you return to Europe?" Perdita asked. She felt herself becoming more at ease in his presence.

"I have no idea," Bastide said. "When circumstances warrant."

"You are in the habit of making extended visits to Europe, I have heard. You were gone nearly fifteen years on your last trip, Hypolitte told me."

"Yes." Bastide nodded. "But only after having spent many years here before that."

"And I understand your forebears were in the same habit: ten or fifteen years here, then the same amount of time there; through many generations, all of them as reclusive as you—unseen, unknown by anyone but servants, agents, or administrators who manage your affairs. Scarcely anyone knows the Bastides personally, and the curious observer cannot, from afar, distinguish one of you, one generation, from another."

"Yes. How do you like the port?"

"It is stronger than I thought and having some effect. Perhaps I have had enough."

"Nonsense." Bastide refilled her glass.

"Isn't it odd," Perdita continued, "that all of your ancestors should live the same secretive, peripatetic life?"

"Is it? I can scarcely say. I have known no other." Bastide glanced at the tall clock that stood across the room. It read nearly midnight. "If you will forgive me, Miss Perdita," he rose, "I must leave you. I am expecting some rare orchids, which should be arriving at the landing within the hour. I must personally look to their handling and loading onto a wagon I have hired. Tertius has prepared a horse for me, I think."

"Of course." Perdita was a little confused by this

sudden development.

"He should be bringing the coach around at any moment now to convey you home. I thank you for a stimulating evening and hope we can have many such in the future. Including Mr. Robert, if you wish."

"I do wish, thank you. Forgive me for asking, but do you need to resume your…your—"

"Prosthesis?"

"Yes."

"No. For an excursion as informal and clandestine as this, a simple linen cowl will suffice." Bastide bowed and disappeared through the main library door.

Perdita rose and walked to the oriel window that looked out on the front drive. Tertius had not yet brought the Rockaway. She turned and strolled casually around the room looking at specimens in cases and books left open on the tables. She noticed through the small doorway that a light had been left burning in the anteroom in which she had seen Bastide's collection of death masks earlier. She entered this room tentatively, a little surprised at her interest in seeing it again. She glanced at the masks cluttering the wall and noticed that some of them had small placards with the names of the deceased written on them in fading ink. Several of the females were nuns. One read: *Sr. Maria Phillipa*. Perdita recognized the name. This was the prioress of the school's convent of a century ago. It was she who acquired the relics of the saints now kept in the Reliquary Chapel, as Hypolitte had told her on the day she first met Solana. Next to this hung the mask draped in the sheet that also partially concealed the chair positioned under it. The sheet was not dust covered like the masks and the chair, the only other objects in the room. Perdita gathered up the sheet and dropped it on the floor, revealing a second death mask resting on the cushion of the chair. Both of the revealed masks were new ones, not grayed or chipped with age like most of the others. Perdita looked at the mask on the wall. It took a moment for her mind to admit to the sensation that washed over her like the waters of the river had done on the day she nearly drowned. The sensation was recognition. She then looked at the mask on the chair. Yes. She knew both faces. On the wall, she was looking at the slightly bloated plaster face of Sister Solana. On the chair, the emaciated face of Marie Delaporte Chardin.

31

Letter from Perdita Badon-Reed to Hypolitte Robert

My dear Hypolitte,

I scarcely know what to think or how to feel! I do not know if I should be incensed, indignant, or "merely" offended. It is late, about one A.M., and I have just returned from a second visit to Jardin Noir. The evening was pleasant enough, I suppose, aside from the harrowing experience of seeing Mr. Bastide's face for the first time. It sounds almost cruel to say it, but that is a vision one is not quickly to forget. He was most gracious and the meal was excellent. The evening ended about an hour ago, when Bastide had to leave to meet a boat at the landing. As I was waiting for the coach to be brought round to bring me home, I took a second look at a collection of death masks Bastide had shown me earlier. Uncovering two that had been concealed under a linen, I was shocked and much distressed to discover that these were the images of Solana and Marie Chardin! I could hardly believe what I was seeing. My first response was to attempt to confront Bastide and ask how it was that he owned these ghastly, and to my heart, offensive objects, but he was gone.

I asked Tertius, the manservant, about them as he helped me into the coach, but he professed ignorance of their existence. What are we to make of this? How and when were these masks taken, and by whose authority? How and why did Bastide come by them? I will demand answers to these questions from Bastide, and Sheriff Aubuchon when he returns from Prairie du Rocher, and perhaps the coroner, if he may be found.

Perdita replaced her pen into the inkwell. She felt upset and agitated, and very tired. This was not the letter she had intended to write to Hypolitte tonight. She arose from her desk and slowly removed her clothes. She washed her face in her basin and slipped into her nightgown. She felt refreshed and more awake now. She sat at her desk again and took up her pen.

Now I will get to the real point of this letter, the letter I had originally intended to write to you this evening. I have given much thought to your letter, and to other things you have said at various times regarding my career aspirations, my place in the community, and my connection to you.

I have come to the conclusion that I have treated you harshly, and am now mortified to recall the things I said to you. And I have also come to understand that the feelings you expressed at the end of your letter are not now, nor have they been for some months, unreciprocated. I wish to talk with you face to face as soon as we may. Would tomorrow evening be possible? It would do me much good, I think, to see your face and talk earnestly about my many failings and missteps as your friend. Fearing that you may be feeling somewhat peevish toward me, I have secured an inducement, a surprise to reward your speedy compliance, if the mere pleasure of my company fails to do the trick!

Yours,
Perdita

Perdita folded the letter and sealed it, and carried it as quietly as she could down the creaking stairs to leave it on the pier mirror in the entryway. It was nearly two A.M. and the effect of the evening's stimulation, its revelations and ethical dilemmas abruptly faded, and she felt exhausted. She returned to her room, quietly closing the door behind her. Though she had never done so in the entire time she had been living at Tranquille House, and could not account for the compulsion to do so now, she locked her door.

She fell into bed. Her mind revived for a few minutes as she recalled the many sensory stimuli of Jardin Noir: art, specimens, books. She thought of the supper Tertius had prepared, and she thought of the evening's many conversations, of Bastide's vehemence when certain topics were broached, and of his face; his ghastly, livid face. She thought of the death masks of Solana and Marie, and recalled her sense of surprise and outrage at first seeing them. These emotions were rekindled as she saw the masks in her mind, but were gradually replaced by another sensation that Perdita slowly identified as dread.

Soon her thoughts settled on Hypolitte and how he would receive her letter. A sense of excitement at seeing him again was growing in her, and she recognized this didn't seem to trouble her in the least, as it might well have done a month ago. Christmas was coming soon. It would be the first holiday they would spend together. During that season in Ste. Odile, there would be the old French observation of The Epiphany and Twelfth Night. There would be the King's Ball, with dancing, and the Galette des Rois, as the Sisters had told her. She and Hypolitte would celebrate these things together.

Perdita slowly realized she did not recognize her surroundings. She found herself in a chamber of high limestone walls under a timbered ceiling. The crowd that milled around her—men, women, and children dressed in medieval jerkins, bodices, and tunics—embraced and consoled one another. An air of doom pervaded the chamber, and the figures dressed in white, whom she somehow knew to be the *perfecti*, led prayers at the far end of the room. The crowd had gathered to pray and extend well wishes to the four men who were to escape that night, taking with them as much of the company's theological and worldly goods as they could carry, so as to preserve some scrap, some memory of the faith for which the rest of the throng would die in the cleansing flames the next morning. She knew the four men's names: Amiel Aicart, his companions Hugo and Poitevin, and Orien Bastide.

Perdita startled herself awake. Some movement on her bureau sent her engraving of St. Cecilia, which she had never gotten around to hanging on a wall, crashing to the floor. A scratching sound on the windowsill was followed by the creak of the sash pushing up a few inches. Perdita sat up in bed. After a moment she gathered her bearings. Had the sash just been raised, or had she raised it earlier and only dreamed that it had just happened? Why would she have raised the sash to make her already chilly room even colder? Had some breeze blown the engraving to the floor? She rubbed her eyes and thought she saw movement outside her window. She rose and walked to the window, but could see no sign of activity beyond the bare, wind-whipped branches of the elm tree that stood outside her room. She closed the sash and returned to her bed. She suddenly felt wide awake and knew she would sleep no more that night.

Letter from Hypolitte Robert to Perdita Badon-Reed

November 27, Afternoon

Dearest Perdita,

I cannot tell you with what excitement and anticipation I received your note. I worried that it must be you who were peevish toward me and feared we would never have the opportunity to talk these things out, and put, what seems to me, small problems impeding a great good, behind us. I am anxious to meet at the earliest possible opportunity. There have arisen some questions regarding assaying results recorded by Karl, my assistant. This demands my urgent attention and will certainly keep me occupied most of the day tomorrow. And tomorrow evening I am to meet your Uncle Tancred. I had a mysterious and urgent telegram from him this morning, saying he hoped to be back in Ste. Odile by seven o'clock tomorrow night. He said he needed my assistance in a matter of such urgency and moment, that he would only discuss it in person. Surely whatever confidence he wishes to impart will be expressed within two hours' time. Shall we meet at Herve's at nine? I will send word if I expect to be late.

I have much to say to you, and I am curious about the surprise you mention. An inducement, you say? As if I would ever require such a thing!

And yes, I am appalled at your discovery of the masks. An explanation must be demanded from Aubuchon, who would have surely known of this; of the coroner, and of the man himself, Mr. Bastide.

P.S. It is probably nothing, but I should mention your letter arrived with its seal broken. I failed to mention it before, but another message you sent me about a month ago arrived in the same condition. Is it safe, I wonder, to leave your letters on the pier mirror as they await being picked up?

32

"You are recovering remarkably well, Anatolia." Perdita smiled. She was slowly brushing the child's hair, and Anatolia had drifted into a dreamy, contented state. "You like this brushing, I think?"

"Yes, Miss…a lot," Anatolia whispered. Her voice was still weak and she had some difficulty in swallowing. A small bandage covered the wound on her throat.

"You are getting stronger and will be completely on your feet again soon and back in class."

"I hope so, Miss Perdita." They were alone in the dormitory, except for the occasional solicitous visitation of Sister Consolata monitoring the comfort of the patient. "Thank you for bringing me soup, Miss," Anatolia continued. "It was good."

"I am glad you liked it."

"You look tired, Miss. Are you tired?"

"Yes. I had little sleep last night. And I have done nothing to improve my appearance today. But I wanted to stop by and see you after class, before I go home to freshen myself up. I am having a late supper tonight."

"You are meeting Mr. Robert, aren't you, Miss?"

Perdita smiled again. "Yes. I should have known that *you* would know that!"

Anatolia looked at Perdita gravely. "I hope all will go well, and that he will meet you," she said.

"Of course he will, Anatolia. Why wouldn't he?"

"I don't know. I can't tell. So many things seem dark to me now. I can't tell if bad things are coming. Everything is dark, and I haven't felt this way before!"

"You are recovering from an illness that nearly killed you. All will be as it was before, you'll see."

"I hope so, Miss."

A cold wind swept across Constantinople Street. Perdita buttoned her jacket and pulled her shawl up to cover her throat. She had decided to say hello to Mrs. Moon while she was so close to the rectory, and to look at her *Beatrice Cençi* too, now stored safely in the barn for winter.

Mrs. Moon seemed genuinely glad to see Perdita. She took Perdita's wraps, ushered her into the parlor to the large chair by the fire, and disappeared into the kitchen to make tea.

"You look tired, child," Mrs. Moon said on her return, carrying a silver tray laden with a silver teapot, two cups, and some slices of cake.

"I didn't sleep well last night. I am tired. I had odd dreams."

"Odd?"

"Yes. Rather like some Sister Solana had told me she'd had. Odd. I will catch up tonight, though: 'The sleep that knits up the raveled sleeve of care.'"

"I am sure you will, dear." Mrs. Moon placed a teacup and cake on the small table next to Perdita's chair. She then seated herself on the sofa.

"I hear from Mr. Robert that Uncle is returning this evening?"

"Yes." Mrs. Moon sipped her tea. "I've been worried about him. He hasn't been well, you know. Insomnia, no appetite."

"Yes. I noticed that a little before he left. *Where* did

he go, and why?"

"It's all very mysterious. All he would say is that it is better that you or I know nothing just yet. In fact, he sent me a message, a telegram this morning, asking me to be gone when he arrives tonight."

Perdita was puzzled. "Why on earth would he make such a request and be so evasive? Is his boat on schedule?"

"I don't know, dear. There was some sort of train accident at Kaskaskia and a fire this afternoon. The telegraph lines are down, and will be for some time, according to Mr. Le Pelletier at the telegraph office."

"Uncle telcgraphed Hypolitte yesterday and asked for an urgent meeting."

"I don't know what to think," Mrs. Moon fretted. "His health cannot take too much more excitement, I'm afraid. What a time this has been since—"

"Since I arrived?"

"No, dear. Things started to go wrong before you arrived. Things always seem to go wrong when there is a Bastide at Jardin Noir. No, you have done nothing but set things right. What a benefit you have been to our little community! If we would all only practice what we preach, as you do."

"Thank you, Mrs. Moon." Perdita sighed. A wave of exhaustion passed over her. She hoped she would be able to sleep well. "I could have done nothing other than what I have done. I had no real choice. I swear, though, at times I feel it has all nearly drained the life out of me."

Perdita finished her tea and picked at her cake, leaving it half eaten. After a pleasant chat of twenty minutes or so, Mrs. Moon rose to finish washing the dishes, which Perdita's arrival had disturbed. Perdita followed her to the rear of the rectory, intending to cross the back drive and look at her *Beatrice* in the barn. When she stepped out the back door, and Mrs. Moon closed it behind her, Perdita found herself unwilling to walk any further toward the barn. She suddenly had no desire to see her statue, a sensation that puzzled her.

"I don't have to do this just now," she said to herself.

Perdita arrived at Herve's at a few minutes before nine o'clock. It had gotten considerably colder during the late afternoon and evening, and despite having borrowed a heavy coat from Mrs. Zell, the walk from Tranquille House had been an uncomfortable one. Every table in the small dining room was occupied, and Perdita had to wait quite some time to be seated.

"Mr. Robert is to join me, Herve," Perdita said, as she was seated at the same window table she and Hypolitte had occupied on their last visit. She gave her coat to Herve.

"Very good, Miss Perdita," Herve said. "Will you have something to drink while you wait?"

"No. Well, yes. I am chilled. I'll have some sherry, I think. The one you gave me before—I forget its name."

"Yes, Miss. I'll get that at once." Herve carried the coat to the cloak room and returned in a few minutes' time with the sherry. The wine was nutty, strong, and comforting. Perdita sipped it casually, savoring its flavor and warmth.

Hypolitte was late, which was unusual for him, but Perdita knew that Uncle Tancred often lost track of time and might easily keep a companion past the comfortable boundary of any appointment. By ten o'clock, Perdita felt nothing more of the chill of the night air, and after a third glass of sherry, she was becoming sleepy. The restaurant patrons were slowly finishing their late meals, settling their bills, and going home. Perdita had been hungry earlier, but now she was just tired.

"Herve," she called. He came immediately to her side. She realized that every other table in the room was empty. "What time is it, Herve?"

"It is 11:30, Miss. I am afraid we must close up soon. It doesn't seem that Mr. Robert is coming tonight."

"No. It seems not. He said he might be delayed. He had some business with Uncle...with Father Condell, you see?"

"Ah, yes."

"But he said he would send word if he was delayed."

"Would you like for me to see you home, Miss Perdita?"

"Thank you, Herve, but no."

The air was still now, but colder. Perdita felt that a brisk walk in the chilly night air might clear her head. Instead of walking south on Bosphorus to Rouen Street and Tranquille House, Perdita decided to go out of her way along Endymion to Gentian Street and Hypolitte's apartments. She was worried about him. She had never known him to be irresponsible or unequal to his word. For him to have missed their appointment and to have sent no word was so far removed from his character or habits as she had come to know them, that she could not help but feel some sense of unease as she tried to imagine their cause.

The streets were completely deserted, except for a random stray dog or cat. The dim oil street lights flickered weakly here and there, and nearly every house she passed was dark and quiet, except for the occasional barking of a dog chained to a fence or napping on its master's bed, disturbed by her footfalls on the sidewalk. At Gentian Street she turned south and immediately came into view of Hypolitte's laboratory and apartments.

No light was visible in any window, either in the laboratory upstairs, or the apartments below. Perdita looked through several of the ground floor windows and saw no signs of life inside. She knocked on the front door, gently at first, then more briskly. No answer. She returned to the windows. There was still no sign of movement to be seen.

Perdita became aware of a rustling in a holly bush a few feet to her right at the front of the building. A sudden disturbance of a branch startled her, and a low chittering sound caused her to back slowly away from the bush toward the street. She wondered if she had disturbed a raccoon or an opossum, as she and Hypolitte had seen these many times on the streets at night. Something emerged from the shadows of the bush that was larger than a raccoon, followed quickly by a second creature. In the dim light of the street lamp she could make out few details. The creatures were nothing she had seen before. The forelegs were impossibly long, almost like arms, and the paws prehensile. The animals moved in an oddly liquid, somehow obscene way that Perdita had never observed in an animal before. Both of the creatures gazed hypnotically at her with eyes that shone yellow in the lamplight. Suddenly, one of them scurried toward her, followed quickly by the other. Perdita gasped and stepped backward, nearly losing her footing. Before she could think to run away, the creatures were upon her. They bit simultaneously into the hem of her skirt, then twisted and writhed in a hideous fashion until they had ripped a length of fabric away. Perdita screamed briefly, but as quickly as they had attacked her, the creatures skittered off, up Gentian Street, seeming to fight over the strip of cloth as they disappeared into the shadows.

33

"Miss Perdita, wake *up*!" Mrs. Zell's voice was animated and insistent. Perdita roused herself. She had hardly slept. The dream she'd had the night before had returned, but in greater detail and in a more sensory and immediate way. Once again, she'd found herself in an unadorned castle chamber surrounded by people she knew to be heretics preparing to meet their doom in the flames of the Inquisition that would soon light up the meadow five hundred feet below. "Miss Perdita! Miss *Perdita*!"

"Yes, Mrs. Zell, I am coming…I have hardly slept. I am coming as fast as I can." Perdita rose unsteadily from her bed. She made her way clumsily to her door and unlocked it. Mrs. Zell pushed it open urgently. "Good heavens, Mrs. Zell!" Perdita gasped.

"Perdita, quickly!" Mrs. Zell's face was drawn in concern. "Mrs. Moon *needs* you. Your uncle, Father Condell —"

"What is it?"

"He was found this *morning*. The doctor thinks he's had a *stroke*!"

Perdita said nothing. A stab of fear shot through her. She dressed as quickly as she could and pinned her disheveled hair atop her head.

"Mrs. Moon's *daughter*, Bess, is waiting for you in the *parlor*," Mrs. Zell said, scurrying behind Perdita along the hallway, helping button buttons, clasp sleeves, and flatten wrinkles. Bess stood as Perdita entered the parlor. Her eyes were red and swollen. Perdita embraced her.

"What has happened, Bess?"

"We don't know, Miss. He's very bad off, though, I'm afraid."

"He was *found*? Where?" Perdita asked.

"On the front walk, outside the rectory. He was in vestments, Miss, in his surplice and stole! And he was covered with a blanket!"

"Covered? Where did he go last night?"

"We don't know. He didn't want Mother to know what he was doing. We know nothing."

At the pier mirror by the front door, Perdita wrapped her scarf around her neck and put on Mrs. Zell's warm coat she had worn the night before. She then guided the sobbing Bess out onto the sidewalk. Perdita and Bess hurried west along Rouen Street, then north on Constantinople toward the rectory. Bess dabbed at her eyes as they walked, continuing to sob audibly every few minutes.

"What will become of Father, if he stays as he is?" Bess mumbled, as though she expected no answer.

"I don't know, Bess. We mustn't assume there is no hope."

"Oh, no, Miss Perdita. I would never do that. I prayed for him all the way over to fetch you." Bess seemed to collect herself for a moment, then broke down again. "What will become of the parish? Who will look after us as well as Father did?"

"We must pray he will recover; believe he will. And, if the worse happens, we must have faith that the archdiocese, through our Lord's guidance, will provide a replacement who will fill Uncle's role admirably well. Father Vannier, perhaps."

"Father Vannier isn't like Father Condell. No one is."

"Of course not, dear. We must put our faith in the church and in God."

Perdita and Bess arrived at the rectory just as Dr. Duclos was leaving.

"Doctor!" Perdita said anxiously.

"Miss Perdita. He isn't well."

"Was it a stroke?"

"Yes. He appears to be paralyzed on his right side and cannot speak. I cannot tell how aware he is of his surroundings. He is generally insensible."

"Is there any hope of recovery?"

"I would not expect it. We must make him as comfortable as possible and arrange to get him to St. Louis as soon as we can manage it. His needs will be beyond our capabilities here."

Bess began to sob loudly again. Perdita embraced her.

"And," Dr. Duclos continued, "there is some ill effect from his exposure overnight. Mrs. Moon and the sheriff are with him now."

"Thank you, Doctor."

Duclos nodded and headed off south, into the cold wind, toward his office. Perdita and Bess let themselves into the rectory and left their wraps draped on the hall tree. They found Mrs. Moon sitting on the edge of Tancred's bed, washing his face with a damp cloth. Sheriff Aubuchon sat in a ladderback chair at the bedside. He rose as the women entered the room.

"Miss Perdita," Aubuchon said. Perdita nodded at him and walked to the bedside. She touched Tancred's forehead. It was warm. His eyes were half open, fixed on nothing. His lower lip was sagging and wet.

"He has a fever," Mrs. Moon said. Her voice was even and calm, full of resignation, Perdita thought.

"Mrs. Moon," Perdita said quietly, "what has happened?"

Mrs. Moon touched Tancred's mouth with a towel. "I arrived at five-thirty this morning, as I do every morning. I found him on the front walk covered in a blanket. There was a black velvet jacket under his head, rolled up for a pillow."

"Someone delivered him here in this condition," Aubuchon said, "and took some pains to protect him from the cold."

"Who would have done this?" Perdita asked.

"No idea, Miss," Aubuchon shook his head. *"C'est le coeur du mystere."*

"And he was in vestments?" Perdita continued.

"Yes," Mrs. Moon said.

"And you have no notion of where he went last night?"

"None at all. As you know, he didn't want me to be here when he got home."

"Where is the black velvet jacket?" Perdita asked. Aubuchon retrieved the jacket from the foot of the bed and handed it to Perdita. She held it open in front of her. It was large and familiar. "I have seen this before," she murmured to herself. "But I can't think where."

"He will need care day and night," Mrs. Moon said tenderly, continuing to stroke Tancred's face with the damp cloth. "I will accompany him to St. Louis on Friday. I will write to the monsignor and ask that he provide a conveyance at the landing. He will know what to do."

"Yes," Perdita agreed.

"We will need a replacement at the parish as soon as possible," Mrs. Moon went on. "Perdita, you and your mother are his only blood relatives. We must go through his things—"

"Yes, Mrs. Moon. There will be plenty of time for that."

"I will send Villiers, or the new man I've just taken on, with you on Friday," Aubuchon said to Mrs. Moon. "You will need help with him."

"Thank you, Sheriff."

"Sheriff—" Perdita said.

"Yes, Miss?"

"Hypolitte was to meet Father last night. Have you seen him, or heard from him?"

"Not a word, Miss."

34

Letter from Moira Keane Parnell to Perdita Badon-Reed

December 2, 1882

Dearest Perdita,

I am beginning to wonder if you have fallen off of the edge of the earth. It has been so long since I have heard a word from you. Two short letters I sent last month have gone unanswered. I hope they have not been lost.The first was to relay to you information regarding Prosper and his family, which I received from his brother, Michel, and the second was to repeat an inquiry I had made in October, I think it was, as to when I could come to visit you. In case that letter went astray, let me repeat: far from being an indifferent parent, your father has revealed to me his great love for you and his concern for your well-being and comfort. Unknown to your mother, he has laid aside money for your use since you were a child. It is nearly a thousand dollars, and he has entrusted it to me to convey to you, fearing you would not accept a direct gift from him. He asked that I keep the source of this money a secret until such time as he could think of a means to make amends for the years of estrangement between you. But, after much consideration, I feel it is important for you to know his heart, and the scope of his love, which he has been, he knows, so ill-suited to express.

His wish is that you would come home so that he may have you near in his old age and make up for the lost years. But, whether you will come home or no, he wants you to have this windfall.

I attempted to send you a telegram yesterday, but was told that the lines are down in your area, probably for some time to come. It is my intention to bring this money to you in person, as I want exceedingly to see you again, and assure myself of your well-being in light of the tragedies and adventures you have known in your time in Ste. Odile. I have sensed a distress in you, and feel the need to be by your side, otherwise I would delay my trip until spring.

I have become friendly with Mr. Bryce-Lancaster of Drummond Lines, who informs me that the quickest and most efficient way to reach you from Boston is by ship to New Orleans, then by steam packet or train up the Mississippi. At least it is in any season but winter. My father fears winter storms off the Carolinas, and hurricanes in the Florida Keys (I thought the season was over), and in the Gulf of Mexico. He tells me he will be uneasy unless I take the overland route: a train either to Cincinnati or Chicago, then a steam packet to Ste. Odile.

I would have left before now, and feel I should have, but I must tell you, Prosper has expressed a wish to accompany me. I know that seeing him will cause you great discomfort, Perdita, but surely you could find it in your heart, for the sake of his years of devotion to you, and your abrupt abandonment of him, to grant him one short, perhaps chaperoned, interview? I have told him I thought you would, that it is your nature to be compassionate, but that he *must* understand that no possibility of reconciliation would be implied by such a meeting.

The complication now is Prosper's health. He remains very ill and in his brother's care at Carcassonne. Poor Michel is also charged with the care of their parents, whose health remains, as I mentioned some time ago, extremely fragile. Knowing Prosper's aversion to travel over water in the best of conditions, I can only imagine how great his dread must be to return across the North Atlantic as winter sets in. I will grant him leave of a few more weeks, then I will make my travel plans without him. I will write again in advance of my departure.

My dearest friend, I cannot help but notice many subtle changes in you since you left us. I fear the life you have lived since arriving in Ste. Odile has driven the side of you that I have so valued and so missed since last summer, into some outer darkness, out of my reach and influence. I do so miss you. I long for, yet fear in some ways, our re-union. I fear to see a Perdita whose energies and thrill of life may be lost. Is this what I will find? Please write as soon as you can.

Yours,
Moira

Letter From Prosper Redon to Moira Keane Parnell

December 5, 1882

Dear Moira,

I am beginning to feel the positive effect of my most bland diet. I have felt stronger for the past several days and have been able to eat two meals a day since Sunday. Michel thinks I may have even regained a tiny percentage of the weight I have lost.

Poor Michel! He has been caretaker to our parents and to me to the near destruction of his financial career. He hired two nurses to administer to our needs, but before a week of their service was out, he had decided that the two need his constant supervision. They continue now in most of their duties, but always under his watchful eye. And he must needs be vigilant, for the nurses are both farm girls and though they are simple and kind-hearted, they have been raised in the skills of husbandry, of birthing, tending, and slaughtering pigs, goats, cows, and all manner of domestic fowl. They are rough-hewn if good-intentioned, and must be often instructed in the gentle and delicate care of the fragile shades of our parents.

But I am not so fragile as I was. My food is very dull and without seasoning or imagination, but it has allowed for the slow recovery of my system and the gradual return of my strength. Monsieur Vatrollier of the district police has been most patient, and I have assured him that if my progress continues unabated, I should be able to see him within the next couple of weeks.

Then, in spite of the weather, I hope to return home to accompany you to Ste. Odile to confront Perdita. That I may avoid the northern Atlantic route back to Boston in what will be late December or early January at the earliest, I wonder if you would agree, dear Moira, to wait for me in New Orleans that I may book a direct Southern route? My sincerest apologies if this is an inconvenience. I would, of course, pay your expenses of waiting in that city for my arrival. I must have you with me when I see her, or I fear she will not see me at all.

Yours,
Prosper

Letter from Perdita Badon-Reed to Moira Keane Parnell

December 12,1882

Dearest Moira,

My sincere apologies for not having answered your last two letters. It was my truest intention to do so, but so much has happened. There was an outbreak of diphtheria at our school and two of our poor girls died. Anatolia nearly did, but for the grace of God, she was spared. It appears Uncle Tancred has suffered a stroke and is all but insensible. He is being taken to St. Louis, to an infirmary for aged priests where he can be properly cared for. This catastrophe happened under strange, and as yet mysterious, circumstances, which also somehow involve my friend, Mr. Hypolitte Robert, who has disappeared without a trace. I am so very worried and will not rest until I know his whereabouts.

And I am exhausted. I have been troubled lately with terrible nightmares and fears for which I cannot account. And something more: I start every day with an inescapable sense of dread and foreboding. It is a feeling which I cannot define and can scarcely put into words, except to say that I almost fear to proceed from one day to the next, as though to do so will acquaint me with some terrible knowledge, some revelation that will alter the world and my place in it, forever. The nightmares and the dread I feel have one thing in common: both are connected in some unaccountable and illogical way, to Bastide. His presence, I swear, overarches my sense of foreboding, as it does the town itself. This is sophistry, most likely, but I am frightened to recall that Solana voiced similar fears to me some weeks before she died. Marie Chardin also recalled to me her experience of having crossed that threshold, gained that knowledge, just before the death of her daughter.

I have scarcely slept in more than a week. For this reason, I must beg your indulgence and will keep this message very brief. When circumstances have settled, and I am myself once more, I will become, again, your faithful correspondent.

Moira, I am thrilled at the prospect of your visit. Your account of my father's concern was, I can tell you, a greater windfall to me than the money he has entrusted to you. Thank you for telling me. I look forward to seeing you, depend upon it, and the comfort of your counsel, concern, and friendship. I must ask you, though, please do not allow Prosper to accompany you. I will write to him, too, to dissuade him, if you will forward his address at his family home. He must not come here.

Affectionately,
Perdita

35

Karl was overwrought, the result, it was obvious, of a workload which, though not excessive, seemed to be beyond his capabilities to manage. He had a young face, but he was no longer young. The lines around his eyes and mouth were more evident, Perdita thought, because of the worry and overwork he'd known in the last few days.

"No, Miss," he said, piling a basket filled with ore samples to be analyzed atop several others on his work table. "I still have not seen Mr. Robert, not since our audit of four days ago. The sheriff has been here four times and his deputy, twice. There has been no sign in his apartment downstairs that he has been there."

Perdita had not wanted to hear that Karl had no news. She had checked with him the day before yesterday, and had walked past the apartment more than a half-dozen times since then. A note she'd left in the door last night remained undisturbed, and Deputy Villiers, with whom she had spoken before coming to the laboratory, had no light, as yet, to shed on the disappearance. The deputy indicated though, that eyewitness accounts had suggested to him to make inquiries at Jardin Noir, which he intended to do later that day.

"I hope nothing has happened to him," Karl continued. "Well, *something* has happened. He has never just disappeared before and left me on my own with no word, at least not for more than a day or two at the outside. The engineers and straw bosses want their results. The work is manageable, even dull for two people, but too much for one!"

"Thank you, Karl." Perdita smiled weakly, remembering Hypolitte's account of how he barely had enough work in the laboratory to keep an assistant busy. "I think I can understand your predicament. Send word if you hear anything."

"You know I will, Miss."

A few snow flurries had begun to fall. The stairs leading from the laboratory down to the street were becoming icy and treacherous. As Perdita walked past the apartment door and the front of the building, she thought again of the strange, muscular creatures which had attacked her the night Hypolitte disappeared. She looked warily at the bushes at the front of the building in which the creatures had been hidden. She wondered why the creatures had behaved so aggressively and wondered, too, if they might have actually been abnormally large and misshapen weasels or ferrets that she was unable to identify in the darkness.

As Perdita turned north from Endymion Street onto Constantinople, the wind increased in its intensity, and seemed to blow right through her, chilling her profoundly. Today was the day that Mrs. Moon was to take Uncle Tancred to St. Louis, and Perdita wanted to help in any way she could to prepare him for his trip and to see him off at the landing. Perdita kept her head down as she walked directly into the cold gusts. She could hear the clopping of horse's hooves in the street approaching her. She glanced up only at the last moment, as the large maroon carriage pulled by two chestnut geldings passed her. It was Bastide's Rockaway. The curtains were drawn, but she could make out, dark against the incoming light from the carriage's far window, the silhouette of a tall, seated figure in a top hat. She was surprised to see, not Tertius, but Aristide's son, Urbain, in the driver's seat.

"Bastide!" she called, as the Rockaway glided past her, but the carriage drove on.

At the rectory, Perdita let herself in the front door. She found Mrs. Moon and a young deputy she did not know in the parlor wrapping blankets around Uncle Tancred, who sat in an ambulatory chair, eyes half closed, insensible.

"Good morning, dear," Mrs. Moon said.

"Miss Perdita," the deputy said, extending his hand. "I have heard a lot about you. I am Deputy Weber, Joseph Weber, from New Bremen. Just sworn in. I'll be helping Mrs. Moon with him, all the way to St. Louis."

"Good morning, and I thank you." Perdita nodded. "How is he today?"

"As every day. All the same, and will be the same from now on, the doctor says." Mrs. Moon looked at Tancred and smiled slightly. "Dr. Duclos left not ten minutes ago. He examined Father to make certain he was strong enough to make the trip."

"The *Fortuna* is due in at eleven," Weber said. "I hope it is on time. I'd hate for him to sit in the cold for too long."

"We could wait in the Vizir office, if we must," Mrs. Moon noted. "Do you think there will be ice in the river?"

"No," Weber said. "Not yet. It hasn't been cold long enough."

"Thank God," Perdita said. "Is someone meeting you at St. Louis?"

"I hope so," Mrs. Moon said. "I wrote to the monsignor early this week. I hope he got my message."

Perdita heard footsteps coming down the hallway. Bess entered the room carrying a large carpet bag.

"I've finished packing this, Mother," she said. "Good morning, Miss Badon-Reed."

"Good morning, Bess." Perdita noted two other carpet bags and a trunk with a carrying strap sitting beside the sofa. "It looks like you will want for nothing on your trip, Mrs. Moon."

"This bag is for you, dear." Mrs. Moon motioned for Bess to place one of the bags at Perdita's feet. "It holds some personal things of your uncle's that I thought you should have. Bess, did you pack *everything*?"

"Yes, Mother. *Everything*."

"Thank you," Perdita said. She picked up the bag and started to open it.

"There will be time enough to go through it." Mrs. Moon said quickly, glancing at Deputy Weber, who had not noticed the tone of her voice. "Plenty of time later, after we are off. We will leave it here, and you can get it on your way back from the landing."

"Of course," Perdita said, a little puzzled.

"We'd better be off," Weber said, glancing at his pocketwatch. "Get your wrap, Mrs. Moon. It's gotten colder in the last hour."

With some difficulty, Deputy Weber pushed the ambulatory chair out the front door and onto the sidewalk. Mrs. Moon and Bess each carried a carpet bag, and Perdita was able to manage the small trunk, placing the strap behind her neck. The wind had picked up a bit, and it cut across Mal Ardents Street. Mrs. Moon had so cocooned Tancred in blankets, cowls, and great coats, that Perdita felt certain he must not be suffering from the cold. The *Fortuna* had arrived early from Belgique and would have left early also, if Deputy Villiers had not arrived on horseback and held the boat for Tancred's arrival.

The *Fortuna*, a sternwheeler, gathered steam as Weber stopped the ambulatory chair at the foot of the gangplank. Perdita handed the trunk she carried to Villiers, who hoisted it aboard the boat, set it down among some others on deck, then returned to Perdita's side. Perdita knelt in front of Tancred and touched his face. His eyes never focused on her.

"Uncle," she said, as tears began to well in her eyes, "you will be well cared for in St. Louis, I am sure. Mrs. Moon and Deputy Weber will see you safely there. You know what faith we have in Mrs. Moon, and you know how well she has taken care of you all of these years. You will be safe ...protected. I want you to know I will pray for your recovery every day. Thank you for taking me in, for helping me to establish myself here, and giving me a chance to make a career, a fulfilling life. Thank you for loving me, though I know you would blush to admit it. Know that I love you, and I will see you as soon as ever I can!" She kissed his cheek. Mrs. Moon embraced her and pressed the rectory door key into her hand. She wiped away Perdita's tears with her handkerchief.

"They will freeze," Mrs. Moon said, smiling. She turned and walked up the gangplank, followed by Weber, gingerly pushing the ambulatory chair. Bess followed Weber onto the deck, left her carpetbag with her mother, then hurried away from the landing, back toward Mal Ardents Street.

Mrs. Moon and Weber waved goodbye and pushed Tancred quickly aft, toward a stateroom booked to keep him out of the cold winds. Within a few minutes, the *Fortuna* sounded its great whistle, backed slowly out into the channel, and began to move ponderously away, north against the current. Soon it was lost behind the profile of bluffs that were crowned, far above, by Jardin Noir.

"Are you all right, Miss?" Villiers asked Perdita.

"Yes." She shook her head. "So, you are on your way to see Bastide?"

"Yes, I am."

"Is the sheriff going, too?"

"No, I am doing this on my own. Do not tell him, if you see him."

"Oh?" Perdita said suspiciously.

"Sheriff Aubuchon can keep the peace, all right,"

Villiers said. "He does his job, and well. No two ways about it. Except…except where Mr. Bastide is concerned."

"Mr. Bastide?"

"Yes. I had two witnesses, people I trust, both tell me they saw Father, Mr. Robert, and Lon Baker on Thermopylae Street headed toward Jardin Noir the night they disappeared."

"Lon Baker is missing, too?"

"Yes. The witnesses knew to tell me this, not the sheriff. He is a good man, you understand, and fair, and I don't envy the lawbreaker who crosses his path. He has the good of the town at heart, above all. He knows what side his bread, *our* bread is buttered on—"

"Yes. I have heard that before. So that means looking the other way if Bastide is implicated in anything?"

"That's it."

"The sheriff seems to share that tendency with Mrs. Morisot and most everyone else I have met in this village."

"Yes."

"Is that why he wouldn't give me Marie Chardin's journal? That business was so odd, so secretive. Marie would only hint at things, and then, the way the sheriff handled it. I've sometimes wondered if it had anything to do with Ste. Odile's first citizen."

"I don't know, Miss, but there could be something to that. Confiscating it was the judge's doing, but I don't know the reason. Are you going home now?"

"Yes. I mean to stop at the rectory for a moment, then I am going home."

"Good. If I learn anything, I will contact you."

"Thank you, Deputy."

Villiers nodded and mounted his horse. He headed west toward Thermopylae Street. Perdita retraced her steps along Mal Ardents, and in a few minutes time she was back at the rectory. She quickly let herself in, retrieved the carpetbag from the parlor, and was out the front door again in a matter of seconds, locking the door behind her.

Constantinople Street was nearly deserted. The cold wind had continued to blow across town, and the sky was completely overcast. Perdita had never felt so alone in Ste. Odile as she did at that moment. Uncle Tancred was gone, separated for the rest of his years from all who loved him: Perdita herself, Mrs. Moon, Bess and all of the parishioners. Solana and Marie were dead, and Hypolitte vanished without a word. Perdita's sense of foreboding returned as she thought about Hypolitte. She was trying to believe that his disappearance had some simple, soon-to-be-revealed explanation, and that he would be with her again in a day or two. But she could feel this belief, this hope, slipping from her with each hour that passed. She missed him terribly. How much easier it would be to take the loss of Uncle Tancred if she'd had Hypolitte by her side to console her.

Perdita was surprised to find Mrs. Morisot's carriage waiting in front of Tranquille House.

"Is that you, Miss Badon-Reed?" Mrs. Morisot called from the parlor as Perdita closed the front door behind her.

"Yes, it is, ma'am." Perdita stood in the parlor door and placed the carpetbag at her feet. She noticed Mrs. Morisot's gaze follow the bag to the floor.

"There you are, dear," Mrs. Morisot said unctuously. She sat in her favorite parlor chair, like the primordial mound emerging from the sea in Egyptian mythology. She was flanked by her two attendant ladies. "I wanted to stop by and tell you personally how much affected my husband and myself are at what has happened to poor Father Condell."

"Thank you, Mrs. Morisot. His life was one of service to others, and to God. I console myself in knowing everyone will feel his loss as keenly as I do."

"Yes, yes. Indeed we will. And Mr. Robert, your

good friend, has disappeared, I am told."

"Yes, Mrs. Morisot. You are well informed, as always."

"Gone, I believe, since Saturday. Did he miss your appointment at Herve's that night?"

Perdita felt her anger rise instantly. "How did you know that? No one knew that but perhaps four intimate acquaintances." She remembered Hypolitte's admonition that some of her letters had arrived opened.

"There, there, Miss Perdita," Mrs. Morisot condescended. "Calm yourself. I'm sure I must have heard it from Herve himself. I dine there often, you know."

Perdita said nothing.

"So, dear, you saw your uncle off at the landing?"

"Yes, I did."

"And is that the bag of his effects?"

Perdita glared at Mrs. Morisot for a few moments. There seemed to be no aspect of her private life that was not of interest to Mrs. Morisot.

"Bess Moon is a confidant of Miss Portia, here, you may remember," Mrs. Morisot went on, indicating the attendant lady to her left. "Portia used to help Mrs. Moon at home when Bess was a child. We saw Bess not twenty minutes ago on Bucephalus Street. That girl couldn't hold her tongue if her soul depended upon it!"

"So it seems," Perdita said.

"Would you like for Portia to take the bag to your room for you, dear? You could sit for a while with me here. Mrs. Zell could bring you a cup of coffee . . ."

"Thank you, no. I am anxious to go up and rest. I am exhausted. If you will excuse me." Perdita grasped the carpetbag and exited the parlor through the dining room, to the stairs.

In her room, she locked the door behind her, as had become her habit in the last week. She dropped the carpetbag on the floor, removed her hat, and tossed it onto the bureau. She sat on the edge of her bed. Glancing down at her dress, she noticed that the hem she had repaired after it had been ripped by the strange creatures on Saturday night had begun to fray again. The last of the three dresses she had brought to town with her was ruined, and she could not afford another, not with the board she was paying at Tranquille House. And now she no longer had the option of moving back into the rectory. She had started to feel self-conscious about her appearance on the street, in church, and even in class in front of the girls. She felt that until Moira arrived for her visit with the money her father had put aside for her, she would look increasingly like a woman whose fortunes are in decline.

She thought about lying down for a while. Her room was cold and it would be comforting to cover herself with her quilt. But she feared falling asleep. She felt increasingly vulnerable in the few snatches of sleep that she had allowed herself. Her dreams troubled her and filled her with apprehension. And there was an increasing sense in her half-waking state that she was not alone.

She retrieved the carpetbag from the floor and opened it on her bed. She began to slowly remove its contents. There was a yellowed, framed tintype of a dour, aged couple, whom Perdita recognized as her grandparents. There was an ebony rosary, a finely carved ivory crucifix, and a tiny photograph of a child of perhaps two years of age. In looking at the picture for a few moments, Perdita recognized a porcelain doll the little girl held and a wooden horse at her feet. She saw her father's eyes and her mother's puzzled expression on the chubby face. It was a photograph of Perdita herself that she had never seen before, possibly the first ever taken of her.

At the bottom of the bag were several bundles of letters tied together with string, and several books: *Lives of the Saints*, a daily missal, a Bible, *The Collected Works of Shakespeare,* and a dog-eared, paper-bound diary. She opened this tattered volume and a folded note fell out. It read:

My dear Perdita,

I can hardly tell you how surprised I was to find this in Father's desk. It was he who stole it and hid it away. He surely intended for you to have it, as was meant all along. Pray for him.

Affectionately,
Effie Moon

Perdita opened the slim volume to the first page. Handwritten in an unsteady script were the words: "The Private and Personal Journal of Marie Delaporte Chardin."

36

Commissary Vatrollier rose slightly from his large desk chair as Prosper entered his office. Vatrollier was a large man in advanced middle-age, balding and well fed, but not fat.

"Good morning, Monsieur Redon," he said in a thin, high-pitched voice that was incongruous with his large frame, "please sit." He indicated an overstuffed but worn chair opposite his desk. He resumed his chair.

"Thank you, Monsieur Commissary." Prosper nodded, and sat. His chair was lumpy and uncomfortable. The desk before him was neat and fastidious at its middle, but disarray increased on it and spread out into the room concentrically in ever-widening rings of chaos, radiating from the epicenter of order somewhere on the writing surface near where Vatrollier's hands now rested. Files, record books, charts, statistical tables, bound dossiers, newspapers, almanacs and other reference books filled worktables and shelves around the room. A small brass birdcage tenanted by two tiny gray finches stood before the room's only window, situated directly behind the desk.

"I hope you are feeling better, Monsieur Redon."

"I am, thank you. I have been quite debilitated for some time."

"Have you found some medicine to improve your condition?"

"Yes, purple loosestrife has been most effective, and I must needs lay on a supply of it to see myself safely home. I apologize for the numerous postponements of our interview."

"Do not trouble yourself. Your family has endured many sorrows, which must, of course, affect you. You are an attorney in America, if I remember correctly?"

"Yes, for nearly twenty years now. Criminal defense."

"Had you remained in France," Vatrollier smiled, "you might have tried to free some of the very same criminals I have apprehended in my career!"

"I don't imagine, the death of my poor sister notwithstanding, that there is much serious crime to investigate in a district such as this?"

"No, that is why I have been involved with your sister's case at Montsegur. Murder is rare, if not unknown there, and they have little experience of investigation. I will admit to you, monsieur, that if not for the prominence of your brother-in-law, Guibord, and the influence of your own family—not so keen as it was a few years ago, but still commanding much respect—we would not be involved in this case now. As for myself, I have only been here ten years. I started my career in Paris."

"That must needs have been much more of a challenge."

"Yes, those were the exciting days. Always something boiling over the fire. Have you ever heard of the Tropmann case?"

"At some time, I think." Prosper frowned. "It does sound familiar."

"Jean-Baptiste Tropmann, a mechanician. Murdered a Madame Kinck and her five children. A savage of a man. That was my last case in Paris, though Inspector Claude got all the credit. I wanted a new start after that business. I moved away from murder investigations."

"Ah, yes, I do remember. It was a sensational affair. I read about it soon after I set up my practice."

"Those were the cases! I had a taste of everything then. I worked a case in disguise against a family of forgers on Menilomontant Street for nearly a year."

Prosper nodded politely.

"And," Vatrollier went on, "if you are in any way interested in the history of crime in your home country, you have doubtless heard of the Romanichels, the powerful crime Bohemians, robbers, and murderers who trace their tribe back to the Middle Ages?"

"Yes, of course. They murdered a business associate of my father's some forty years ago when his family could not pay the ransom they demanded."

"At Auteuil, the Isle of Aux Singes at Greville, and the Carriers d' Amerique at Belleville, I lived with them, the cutthroats! I gained their confidence, became one of them. I gathered information incriminating three ringleaders of the time, and in the fall of '61 they were arrested. All three went to the guillotine! I had a price on my head for years afterward. That is one of the reasons you find me down here today."

"I see," Prosper said. "Well, you have given up a lot to come to this area, but, on the other hand, it may have lengthened your life."

"No doubt." Vatrollier smiled wryly. "No creature lives so long as the tortoise, through its natural dullness and immobility, and none has a life so tedious."

"Well, there it is in a nutshell."

"Except," Vatrollier put his hand on a thin cardboard portfolio on the desktop, "for the rare case such as this. The Guibord Case. The death of your sister." He removed the contents of the portfolio, which consisted of several collections of papers, including a folded document which once had been sealed with wax. "This is the *proces-verbal* written by myself and sealed by my clerk. The seal is, as you see, broken. This was done by the Prefecture of Police. It has since been returned to me and has been unaltered, unchanged."

"I see. Very well."

"I inspected the scene of the murder, your brother-in-law's house at Montsegur, on the morning after Inspector Amoreaux did the initial investigation and examination. Your family and Monsieur Guibord requested the body be examined by a physician, a Dr. Boyer. His report is here, too." Vatrollier handed the documents to Prosper.

He glanced over them, but the words made little sense. He was too distracted, he found, to decipher anything on the pages.

"It was, as you see, a sexual assault," Vatrollier continued. "It pains me to tell you this, but there it is before you, black on white. The assault was quite brutal. There was much bruising and tearing of the flesh around and within the sexual orifice."

Prosper felt himself getting light-headed.

"And," Vatrollier went on, "there was considerable damage to the cervix—"

"Yes, Monsieur Commissary," Prosper blurted out, "I know it was a sexual assault and that it was savagely done. I don't think specific details on that point are necessary."

"My apologies. Let it be sufficient to say that Dr. Boyer, having treated many rape victims in his career, had never seen that sort of damage, not but once, some fifteen or twenty years before."

"He *had* seen it before?"

"Yes. Soon after he moved to the district from Brittany. The violence…and damage were almost beyond human ability, if you follow my meaning."

"Yes, I think I do."

Vatrollier took the portfolio gingerly from Prosper's hand. He leafed through it and removed the physician's report, which Prosper had found indecipherable. "Yes, there is something else," Vatrollier said. "The previous victim, a young schoolteacher, apparently had been assaulted twice before her death, and oddly, had reported being attacked several times by some sort of animals she could not identify."

Prosper looked puzzled.

"I only mention it," Vatrollier continued, "because one of your sister's house servants said that Mrs. Guibord had been frightened by an encounter with strange animals soon before the murder. Murders, I should say."

"Yes, the maidservant."

"Estelle. She was not assaulted. Her throat was just ripped away. She couldn't have made a sound."

"Do these animals you mention have anything to do with these murders, do you think?"

"I cannot see how. Odd coincidence though. And something else—"

Vatrollier's eyes skimmed further down the report. "Your sister's ribcage was crushed. That is the oddest fact in the crime: how that much weight or pressure could have been applied. I am afraid if she had not died from hemorrhaging, this compression of her lungs and heart would have killed her. These are painful facts, Monsieur Redon, and it is with the severest regret that I convey them to you. But you wanted to know."

"Yes, I did. Thank you." Prosper's light-headedness increased, and the room went dark around him for a moment. He was beginning to feel distress in his stomach.

"Again, everything is here in Boyer's report, if you wish to see it. Are you well, sir?"

"I will be. It is much more terrible to hear these facts first hand. I thought I would be more prepared than this." Prosper rested his head in his hands for a moment.

"Such a horrible death!" he said at length. "What of the investigation? Do you have a suspect?"

"I wish I could tell you we had advanced further in the case." Vatrollier stood. Taking a few tiny seeds from his waistcoat pocket, he dropped them through the bars of the birdcage. "This is such an unlikely crime, calling for almost superhuman faculties. We have found no suspect who fills those requirements. There is the occasional lunatic and sexual predator, but no one we know of who can be implicated."

"What of the schoolteacher of twenty years ago?"

"She was also a well-educated woman, of course, like your sister. Her death was nearly an identical crime, and, I have found, part of a cycle of similar crimes which seem to recur over long intervals of time. There are many superstitions in these hills and mountains: spirits, demons, monsters. The business at Geauvidan a hundred years ago is by no means an isolated incident. I do not give any weight to these things. There is one additional point of commonality between your sister's death and the schoolteacher, Mademoiselle Brouchard, I think she was called."

"What is that?"

"Both were intimately acquainted with a local scion, a baronial figure known as Orien Bastide."

Prosper recognized the name immediately. He had seen it in a letter Moira had written to his brother, Michel. She had remarked on the coincidence of Bastide's living in Claire's small village of Montsegur, and also in Ste. Odile, as a recent acquaintance of Perdita's.

"The name is familiar to me, Monsieur Commissary. This Bastide, ironically, has an estate in a small village on the Mississippi, a place where my fianceé…my former fianceé has gone to teach at a female seminary."

Vatrollier frowned and looked at Prosper intently. "And does Bastide know this lady? Have they met?"

"Yes, I believe they have formed a friendship."

Vatrollier returned to his chair and sat. He said nothing for a few moments. He leaned forward on his desk toward Prosper.

"In an investigation such as this," he said, "many people are questioned. In some rare cases, witnesses come from various unexpected places, voluntarily, to tell what they know. This was such a case. Ignorance and superstition hold sway with the simple people, but sometimes with those of a higher estate as well. I kept hearing the name Orien Bastide, in connection with your sister's murder, as a point of possible focus, and with Mademoiselle Brouchard's also… and fantastically, even to others going far back in time, so one can only suppose that these are stories and gossip that have become confused over the years, in local memory. I can hardly credit them without proof, but they are consistent and often repeated. As these witnesses would have it, to be a young woman of some learning, some experience of the world, and to know Bastide…is perhaps, coincidentally somehow, in some way, a sentence of death. Or so they say. If I were to credit these accounts, Monsieur Redon, I would fear that your friend, your former fiancée, is in great need of protection."

37

Letter from Moira Keane Parnell to Perdita Badon-Reed

December 12, 1882

My dear Perdita,

I am told by the telegraph office that the damaged lines in your area have not yet been repaired. I am writing this as I arrange to come to you (sooner than I thought) and hope to post it in the morning. I had a strange and troubling cable from Prosper today. He said he had reason to believe, after speaking to the commissary in charge of his sister's murder investigation, that *you* may be in danger. In danger, he fears, at the hands of your new acquaintance, Mr. Bastide. I do not know what to make of this, and I would be hesitant to credit his outlandish suspicion before I read your last letter. But, there it is, and I'll be sunk if Prosper does not seem nearly frantic about it. There is the coincidence of Bastide having come from the village of Montsegur, and beyond that, there were evidently aspersions cast upon him by some of the local people, who, in my experience, always resent and wish to discredit the local gentry.

Trusting in your good judgment and discrimination, I hope you will not worry yourself unduly about this. You know, we know, how high strung and imaginative Prosper can be, yet I must say he has nearly convinced me too, and I have not been able to completely dismiss his fears. He has booked a passage from Marseilles to New Orleans and asks that I meet him in that city in ten days' time. I am sorry he will be coming to see you, against your wishes certainly, but there seems to be little I can do to stop him.

I am leaving in the morning on a sailing ship called the *Senate*. It is an old vessel, and my father is most distressed that I am sailing around the Carolinas in winter, but there is nothing to be done about it, and I have never been one to see the object of worrying about a thing ahead of time. It was the only ship upon which I could book passage to New Orleans so quickly. I will have a fine beef dinner tonight, get a good night's rest, and be off by seven tomorrow.

I do not know when to say with certainty I will be with you. I have it on good authority that a steamboat trip up the Mississippi to Ste. Odile could take nearly two weeks, whereas a train can cover the distance in less than two days, under the best of circumstances. I will wait for Prosper, as agreed, for no more than three days past his expected arrival time, then, whether he is with me or no, I will book passage north to Ste. Odile, and be with you as quickly as possible.

I cannot tell you how good it will be to see you again. The world is much duller for me without you in it.

Yours,
Moira

Journal of Prosper Redon

December 11, 1882

I know I will not make my brother understand. To be sure, I scarcely understand my motivation myself. With our parents at death's door, and his career in jeopardy and disarray as a result, I am contemplating abandoning him.

The only justification I can conjure for this act, is that I feel there is little I can do to influence this situation. I have been little help and little succor to Michel in the care of our mother and father; in fact, I have been nothing but a further burden and responsibility to him. I know I cannot rest if there is the remotest chance that Perdita is in danger. Vatrollier did his best, at the end of our interview, to underplay the likelihood of her peril. But the cat was out of the bag, and her safety has remained at the forefront of my thoughts since. Random inquiries I made yesterday, both personally and through agents, amongst tradespeople and farmers having connections to the village of Montsegur, have only validated my fears. The deaths and disappearances of any young women from this region, in those periods when his ancient chateau has been occupied, all have the figures of the Bastides in common, it seems.

In some sense, I cannot justify why I should feel it is within my province to protect Perdita, even though I still love her, considering what I leave behind here. Moira tells me there is no communication via telegraph possible to Perdita at Ste. Odile for the near future, and Moira has further stated that some letters to and from Perdita have been lost. Nothing else will do to ease my mind but to see Perdita face to face. I have also resolved that I must needs confront this Bastide. With the suspicions regarding him which are rife in the Albi, nothing less will satisfy me.

38

Perdita was cold. Her windows shuddered as the frigid winds howled across the sleeping town toward the river. She sipped from a glass of wine she had poured for herself and settled back in her bed to read.

The Journal of Marie Delaporte Chardin

April 13, 1882

I have had my second visit to Jardin Noir. I am overwhelmed! Awestruck! Breathless! I have not had such an evening since my early courtship with my Louis. My brain is still reeling! There has been no test, no challenge to my wits as I experienced tonight since Louis goaded me to define the progress of the rights of women in light of Mrs. Wollstonecraft's writings and their application to our present time. The conversation jumped from one topic to another, sometimes at breakneck speed, other times at a deliberate, meandering pace, as the subtleties of any particular topic might demand. I held my own in the conversation, it seemed, and I flatter myself to think that Bastide appeared (from what I could discern under his waxen mask) to hang on my every word. I nearly suggested at one point, after the aperitif, that he remove his mask to be more comfortable, but I could not bring myself to do it.

Tertius, the manservant and *cordon bleu*, prepared a passable lamb, but profusely apologized for its flat, underseasoned state. Having only arrived from Europe less than two weeks ago, he declaimed that he has not yet received those spices he ordered from New York which will replenish his racks and larders.

Bastide asked that I return soon and often, and agreed to my request to bring Michee with me some time to see the wonders of his collections. What better opportunity will I have to expose her to the sciences and art of the world than in this great hermitage which, by our great fortune, exists in our very village? These things would be otherwise far beyond my ability to reveal to her first hand.

As I stepped into Bastide's coach at evening's end to be carried home, the feeling of apprehension and misgiving that washed over me when I crossed his threshold hours before seemed like a silly, distant memory. As I seated myself, Bastide generously offered me an old Roman coin as a keepsake of the evening. At another time, I should have declined such a gift, but I have struggled since Louis's death to feed and support Michee and myself, and keep the wolf in abeyance. I accepted it gratefully. It is solid gold!

April 15

I had terrible dreams last night. I dreamed I was one of a group of condemned heretics confined in some medieval mountaintop keep, awaiting an horrendous death by fire. I remember trying to tell the others I was not one of them, but I could not say the words. After a time, I found I could speak, but by then I had seen their devotion and their level of faith and love for one another, and I seem to have chosen not to speak, as if to do so would diminish their sacrifice in some way. The honor of their act became more important than the preservation of my life, so I kept silent, and with terror in my soul, but also with some level of pride, I resolved to share their fate.

As I awoke from this nightmare, I thought I heard movement in my room. I thought perhaps Michee had experienced one of her night terrors and was coming to my bed to be comforted. I called her name, but there came no answer. As I sat up in bed, I thought I saw, out of the corner of my eye, the movement of some vague, indescribable form: dark enough as to be almost a "hole" in the fabric of the room; sinuous, fluid, and obscene. I cannot describe it better than this, I am sure, if I sat at my desk all night. I slept no more.

April 16

I fear I have made a mistake. I swear, I am astonished at myself in those instances when any sense of good judgment I may have thought I possessed, seems to be nowhere in evidence. My decisions can seem so ill-advised, so obviously wrong, in retrospect, that I fear a time when I will make some great miscalculation that will badly affect the prospects of my daughter and myself. I do not know why it should not have occurred to me that a visit to Jardin Noir might be upsetting to my sensitive Michee. I had foolishly forgotten my own shock at seeing Bastide, masked though he was, for the first time, but I was reminded when I saw her recoil from him at their introduction. Added to this, she became noticeably more agitated on touring the house, as our host showed us from room to room, and she took in his collections of dessicated mummies, hideous mounted apes and various monstrous specimens preserved in jars. Midway through the tour, I felt compelled to end it, and to request we return to the front parlor adjoining the dining room.

To this Bastide consented most graciously, and apologized for any distress his collections might have caused Michee. In a quarter-hour, refreshed by lemonade served by

Tertius, Michee was herself again. I have never spoken to her as a child, and often her precocious wisdom and surprising skill with words have amazed and charmed adults who have made her acquaintance. This was no less true of Mr. Bastide than of others of my friends. Michee had written a sonnet of welcome and gratitude for his warm hospitality, which she read out to us before our supper. Bastide was most impressed and fairly fawned praise upon her. His praise was so solicitous and of such duration, in fact, that I began to feel a strange discomfort in it. This attention, added to a prolonged and intent manner that, some once or twice, I noticed him looking at her, resulted in (I hate to say it) a sense of some unease and distaste in me throughout much of the evening.

It was an early evening, and we were conveyed home at nine o'clock. It took Michee quite some time to set aside the many disturbing sights of the mansion and its master, and fall asleep. I also found it difficult to calm myself enough to rest. The stimuli of the evening were many, and my reluctance to sleep is growing, it seems.

April 18

It becomes more difficult to describe what is happening to me and harder still to understand it. I am so very exhausted that I feel I am beginning to see and hear things that aren't really there. I see things flitter and move out of the corner of my eye, disappearing, always, as I turn to look. I hear things scuttling and skittering under my bed, in the wardrobe, and seemingly within the very walls. I thought I heard scratching on the floorboards, and saw a hint of something, a tail perhaps, disappearing into the gloom as I settled into my bed last night.

I have a fear of losing my wits as my grandmother and aunt did, and I am terrified to think this may be the beginning of an irretrievable decline. What would become of my Michee? Who would protect her in the world? My mother is too old and infirm, and Kathryn, my sister, is ill-suited by her high-strung nature and melancholia to take on the responsibility of another child.

The dream of the heretics returned last night. I kept the candles burning and meant to stay awake as long as I could, but I drifted off sometime after three, I think. I found myself in the process of being bound to a stake with some five or six *credents* atop a pile of fagots and logs. We were downwind from two other stakes which had already been set alight. A scorched, sweet, nauseating smell, the smell of burning flesh, was borne in the smoke, and it enveloped us. I thought of how our immolating bodies would soon compound the smoke and odor that was beginning to choke the meadow. Would herdsmen miles down the valley credit the strange, sickening odor to the suffering that produced it?

At that moment, I jolted myself awake. It wasn't so much fear of the imminent pain I was to endure that roused me, but more an excitement, a shameful kind of dark lust that seemed to be suffocating, crushing me. I could not move. My face was buried in my quilt and I could see nothing. As my head began to clear, I became aware of a presence that seemed to overwhelm and oppress me, and I understood that the odor filling my nostrils was not the burning flesh of martyrs, but wave after wave of stinking breath.

I lay frozen with fear. At first I felt the terror of acknowledging that what was happening to me was real, then in an instant, I faced the almost greater terror that it wasn't. In another moment (I hesitate to write this, but I am compelled to do so) I could feel my legs being forced apart. I felt a kind of barb embedded in each knee, making it impossible to resist this movement. I screamed a muffled and breathless scream, and in the distance I could hear Michee calling for me. Immediately, the presence, the odor were gone. I sat up weakly in bed and looked around me, gasping for breath and feeling a terror of powerlessness. The room was empty.

Michee scurried into my room, where she found me trembling helplessly, drenched with perspiration. At that moment, a thought pierced my brain like a lance: how can I protect her?

April 22

I cannot rest; I cannot think. I feel as though I am safe nowhere, and that I can do nothing to make Michee safe. I feel as though I am never alone, that I am always being watched, even in the daytime. I hear movement around me, under chairs, under my bed, always just out of sight. As I walked to my room last night after putting Michee to bed, I felt something brush across my ankle in the dark, something sinuous and covered with a wiry fur. Am I imagining this? Are any of these things real? I see a difference in the way Michee looks at me. I see worry, concern, uncertainty, fear. I look at myself in the glass to see if I can discern a difference in my face. I think I can.

Later—

I have seen Mother today. She is just returned from her trip to Baton Rouge. She is most concerned and distressed to hear of my nightmares, of the things I think I have seen and heard, and of my association with Orien Bastide. She has been on her visit for four months, and she did not expect Bastide to return from the Continent so soon, she said. She said she must tell me about *Le Vorace*. She is most distressed to hear that Michee has come under B's notice.

A tap on the window sent a stab of terror through Perdita. She jumped from her bed, dropping the journal on the floor. The tapping was repeated, gentle but insistent. In the darkness Perdita could barely see movement in the tree outside her window. She approached the window cautiously and peered into the gloom. After a moment she could make out a face through the glass, drawn and scowling in anguish and desperation. It was Tertius.

39

Perdita struggled to lift the sash. Tertius climbed over the sill and fell into the room.

"My God, Tertius," Perdita gasped.

"Thank you, Miss Perdita," Tertius mumbled. "Forgive me."

She helped him to his feet. He closed the sash and tried to rub some warmth into his arms.

"What has happened Tertius? What is the meaning of this?" Perdita's voice was overwrought and quivering.

"I am so sorry to have frightened you. I am…a fugitive. I have left Monsieur Bastide's service. I can never go back!"

"But why? What has happened?"

"Terrible things. I must sit."

"Of course." Perdita pulled her rocking chair from beside the bureau to the middle of the floor. Tertius sat. Perdita pulled her quilt from her bed and covered him with it. "Do you want me to go downstairs and make you some tea? I'm sure Mrs. Zell has gone to bed, but it wouldn't take much to get the fire going again."

"No, thank you."

"I have wine here also."

"No, thank you, Miss. I will be fine in a few minutes."

"The wine will warm you; are you sure?"

"Well, perhaps. Yes, I think I need it."

Perdita opened a deep drawer of the large bureau and withdrew a corked, half-empty bottle. She removed the cork, filled her glass and gave it to Tertius. He took it and drank. Perdita took a drink directly from the bottle.

"I only have the one glass," she said. "I only need one."

"Thank you, Miss." Tertius rubbed his cheeks and then his hands with the quilt. "Again, I am sorry to have startled and frightened you," he said.

"What is this about, Tertius?" Perdita sat on the edge of her bed.

"I have left Monsieur Bastide's service," he repeated. "I have to make my way south and try to find another situation. My family depends upon me. I must find another situation! How will I do so looking like a vagabond? I have no…"

"You left with nothing?"

"Yes, just as you see me." Tertius went silent for a moment. "For many years in this country and elsewhere I have seen evil being done. It is a sort of helpless evil, if I may call it that, but evil none the less. I have met many a young woman since I have been in service, and I have foreseen what they could not foresee: their destruction and their doom."

"I am not understanding you, Tertius."

"I was complacent at best and fearful at worst. I had my family to think of."

"Yes? "

"Like everyone else in this village, there was the well-being of my family to consider. They depend upon my support, and I had become comfortable. Monsieur Bastide is quite generous. We all became like the Athenians of old. Generosity and prosperity buys much complacency…and silence."

"Tertius—"

"It was I who brought your uncle home."

"You?" Perdita was dumbstruck.

"Yes. I covered him and made a pillow for his head, and I have not been back to Jardin Noir since."

"Of course! It was your jacket. I remember now. But why, what happened?"

"He had come to Jardin Noir with a grave purpose that night."

"And Hypolitte?"

"Yes, Mr. Robert and the Baker lad."

"Where are they, Tertius? Where is Hypolitte?"

"Miss," Tertius said quietly, "the situation deteriorated very quickly. Bastide was under attack and in a rage. I had to intervene."

Perdita felt herself becoming weak, and tears began to well in her eyes. "Where is he?"

"He is dead, Miss."

It seemed at first to Perdita that she had not really heard his words. She looked at Tertius expressionlessly, puzzled by her lack of response. After a moment, she could see nothing in the room but Tertius' face, as all else went dark around her. Then she felt a stab of anguish and fear pass through her, and she gasped for breath

"No, Tertius," she had begun to sob. "No, no, please do not tell me this!" She felt the room reeling and herself fall forward onto the floor. "I cannot hear this, I can't!"

Tertius helped her back onto her bed. She buried her face in her hands. "No more," she went on, "no more. I cannot take anymore. It can't be true, Tertius!" She sobbed helplessly and bitterly for many minutes.

Tertius sat beside her and put his arm awkwardly around her for a moment, but quickly withdrew it. She could not be comforted.

"I am sorry, Miss Perdita. I am very sorry."

Perdita did not gain any measure of composure for a long time.

"How could this be God's will? How could this please God?" she whispered.

"I do not know, Miss."

"How much can God ask? How many trials, how much suffering? Hypolitte dead, Uncle lost to us…Solana, Marie, the girls at school…I have tried to believe, have needed to believe. But how can it all mean anything?"

"Miss, would you lie down?"

"No. But how, Tertius, how did it happen? What happened to Uncle and Hypolitte? And the Baker boy, too?"

"Yes, he too." Tertius removed the quilt from his shoulders and wrapped it around Perdita. He returned to the rocking chair. "Your uncle, Mr. Robert, and the Baker boy came to Jardin Noir on Saturday night. Your uncle, as you may know, had been an exorcist in his younger days, until the tragic death of a subject, a child, I am told. Your uncle came to the house in his vestments, his surplice and purple stole, and with his valise."

"But why?"

"He meant to perform an exorcism."

"An exorcism? But on whom?"

"On Monsieur Bastide."

"Bastide?"

"Yes." Tertius thought for a moment. "I was in the back of the house when they arrived. I had come in from the garden, and Monsieur Bastide didn't know that I had come in. I could hear voices in the library. I came to the ante-room where I could see and hear everything. They were speaking in subdued tones at first: Father Condell, Mr. Robert, and Baker, to Bastide. Your uncle opened his valise on a table and withdrew a crucifix, a bottle of water, an aspersorium and its aspergillum, a cruet of wine, and what looked to be a salt cellar. 'The Archbishop is ill and can give no authority,'

I heard him say. 'I do this by the grace of God, and with the help of these good men, on my own authority.' He blessed himself, and, pouring the contents of the bottle into the aspersorium, he dipped the aspergillum into it, then sprinkled holy water on all present. Father seemed surprised the blessing had no effect upon my master. Bastide humored him. 'You are tired, Father,' he said, 'and I have heard you have not been well.'

To this Father made no answer, but began to recite the Litany of The Saints. Mr. Robert and Baker made response to each invocation. Still, I watched from the darkness."

"Why did you hide yourself?"

"I don't know, Miss. To have shown myself then would have interrupted, or ended, the proceedings, and I felt I should see what happened. I had to see. I knew the proceedings should not be interrupted. I had the greatest respect for your uncle."

Perdita nodded in understanding.

"After several minutes," Tertius continued, "the Litany was over. Then Father said: 'From all sin, from sudden and unprovided death, from the snares of the Devil, from anger, hatred, and all ill will, from all lewdness. Lewdness!' He repeated the word. Bastide began to appear agitated. Robert and Baker moved closer to Bastide, as if preparing to restrain him. I knew if they laid hands upon my master, that I would have to intervene."

"What happened?"

"Father muttered a quick Pater Noster, to which his deacons replied, 'Deliver us from evil.' Then Father repeated a psalm. 'Enough of this, Father,' Bastide said. Father made the sign of the cross. He began to recite another prayer. Bastide became more agitated, more furious. 'You will leave now, Father. Leave my home!' Father ignored this. He said: 'I command you, unclean spirit, whoever you are, along with all your minions now attacking this servant of God…' Bastide moved forward toward Father. Robert and Baker took hold of him, each grasping an arm. I knew then I must act. It was my duty. God in Heaven knows I did not want to do harm to any of those men."

"Did you do harm to them?" Perdita asked tentatively.

"Bastide…the nature of Monsieur Bastide is unknown to you. It is not for me to tell you, it is beyond me—"

Perdita was becoming impatient. "Tertius, what happened to them?"

"Bastide easily cast Robert and Baker away from him. Baker fell with great force against the fireplace mantel, dashing his head upon the marble. He fell dead on the floor. Robert was thrown across a table, and seeing his friend mortally injured, was on his feet in a second, and approached Bastide again, cautiously, but with a look of great determination. Your uncle called for Robert to stay back. Father lunged forward with a crucifix outstretched toward Bastide. My master took hold of Father by the throat and cast the crucifix into the fireplace. He then hurled Father against a glass specimen case which splintered into a thousand shards of glass. Father lay motionless on the floor. From that moment on, your uncle was no longer himself. Robert was immediately upon Bastide. I rammed Robert from behind, knocking him away. He fell next to Father, and I heard him gasp a shallow breath, moan, then lay still. He had fallen on a large dagger of glass. In a few seconds, he was dead. I had killed him."

Perdita was speechless for a moment as she repeated in her mind the admission Tertius had just made. "You, Tertius," she said in disbelief, "you killed him?"

"Yes, Miss," Tertius said mournfully. "It was a terrible mishap. I had to tell you before I disappeared. You had to know, even if you set the sheriff on me."

"The sheriff?" Perdita said sardonically. "You are too closely allied with Bastide to worry about the sheriff."

"No, the law will come for me."

A loud knocking on Perdita's door startled them.

"Miss Badon-Reed!" It was Mrs. Morisot. "Miss Badon-Reed, will you let me in?"

"Please, Miss, please!" Tertius implored her. He hid himself, crouching beyond the far side of the bureau.

"What is it, Mrs. Morisot?" Perdita called.

"Will you let me in?"

"I am very tired, ma'am. Won't it wait until tomorrow?"

"It will not, Miss Perdita! Please open this door!"

Perdita unlatched the door and opened it. Mrs. Morisot stood in the hallway alone, holding a lamp. She stepped into the room and closed the door behind her.

"What is it?" Perdita asked irritably.

"I think you know very well why I am here, Miss Perdita Badon-Reed!" Mrs. Morisot said grimly.

"I haven't the slightest idea—"

"You are no fool, Perdita, nor am I. I know Marie Chardin's journal was among your uncle's effects, and I know Bess packed it for you. I believe that must be it there on the floor. I want it."

Perdita stooped and picked up the diary.

"Why do you want it, Mrs. Morisot?"

"You know why I want it. Mrs. Chardin was a deranged woman. There was insanity in her family. Her journal cannot be taken at face value, as truth. I want it so you cannot use it against us."

"What?"

"I have had my eye on you since the day of the execution. I knew then that you bore watching, that you would bring trouble."

"I have done nothing." Perdita clutched the diary to her breast.

"You will. I have followed your progress. You have more regard for the deaths of an insignificant widow and a silly nun than for the well being of hundreds."

"You have intruded upon my privacy enough, Mrs. Morisot," Perdita said angrily. "You have read my letters and spied upon me!"

"I won't allow you to ruin the…the balance of things. You think you know what is right, and that you must act in a certain way, no matter the damage it causes. This is your nature, I know it is!"

"I will be leaving Tranquille House in the morning," Perdita said through her teeth.

"You will leave tonight, but not as you think." Mrs. Morisot reached into the pendulous folds of her great skirt and produced a small, brightly-plated revolver. She pointed it at Perdita. "I have come up from nothing," Mrs. Morisot continued bitterly. "You will not threaten what I have!"

"It is you," Perdita said ironically, with no trace of fear in her voice. "It is you, not the village, isn't it, Mrs. Morisot?"

"Give me the diary!"

There was a crash as the bureau fell suddenly on its side. Tertius leapt up from the shadows and threw himself against Mrs. Morisot. Perdita heard the pop of a gunshot and dropped the journal as Mrs. Morisot fell against the wall, Tertius falling on top of her. The lamp crashed to the floor, spreading flames instantly across the wool rug, under the bed, and up a wall. Tertius and Mrs. Morisot lay dazed behind an already fierce wall of flame, cut off from the door. Perdita could see that first Mrs. Morisot's clothes, then Tertius's, were on fire.

"Tertius!" Perdita screamed. "Get up, I can't reach you!" She saw him move slightly. She could see an expanding bloom of red spreading across his stomach.

"Get out," he said weakly. "Get out!"

40

Mrs. Zell heard the commotion and the gunshot upstairs, and came to investigate. Throwing open Perdita's door, she quickly saw she could not approach the conflagration or its victims. She helped Perdita out of her room and then out the front door, thinking to grab coats and shawls from the hall tree, and the rectory key from the pier mirror on their way out.

As soon as the women were safely outside, it was clear that there would be no saving Tranquille House. Most of the second floor was aflame, as was the southwest corner of the third floor. A crowd quickly gathered to watch the blaze and to offer help to the fire brigade when it arrived.

The alarm had been raised by several neighbors, and the fire bell could be heard ringing across town. The shed that served as the fire station was close by, at the corner of Bosphorus and Rouen Streets. In a few minutes' time, eight or nine volunteers appeared on the scene pulling a small, frail-looking fire engine behind them. The device consisted of a copper holding tank mounted on four legs, upon which a four-man hand pump was mounted. A thick suction hose protruded from the rear of the tank, and a smaller spray hose from the front. This was coiled onto a hose reel affixed to a delicate wooden carriage on four wheels which supported the whole device.

"The well is on the *west* side," Mrs. Zell called to

the volunteers. "Toward the *back*."

Four volunteers loosened the clamps holding the engine to its carriage and lifted it off, carrying it quickly to the west side of the house. In a few moments' time, they had dropped the suction hose down the well, and, two to each side of the engine, were furiously manning the reciprocating pump levers, while others of their number directed the hose and its intermittently forceful spray of water onto the fire.

Mrs. Zell threw a coat over Perdita's shoulders. Perdita's jaw had begun to tremble with the cold, and her soot-covered face was streaked with tears. As she watched the activity around her, Perdita had the sensation that the town and its people, familiar to her since the summer, were transforming before her eyes into something alien and unfamiliar. The faces of neighbors and acquaintances milling around her seemed to have no connection to their names and personalities. Each face, though etched with what appeared to be a determination to contain the fire, and concern for its victims, now also seemed to carry a monition of malevolence.

"Hypolitte is dead," Perdita said, as if in a trance.

"No," Mrs. Zell gasped.

"Tertius killed him," Perdita continued. "He said it was an accident. He said Uncle was trying to perform an exorcism." She looked pointedly at Mrs. Zell. "Do you know why Uncle would want to do that?"

"No, Perdita. Mr. Robert *dead*!" Mrs. Zell made the sign of the cross.

Perdita continued to look deeply into Mrs. Zell's eyes to see if she could recognize any sign of deception. "It seems to me, Mrs. Zell, that townspeople like you whose families have been here for generations, have secrets to keep. Evil secrets. I think I have been denying that fact to myself, trying insipidly to remain naïve because I need to believe in good. But I think I have been wrong. There *is* evil here. I cannot deny it any longer."

"Yes, Perdita. Like Marie and many others, I have the *welfare* and safety of family to *consider*. People have *disappeared* for looking too deeply into things, asking too many *questions* which could jeopardize the well-being and livelihoods of the *many*."

"Why? What do you mean?"

"You should leave town, Perdita. I think you should leave *immediately*."

Perdita started to press Mrs. Zell further, but her resolve was overwhelmed by her exhaustion. There would be time for that tomorrow. She was chilled to the bone and could see that Mrs. Zell had started to shiver, too. They needed to get out of the cold.

"We need shelter. What will you do, Mrs. Zell, now that your employer is dead and your home destroyed?"

"I don't *know*. I have never known a time when there was a *shortage* of work in the *town*."

"Everything I had is lost," Perdita continued. She remembered how quickly the flames had spread across her room, engulfing Tertius and Mrs. Morisot. She thought about her few possessions, now consumed in the conflagration. "Uncle's things are gone and the *Moby Dick* Solana gave me. Mrs. Morisot wanted Marie's diary. That is what this was about."

"Yes, I know. There are *things* she did not want you to know. Things the old *families* know, as you have said. You were more of a problem than any *newcomer* before you."

"Why?"

"Don't *ask* me about it, Perdita. do not know *what* to tell you. I have the rectory key. We must get you *there* for the night, though I expect the *sheriff* will want to speak to you."

Aubuchon and Deputy Villiers emerged from the crowd and approached the women. They had been directing onlookers to aid the firefighters. Now they seemed to be having an animated debate.

"This is why we need a steam engine," Villiers said. "This Taylor contraption can't throw water high enough."

"Nonsense!" Aubuchon scoffed irritably.

"They're barely reaching the third floor. With a fourth floor, we'd be lost."

"They aren't pumping to full capacity yet," Aubuchon barked. "A steam engine takes twenty minutes to build up a head. Fire like this'd be nearly over by that time. It's not the money, we can afford it; it's how useful it would be. We'll talk to Chief Lamarck tomorrow when he's done with this mess, and after he's had some rest. Excuse us, ladies. I wanted to be sure you were both uninjured—?"

"Yes, Sheriff," Mrs. Zell said, "Perdita just got out with her *life*."

"You were near the fire?"Aubuchon asked. "Was there anyone else in the house? Your neighbors said they only saw light in your room upstairs, Miss."

"Yes, there were others, but I am certain they are dead. It was Mrs. Morisot's doing. She and Tertius were there. They are dead."

"Tertius?" Deputy Villiers said.

"Yes."

"Lamarck told us he thought the house was empty. We'd better try to get in there and make sure," Aubuchon said, running away toward the burning house. Mrs. Zell gave the rectory key to Perdita and followed Aubuchon.

"Did you get the note I sent a few days ago?" Villiers asked Perdita.

"No. Much of my correspondence was tampered with by Mrs. Morisot."

"I went up to Jardin Noir after we spoke the other day."

"Yes, I had wondered what had happened."

"Tertius was gone by then, disappeared. Aristide's boy Urbain answered the door. He claimed that Bastide was away and that Tertius had been gone since Sunday. Run off."

"He killed Hypolitte."

"Killed him?" Villiers was aghast.

"It was an accident. Uncle and Hypolitte and Lon Baker went to Jardin Noir on Saturday night."

"Why?"

"To perform an exorcism."

"An exorcism?" Villiers repeated incredulously.

"Yes."

"I don't understand."

"Neither do I."

"You need to get out of the cold. Where will you go, Miss Perdita?"

"The rectory."

"We'll have questions for you tomorrow."

"I will come by the office in the morning." Perdita nodded at Villiers and made her way through the onlookers toward Constantinople Street and the rectory.

It was a cold, still night. A little snow had fallen earlier in the evening, but now all was clear, and the streets gleamed in the silvery moonlight. Perdita thought Anatolia would be concerned when she heard about the fire. She resolved to stop by the dormitory to see the child the next day.

The northern end of town seemed to be overlaid by a shroud of utter stillness. It appeared that everyone had gone to Rouen Street to watch the fire. As Perdita approached the rectory, her footsteps echoing off the damp pavement, she saw movement on the moonlit street ahead of her. A muscular, slithering body darted across the street, thirty feet ahead, running from east to west, toward the rectory. The figure was quickly followed by another. Perdita stopped and peered into the shadows which had swallowed up the forms. She looked at the spot for several minutes, but saw no more movement.

Perdita opened the rectory door and locked it behind her. She felt suddenly hungry. In the kitchen she found bread, which she spread with butter and honey. She ate this quickly. In a cabinet she found a nearly empty wine bottle, which she uncorked and drained. She left the bottle on the kitchen table.

Her old room was unchanged since the day she'd moved out. She dropped her coat and shawl onto the desk and fell across the bed. In seconds her eyelids were heavy, but she could *not* go to sleep. She tried to keep herself awake by focusing on some sound, inside or out, but there was nothing to be heard. The room was quite cold. She pulled the blanket over herself and focused her attention on some Creole houses and skeletal trees bathed in silvery moonlight visible through her window across Mal Ardents Street.

She had begun to feel as though the night was a palpable barrier, a mantle that lay over her, restricting her movements, suffocating her. She needed something to occupy her mind, to keep it active and awake. She thought of Marie, Solana, Hypolitte, and Uncle Tancred. Soon her memories of Hypolitte crowded out every other thought. For years, he had been here waiting, though he didn't know it, for her to arrive. And she, too, had been abiding coincidence and circumstance, waiting for the proper conjunction of events to result in her traveling to Ste. Odile to find him. When she had found him, she wasted more time in resisting the simple truth, that he was the force drawing her there. He would not have been a deterrent to achieving her artistic goals. He would have been quite the opposite, a source of constant encouragement. She understood that now. He had told her this, and she had finally believed him, but at that moment, she understood it profoundly.

But whatever love and commiseration she might have enjoyed with Hypolitte would never happen. Marie would never see her daughter grown, Solana would never again shamefully delight in the latest Paris fashions or the beauty of an illuminated medieval text, and Uncle Tancred would never re-read his Shakespeare, discovering subtleties and brilliant turns of phrase that he had somehow missed in fifty years of study. All of this, Perdita understood, could be laid at Bastide's door.

She wondered *how* it was that Bastide was responsible for these things. She could see him now, looking very different, but recognizable, with three other men, preparing to slip out of the fortress by night, laden with sacred books and as much gold as each of them could carry. They were to lower themselves down the mountainside and escape the martyr's death awaiting the rest of their compatriots. They were to escape to salvage some vestige of the beliefs that sustained them, and for which the company was willing to die. These four would preserve perhaps the last evidence that the Cathars had ever existed at all.

As Perdita watched the four men making their preparations, she could not account for the sensations that were overtaking her. Some of the children of the new converts were gathered around her, touching and stroking her, expecting from her some explanation, apparently, of what was happening to all of them. She could not answer the children's questions or respond to their attentions. She could not take her eyes off Bastide, nor think about anything else.

She was distracted in the extreme from the questions and demands assaulting her at that moment. Her limbs were weak, her thighs and stomach flushed with blood and tingling. She felt overheated and excited by a lust that horrified her. But still the children pulled at her skirt, prodded her.

Perdita jolted herself awake. She was covered with perspiration in spite of the coldness of the room. She felt drained and weak, too weak even to lift her head. A stab of fear shot through her as she realized that the nudging and prodding she'd dreamt of were continuing, were real. It was not the children she had felt. She became rigid as death and dared not to move. A cold prod at the top of her thigh, a probe against her groin, a paw, a snout, the brush of coarse fur. She screamed a muffled scream. Forms writhed under her blanket, against her, front and back. They chittered, growled, nipped at her flesh. She tried to throw herself over the side of the bed, but could not. She could not move.

She wanted to kick at the creatures that were swarming furiously over her, scratching and biting her, but her legs would not respond. Suddenly the creatures burst violently from under the blanket and leapt upon the desk. There were two of them, *Le Vorace*, silhouetted against the window. One of the creatures abruptly and savagely attacked the other. There was a squeal of pain, and in an instant, they crashed through the window and onto the snowy hedge outside.

Perdita closed her eyes and tried to catch her breath. What was happening to her? She did not want to see or hear anything else; nothing else that might still be near her that was unnatural or horrifying. She wanted a moment to recover before her senses could admit stimuli of any kind. A cold wind from the broken window bore heavily against the back of her neck and head. She would have to block it with something, then spend the rest of the night in some other room. Perdita became abruptly aware of a rank odor that surrounded her, which became stronger with each gust of breeze. She tried again to move her legs, but they would scarcely budge. She moved her heel just enough to feel something against it, behind her in the bed. She heard herself whimper slightly. An eddy of numb terror washed over her as she sensed a presence in the room. It was pressure she felt against her back, from a form that seemed to extend beyond hers at head and foot. And it was wave after wave of breath she felt against her neck.

Perdita could not force herself to open her eyes completely, not so horribly close to the thing she did not want to see. Through barely parted eyelids she saw an unfocused gray mass—liquid, obscene and monstrous—forcing her onto her back. A limb with a texture she could not identify either as fur or skin, slid up her leg, pushing her skirt aside. She felt a sharp, stabbing pressure on the inner surface of each knee as if a barb or thorn were being snagged into them. To her horror, she realized the pressure was forcing her legs apart. She thought she heard a voice, it may have been behind her, or inside her head. It said one word, a guttural spitting of the word, an infernal ululation delirious with craving: "You… you."

Perdita tried to scream for help but could not draw breath deep enough to do so. A great pressure was overwhelming and suffocating her. In another second, she felt a stab of pain at her secret and unbroken core. It was broken and breached now, over-gorged, surrendering, with a tearing and searing inside her.

41

Perdita awoke to the smell of asafetida. Before she opened her eyes, the scent wafted past her, then was gone, bringing her back from a dimensionless region of pain and infernal darkness. She drew breath. She felt an aching in her left ribs as she inhaled. She exhaled quickly. Her left leg was bent. When she straightened it, she gasped at a burning, abrasive pain in her groin and upper thighs.

She opened her eyes. The ceiling of the room was a patchwork of logs and milled timbers with tangles of roots hanging between them.

"Here she *is*," a voice said.

"Good. Lie still, child," another voice said.

Perdita turned her head slightly to the left. Mrs. Zell was standing over her. Next to her, just within Perdita's field of vision, stood Euphrosine, the wildcrafter.

"Mrs. Zell, Euphrosine," Perdita said weakly.

"You'll be *safe* here, Perdita," Mrs. Zell said. "As safe as anywhere *else,* I reckon."

"Yes, safe for a while." Euphrosine's tone was one of conditional agreement. "He'll know you are here, but won't come for you, I think."

"What? What do you mean?" Perdita tried to sit up, but could not. She could see that she was on the cot in Euphrosine's cabin. There was daylight visible through the cabin's two small windows.

"Don't move yet." Euphrosine put a gnarled hand gently on Perdita's chest. "I have applied a poultice, and I will give you something for the pain."

"How did I get here?"

"I came to look *in* on you after the *fire* had burned out," Mrs. Zell said. "I found *this* in the rubble." Mrs. Zell picked up a blue leather-bound book from the foot of the cot. It was dirty, but scarcely burned. It was Perdita's copy of *Moby Dick*.

"Odd that it *survived*," Mrs. Zell continued. "I salvaged a few things from the *kitchen,* and my room that had not been too badly *burned*. I hired a *wagon* from Aristide, and was taking everything to my *cousin's* house on Chartres. I stopped at the *rectory* to return this to you. I found you *unconscious*. I had to get in to you through a broken *window*. When I saw the *state* you were in, I knew what had *happened*. I knew I had to bring you *here*."

"You have lost much blood," Euphrosine said. "You will be weak. We have cleaned you and treated you. In a few days, your strength will be back. We will watch over you as you sleep."

"Yes, we *must* watch over you," Mrs. Zell said.

"What is this about? All of this?" Perdita whispered.

"Sleep for a while longer." Euphrosine smiled.

"Euphrosine, I need to see a doctor." Perdita's voice could barely be heard.

"Nothing he can do for you. You are with me now."

When Perdita awoke again, the light coming in through the small windows was nearly gone. Mrs. Zell sat at her bedside, and Euphrosine, smoking her clay pipe, sat near the hearth in her large walnut chair piled with pillows. Her enormous dog, Potiphar, lay at her feet. Mrs. Zell smiled when she saw that Perdita was awake, and she touched her forehead.

"You had a bit of a *fever*," Mrs. Zell said. "It's gone now. You have slept all *day*."

"I have?"

Euphrosine stood and poured a clear, green liquid from an iron kettle hanging in the fireplace into a bowl. She brought the bowl to Perdita. "Drink some of this," she said. "The leaves, too."

Perdita sat up on her cot. Sitting upright was painful. She leaned against the cabin wall. The room went dark for a few moments, but the sensation quickly passed. She sipped from the bowl. The liquid was nearly flavorless.

"You will need to get up soon and walk," Euphrosine continued, "or soreness will set in too much."

Perdita returned the bowl to Euphrosine. She moved herself to the edge of the cot. Mrs. Zell stood and took Perdita's arm. Perdita stood slowly. The room once again went dark for a few seconds.

"Are you *all right*?" Mrs. Zell asked.

"Yes, I think I am."

"Walk to the fireplace and back," Euphrosine said.

Perdita took a few steps. She felt some pain and discomfort, but they were not unbearable. Her legs quivered. "I am weak," she murmured.

"Yes," Euphrosine said. "You need meat. I have some squirrel and rabbit to give you. Never mind if it is a bit bloody, you need it."

Potiphar lifted his huge head as Perdita stepped gingerly past him, then quickly dropped it again and went immediately back to sleep. Perdita reached the mantel and rested there.

"Now come back," Euphrosine said in a pointed tone. "Lie down and listen to what I have to tell you. You have many questions."

"I do; yes, I do." Perdita made her way slowly, but with growing stability, back to the cot. She sat carefully, then lay back. Euphrosine pulled her chair from the hearth to Perdita's bedside. She sat and puffed her clay pipe back into ignition. The aged woman's eyes looked intently into Perdita's. They were bleary and exhausted, but held a spark of purpose and resolve.

"I have been here many years," she began, "more than you can know, or before today, would believe. But you begin to believe now. I said this to you before: what is faith without belief?"

"Yes, I remember."

"And I also said you would come to see me someday."

"Yes."

"And now you are here."

"Just as you said. I am grateful for your care. But I am so confused. What is happening to me? What attacked me? What…happened to the others? Marie, Solana?"

"They came to me, so have you, though not of your own doing. Now you are ready to hear what I have to say. Before this day, you were not. She who has the answers? *C'est moi.*" The ancient woman, known as *Mere de Siecles,* the Mother of Centuries, settled deeper into her chair. "You know my name, all know my name as Euphrosine. Euphrosine the wildcrafter, the *traiteur*, the wise woman. But there was a time when I was known by another name, and that name was Scribonia. Scribonia the seer, the oracle, the servant and follower of Circe, witch of Aeaea. I was more powerful then. Years have weakened me, but I do what I am still able to do. I *must* do what I am able to do. I must tell you, with sorrow, that the deaths of your friends, and countless others, all of it was my doing."

"*Your* doing?"

"Yes, because when I was powerful, I did what I could not undo. I brought this abomination into being. The suffering of generations has been my doing. You have suffered the same violation as your friends. Yes, you are reliving the horrors they knew. Yes, it is all the scourge of one entity. I am only strong enough now to keep him at bay, and help, in small ways, those he has chosen."

"What abomination? What scourge?" Perdita asked the questions reluctantly. She felt she was on the brink of that knowledge which she had foreseen that would never again allow the complacency, the untroubled sleep she had known before stepping onto the landing at Ste. Odile.

Euphrosine puffed her pipe. Potiphar rose from his spot near the hearth, walked slowly to Euphrosine's side, and lay down again.

"The gods of old," the ancient woman said, "the spirits of forest and spring, of anger, lust, revenge, became the demons of the new faith, the Christian faith. I lived at the confluence of these two worlds, and knew the mysteries of both. I kept familiarity with these spirits, these demons, for their power could not go completely out of the world, but instead grew more malevolent in its suppression: Asmodeus, Isaacaron, Balphoroth…and others. You must receive what I say, Perdita. Here is where faith and belief are one."

Perdita looked incredulously at Mrs. Zell, who had not resumed her seat but stood just behind Euphrosine. She saw no sign of doubt or contradiction of the story being told on Mrs. Zell's face, only a grave concern.

"I tell you now," Euphrosine continued, "that all of my craft, my knowledge, and my remorse, too, meet in one being. It is he who has done this to you, as he did to your friends, to your fiancé's sister, and numberless others: it is Bastide."

"Bastide," Perdita repeated, as though the word were an affirmation.

"You have heard some speak of the family, the lineage of Bastide," Euphrosine said. "There is no family. There is *only* Bastide."

"Only?"

"The Bastide who helped to found this village is the same Bastide who lives now at Jardin Noir."

"The same—"

"The same," Mrs. Zell said. "It is true, child."

"Yes, it is true," Euphrosine went on. "He was condemned to live through the centuries, as I was, because I could not undo what I had done. I had to follow him to mend, or even prevent, some of the suffering that his nature must cause. I must do this because I was Scribonia, the disciple of Circe." Euphrosine took her pipe from her mouth. It had gone out. She placed it on the floor.

"During the time of Diocletian," she continued, "during his later years, the garrison at Lyon in Gaul was under the command, briefly, of a minor general named Quintus Tacitus Gabro. During his duty there, he and his wife, Vipsania, lived in a villa well protected by walls and many troops. It was a good marriage, they say, the joining of two old families, but childless. There was a native family in the town who were the descendants of once-powerful chieftains of the Gauls: a distant branch of the line of Vercingetorix, who led an army against Julius Caesar centuries before. This family, the last of their race, was killed by a tribune under orders of Gabro, for inciting revolt. All were killed but an infant boy. He was a beautiful child, and of a distinguished family, so Vipsania, the wife of Gabro, took him into her household. They adopted him as their own son. He was given the Roman name Medullinus, and was raised with all deference and comfort as the heir of Gabro.

"I was born in Thrace. My father was in the army and was elevated, in time, after many campaigns and much distinction, to the rank of centurion. He finished his years of service at Lyon, and upon his honorable discharge, he sent for his family: my mother, my younger brother Titus, and myself.

"The women of my mother's family had always preserved the tradition of wildcrafter, herbalist, and seer. I was to continue this tradition. We honored the gods of Rome and acknowledged the divinity of the emperor, yet we held much congress with a small Christian group of the region and found ourselves praying with them, and were persuaded, as the months passed, by their example.

"Unusual as it was for the time, I was educated alongside my brother. My passion was the classics, especially the stories of Circe. I was so impressed by her power, and how it freed her from all the constraints of men, that I resolved to form a cult to her and learn the secrets of her craft.

"At Lyon, my father had made a comfortable life for us. After twenty years of warfare and killing, he was weary of the demands and practices of the empire, and he readily embraced my mother's new Christian religion. But I was conflicted. I saw no power in the new faith, nor any immediate, earthly reward in it. I did not understand the thought of foregoing hope for comfort and fulfillment in this life in favor of the promised comforts and fulfillments of the next. At Lyon I met Livilla, the oracle and witch. She could see the seed of enlightenment and power in me, and for three years I was her secret student. I learned the wisdom of centuries and the coercion of nature. I have little of that left now.'

"One winter, a decree came from the emperor to arrest and eliminate all Christians in our region. They were seen as a threat to order. They could have practiced their faith unmolested if they would acknowledge the divinity of Diocletian and pay homage to him as such. But none of the Christians who could be found, including my parents and my brother Titus, would agree to this affront to their new God. When the soldiers came to arrest them, including Eusebius, Father's old comrade in arms, I was with my mentor, so I escaped.

"I was told that Father believed his years of service to the empire would deliver his family from harm. Instead, my mother and Titus were torn to pieces by starved bears in a public spectacle for the amusement of Gabro, Vipsania, Medullinus, and the citizens of Lyon. Father was considered a traitor to Rome. He was devoured by eels in a pool as after-dinner entertainment at Gabro's villa.

"I went into hiding. My father's line had been wiped out, for I had vowed, in exchange for my powers, never to marry. I planned a revenge equal to Gabro's savagery. Livilla advised me that it would discredit my martyred family and all their descendants, who would now never come into being, to destroy Gabro alone. She said she heard the wailing and lamentations of hundreds of generations who would now have no ingress into being. It would be fitting, she said, to curse Gabro's line forever.

"In Gabro I caused, on the instruction of my mentor, for a vile, infected lesion to open at the deepest part of the fundament. This became suppurated, filled with pus. He became fetid and rank, abiding in a miasma of his own decay. He was a figure of disgust to his family and all those who served him. After a time, when his suffering had grown beyond all bearing, I caused wasps to invade this fissure, to lay their eggs. The larvae that emerged from these fed on his flesh from within, until he was mad with pain. After two weeks, he fell on his own sword.

"Then I directed my vengeance upon Gabro's son. Medullinus was a young man of many possibilities, and he was engaged to be married. He had an active, hungry mind, and wanted to consume all possible knowledge within his realm of experience. He was a patron of the arts, and an eager conversationalist. For him I planned another parasite, but one whose infestation would be eternal. A slave in the household of Xanthippe, the young man's sweetheart, was bribed to steal a lock of his hair and an ivory pin he had given her as keepsakes. With these cut to bits and mixed with the fat of a goose which had never flown, the oil of a fish caught in darkness, and the hearts and heads of three asps, I ignited the beckoning flame, the flame which must burn for three nights and two days. With very much effort, and the aid of my mentor, with three midnight conjurings, prayers, and incantations, and the recitation of the *Invocabo,* I caused the demon of old, the great spirit known in the East as Balphoroth—Balphoroth the incubus—to claim Medullinus as host."

"Incubus?" Perdita whispered.

"The bringer of nightmares," Euphrosine said. "The oppressive spirit, the demon of lust, of monstrous appetites, and death." Euphrosine's gaze at Perdita softened. "There was a time when you would have denied what I am telling you, disdained to hear the truth. But now, you have seen too much."

"Yes, I have seen too much."

"I drove the demon into the young man. The demon was made to visit the victim as he slept, first entering his open mouth as a wisp of spirit, but becoming monstrous, glutinous flesh at the first moment of infestation. The terrified young man struggled and tore at the insubstantial assailant and resisted its defilement, unable to scream or breathe for a time, or seize in any way the substance of the vile thing. Medullinus became the host, the carrier of the parasite. By this act, the demon and the host are bound together for all time, for the demon, once immortal, becomes subject to the lifespan of the host, so the parasite must keep the host alive to continue to be. Together they are immortal, but not indestructible. The fate of one is tied to the other. The demon *must* keep its host alive."

"That is why Uncle tried to perform an exorcism!"

"Yes." Euphrosine nodded. "As a younger man your

uncle would have been a demonologist. He should have remembered that the incubus, of all evil spirits, is impervious to exorcism."

"But why? Why wouldn't it work?"

"Because, child, the incubus is a unique spirit of evil. He does not seek to ruin your salvation. His aim is not to drag you to the depths of Hell. He does not want your soul: he wants *you!*"

Perdita shuddered at the thought of the being which had held her in its grasp.

"And he will have you until there is nothing left, or —"

"Or, what?"

"Or you are contaminated with his spawn."

"His *spawn?*"

"It is never but one girl under his gaze at a time. Often, she finds that the attack has left her with a parasite of her own."

"My God!" Perdita gasped in understanding.

"They can be conceived as nothing other than vile entities, filthy harbingers of the demon's attentions."

"*Le Vorace!*" Perdita whispered.

"Yes, The Ravenous. They are misbegotten and of another plane. They can live only a short time among us and must feed voraciously to do that. They will feed upon each other in time, or die, as their vile energy is spent."

"You called them harbingers?"

"They are a part of their master. They are sensitive to his awareness, if not his will. When Bastide becomes aware of a woman, *Le Vorace* are also aware of her."

"They do his bidding?"

"No. They are beneath commanding, incomplete. They are merely drawn to whom their sire is drawn, for his essence is irresistible—for Bastide's nature, in both mind and flesh, is also insatiable."

"Marie said that seeing them, that was how you knew you were chosen."

"Yes, and there is another way, also."

"The dreams!" Perdita exclaimed.

"Yes, the dreams. When you are drawn into his influence, his nature is to devour all that is you, every thought and idea: this is the remnant of Medullinus, but overtaken by the demon. A connection is made, a symbiosis of spirit and essence. The dreams are nothing of your experience—they are Bastide's."

"The heretics, the burning at the stake?"

"These were things he knew and still remembers. As Scribonia became Euphrosine, so too did Medullinus become Orien Bastide. Bastide, captured by the fire of inquiry and debate, fell in with the Duallists, the Cathars, in the hills and mountains of the Albi. He knew first hand that their doctrine of the wickedness and imperfectability of the flesh was true. He never became a *credent*—his secret would not allow that—but he felt a strong attachment to them. He fought in the Albigensian Crusade, and he made a last stand on the mountaintop fortress of Montsegur in 1244."

"Could he have been killed?"

"Yes. He is immortal because the demon must keep him so, but he is not indestructible. As Bastide the man, he is stronger than most men, but not supernaturally powerful, not anymore. In moments of great distress, often his strength fails him. He could have died on the *Prat dels Crematz* with his comrades. Bastide was one of four chosen to escape martyrdom to preserve the teachings and treasure of the Cathars."

"But what of you, Euphrosine, how is it that you are immortal?"

"Not immortal. I have not cheated death. I will die someday. When I saw the suffering I had caused among the innocents, I asked Livilla to help me destroy the demon and drive it out of Medullinus. But even Livilla could not do this. It was a thing that could not be undone, because the demon became too strong in its host. I decided I must follow the entity, to watch him and help, as I could, those who came under his notice. Livilla was able to give me long life, and the knowledge to extend it, to restore myself as long as I wished to, with the secrets of her herbs and art. This is not a coercion of nature, but it is an affront to it. I will not do it much longer."

Perdita thought for a moment.

"Euphrosine," she said at length, "could you not have prevented these attacks, warned all the women in the countryside, rather than just treating the victims?"

"Like Bastide," Euphrosine said, "I, too, can be killed. Livilla warned me that I must never interfere or thwart the will of the demon, of Balphoroth. Even at my most powerful, to have done so would have meant my death. Now I have much less power against him."

"How did Bastide come to be here?"

"After the destruction of the Cathars, he lived as he could, always near to what was left of the heretical sect. They had gone into hiding and maintained their faith in secret for centuries. He followed Champlain to Canada, as I did, and eventually he met Monsieur de Castres, and his brother, and the young son of a Paris iron monger named Renault. Like Bastide, de Castres was secretly, philosophically at least, a Cathar. They joined Father Lothair Moussaut in his expedi tion down the Mississippi to further explore lands seen by Joliet and Father Marquette. Moussaut did not know that de Castres was seeking a place of religious refuge, to make a settlement, like that in New England, where he could practice and reestablish his faith, unmolested. They found this safe harbor, this all but hidden refuge on the river. Bastide's zeal seemed to match de Castres' at first, until lead was found here by Renault. Then his focus changed. There was a fortune to be made, and Bastide saw this more clearly than anyone. By then, a settlement was well established and trying to live in harmony with the sometimes hostile local Indian tribes. But in 1689 bands of the feared Osage came through, and de Castres and Moussaut were killed in a raid. Bastide and Renault escaped back to Quebec. They returned ten years later to found the permanent settlement. That is when I discovered him here. Eventually Bastide removed Renault and any other claimants to the region's mineral resources. He was becoming rich."

"I heard some of this from Hypolitte."

"Immortality is difficult to hide," Euphrosine continued, "so Bastide purchased his chateau at Montsegur in 1761, and hiding away from most society, he was able, by disappearing from Ste. Odile to Montsegur and back every generation or so, propagate the illusion that these houses were occupied by many generations of a family, not by one man. Both places have traditions, going far back in time, of the deaths and disappearances of young women."

"Yes."

"It has been often repeated. When Bastide takes up residence in one of these homes, some young woman—refined, educated, cultured—becomes the focus of his attention. The demon and its host will be thought fascinating, deferential by her, yet it does not have unchecked access to these victims until—"

"Until," Perdita frowned in a sudden insight, "until they freely accept some token or gift from him."

"Yes. An old coin, usually. When this token has been freely accepted, the victim has sold what protection from the entity she had before. It is a fatal act."

Perdita shook her head speechlessly at this revelation, remembering for a moment her doubts, and Solana's, about accepting the gift.

Euphrosine retrieved her pipe from the floor and relit it with a match. Potiphar raised his head again for a moment, then dropped it to the floor and went back to sleep. "I have the art of Livilla to sustain me," she went on. "Bastide has nothing but the will of Balphoroth to animate his spirit and body. The toll of the centuries, the living decay, cannot be denied. His flesh shows its unnaturally prolonged decline and dessication. Thus he must hide his face behind wax. The entity, a fusing of two beings, will transform in the dead of night, when dreams are abroad. The essence of Bastide diminishes, and the essence of Balphoroth emerges, dominating the entity that now becomes the monstrous coalescence of both. Whomever fascinates Medullinus is consumed and destroyed by Balphoroth."

Perdita said nothing for several minutes. "All you have told me," she said at length, looking at Mrs. Zell, "is known by the town. The nature of Bastide is known, accepted?"

Mrs. Zell nodded sadly. "Yes," she said. "Known by the *old* families. Nothing is said to newcomers. Some of us help them, if we can, if necessary, but we do not *speak* of the secret. Mr. Robert and Father knew *nothing* of it. In the twenty *years* or so of Bastide's absences, it is a secret easy to keep."

"Have you heard the story of Theseus and the Minotaur?" Euphrosine asked.

"Yes, of course."

"King Minos held dominion over Athens and to maintain his favor, the Athenians were willing to sacrifice numbers of their young men and women to the Minotaur. The citizens were willing to pay a terrible price to be left unmolested, prosperous, and complacent. In time, the sacrifice just became a way of life, a part of the order of things."

"Once Mrs. Morisot told me that prosperity was a fragile thing," Perdita said. "She said I would upset that order here and threaten her way of life."

"It is *why* she wanted Marie's *journal,*" Mrs. Zell

said. "Marie came to understand what was *happening* to her. She wanted to keep a *record* of it. There was *insanity* in her family, and she always *feared* she would lose her wits. She *murdered* her daughter in a misguided and *frantic* effort to protect the child from an *unspeakable* fate. The journal could *implicate* Bastide beyond doubt to the *outside* world, to the authorities, madam thought. Then all of this *prosperity* would end. You had no *history* here, and she saw *strength* in you. You were to be *feared,* Perdita!"

"To Mrs. Morisot and others," Euphrosine put in, "the sacrifice was a very small price to pay. I think these revelations have overwhelmed you. You look tired, Perdita. Rest. In a day or two you will be strong enough to go, to escape from his reach."

"I will *come* for you the day after *tomorrow,"* Mrs. Zell said. "Conserve your *strength*. Occupy yourself with this." She picked up Perdita's copy of *Moby Dick* and placed it gently in her lap. "I have *told* Sister Clotilde at the *school* that you are gravely ill, and, of course child, you must *prepare* to leave Ste. Odile!"

42

"I am loath to think what I will be leaving behind," Prosper said, avoiding his brother's gaze. "You will not forgive me, I suspect. I can sense your resentment."

Michel did not speak for a moment. Prosper was hoping for absolution from him, he knew, but Michel could not give it.

"Mother has become nearly comatose," Michel said at length. "She must be lifted in and out of her bed by the nurses and can eat nothing now but thin liquids. Your own illness has prevented you from helping me with her care and Father's. You have been unavoidably removed from the situation. When the nurses are busy with Father, I feed Mother or bathe her and so on. I do whatever must be done to comfort and care for them. Yesterday while you were meeting with the policeman, Father had another small paroxysm, and though he can still see and hear, he has but brief interludes of consciousness."

"Oh, I didn't know," Prosper said. "I got in late last night. Is he improved today?"

"He has great difficulty in breathing, and he cannot speak. His physician was called, and after a lengthy examination, he told me he would not expect Father to live out the month. Mother will not be far behind, if she does not, in fact, precede him."

Prosper at last looked Michel in the eye. "I know

what you have done for them. I know how you have cared for them, and I am sorry I have not been well enough to help you. It is because I have been of no help that my departure would not be a detriment, but rather a lessening of your burden."

"You are getting stronger," Michel said sternly. "Soon you would be able to help with their care. At any rate, they will be gone in a matter of weeks, if not days. I would think you would want to be here at the end. *That* would give them comfort. And when the time comes, you could help me with the final arrangements."

"Of course, I should *want* to stay," Prosper admitted remorsefully. "To see beloved parents through to their final moments. After that, there would be a wake, funeral, and burial. A good son, showing proper love and respect, should gladly participate in these rituals. I cannot."

"You *cannot?*"

Prosper could see renewed anger and disbelief on Michel's face.

"No," Prosper said. "I must go. I must keep to my travel plans."

"I do not understand you, Prosper. You leave your parents at their deathbeds for that woman? The woman who has cast you aside…abandoned you?"

"Mother and Father and God in heaven know I love my parents. My absence will not signify a lapse in those affections. My connection to Perdita and her treatment of me are beside the point. Our sister was horribly murdered, and if my actions could save *anyone* else from the same end, I must needs do what I can."

"You do not know that any harm will come to her."

"No, but I sense it will. She is exactly the type of woman who has fallen victim before—"

"You *sense it?*"

"Yes. Quick communication with her is impossible.

I must go there. I will leave you with enough money to pay for Mother and Father's care and final disposition. There is nothing more I can do here. I must go."

"Then go, Prosper. I have nothing else to say to you."

Letter from Moira Keane Parnell to Edward Badon-Reed

Mr. Edward Badon-Reed
511 St. Columba Square
Boston, Massachusetts
December 20, 1882

Aboard the Senate

Dear Edward,

As Father and you both predicted, a storm off Cape Hatteras has provided the voyage's greatest excitement so far. The seas have been choppy and the weather brisk, but we have had no real danger yet, as I can see, aside from that one, rather minor, squall. A steward did tell me the bilge pumps have been taxed in the last two days, but he said that was nothing unusual for a passage at this time of year.

We are in more settled and calm waters now, having passed the Straits of Florida and the Keys, and are now heading northwest, toward New Orleans. I want to assure you that your parcel is safely stored in my trunk, which I hardly ever let out of my sight. I have a hotel room waiting for me in the city. As I told you last week, Prosper had wished to accompany me to Ste. Odile. Six days ago he wired me from Gibraltar and most urgently asked that I not wait for him at my hotel after all, but get to Perdita's side as quickly as possible. He has become concerned, nearly distraught I'd say, about Perdita's safety. Knowing him as I do, I did not at first give much thought to his fears, but having reread his message many times, I see a genuine desperation in it, and have found that I, too, feel a growing sense of unease about her well being. I noted a changing tone in her letters recently, and I am more anxious than ever to assure myself that all is well. Prosper will follow as soon as he can. I think above all he too wants to see for himself that she is safe.

I had a letter from Perdita dated the 12th. She seemed tired and preoccupied, but in good health. Who could not blame her for her exhaustion, given all that has happened to her in the town?

I do not think, I cannot imagine, that Prosper still has any hope for a reconciliation. At first, he just wanted an explanation from her, but now it is assurance of her safety. This concern is a quality, I know, that helped to convince you he would make a good husband and helpmate for Perdita. And he had many other good characteristics to recommend him, not the least of which were his devotion to her, and—let us face the fact—that he makes a very comfortable living in his profession. When she abandoned him, I knew you and Mrs. Badon-Reed were upset, angry, and puzzled. I believe I heard you say, Edward, that Perdita had thrown away her last and best hope for happiness.

If I may be allowed an opinion and an observation: during the course of these events, Prosper has looked to me to become his confidant and confessor. I have always liked him, and been sympathetic toward him, but as I have come to know him better, I must say I now understand more fully why Perdita could not accept him as her partner in life. Though his heart and intentions are good, his enamorment of her is of such an obeisant kind, if I may call it such, that far from being an equal to her in marriage, he would more likely live by her leave and at her command. He would be more of a lapdog than a husband. I hate to speak so of him, but there it is; not a condemnation, just an observation.

For myself, I have never thought I was of a temperament to live well in the married state. I know I am not of a compromising nature, or patient enough to cater to the needs of another being on a daily and routine basis. I have been satisfied with the life I have had. I am neither romantic nor affectionate, and I would much rather occupy my time with doing good works in the community and with enjoying cultural and artistic diversions with a few good friends. That is all there is to me, nothing more. But that is not true of our Perdita.

I have had no friend with whom to share my diversions who fills that role better than Perdita. Even so, Perdita is not like me. As I have said, all that is in me is visible, there is nothing deeper than that. She has a sense of duty and moral purpose that I lack. For all of her former meekness and shyness, I'll be sunk if I haven't come to understand she is much stronger, much more complex, and more resilient than me. She has a romantic and compassionate spirit that I have sometimes envied. Music, the arts, great ideas, and the notion of love can send her on flights of fancy that I can scarcely imagine. To her, all of these things are a part of the same great whole: the life that she seeks, the path to happiness. Yet, to paraphrase what was said of Lear, she hath always but slightly known herself. I don't think she grasps this basic fact of her nature. Being frustrated and let down by Prosper's affections—he could never live up to her ideal of a partner to truly commiserate with—she came to the conclusion that finding that ideal in a man was unlikely, if not impossible. Failing that, she felt she must apply her life and energies to some other purpose without delay, as she approached middle age. Her art, her sculpture, became that focus. To pursue that purpose, she thought to the disapproval of all who loved her, she left to start a new life elsewhere, to make something, or do something she could leave behind her when her life was through, and prove she was of some benefit to the world.

I like to think that you, Edward, have come to these same conclusions. Better yet, perhaps that you have *not,* but that your love for your daughter and your great wish to make amends to her, make any choices she has made of which you disapprove, small and irrelevant issues. It would give me great pleasure to think so. It would give even greater pleasure to Perdita, who I know has always sought some confirmation of your love and approbation.

I have great expectations of happiness for her with this Hypolitte, the suitor I mentioned whom I expect is to become the new beau in her life. From what Perdita has told me of him, and from the affection I have read between the lines of her letters, I truly think they are "made for each other." In her last letter she mentioned he had gone missing, which he has reportedly done from time to time. This may have been triggered by one last effort she made to deny her needs and keep him at arm's length. I hope they are reunited by now, and have put whatever differences they had behind them. As she describes him, I can't imagine a man better suited to love her and support her search for self expression. I am excited to think of the happy future that I believe my dear friend will now have, one which she has so definitely earned. And this happiness will be warmly enhanced, because she now knows she also has the conditionless treasure of her father's love.

Yours,
Moira

P.S. I will write to you again from New Orleans before heading north.

Journal of Prosper Redon

December 16, 1882

I was able to catch the sloop *Jour de Fête* a quarter-hour before its departure at Sete. I am very glad I did not go all the way to Marseilles to find a ship, and lose perhaps two more days. I must needs be across the Atlantic as soon as possible. I had no privacy aboard the boat, and felt quite sick for more than ten hours. The master, Anatole DuFore, I found to be quite solicitous and provided for my comfort as best he could, under the circumstances.

Late on the second morning we made Gibraltar. By a great stroke of luck, the British merchant vessel, *Boudica*, bearing both steam and sail, was an hour from departure to New Orleans. I was doubly fortunate to secure a tiny cabin aboard her. That was two days ago. The seas have been but slightly choppy, and the weather well above freezing. If this string of luck holds, we may see New Orleans in six or seven days' time.

Moira has by now departed from Boston to New Orleans. An agent has wired ahead to the Hotel Josephine on St. Agnes Street so as to secure her a room. In her last letter she promised, reluctantly, to wait for me there until Christmas Day, then book passage alone to Ste. Odile. I urged her not to wait, but to get to Perdita's side as soon as she can. Even if Moira does not entirely share my concerns, I know that her communications with Perdita have germinated a disquietude in her which nothing short of their reunion will allay.

The *Boudica* is expected to reach New Orleans on the 24th, if the weather holds. Captain Gillian has told me that the mild weather of the last two weeks should make river travel safer. I pray these conditions persist until my departure up the Mississippi. I cannot abide the delay of a single hour, much less days. In a few days' time I should be looking Perdita in the face. Whether at that moment I may accomplish nothing more than knowing she is safe, or change her attitude toward me, or understand, finally, her intractability, all will be known then.

43

The extra jacket and shawls Mrs. Zell had brought were enough to keep out the early morning chill. Perdita's face burned with the cold, though, as an occasional gust blew across the road, bringing flurries of snow with it. The mare pulling the trap seemed unaffected and trotted on hypnotically, along the Saline Road, which became Constantinople Street in town. Neither woman had spoken for twenty minutes, not since passing Theophraste, Aristide's youngest son, making his weekly delivery of bread, cheese, tobacco, and whiskey to Euphrosine back in the salt marsh.

The rim of the sun appeared over the tree line to the east. Perdita pushed her cold feet under a canvas bag on the floor that Mrs. Zell had brought for her in which to carry her last few remaining possessions: unguents and salves from Euphrosine, and her *Moby Dick*.

"I will give you a *valise* and some clothes," Mrs. Zell said at last.

"Yes, thank you," Perdita said weakly.

"I will give you some *money* too," Mrs. Zell continued. "It won't be much, but it will buy you a few days' lodging and get you *back* to St. Louis."

"Thank you for your generosity, Mrs. Zell, but I should not accept any money from you. You have lost everything in the fire, too."

"Not *everything*. I had *money* in the bank. You will

need *something* to get you out of town. If you don't *take* the money, you are *lost*. You would not *survive* another night!"

"Yes, I cannot stay here another night."

"Certainly *not*. I must stop at the *bank* to get my money, then to my *cousin's*. You will want to get to the *rectory* to get whatever you may *want* of your uncle's, as you must *never* look back, never come to Ste. Odile *again!*"

"No, I never will."

"Then I will take you to *Belgique*, where you can catch the train *north*."

"Yes, that is what I will do. If you could drop me at the seminary, I want to say good-bye to the sisters, and to Anatolia."

"Certainly."

"I must leave word with you for my friend Moira, who will be traveling to Ste. Odile now. She will be here soon, at any moment. Tell her to follow me to St. Louis."

"Yes, very *well*."

"I will go to…the Hotel Essex. I stayed there before. Moira has money for me. Keep what you advance me from that, and the rest will get me home."

"Good." Mrs. Zell nodded.

Perdita intended to thank Mrs. Zell again for her help and generosity, but was interrupted by the sound of horse's hooves approaching them at a frantic pace from behind. Both women looked back to see Theophraste galloping toward them. The boy's face carried an expression of urgency and terror. He reigned in his horse alongside the trap.

"Mrs. Zell, Mrs. Zell!" he shouted, breathless.

"What is it, boy?"

"It's terrible! Terrible! Euphrosine and the dog, both are dead! Torn to bits!"

"Dead?" Both women gasped at once.

"Dead! Torn to pieces. Blood everywhere! I'm going for the sheriff!"

Perdita and Mrs. Zell looked at each other gravely. Perdita felt a stab of terror in her stomach followed quickly by a flood of remorse.

"This is my fault. It was her connection to me—" she murmured.

"Try to *calm* yourself, son," Mrs. Zell said.

"I never seen anything like that!" the boy said with tears in his eyes. "Must have just happened. Blood was still flowing. And it looked like parts of them were gone, like they were eaten!"

"Should we go back?" Perdita asked. "This is my fault! Because she tried to help me. She is dead because of *me!"*

"No!" Mrs. Zell said sternly. "It was *Le Vorace*. It means Bastide knows you were *there,* and Euphrosine's *powers* were too far gone. This was *fated* to happen someday. You must *not* go back. Ride on to the *sheriff,* Theophraste. Perdita, we must not *fail* to get you out of town before *nightfall!*"

Mrs. Zell stopped the trap at the front gate of the seminary. Perdita pulled her bag from the floor and stepped out.

"I must go to my cousin *Audrey's* house, Perdita. I will be back to pick you *up* at the rectory in two *hours*."

"I will be there," Perdita said.

Mrs. Zell turned the mare around and headed back toward Rouen Street. Perdita walked along the avenue of cypresses toward the dormitory. Wisps of snow were beginning to collect on the ground. She thought of nothing as she approached the gloomy brick buildings. She no longer felt the cold, nor any sense of shock at the morning's events, nor anything, it seemed, that had happened in the last six months.

Sister Consolata, emerging from the dormitory and

walking toward the school, saw Perdita approaching. Sister stopped when she saw Perdita and bore an expression that conveyed both surprise and concern.

"Miss Perdita," she exclaimed, "is that *you?*"

"Yes, Sister," Perdita said wearily. "I must look a sight."

"You have been ill, we heard. What has happened to your dress?"

"Many, many things. Sister, I must leave Ste. Odile. I have come to say good-bye to you, the sisters, and to Anatolia."

"Oh no, Perdita," Consolata protested. "You're not going! Whatever will we do without you? And the girls love you so!"

"I feel I have let them down. I have not opened their eyes as I thought I would, as I promised Sister Clotilde. So much has happened."

"Oh, no, you are their favorite; I hear them say it all the time!"

"Thank you, Sister, but I must go. I am bound to go."

"We will miss you," Consolata said sadly. "I will miss you. Anatolia is in her room. I will tell Sister Clotilde, Sister Elizabeth, and Sister Rose Agnes you are here."

"I will come to the convent after I see Anatolia."

"As you wish, Perdita. Very well." Consolata embraced Perdita and disappeared into the school.

The dormitory was nearly vacant, as most of the girls were in the gymnasium preparing for the Christmas pageant. Anatolia's room was on the third floor. The stairs seemed daunting to Perdita, and she found she needed to rest at each landing to catch her breath. Anatolia's room was the first one at the top of the stairs. No sooner had Perdita reached the third floor corridor than Anatolia burst from her room and embraced her.

"Miss Perdita!" she said. "I knew you were coming!"

"Anatolia! It is so good to see you."

"I knew you were coming. I *knew* it!" Her voice was still raspy and dry. "Come into my room, Miss." Anatolia took Perdita's hand and led her urgently into her small room.

"You seem well, Anatolia," Perdita said squeezing the child's hand. "I can tell you have your energy back."

"Yes, I feel very well. I have seen so many things I wanted to tell you about," Anatolia said excitedly. "Sister told us you were sick, but I knew you were hurt and frightened."

The room was a tiny garret with one window, two small tables, and a cot. Anatolia was the only girl at the seminary designated by Sister Clotilde to have a room to herself. The walls were covered with Anatolia's visionary drawings, verses, and pictures of Christ and the saints. "I have been making lots of drawings," the child continued, "and today, I have been making one for you!"

Perdita smiled warmly at the child, and sat on the edge of the cot. "I am so glad to see you, Anatolia! This has done me very much good, I can tell you." Perdita looked around her at the drawings and holy pictures covering the walls. Anatolia was rifling through a stack of drawings on the table near her window.

"But I have to leave Ste. Odile, Anatolia," Perdita continued. "I wanted to say good-bye."

Anatolia did not respond, but continued to look through the drawings.

"Did you hear me, child?" Perdita went on. "I have to leave today. I wanted to say good-bye to you first. If it ever happens that I have a little girl of my own, I would hope she will be just like you."

Anatolia found the drawing she was looking for and pulled it out of the stack.

"Have you heard anything I have told you?" Perdita asked.

"Yes, Miss, and I know it makes you sad to say it. I have to tell you that you won't have a little girl of your own."

"I won't?"

"No," Anatolia said earnestly. "In our souls, I am your little girl! We are connected that way."

"Well, I can almost believe that, Anatolia. Someday I hope to see you again. I would hate to think we would never meet again, but I know I must go. I must go today and never come back. Except for missing you, I will thank God to be away from this town!"

"I have not *seen* you leaving Ste. Odile."

"I must go today."

"I have not *seen* it."

"Sometimes you miss things, isn't that true?"

"Yes, but look at this." Anatolia showed Perdita the drawing she held. It showed a black man in a blue suit surrounded by flowers and green trees. He was striding across a river. In the upper left corner of the drawing was written "Asmiel Returns for His Daughter."

"It is my father!" Anatolia said excitedly. "I have seen him coming for me. I know it won't be until the weather is warm next year, but he is coming!"

Perdita smiled compassionately. "I hope that is true, child. Remember you don't always see things aright. I hope he will come, but if he doesn't—"

"I think he will."

"I had almost decided to ask Sister if I could take you with me when I go today."

Anatolia embraced Perdita. "I must be here where my father can find me—if he comes."

"Anatolia, aren't you sad to see me go?" Perdita looked earnestly into Anatolia's eyes.

"But you aren't going. You *aren't* going, Miss."

Anatolia left Perdita's embrace and retrieved the top drawing on her work table, one she had been working on minutes before. She gave it to Perdita. It was a drawing of Perdita herself, floating above the ground as if in an ecstatic state. Across the top of the drawing were written the words "The Life's work is Satisfyed. Love, Love. And so important, if known by those who live in it or not."

"Thank you," Perdita said, perplexed. "What does it mean?"

"Goodness, Miss, I don't know."

"I am going to miss you, my girl!" Perdita embraced the child again, and as she released her, she noticed a folded note on heavy, expensive paper lying on the small table next to the cot. Perdita had seen the paper before. She picked up the note and opened it. Her hands began to tremble.

"Oh, that came for me last night," Anatolia said.

The note read:

My dear Anatolia,

You do not know me, but perhaps you have heard my name. I have heard yours mentioned in the most radiant terms from Miss Badon-Reed, our mutual friend. She has described you as the most gifted and promising of artists and poets. I would hope someday soon to see some of your works for myself. Yours is an acquaintance I am most anxious to make.

Your friend,
O. Bastide

44

Letter from Moira Keane Parnell to Edward Badon-Reed

December 23, 1882

Dear Edward,

I arrived in New Orleans yesterday morning soon after dawn. It was an arduous trip and has very nearly killed any romantic notions I may ever have had about ocean travel. Perdita and I spent many a Sunday afternoon imagining a time when we might make the "Grand Tour" of Europe, as has become so fashionable in recent years. I would think the better of such a plan today, if the opportunity should present itself.

Even at the early hour of our arrival, the dock and quays were bustling with activity. My steward carried my two small trunks to the quay for me, where I hired a trap to take me to the Josephine on Ste. Agnes Street, some half mile or so to the north.

The hotel was rather threadbare, to my taste, and located in a run-down part of the city. We passed crumbling brick buildings festooned with rusting decorative ironwork; tiny wooden houses with three or four rooms situated one behind the other to save space; and many warehouses used, my driver told me, for the cotton trade. One great advantage I found, however, in the location of the Josephine, was that it is but two city blocks from the train station.

The hotel's proprietress is an elderly widow, Mrs. Trincant, whom I found to be most solicitous and responsive to the needs of her guests. The Josephine's lobby, though wanting some superficial repairs, is well kept and tidy.

Mrs. Trincant's grandson, Jean-Baptiste, a young man of about twenty, carried my trunks to my modest room on the second floor, and later accompanied me to the train station to purchase my ticket. He did this, he said, because my route to the station led past an opium den, and he wanted to ensure that I accomplish my mission unmolested. I asked him why a new train station had been built in such a neighborhood. He told me that the St. Louis and Southern Railroad had many enemies amongst the owners of the packet lines, who saw a train route paralleling the river as a threat to their domination of the business of moving goods and passengers up and down the Mississippi Valley. These packet men have many friends in the city government, and amongst the less sympathetic decision makers they are able to administer timely bribes. I purchased my ticket, and we quickly retraced our steps. Being exhausted, I had little desire to see anything of the city. Back at the hotel, I rested most of the day, bathed, had a light supper, and retired early.

My first class ticket to Belgique, the nearest train station to Ste. Odile, cost eighteen dollars. Since the trip is scheduled to take twenty-two hours, and my train is equipped with a Pullman car, I paid an extra two dollars for a sleeping chair. In that comfortable leather chair is where I now find myself.

I suspect I am focusing on these minutiae of my trip, and outlining them to you, as a means of diverting my thoughts from Perdita. The more I have thought about Prosper's telegram, the more Perdita's safety obsesses me.

Moira put down her pen. Perhaps it was wrong to continue a letter to Edward expressing these concerns. She wished, though, that she could express them to someone. She wished she had been able to wait for Prosper so that, far from reassuring each other of Perdita's safety, which was unlikely, they could at least commiserate about their uneasiness regarding her safety.

Over the years, Moira had found that she and her friend had developed a spiritual connection, much like the one she often observed in her parents after decades of marriage. At a museum, or concert, Perdita would often express an observation which Moira, at that very moment, was thinking. And each could sometimes sense, at a considerable distance, that the other was happy, sad, fearful, or distracted. For the most part, both of them dismissed these events as coincidence, but now, after months of growing preoccupation with them, Moira was not so certain.

Since the day she discovered Perdita was gone, Moira thought she sensed a slowly growing anxiety and unhappiness in her friend. She had not permitted these feelings to incite any real sense of alarm in her until about a week before Prosper's telegram expressing his concerns about Bastide. After receiving it, her sleep was troubled for two nights by dreams of Perdita experiencing great distress, pain, and eventual death.

"If nothing else," Moira whispered to herself, "I will put these fears to rest."

From her sleeping chair, Moira watched an alien landscape flowing past her window. Lush river bottoms gave way to impenetrable thickets, then to live oaks with branches grotesquely splayed and dripping with Spanish moss. Between Baton Rouge and Natchez she saw many ruined plantations with fields overgrown and mansions burned out, interspersed with numerous small working farms.

She shared the coach with only five other passengers: two prosperous-looking couples and another single woman, who sat behind Moira. The men napped as the women looked out the windows, or read. The single woman, perhaps ten years younger than Moira, worked intermittently on a needlepoint of two bluebirds Moira had glimpsed when she stood to stretch her legs.

In the late afternoon the train stopped at Natchez. The station had a refreshment saloon, and from her window Moira could see second-class and emigrant-car passengers scramble off the train to eat as much of a long-overdue meal as they could manage in the twenty minutes that the train was scheduled to stop. A conductor, a tall, thin man in blue, entered the Pullman from the front. Moira asked him if he would ask at the station if the telegraph wires were yet repaired and send a wire to Belgique, asking that a carriage meet her there when she arrived the next morning. He nodded and exited the coach from the door through which he had entered.

A news butcher, a boy of about twelve, stood shivering on the platform just outside the coach, selling newspapers, magazines, and candy. Moira removed two silver dollars from her coin purse and stepped out into the vestibule, then outside. She bought a copy of *The Sentinel*, a journal of literature and opinion to which she had once held a subscription. She told the boy to keep the change from the dollar.

Moira reentered the train at the dining car, one car ahead of the Pullman. The elegant diner, walnut-trimmed and upholstered in red velvet, was attended by two waiters dressed in white jackets. The older of the two, a tiny and aged bald man, greeted Moira and showed her to a table at the middle of the car. There was only one other diner in the car, the young woman who had been working on the needlepoint earlier. Moira nodded to her and she smiled in return. Moira sat and ordered beefsteak, boiled potatoes, and coffee. The food arrived in a few minutes, and she ate slowly, barely taking note of its flavor.

She tried to read from her magazine, first an excerpt from Joseph Sheridan LeFanu, then an essay postulating on the culture and physiognomy of hypothetical denizens of Mars, but she was distracted. All day, now that her trip was nearly over, she had found herself becoming increasingly anxious and preoccupied with thoughts of Perdita's safety. Was Bastide a dangerous, possibly murderous figure, as Prosper feared? If so, had Perdita learned to be wary of him, or had she formed a more intimate connection since Moira had last heard from her? There had been a sameness to the accounts Perdita had given her of the histories of Marie Chardin and Sister Solana, and in Prosper's description of Claire's last months, also. Perdita seemed to be following that same pattern, and the more Moira thought of this, the more urgently she wanted to be at her friend's side.

After the engine had taken on fuel and water, the bell was sounded, warning of the train's imminent departure. Just as they had scrambled off the train twenty minutes earlier, the lower class passengers rushed out of the refreshment saloon and back on board, many with their mouths and pockets full of food. Moira left a dollar on her table and returned to the Pullman.

As the evening progressed, she managed to read most of her magazine. Reading, combined with the movements of the train, made her a little queasy from time to time, but this condition was easily remedied by putting down the magazine and closing her eyes for a few minutes.

By ten o'clock, she was exhausted. She dreaded the prospect of attempting to sleep in her reclining chair. Recently she had read accounts in *The Atlantic Monthly* of transcontinental train trips. She considered how much more uncomfortable the emigrant-car passengers must be, cramped together on poorly upholstered benches with their coats and jackets draped over them, or bunched up to serve as pillows against the oak bench backs or arm rests. The discomfort, coupled with the snoring and coughing of other passengers, plus the wailing of children, inconsolable in their weariness and sense of displacement, made the probability of rest unlikely for any but the soundest sleeper, Moira imagined.

She lowered the back of her chair by a few inches and settled in, prepared to make the best of what promised to be a futile attempt at a night's sleep. Turning her head toward the window, she was entranced by the moonlight on the hillsides and fields, and by the silvery bands of rivers slowly beginning to freeze, winding off into the dark forests. After a few minutes her eyelids grew heavy.

Sleep came intermittently throughout the night. She nodded off and reawakened at about eleven. By midnight, having resigned herself to insomnia, Moira was surprised to be startled awake from a nightmare of Perdita being buried alive. In the dream, Moira saw herself at a distance, tearing frantically and bare-handed at the loose earth of a fresh grave, knowing that her friend lay terrified and suffocating below her. With no chance of reaching Perdita in time, Moira awakened suddenly, nearly pitching herself from her chair in panic. She found herself covered in perspiration and gasping for breath. She tried to clear her mind and calm herself.

It took several hours for her to drift off again. She slept a deep, dreamless sleep, awakening only when she felt the sunlight warming her face. The dining car served a breakfast of coffee, fried eggs, and steak. Moira ate only the steak and sipped her black coffee, thinking nothing as she stared blankly at the frosty landscape spreading off to the east. Her shoulders and lower back ached, and she had a small pain behind her left eye. The old waiter refilled her coffee cup, and as she slowly drank, she began to feel revived.

At five minutes past eleven, almost exactly on time, the train stopped at the tiny clapboard station at Belgique. A cold wind was blowing from the north as Moira stepped onto the platform. A porter, an elderly but wiry black man, carried Moira's trunks to a waiting spring-platform wagon with a two-mule hitch. The driver, an equally aged black man, helped the porter lift the trunks onto the back of the wagon. Moira gave the porter fifty cents. He bowed, touching the bill of his cap, and returned to the Pullman.

Moira buttoned her jacket and pulled her shawl tightly around herself. The driver said nothing and made no attempt to help her climb up to the seat.

"I requested a carriage," she said.

"I got no carriage. I got this wagon only today," the driver said, never looking at her. "It take two mule, so you got one more than you need."

Moira could detect a slight French accent in his speech.

"And what is your name, sir?" Moira asked, as the driver turned the wagon around and onto a dirt road dusted with snow.

"Aristide," the old man said.

"Aristide of Ste. Odile? I have heard of you, from my friend, Miss Perdita Badon-Reed."

"Miss Perdita?" Aristide repeated.

"Yes."

"You have come to take her away from here?" Aristide asked gravely.

"Well, no. I am concerned for her. I was planning a visit in the spring, but I have become concerned—"

"She is in danger," Aristide interrupted. "You are here for a reason. I know she has not been well, and she will get worse. We will look for her at de rectory first, then de convent. Anatolia maybe can tell us where to find her. She has meant much to us here, but you must take her away."

Aristide looked solemnly at Moira for a moment with his sad, ageless eyes. She felt a sudden stab of fear in her stomach.

"As quickly as we can, Aristide…we must find her!"

45

As Perdita walked north into the wind on Constantinople Street, toward the rectory, she felt a violent sickness in her stomach. A stab of horror had shot through her when she read Anatolia's note, but now she could not settle on a way to interpret her feelings. She noticed her tongue was dry and her throat sore, and she realized she had been inhaling the cold air through her mouth. She quickly forgot the pain in her throat and her frozen feet and burning face. Now she could identify what she was feeling: it was anger.

There were so many components to her anger, she could not settle on one above all others to explain its intensity. She soon gave up the effort. The fact of it was enough: the intensity that seemed to be animating her now and reviving her from her exhaustion and discomfort. As she acknowledged her anger, it evaporated every other thought from her consciousness and left itself as all she knew. It was all she needed to know.

At the rectory she let herself in, and left her borrowed jackets and shawls draped on the hall tree in the entryway. She carried the canvas bag Mrs. Zell had given her back to Uncle Tancred's room. She removed Euphrosine's unguents and salves from the bag and left them on a night table to make room for any keepsakes of Uncle's she might find. On his bureau she found a silver and ebony rosary, a small print of Christ driving the money changers from the

Temple, and a copy of *The Consolation of Philosophy* by Boethius. She put all of these in her bag slowly and uncertainly. Glancing around the room, she saw nothing else she wished to claim.

As she walked down the hallway toward her old room, she passed the open door of Mrs. Moon's sewing room and caught a glimpse of her reflection in a mirror above a table. She stopped and looked at herself. Now she could understand why Sister Consolata had looked at her with such disbelief. Her hair was disheveled, her expression haggard and worn, her dress dirty and tattered. She looked like a deranged woman, a denizen of alleys and doorways, homeless, and without a dollar to her name.

After a moment, she went into the dining room and left her bag on the table. She then walked back through the kitchen and out the back door. With a sense of inexplicable urgency, she ran across the drive toward the barn. With difficulty, she opened the single door and entered. The space was poorly lighted by too few windows. At the center of the floor sat her workbench, upon which were arranged her points, chisels, rifflers, and hammer. In front of this, dominating the small space, rested her unfinished *Beatrice Cenci*. She approached the statue with emotions that seemed to be a mixture of curiosity, reverence, and fear. Months of dust had settled on the marble, and it was draped here and there with garlands of cobwebs.

Perdita walked slowly around the statue, regarding it from all sides. She felt as though she were seeing it now with an objectivity which would have been impossible for her before that moment. She felt her spirits, her expectations, fall as she realized for the first time that this ankle was too long, this forearm too short, and the neck was turned at an impossible angle. None of these flaws could be fixed or underplayed. The statue was awkwardly proportioned, poorly conceived, and unsalvageable. She was mortified to think

Hypolitte had seen the piece as it was, noticed the flaws, surely, and out of kindness or love for her, offered no criticism.

Tears welled in Perdita's eyes, but she would not let herself cry. She ran out of the barn and back into the kitchen door. In the kitchen, she collected an opened bottle of Burgundy and a glass. Returning to the dining room, she removed her uncle's keepsakes and placed them on the dining table. She sat in Uncle's old chair at the head of the table and filled the wineglass. She sipped from it tentatively and stared out at the gray and white expanse of freezing space that was the lawn and drive and hedges bordering Mal Ardents Street. Her mind was a turmoil of thoughts, memories, of half-formed, abstract moral propositions, and a bafflement at the now vague creative urgings that had reformed her life. She thought of the treasures and curiositics shc had seen in Bastide's possession, and wondered at the skill and insights which had produced each illuminated book and each carved statue. She marveled at the fact that each great work she had ever admired had arisen out of a life which had also known turmoil and fear, compromise and disappointment, as hers had, as every human life must. She wondered if she had any part of the insight to express the human condition, the state of the soul, as she now viewed them. After twenty minutes she had finished the wine. She arose from her chair.

From a small secretary near the bay window, she removed a sheet of paper, a pen, and ink. She thought Theophraste might still be at Aubuchon's office, and if he were recovered from his morning's shocks, he may be able to deliver a note for her. She wrote:

Mr. Orien Bastide,

I cannot help but think that my remaining days in Ste. Odile are few. Whether I go or not, I have greatly missed your company and conversation, and the treasures of your collections. I wonder if you would indulge me with the very great beneficence of showing me once more your treasures cached in the mine shaft? I would deeply value the chance to look again upon the *Hercules* by Polydorus, and to hear from your own lips the histories of these wonderful works. I shall anticipate your acquiescence to my presumptive request, and await you at the headframe at noon tomorrow.

Gratefully your servant,
Perdita Badon-Reed

46

Karl had overslept and was late getting into the laboratory. The day had become overcast and dark, and he had misjudged the time. He had never been able to catch up on his workload since Hypolitte had disappeared, and had gotten in the habit of working on his samples until after dark most days to avoid falling too far behind. He now no longer hoped each new day was the day Hypolitte would return. He knew that, for whatever reason, Hypolitte was never coming back.

Karl lived in a men's boarding house on Chartres Street, and had a walk of only two blocks north on Gentian each morning to the laboratory. The biting wind of the last few days had made the walk seem three times as far, and carrying the tin pail his landlady had packed with his lunch of bread, pork and cheese, had left his fingers exposed and numb in the cold. He thought he might run part of the way, but his ankles were bad, and the streets and sidewalks had occasional patches of ice and light snow that made too much haste unwise.

In five long minutes, he was there. Karl had gotten out of the habit of looking through the windows of Hypolitte's apartment for any signs of life. This morning, though, he did notice smudges on the glass of the door that he did not remember seeing before.

"Someone else has been checking on him," Karl

mumbled to himself. A light dusting of snow that had begun to accumulate on the laboratory stairs in the last few hours, showed small footprints coming down, but not going up. "Whoever it was, must have waited here a long time."

At the top of the stairs, Karl was surprised to find a pane of glass on the front door broken, and the door unlocked. He apprehensively pushed the door open and entered. The large room was bathed in orange early-morning sunlight streaming in now under the cloud cover, through the bank of east-facing windows. There was no intruder visible. Karl left his lunch pail on his work table and looked around the room for any sign of theft, or disturbance of assaying records. Nothing was out of place in his work area. In Hypolitte's area, however, he noticed some papers and charts had been moved, and that the blanket Hypolitte kept there to wrap himself in on cold days, and the cushion from his desk chair had been arranged on the floor under one of his tables to form something like a makeshift bed. Karl looked over the counters and shelves above the table. The jars and pots may have been gone through: the order of their storage seemed different, and there was an empty space, as if one of them were missing. And in the corner by the bookcase, he noticed that Hypolitte's fishing gear had been rifled. The netting had been cut from the fishnet.

Moira recognized the strange, European character of the town that Perdita had described to her in many letters. The Creole houses, the church, the seminary, even the names of the streets left an impression in her of decadent anachronism and dislocation. Aristide reined in the mules behind a small trap parked in front of the Gothic brick rectory. A pale woman with a drawn face and black hair accompanied by a child, a mulatto girl of about twelve, were approaching the trap on the front walk.

"Mrs. Zell, Anatolia!" Aristide called. The two approached the wagon.

"Aristide," Mrs. Zell said. "We have come for Perdita. Have you *seen* her?"

"No. We are looking for her."

"Mrs. Zell," Moira said. "I am Moira, Perdita's friend."

"Miss Parnell." Mrs. Zell smiled slightly. "I am glad to *meet* you at last. This is *Anatolia*. We have come to find your *friend* and get her to the train station. Thank God you are *here*. You can see her safely away—"

"But where may she be?" Aristide asked.

"I am afraid for her," Anatolia said quietly but firmly. "I wanted to come with Mrs. Zell. I saw Miss Perdita in a vision just after she left me. I could not tell what was happening to her, but I saw her walking under rocks, under rocks that hung over the road."

"Dat is north of town," Aristide said. "Nothing up dere but dat old headframe. Help the chile, Mrs. Zell, an' get into de wagon."

Although Perdita assumed Mr. Behr had been expecting her, she could see the surprise on his usually congenial face.

"Miss Perdita!" he said, with a hint of concern in his voice.

"Yes, Mr. Behr. You were expecting me?"

"I was told by Mr. Bastide to expect you. Are you well? Have you walked all the way from town in this cold?"

"Yes, I have." Perdita was exhausted. She removed the canvas bag from her shoulder and let it slip to the ground. "I couldn't afford a horse, so I walked."

"I heard about the terrible fire. Did you lose everything?"

"Nearly. Nearly. There is nothing left to keep me here, so I am leaving. I asked Bastide if I could see his treasures one last time. I'll never be back...never see them again."

"Well, yes, I got word last night. Everything is ready. The lamps are lighted and the mules harnessed, as you can see. I am surprised, though. I remember your great dislike of enclosed places. I didn't think you'd care to go down there again."

"I overcame it once; I will again."

"Would you like to wait in the shed, to get out of the wind? I have a stove in there. Oh! It looks like Mr. Bastide is right on time. Here he is!"

The sound of trotting horse's hooves could be heard from the road. Perdita turned to see Bastide's Rockaway turn onto the drive that dipped into the limestone basin and up through the snow-covered glade. She slipped the strap of her bag back onto her shoulder and turned to face the carriage. In a minute, Urbain was reigning in the geldings in front of Perdita and Behr. The carriage door opened and Bastide stepped out. He wore no prosthesis. A voluminous black cloak covered his gaunt frame, and his silk top hat sat upon his shock of gray hair. In the cold, overcast light, he looked particularly spectral and horrific, Perdita thought.

"Mr. Bastide, good morning," Behr said cheerfully.

"Good morning, Mr. Behr," Bastide said in his guttural, wet voice. "Good morning, Miss Perdita."

Perdita nodded. "Thank you for indulging me, sir," she said flatly.

"I am more than glad to do so," Bastide said, with something like a smile. "I am grateful we may once again pass an agreeable hour together."

"Yes, an agreeable hour," Perdita repeated.

"You do not look well, Miss Perdita," Bastide said. "That would explain your visit to the old *lamia*, Euphrosine. A waste of your time, I assure you."

"I am not well, and I have seen her, as you know.

Well or not, I am determined to see your treasures once more before I go."

"Yes. The town will miss you, as I will. Very well. Have you walked all this way this morning?"

"Yes." Perdita nodded slightly.

"Where will you go?"

"Home."

"Well, it is cold, sir," Behr said, as he started toward the shack that held the elevator cage. The boy François stood ready with the huge mules harnessed to the cage ropes. "You will be more comfortable underground."

"That we will, Mr. Behr," Bastide said. He allowed Perdita to precede him, and they followed Behr up the small hill.

At the cage, Perdita stepped inside and felt her breath becoming short. This sensation increased as Bastide stepped in after her. He closed the cage door and signaled to Behr, who relayed the signal to François. The boy slowly guided the mules forward, and the cage began to descend.

Perdita felt herself becoming faint, as there didn't seem to be enough light or air in the shaft. The overcast day had made the light filtering down from above much dimmer than on her first visit.

"Are you sure you are well, Miss Perdita?" Bastide asked after a moment. "You look rather a sight, if I may say so."

"I haven't been well, or strong, for several days. I do not care to be enclosed like this."

"Yes, I remember."

"And surely we know each other well enough that you may call me Perdita, as you have done before."

"Perhaps you do not know me as well as you may think…Perdita."

"I might surprise you, sir."

"No." Bastide looked at her with his watery, lidless

eyes. "No, you do not. There is a private, artless, and empathetic self that you have not seen. I can see you are not well, and I am concerned for you."

Perdita smiled sardonically. "Thank you. I truly think you are. What a benefit it would be if my condition and your empathy could find some conjunction, some mutual benefit."

Bastide looked at her quizzically. "I am concerned for you," he repeated. "I will drive you back to the rectory this afternoon, or better, to see Duclos."

Perdita said nothing. In another minute, the cage had reached the bottom of the shaft. Perdita threw open the door and leapt out, drawing deep, rapid breaths. The torches had been lighted as far down the left tunnel as she could see.

"Perdita," Bastide said, "you do not seem to be up to this today. Would you prefer to come again another time?"

"No," Perdita said, trying to control her breathing. "No, I must see the Polydorus. There will never be another opportunity for me."

"Very well. One moment, if you will. The cold affects me." Bastide removed his vial of distilled water and his glass rod from a pocket inside his cloak. He dropped a few drops of water into each eye and returned the paraphernalia to his cloak.

"Will you follow me?" he said. Bastide proceeded down the boarded walkway toward drift number four. Perdita did as he invited, finding, as she had on her first visit, that she could not help but fix her gaze downward, to the boards, as she walked. Bastide walked slowly ahead of her, turning to check her progress every few minutes. She thought of scraps of music to distract her: Bach's Toccata in D, and the Allegretto from Beethoven's Seventh.

"Are you all right?" he asked.

"Yes, yes," she said desperately. She felt as though her skin were crawling to escape the enclosure of the tunnel.

At moments the walls seemed as though they were mere inches from her, and the ceiling oppressing her from above.

"Shall we continue, Perdita? Have you had enough?"

"No, no, we must continue. I will do this. I *will*. Please...lead on."

Bastide nodded and continued to walk. "I commend you, Perdita," he said. "I can easily see the difficulty you are having. There are few, I dare say, who would endure the suffering I see on your face...to be in the presence of genius. Such an homage would be valued by any artist, surely."

"Yes, an homage must be paid. This kind of opportunity is rare—" Perdita could not lift her gaze, but kept her eyes nearly closed, locked on the boards of the walkway. When she heard Bastide stop, she lifted her eyes.

Mr. Behr was surprised to see visitors approaching the headframe. As the wagon emerged from the limestone basin, he recognized Aristide and Mrs. Zell. He did not recognize the second woman and the child.

"Aristide!" Behr called. "What could bring you out here in this weather? I have no permission to allow visitors in. Your son here could tell you that."

"That is Bastide's coach," Mrs. Zell said, as the wagon stopped alongside the Rockaway. She and Anatolia climbed down from the back of the wagon. "Is Miss Perdita here? Has she gone underground?"

"Yes, she is here." Behr was confused. "She and Mr. Bastide have gone down. They will be back up soon. What is the matter?"

"We can't wait for that," Anatolia said firmly. "We must see her. You must let us go down to her *now*."

Drift four looked exactly as it had the first time Perdita had seen it. She had remembered it perfectly. Nothing had been done to reinforce the post supporting the archway overhanging the drift. The old iron gate still sagged precariously on its frame, and untouched beams and planks of new lumber still lay scattered about. The two Davey's lamps on opposite sides of the post flickered as Bastide walked past them.

"Your courage has been rewarded, Perdita," Bastide said. "We are here."

"Yes," Perdita said painfully, "we are."

Bastide produced a rusted iron key and unlocked the gate, which nearly fell to the floor as it swung open. The lamps inside the enclosure had not been lighted. Bastide withdrew a small box of matches from within his cloak and soon had illuminated the entire chamber.

"Ah!" he said with delight. "I had forgotten what treasures are buried down here!" He walked among the Roman marbles and bronzes, the paintings and gilt work, the Restoration portraits and the Mannerist allegories.

Perdita felt her breath coming a little easier as she tried to accustom herself to her confined surroundings. At length she followed Bastide into the enclosure. For a moment she wished she had some wine to steady her nerves, but she quickly knew her composure would have to come from someplace inside herself.

"Do you think, Perdita, that it is gauche for one man to own all of this?" Bastide asked almost giddily.

"Yes, I do. I said as much to Hypolitte."

"You may be surprised to learn that I agree with you. I have plans to build a great museum to house all of this, and more."

"I have heard of those plans."

'This is the world's legacy. I never meant to keep all this for myself. It is the inheritance of all peoples."

Perdita walked past Bastide. She pulled the tarpaulin off the large object on the floor. The smooth, aged marble of Polydorus's *Hercules* gleamed in the lamplight. Perdita smiled slightly, with the pleasure of the form, its textures, volumes, and lines.

"I wanted to see this one more time," she whispered.

"And so you have," Bastide said.

"And I wanted...*want* to show these things to Anatolia," Perdita said wistfully. "I want to show her these things and watch her come to understand them and enjoy them. I would appreciate them anew through her enjoyment. But, I can't. I cannot do that. It is impossible."

Perdita recovered the statue with the tarpaulin. She stepped past Bastide toward the gate. "You seem nearly ecstatic, Monsieur," she said.

"Who would not be, who has any sensibility, or any soul? I will share all of this, display it for all to see. I have never known a time when I was not captivated by all that humans may think, conceive, or make. I am starving for the knowledge that elevates this life above deadly tedium. These keep me alive, I would say, and anxious for life."

"Yes." Perdita nodded. "I have seen that quality in you. Truly, you seem to want to sap the intellectual, the human energy out of all around you."

"Perhaps," Bastide said, "that is an accurate description. No, now I think of it. I do not want to sap it, but rather to understand it, to share in it."

"I think of the similar fire that burned in the hearts and minds of those who are gone now: Marie, Solana, Uncle, Hypolitte. Active minds, burning with life, now gone cold."

"Yes, they will be missed: your uncle helpless; Hypolitte disappeared."

"They *are* missed. Hypolitte is dead."

"We must hope not."

"And Uncle is himself no more. He loved the light of human brilliance too, as you said. Shakespeare, in particular."

"Yes, he was known to be something of an authority, as I am. I know he was fond of quoting the plays and poems to illuminate any circumstance, which is unendingly possible, with Shakespeare."

"Yes, he was."

Bastide was silent for a moment. He seemed to be gathering his thoughts.

Then he quoted:

"The idea of her life shall sweetly creep
Into his study of imagination,
And every lovely organ of her life,
Shall come apparell'd in more precious
Habit
More moving—delicate and full of life
Into the eye and prospect of his soul."

"Well quoted," Perdita said. "*Much Ado about Nothing.*"

"You are an authority, too," Bastide remembered.

"Somewhat. It is the fire and essence of women that most enthralls you, isn't it?"

"Yes." Bastide admired a gilt crucifix on the table near him. "It is true. The soul and essence of women are everything…*everything*. I want to keep a part of those qualities always, to never forget the uniqueness of each, if possible. To keep some remembrance of each essence. I revere it, and…desire it beyond my own ability to contain and understand."

"If you are helpless to these feelings," Perdita said evenly, "how much more helpless are the women themselves? Marie? Solana? Claire Guibord? Or worse, a child…a child like Anatolia?"

Bastide looked at Perdita sharply. He quickly softened his expression. "I do not understand you, Perdita."

"Hypolitte is *dead!*" she hissed. "I will never know

a life with him, or what it truly would have meant to love him. I will never fully warm my heart to him, to know him that way. I have only a monstrous, savage violation to turn my heart to stone! I have thought of another passage worth repeating:

> "A hungry lean-faced villain
> A mere anatomy…
> A needy, hollow-eyed, sharp-looking
> Wretch,
> A living dead man."

"Very good, Perdita." Bastide reached into his cloak and withdrew his bottle and glass rod. "*A Comedy of Errors,* unless I am mistaken." He unstoppered the bottle, dipped the rod into it, then held the rod above his eye.

"You are right, Bastide, but I have recently discovered Mr. Melville, a more modern author worthy of reference." She reached into her bag and removed her blue-bound *Moby Dick*. She dropped her bag to the floor and, grasping the book with both hands, drove it down upon Bastide's hand, and the glass rod it was holding. The rod plunged deep into Bastide's eye, and black fluid shot up through the center of the rod and far out its end. Bastide roared in pain. Perdita lunged at him as hard as she could. He fell backwards across the *Hercules*. Perdita grasped a large bronze candlestick sitting on the floor under the table nearest her.

"Perdita!" Bastide screamed.

Perdita spat the words: "'To the last I grapple with thee; from Hell's heart I stab at thee; for hate's sake I spit my last breath at thee!'"

Bitter tears began to stream from Perdita's eyes. "Now I will ensure that you cause no more suffering and death."

Grasping the candlestick with both hands, she stood

over Bastide and raised the heavy bronze stick above her head. She slammed it down as hard as she could onto Bastide's left arm, lying against his chest, but the blow glanced off. Bastide rolled away from her to his left and scrambled to his feet. He swung his right arm savagely at her and struck the right side of her face. She fell backward against a table, stunned. A searing pain shot across the side of her face. She opened her mouth slightly and knew her jaw was broken. As Bastide reached for the glass rod protruding from his eye, Perdita rammed the large candlestick she held into him, and he stumbled backward. Finding an ornate medieval chasuble folded on the table next to her, Perdita set down the candlestick momentarily and, grasping the ancient fabric, she held it in the flame of a flickering Davey's lamp nearby. She threw the burning vestment onto Bastide.

"The rings of sorrow spread for centuries, the contagion of you, will end," Perdita sobbed.

As Bastide threw off the burning chasuble onto a stack of Dutch paintings which immediately ignited, Perdita took up her candlestick again and rammed him a second time with all her might. He fell backward across the Polydorus and onto the floor. He slapped at several growing flames that the chasuble had left on his chest. Perdita ran to his side and stood over him.

His features seemed to be melting, transforming before her eyes; at first glutinous and unfixed, then hideously incunabular. The flames spread across Bastide's shoulders, and he swung an arm furiously at Perdita as he attempted to rise again, breaking the small and ring fingers of her left hand. He slapped desperately at the flames on his chest. Perdita managed somehow to grasp Bastide's arm and, pulling it away from his chest, forced it down, the wrist resting against a small jeweled cabinet on the floor. She held it there with her foot. With all her strength, she slammed the candlestick down again against the forearm, snapping it instantly into a sickening right angle. Bastide screamed in pain. Perdita felt herself beginning to retch, but she controlled the impulse.

"By God, it will end here!" She raised the candlestick again and brought it down on Bastide's right hand just as he was reaching for her. The blow struck the hand end-on and broke the wrist instantly. Bastide gasped in agony as the hand flopped uselessly on its wrist like the head of a dead bird retrieved by a hound. Perdita shivered in horror at the sight of Bastide's mangled arms and the violence of what she had done. Her gorge rose again, choking off an anguished sob of remorse. She dropped the candlestick in disgust. Perdita grabbed her canvas bag from the floor and ran from the enclosure.

"PERDITA, PERDITA!" Bastide growled blindly, as he struggled agonizingly to his feet.

Perdita still thought she could see a transition, a metamorphosis continuing in him, a fiendish transfusion of two beings, rising and falling, both elements equally insubstantial, as he thrashed in pain. But she was light-headed and could not be certain she was not imagining it. She slammed the rickety gate behind her. It barely stayed closed. She clasped the rusted lock shut, knowing it would, at best, only temporarily contain him, even in his injured state. She removed from her bag the last item it contained: the pot of Greek Fire Hypolitte had shown her long ago. Perdita had placed the pot in the netting she had cut from Hypolitte's fishing net. She held the net by its end and approached the support post. She swung the net in a rocking motion a few times, then, with all of her strength, smashed it into the burning lamp.

Flames flew instantly up and down the entire length of the post and along the oil-soaked beams it supported. In another few seconds, the mouth of the drift was an inferno.

"Perdita, damn you!" Bastide screamed, now covered in blood. He pulled the rod from his eye awkwardly with his maimed arms. Perdita ran back to the gate and, lifting a plank from those scattered on the floor, she placed one end against the gate's lock panel and wedged the other end into the floor, against a ridge in the limestone. The plank lay above the iron ring anchor set in the floor.

"Let me out!" Bastide howled. "I will be out!"

Perdita lay herself face down on the plank. She reached from each side down to the floor and grasped the iron ring with both hands as tightly as her remaining energy allowed. She hoped her strength would hold out long enough to keep Bastide from pushing the plank aside.

"No, you will not!" she murmured.

Bastide pushed weakly against the gate with the stump of his right arm. The gate shook precariously, but would not give way. His vigor was sapped by the mortal shock to his body. He slipped his right arm under the plank and tried to lift it away from the lock panel, but could not dislodge it.

Perdita held on until her hands, arms, and tendons ached. She heard a snap and groan of fire-consumed beams behind her, and the falling of dust and fragments from the fracturing mass of ceiling above.

"There is nothing more important than this," she whispered.

47

Letter from Moira Keane Parnell to Edward Badon-Reed

January 9, 1883
Ste. Odile

Dear Edward,

The shock and sorrow that my telegram of yesterday must have caused you, I can scarcely imagine. The telegraph lines in this area have only just been repaired, or I should have not been able to notify you immediately of these terrible events. A more complete account of this disaster will be formulated in the next few days, I am told, by the sheriff and officials of the mining company.

Prosper arrived on Wednesday and left town yesterday. He will call upon you in Boston when he returns. He seems a broken man. In addition to this tragedy, he received word that both of his parents died within four hours of each other on New Year's Day. He swore in his teeth that Bastide, the man lost in the cave-in with Perdita, was the begetter of all of the sorrows known by him and his family, going back to his sister's death. He had resolved, after speaking to a policeman back home, to confront this Bastide, after sorting things out with Perdita, but he arrived a week too late. By the time Prosper made the landing at Ste. Odile, the town was ablaze with excitement, concern and uncertainty.

Mr. Behr, the caretaker at the mineshaft used by Bastide to store art treasures, said we had missed intercepting Perdita before going underground with Bastide by not ten minutes. He was obliged, on explicit instruction from his employer, to permit no one to descend to the storied repository without permission. As he explained his position to us in spite of our concerns, we saw smoke billowing up through the mine shaft, and heard the unmistakable rumble of a cave-in. The locals say these fires can burn literally for years. Mr. Behr told me there was no route of escape for Bastide and Perdita.

The town seems to be in a state of sad disbelief at the loss of our Perdita. She touched many hearts and souls in her short time here. Her friend, Mrs. Zell, and several nuns at the seminary, seem deeply, painfully inconsolable. I met the child, Anatolia, who had become Perdita's special favorite. There is a light in her I have never seen before. She called herself Perdita's daughter of spirit, and said she will, for the rest of her life, acknowledge no other claimant as her mother. She gave me a drawing she made for Perdita, but had held onto for safekeeping. It showed Perdita in an ecstatic state and was illuminated with an abstruse inscription. Anatolia says that now she understands its meaning.

I have come to know Sister Clotilde, the Mother Superior at the convent. I have asked her if I might fill Perdita's position at the seminary, and she has agreed. She is most grateful to learn of your wish to apply Perdita's windfall to the support of the orphan girls under her care.

And so, our Perdita is gone. I can scarcely believe this is the same world we knew in her salad days. Perhaps, for me, it is not. Where is there an idea, a philosophy, a great work—whether in stone, paint, or verse—that will not be diminished in my experience and enjoyment, at the loss of her understanding, her praise, her sheer delight? The rest of my years will feel her loss, and I will wonder how her kindness, resolve, and courage would have enhanced each remaining and now solitary discovery of my life.

None of these things will ever seem the same to me, as the light of her is gone: your daughter, my friend, our Perdita.

Until we meet again,
Moira

About the Author

John S. McFarland's horror fiction has appeared in *The Twilight Zone Magazine; Eldritch Tales; Charon*, and in the anthology *A Treasury of American Horror Stories,* along with Stephen King, H. P. Lovecraft, and Richard Matheson. He has published mainstream fiction in numerous literary journals and has been a guest lecturer in fiction at Washington University in St. Louis. McFarland has also written extensively on historical subjects ranging from Jack the Ripper to Hollow Earth theory to early twentieth century spiritualism. He lives in St. Louis.